**JPod** by Douglas Coupland

'Introducing Generation Xbox: a whole new breed of techno-geeks from the master of the modern cult classic. Very evil . . . Very funny'
*Publishing News*

'Douglas Coupland once again captures the zeitgeist in his latest novel about the techno-geek underworld'
*Harper's Bazaar*

'This bright, shiny, magpie-friendly package shows a reliably unreliable narrator unafraid of experimentation and canonical rule-breaking having the time of his jet-setting, cool-hunting life' *I-D*

'Blending biting satire and fast-paced farce with high technology and low life, *JPod* reflects modern living in a darkly humorous glass'
*Waterstone's Books Quarterly*

'This is vintage Coupland, a spookily normalised account of an insane world, and it's great fun to read'
*Evening Standard*

'This is a wonderfully inventive book, fizzing with wit and black humour . . . It's good to have [Coupland] back'
*Sunday Tribune*

'*JPod* turns out to be the perfect vehicle for his funny and poignant evocations of near-term nostalgia . . . there is brilliance at work in *JPod*. Not to mention more LOLs than you could shake a bong at' *Los Angeles Times*

'Zeitgeist surfer Douglas Coupland downloads his brain into *JPod*' *Vanity Fair*

'I admired *JPod* enormously . . . I found myself enjoying every minute of it . . . buy the book and get some conceptual art free' Liz Jensen

'Classy Canadian's irony-packed follow-up to 1995's *Microserfs*' *Zoo*

'As a cultural artefact *JPod* rocks' *Financial Times Magazine*

'Coupland's on top comic form . . . Class' *Arena Homme Plus*

'An extraordinary book, wide-ranging and wildly inventive' *London Review of Books*

'As ever with Coupland, the detailed characterisation is a joy to read' *Scotland on Sunday*

'A lethal joyride into today's new breed of techno-geeks . . . *JPod*'s universe is amoral and shameless' *Nation*

# JPod

**By the same author**

Fiction

*Generation X*
*Shampoo Planet*
*Life After God*
*Microserfs*
*Girlfriend in a Coma*
*Miss Wyoming*
*All Families Are Psychotic*
*Hey Nostradamus!*
*Eleanor Rigby*

Nonfiction

*Polaroids from the Dead*
*City of Glass*
*Souvenir of Canada*
*Souvenir of Canada 2*

# JPod

a novel by

## Douglas Coupland

BLOOMSBURY

First published in Great Britain in 2006
This paperback edition published 2007

Copyright © 2006 by Douglas Coupland

The moral right of the author has been asserted

Bloomsbury Publishing Plc, 36 Soho Square, London W1D 3QY

All papers used by Bloomsbury Publishing are natural, recyclable products made from wood grown in well-managed forests. The manufacturing processes conform to the environmental regulations of the country of origin.

A CIP catalogue record for this book is available from the British Library

ISBN 9780747585879
10 9 8 7 6 5 4 3 2

www.jpod.info
www.bloomsbury.com/douglascoupland

Design by Douglas Coupland
Printed in Great Britain by Clays Limited, St Ives plc

# JPod

## "Winners Don't Do Drugs"

William S. Sessions, Director, FBI

**FINAL**

**FINAL.FINAL**

**final.FOR REAL**

**FINAL.version 2**

**absolutely.FINAL**

**FINAL.2**

**FINAL.3**

**FINAL.3.01**

**FINAL.3.02**

**FINAL.working**

1ne
2wo
3hree
4our
5ive
6ix
7even
8ight
9ine...

# ...Best!

# ...Dream!

# ...Ever!

**Play as Gene Simmons**
**Play as Iron Man**

watch_me_xplode

# Universal Goo

Chihuahua Death
Drive the hot dog wagon onto the hockey rink
**Fatality gap**
Do the Boneless

Want to take your business to the next level? Use new strategies to improve your income, and locate parks and truck stops where purchased orgasms are a snap. Make your elevator banter funny but not witty. Get free publicity even though you're promoting nothing. Business network with scary people you don't respect and whose haircuts obviously cost way more than your own. Establish credibility for tasks you hate performing. Clarify values but remember, a million times nothing is still nothing. Read business magazine articles written by children and adults who've never owned businesses. Get more referrals by grooming better and by shooting out more pheromones; basically, don't wash your perineum, that little strip of skin between the genitals and anus. This goes for both sexes. Sex is everywhere in even the drabbest office environment. But then, so is death. Find the middle ground. Overcome objections by pretending you have a non-existent education. Nobody will ever check your credentials unless you run for public office or become head of a school; the secret message is "don't aim for the top—aim for someplace two notches below the top." Having said this, you will still become bitter for not having made it to the top. Even when life is good, it isn't really good. Get commitments, then let people down. Increase sales and get nothing for it. Sell more with your Internet marketing and your website, but don't show too many teeth in your press photo. Make spelling mistakes in your resumé and then wonder why nobody calls you. Play Freecell and contribute nothing to the world but have fun doing it. Yes! You can improve your marketing strategy and your sales, but people will find you kind of boring while you're doing it, and if it works out, people will still think you're not that nice person who showed promise in high school. Also remember that high school is a North American obsession. Europeans think this obsession is juvenile, and the moment you use a high school metaphor, their minds will wander. They're just jealous. There is a much better way to market your products and services, but it's maybe *too* fresh, and maybe you're not ready for that new freshness. If you want to grow your business with less wasted effort, then you're living in dreamland. Whether you're just starting out or you made a million from your business last year, it's all kind of scary and futile, isn't it? There are simply too many people on earth. Oil is going to run out in your lifetime. What's your follow-up strategy to increase sales and profits? Honestly, if you haven't joined a local Kiwanis-type organization, then do it right now. Most of the business decisions in your city are made by older guys who eat mediocre chicken dinners in hotel ballrooms and then go off and have naked whipped cream go-kart rides. It doesn't matter how savvy your proposal is, if the guys in the fezzes have chosen Murray to take over the lease to that office space you were eyeing, then you're totally fucked and Murray will get the lease. One person's testimonial: "Requests for my services went up by 300% as a result of working with Ken, because he's way better-looking than the earnest blank before him, Ron. We fired Ron under the pretext of catching him swiping Post-it notes and bond paper from the storeroom, but really it was because he was boring, didn't like golf, and Tracy at the front desk thought he was, quote, 'Kind of pervy.'" If you're trying to stay more focused on what you do, then simply do what most genuinely successful people do, which is take Ritalin. Most people think Ritalin is a kiddy drug, but what it actually does is allow you to stay focused and stop your mind from wandering. Hi, I'm Denise from HR. This morning I crumpled up a piece of paper and then I held it in the palm of my right hand and I looked at it and I thought, "Denise, this is your life. This is as good as it gets." Hi, I'm Jeremy. I'm that high-energy new guy they stole from Remtech across the Parkway. I'm young, smart, good-looking and I'm using ever-escalating amounts of crystal meth to make me seem more alive than you. I'll either end up winning everything or be found holding up a cardboard sign and talking to myself at the Exit 23 off-ramp. Hi, I'm Rick and I hate everything in the world because I lost everything I owned in the tech bubble in the late 1990s. I really thought I'd be on a beach right now. Instead, I piss in the men's room urinal and have to listen to Jim in the stall beside me flip through the sports pages. It's all he does. I don't know how he gets away with it. He's there for two hours a day. Please turn off all cellphones and personal computer systems. Engineers aren't funny or cute or nerdy. They're damaged. I might be damaged, but they're way more damaged than in any other division of the company. I resent the fact that nerds are somehow cool. They're just losers. Would you like another transaction? People say that everyone can be a success, but you look at the numbers and no, the world is way more about failure and compromised standards than it is about winning. The older the culture is, the less cutesy it is about saying, "Well, you're a winner because you tried your best." Can you imagine a Chinese person saying that? They'd just think you're a loser and buy all of your goods at fire sale prices during your bankruptcy yard sale. You're always hearing about "following your dream," but what if your dream is boring? Most people's dreams are boring. What if you had a dream to sell roadside corn—if you went and sold it, would that mean you were living your dream? Would people perceive you as a failure anyway? And how long would you be happy doing it? Probably not long, but by then it's too late to start something else. You're fucked.

Communists are smart in some ways. They actively discourage hoping or dreaming. At least that way, when you finally get a shitty little AM radio after being on the waiting list since 1988, you'll feel both cheered and kindly towards the regime in power. Okay, I'm kidding. The only way to the top is killing and greed. Okay, I'm kidding. But killing helps. Greed kind of helps, but it looks ugly, and at parties people avoid greedheads, so there goes your social life. Life is a contest between you and everyone else. Don't you get an empty feeling in your soul when you have a blank to-do list? Hasn't it been a long time since you had a flying dream? Workshops and seminars are basically financial speed dating for clueless poor people. TV and the Internet are good because they keep stupid people from spending too much time out in public. There are too many old people coming down the chute in the next few decades. Heaven help you if you can't hold your job act together. Put a smile on it, or it's cat food for dinner tonight. A decade of cat food is 3,652 cans. Incorrect password, please try again. People who advocate simplicity have money in the bank; the money came first, not the simplicity. Invitation to All Staff Members: Thursday bowling, pizza and drinks, sponsored by the company. Black lights and music galore. Dancing and bowling shoes provided. Bowling Skills Not Required!!! People who use the phrase, "In these changing times, when the only thing that's certain is change itself" are idiots. Think about it and read the following sentence: "In these static days, when the only guarantee is stasis itself . . ." You see what I mean. Sometime when you're all alone in a room, ask yourself if what you do for a living can be done by someone in India. If there's even a flicker of doubt, then you have to admit that you're doomed. Which is more humiliating: losing your job to a robot, or losing your job to someone who lives in a country whose standards of living you consider inferior? You can't fake creativity, competence or sexual arousal. If you have none of these three attributes, then pack it in right now. Go sell roadside corn in India. Your call is important to us. As you know, Jessica is away for two more days—could you please be sure all of your dirty dishes are put into the dishwasher (not the sink) before the end of the day so that when Katie or Kirsten comes down to turn it on, it is ready to go. Nobody has ever been happy in a job they obtained by first handing in a resumé. Most people have no idea how to politely answer a phone. The English do, and it's been their only major business advantage for the past two centuries. Using the keypad, spell the last name of the person you wish to speak with. Women can discern shitty clothes at thirty paces. Even seasoned recruiters base their first impression on the basis of fuckability. The second thing they look at is whether

you're competent, and the third thing they see is whether you're creative in disguising your lack of competence and/or fuckability. A big Thank You to everyone who participated in Jeans Day this year. We did really well and were able to raise $230.00 for the kids. My friend Josie used to apply for jobs she had no interest in getting, and she liked to mess with people's minds. She'd talk about cramps and abusive boyfriends and her daydream about one day breastfeeding her baby and she always got offered the job. Most people are at their most robotic when interviewing, which is obviously ironic because you're trying to put forth the most concentrated essence of yourself that you can. Most resumés are as boring as yours, and nobody ever reads the second page. There are people out there who will hate you for the way you use your knife and fork. Put the word "implement" in your resumé and you won't get phoned back. College will guarantee you a higher lifelong income, and friends made in college last longer than those made in real life. Men turn bitter around forty. The easiest way to get a job is to fill in for women on maternity leave. They almost never come back. Watch out for post-grad students. They wreck more marriages than drugs and alcohol combined. Needy people never last more than two years at any job. I used to get straight A's my whole life, and then in college I started getting D's and it was like morphine. It was great. If someone's bothering you at work, ask him or her to make a donation to a charity. Keep a can and donation envelopes in your desk. They'll never bug you again. It works.
$$$$$$$$$$$$$$$$$$$$$$$$$$$$$$$$$$$$$$$$$$$$$$$$$$$$$$$$$$$$
$$$$$$$$$$$$$$$$$$$$$$$$$$$$$$$$$$$$$$$$$$$$$$$$$$$$$$$$$$$$
$$$$$$$$$$$$$$$$$$$$$$$$$$$$$$$$$$$$$$$$$$$$$$$$$$$$$$$$$$$$
$$$$$$$$$$$$$$$$$$$$$$$$$$$$$$$$$$$$$$$$$$$$$$$$$$$$$$$$$$$$
$$$$$$$$$$$$$$$$$$$$$$$$$$$$$$$$$$$$$$$$$$$$$$$$$$$$$$$$$$$$
$$$$$$$$$$$$$$$$$$$$$$$$$$$$$$$$$$$$$$$$$$$$$$$$$$$$$$$$$$$$
$$$$$$$$$$$$$$$$$$$$$$$$$$$$$$$$$$$$$$$$$$$$$$$$$$$$$$$$$$$$
$$$$$$$$$$$$$$$$$$$$$$$$$$$$$$$$$$$$$$$$$$$$$$$$$$$$$$$$$$$$
$$$$$$$$$$$$$$$$$$$$$$$$$$$$$$$$$$$$$$$$$$$$$$$$$$$$$$$$$$$$
$$$$$$$$$$$$$$$$$$$$$$$$$$$$$$$$$$$$$$$$$$$$$$$$$$$$$$$$$$$$
$$$$$$$$$$$$$$$$$$$$$$$$$$$$$$$$$$$$$$$$$$$$$$$$$$$$$$$$$$$$
$$$$$$$$$$$$$$$$$$$$$$$$$$$$$$$$$$$$$$$$$$$$$$$$$$$$$$$$$$$$
$$$$$$$$$$$$$$$$$$$$$$$$$$$$$$$$$$$$$$$$$$$$$$$$$$$$$$$$$$$$
$$$$$$$$$$$$$$$$$$$$$$$$$$$$$$$$$$$$$$$$$$$$$$$$$$$$$$$$$$$$
$$$$$$$$$$$$$$$$$$$$$$$$$$$$$$$$$$$$$$$$$$$$$$$$$$$$$$$$$$$$
$$$$$$$$$$$$$$$$$$$$$$$$$$$$$$$$$$$$$$$$$$$$$$$$$$$$$$$$$$$$
$$$$$$$$$$$$$$$$$$$$$$$$$$$$$$$$$$$$$$$$$$$$$$$$$$$$$$$$$$$$
$$$$$$$$$$$$$$$$$$$$$$$$$$$$$$$$$$$$$$$$$$$$$$$$$$$$$$$$$$$$

$$$$$$$$$$$$$$$$$$$$$$$$$$$$$$$$$$$$$$$$$$$$$$$$$$
$$$$$$$$$$$$$$$$$$$$$$$$$$$$$$$$$$$$$$$$$$$$$$$$$$
$$$$$$$$$$$$$$$$$$$$$$$$$$$$$$$$$$$$$$$$$$$$$$$$$$
$$$$$$$$$$$$$$$$$$$$$$$$$$$$$$$$$$$$$$$$$$$$$$$$$$
$$$$$$$$$$$$$$$$$$$$$$$$$$$$$$$$$$$$$$$$$$$$$$$$$$
$$$$$$$$$$$$$$$$$$$$$$$$$$$$$$$$$$$$$$$$$$$$$$$$$$
$$$$$$$$$$$$$$$$$$$$$$$$$$$$$$$$$$$$$$$$$$$$$$$$$$
$$$$$$$$$$$$$$$$$$$$$$$$$$$$$$$$$$$$$$$$$$$$$$$$$$
$$$$$$$$$$$$$$$$$$$$$$$$$$$$$$$$$$$$$$$$$$$$$$$$$$
$$$$$$$$$$$$$$$$$$$$$$$$$$$$$$$$$$$$$$$$$$$$$$$$$$
$$$$$$$$$$$$$$$$$$$$$$$$$$$$$$$$$$$$$$$$$$$$$$$$$$
$$$$$$$$$$$$$$$$$$$$$$$$$$$$$$$$$$$$$$$$$$$$$$$$$$
$$$$$$$$$$$$$$$$$$$$$$$$$$$$$$$$$$$$$$$$$$$$$$$$$$
$$$$$$$$$$$$$$$$$$$$$$$$$$$$$$$$$$$$$$$$$$$$$$$$$$
$$$$$$$$$$$$$$$$$$$$$$$$$$$$$$$$$$$$$$$$$$$$$$$$$$
$$$$$$$$$$$$$$$$$$$$$$$$$$$$$$$$$$$$$$$$$$$$$$$$$$
$$$$$$$$$$$$$$$$$$$$$$$$$$$$$$$$$$$$$$$$$$$$$$$$$$
$$$$$$$$$$$$$$$$$$$$$$$$$$$$$$$$$$$$$$$$$$$$$$$$$$
$$$$$$$$$$$$$$$$$$$$$$$$$$$$$$$$$$$$$$$$$$$$$$$$$$
$$$$$$$$$$$$$$$$$$$$$$$$$$$$$$$$$$$$$$$$$$$$$$$$$$
$$$$$$$$$$$$$$$$$$$$$$$$$$$$$$$$$$$$$$$$$$$$$$$$$$
$$$$$$$$$$$$$$$$$$$$$$$$$$$$$$$$$$$$$$$$$$$$$$$$$$
$$$$$$$$$$$$$$$$$$$$$$$$$$$$$$$$$$$$$$$$$$$$$$$$$$
$$$$$$$$$$$$$$$$$$$$$$$$$$$$$$$$$$$$$$$$$$$$$$$$$$
$$$$$$$$$$$$$$$$$$$$$$$$$$$$$$$$$$$$$$$$$$$$$$$$$$
$$$$$$$$$$$$$$$$$$$$$$$$$$$$$$$$$$$$$$$$$$$$$$$$$$
$$$$$$$$$$$$$$$$$$$$$$$$$$$$$$$$$$$$$$$$$$$$$$$$$$
$$$$$$$$$$$$$$$$$$$$$$$$$$$$$$$$$$$$$$$$$$$$$$$$$$
$$$$$$$$$$$$$$$$$$$$$$$$$$$$$$$$$$$$$$$$$$$$$$$$$$
$$$$$$$$$$$$$$$$$$$$$$$$$$$$$$$$$$$$$$$$$$$$$$$$$$
$$$$$$$$$$$$$$$$$$$$$$$$$$$$$$$$$$$$$$$$$$$$$$$$$$
$$$$$$$$$$$$$$$$$$$$$$$$$$$$$$$$$$$$$$$$$$$$$$$$$$
$$$$$$$$$$$$$$$$$$$$$$$$$$$$$$$$$$$$$$$$$$$$$$$$$$
$$$$$$$$$$$$$$$$$$$$$$$$$$$$$$$$$$$$$$$$$$$$$$$$$$
$$$$$$$$$$$$$$$$$$$$$$$$$$$$$$$$$$$$$$$$$$$$$$$$$$
$$$$$$$$$$$$$$$$$$$$$$$$$$$$$$$$$$$$$$$$$$$$$$$$$$
$$$$$$$$$$$$$$$$$$$$$$$$$$$$$$$$$$$$$$$$$$$$$$$$$$
$$$$$$$$$$$$$$$$$$$$$$$$$$$$$$$$$$$$$$$$$$$$$$$$$$
$$$$$$$$$$$$$$$$$$$$$$$$$$$$$$$$$$$$$$$$$$$$$$$$$$

ramen noodles, ramen noodles, ramen noodles, ramen noodles, ramen noodles, ramen noodles
ramen noodles, ramen noodles, ramen noodles, ramen noodles, ramen noodles, ramen noodles
ramen noodles, ramen noodles, ramen noodles, ramen noodles, ramen noodles, ramen noodles
ramen noodles, ramen noodles, ramen noodles, ramen noodles, ramen noodles, ramen noodles
ramen noodles, ramen noodles, ramen noodles, ramen noodles, ramen noodles, ramen noodles
ramen noodles, ramen noodles, ramen noodles, ramen noodles, ramen noodles, ramen noodles
ramen noodles, ramen noodles, ramen noodles, ramen noodles, ramen noodles, ramen noodles
ramen noodles, ramen noodles, ramen noodles, ramen noodles, ramen noodles, ramen noodles
ramen noodles, ramen noodles, ramen noodles, ramen noodles, ramen noodles, ramen noodles
ramen noodles, ramen noodles, ramen noodles, ramen noodles, ramen noodles, ramen noodles
ramen noodles, ramen noodles, ramen noodles, ramen noodles, ramen noodles, ramen noodles
ramen noodles, ramen noodles, ramen noodles, ramen noodles, ramen noodles, ramen noodles
ramen noodles, ramen noodles, ramen noodles, ramen noodles, ramen noodles, ramen noodles
ramen noodles, ramen noodles, ramen noodles, ramen noodles, ramen noodles, ramen noodles
ramen noodles, ramen noodles, ramen noodles, ramen noodles, ramen noodles, ramen noodles
ramen noodles, ramen noodles, ramen noodles, ramen noodles, ramen noodles, ramen noodles
ramen noodles, ramen noodles, ramen noodles, ramen noodles, ramen noodles, ramen noodles
ramen noodles, ramen noodles, ramen noodles, ramen noodles, ramen noodles, ramen noodles
ramen noodles, ramen noodles, ramen noodles, ramen noodles, ramen noodles, ramen noodles
ramen noodles, ramen noodles, ramen noodles, ramen noodles, ramen noodles, ramen noodles
ramen noodles, ramen noodles, ramen noodles, ramen noodles, ramen noodles, ramen noodles
ramen noodles, ramen noodles, ramen noodles, ramen noodles, ramen noodles, ramen noodles
ramen noodles, ramen noodles, ramen noodles, ramen noodles, ramen noodles, ramen noodles
ramen noodles, ramen noodles, ramen noodles, ramen noodles, ramen noodles, ramen noodles
ramen noodles, ramen noodles, ramen noodles, ramen noodles, ramen noodles, ramen noodles
ramen noodles, ramen noodles, ramen noodles, ramen noodles, ramen noodles, ramen noodles
ramen noodles, ramen noodles, ramen noodles, ramen noodles, ramen noodles, ramen noodles
ramen noodles, ramen noodles, ramen noodles, ramen noodles, ramen noodles, ramen noodles
ramen noodles, ramen noodles, ramen noodles, ramen noodles, ramen noodles, ramen noodles
ramen noodles, ramen noodles, ramen noodles, ramen noodles, ramen noodles, ramen noodles
ramen noodles, ramen noodles, ramen noodles, ramen noodles, ramen noodles, ramen noodles
ramen noodles, ramen noodles, ramen noodles, ramen noodles, ramen noodles, ramen noodles
ramen noodles, ramen noodles, ramen noodles, ramen noodles, ramen noodles, ramen noodles
ramen noodles, ramen noodles, ramen noodles, ramen noodles, ramen noodles, ramen noodles
ramen noodles, ramen noodles, ramen noodles, ramen noodles, ramen noodles, ramen noodles
ramen noodles, ramen noodles, ramen noodles, ramen noodles, ramen noodles, ramen noodles
ramen noodles, ramen noodles, ramen noodles, ramen noodles, ramen noodles, ramen noodles
ramen noodles, ramen noodles, ramen noodles, ramen noodles, ramen noodles, ramen noodles
ramen noodles, ramen noodles, ramen noodles, ramen noodles, ramen noodles, ramen noodles
ramen noodles, ramen noodles, ramen noodles, ramen noodles, ramen noodles, ramen noodles
ramen noodles, ramen noodles, ramen noodles, ramen noodles, ramen noodles, ramen noodles
ramen noodles, ramen noodles, ramen noodles, ramen noodles, ramen noodles, ramen noodles
ramen noodles, ramen noodles, ramen noodles, ramen noodles, ramen noodles, ramen noodles
ramen noodles, ramen noodles, ramen noodles, ramen noodles, ramen noodles, ramen noodles

Click here.

**Part One**
Never Mess with the Subway Diet

"Oh God. I feel like a refugee from a Douglas Coupland novel."

"*That* asshole."

"Who does he think he is?"

"Come on, guys, *focus*. We've got a major problem on our hands."

The six of us were silent, but for our footsteps. The main corridor's muted plasma TVs blipped out the news and sports, while co-workers in long-sleeved blue and black T-shirts oompah-loompahed in and out of laminate-access doors, elevated walkways, staircases and elevators, their missions inscrutable and squirrelly. It was a rare sunny day. Freakishly articulated sunbeams highlighted specks of mica in the hallway's designer granite. They looked like randomized particle events.

Mark said, "I can't even think about what just happened in there."

John Doe said, "I'd like to do whatever it is people statistically do when confronted by a jolt of large and bad news."

I suggested he ingest five milligrams of Valium and three shots of hard liquor or four glasses of domestic wine.

"Really?"

"Don't ask me, John. Google it."

"And so I shall."

Cowboy had a jones for cough syrup, while Bree fished through one of her many pink vinyl Japanese handbags for lip gloss—phase one of her well-established pattern of pursuing sexual conquest to silence her inner pain.

The only quiet member of our group of six was Kaitlin, new to our work area as of the day before. She was walking with us mostly because she didn't yet know how to get from the meeting room to our cubicles. We're not sure if Kaitlin is boring or if she's resistant to bonding, but then again none of us have really cranked up our charm.

We passed Warren from the motion capture studio. "Yo! jPodsters! A turtle! All *right*!" He flashed a thumbs-up.

"Thank you, Warren. We can all feel the love in the room."

Clearly, via the gift of text messaging, Warren and pretty much everyone in the company now knew of our plight, which is this: during today's marketing meeting we learned we now have to retroactively insert a charismatic cuddly turtle character into our skateboard game, which is already nearly one-third of the way through its production cycle. Yes, you read that correctly, a turtle character—in a *skateboard* game.

The three-hour meeting had taken place in a two-hundred-seat room nicknamed the air-conditioned rectum. I tried to make the event go faster by pretending to have superpower vision: I could see the carbon dioxide pumping in and out of everyone's nose and mouth—it was purple. It made me think of that urban legend about the chemical they put in swimming pools that reveals when somebody pees. Then I wondered if Leonardo da Vinci had ever inhaled any of the oxygen molecules I was breathing, or if he ever had to sit through a marketing meeting. What would that have been like? "Leo, thanks for your input, but our studies indicate that when they see Lisa smile, they want a sexy, *flirty* smile, not that grim little slit she has now. Also, I don't know what that closet case Michelangelo is thinking with that naked David guy, but Jesus, clamp a diaper onto him pronto. Next item on the agenda: Perspective—Passing Fad or Opportunity to Win? But first, Katie here is going to tell us about this Friday's Jeans Day, to be followed by a ten-minute muffin break."

But the word "turtle" pulled me out of my reverie, uttered by Fearless Leader—our new head of marketing, *Steve*. I put up my hand and quite reasonably asked, "Sorry, Steve, did you say a *turtle*?"

Christine, a senior development director, said, "No need to be sarcastic, Ethan. Steve here took Toblerone chocolate and turned it around inside of two years."

"No," Steve protested. "I appreciate an open dialogue. All I'm really saying is that, at home, my son, Carter, plays SimQuest4 and can't get enough of its turtle character, and if my Carter likes turtle characters, then a turtle character is a winner, and thus, this skateboard game needs a turtle."

John Doe BlackBerried me: **I CAN'T FEEL MY LEGS**

And so the order was issued to make our new turtle character "accessible" and "fun" and the buzzword is so horrible I have to spell it out in ASCII: "{101, 100, 103,  121}"

**ORIENTAL
NOODLE SOUP**

**NISSIN**

70622 03503

2¼ oz. x 6 CUPS

# Chicken Flavor

• • •

Back in our cubicle pod, the six of us fizzled away from each other like ginger ale bubbles. I had eighteen new emails and one phone message, my mother: "Dear, could you give me a call? I really need to speak with you—it's an emergency."

An emergency? I phoned her cell right away. "Mom, what's up? What's wrong?"

"Ethan, are you at work right now?"

"Where else would I be?"

"I'm at SuperValu. Let me call you back from a pay phone."

The line went dead. I picked it up when it rang.

"Mom, you said this was an emergency."

"It is, dear. Ethan, honey, I need you to help me."

"I just got out of the Worst Meeting Ever. What's going on?"

"I suppose I'd better just tell you flat out."

"Tell me what?"

"Ethan, I killed a biker."

"You killed a *biker*?"

"Well, I didn't *mean* to."

"Mom, how the hell did you manage to kill a biker?"

"Ethan, just come home right now. I'll be there in twenty minutes."

"Why doesn't Dad help?"

"He's on a shoot today. He might get a speaking part."

She hung up.

• • •

On my way out of the office, I passed a world-building team, standing in a semicircle, staring at a large German-made knife on a desktop.

"What's up?" I asked.

"It's the knife we're using to cut Aidan's birthday cake," a friend, Josh, replied.

I looked more closely at the knife: it was clownishly big. "Okay, it's hard-core *Itchy & Scratchy*—but so what?"

"We're having a contest—we're trying to see if there's any way to hold a knife and walk across a room and not look psycho."

"And?"

"It's impossible."

A few desks away, Bree was showing someone photos of her recent holiday visiting Korean animation sweatshops. She was bummed because she couldn't get into North Korea: too much legal juju. "It's a real blotch to have on your passport. I just wanted to know what it's like to be in a society with no technology except for three dial telephones and a TV camera they won from Fidel Castro in a game of rock paper scissors."

Bree is right. For those of us who are too young to have visited Cold War East Germany or the USSR, North Korea remains as the sole boutique nation with a quack low-technology dictatorship. "Owning a 56K floppy disk can land you two decades of hard labour."

I suggested North Korea should change its name to something friendlier, more accessible.

"Like what, Ethan?"

"How about Trish?"

"As in Patricia?"

"Yeah."

"I like that. It's fresh."

"Thanks."

• • •

Through a rare and cheerful accident of freeway planning, I can get from the campus to my parents' place by making two left turns and two right turns, even though they live 17.4 miles away in the gloomy evergreen cocoon of the British Properties. I find this elegant and pleasing.

When I pulled into the driveway, nothing seemed out of place. It could easily have been 1988, right down to the 1988 Reliant K-car wagon. Inside the front door, I heard Mom call from the kitchen, "Ethan, would you like a sandwich? I have egg salad."

I walked into the kitchen, unchanged since Ronald Reagan ruled Earth. My brother, Greg, and I once found a pile of cleaning products that predated bar-coding on a hallway shelf. "No sandwich, thanks, Mom. Am I, or am I not, here about a dead biker?"

Mom cut her own sandwich in two. "I know for a fact that your diet is appalling. Greg tells me that all you eat is Doritos and fruit leather."

"Mom, the *biker*?"

"I was going to eat my sandwich, but okay, Mr. Impatient, follow me."

We walked out of the kitchen and down the main hallway, past my old bedroom, over which my beer-bottles-of-the-world collection had once stood sentry—a room that now housed Mom's sewing machine, her cigarette-making machine and the machine she uses to roll up old newspapers to convert them into fire logs. Where my bong once sat now rested a balsa wood mallard duck, sitting in a basket of silk freesia.

Farther down the hall we descended a set of stairs into the back hallway, rife with the aroma of mildewed sporting equipment, and from there, down another set of stairs that led into the basement proper. Mom reached into a basket and handed me a pair of Ray-Bans and put a pair on herself. She said, "I'd lower the lights, but it confuses the chlorophyll cycles."

Mom also keeps her grow-op at nearly a hundred percent humidity, and I hate humidity. Humidity feels like hundreds of strangers touching me.

At the far end of the basement, where the air hockey table had sat dormant for decades, amid a cluster of astonishingly fertile female plants decked out in coloured ribbons (Mom's genetic bookkeeping system), lay the beefiest, scariest death star of a biker I'd ever seen. "Holy *crap*, Mom, you've done some weird stuff in your life, but this tops it. What happened?"

"I electrocuted him."

"You *what*?"

"I rigged up this corner of the room so that if I ever got into trouble, I could electrocute anybody standing in that puddle." I looked down—the biker *was* lying in a puddle.

"You set up a death trap in your own house?"

"This is a grow-op, dear. I'm not raising miniature ponies down here."

"So why did you electrocute him?"

"His name is, or was, Tim."

"What did young *Tim* do to you?"

"He was trying to extort me into giving him a share of the crop."

"How much?"

"Fifty percent."

"What an asshole."

"It really was an accident, Ethan. I wasn't sure if it was going to get ugly, so I arranged things so that he was standing in the puddle. And then his cellphone rang, and I had a panic reflex and flipped the switch."

I wanted to know what sort of ring tone a biker would select for his cellphone, but that could wait until later. I stared down at Tim. He looked heavy. And his—for lack of a better word—*deadness* was hard to absorb.

Mom said, "If you could drag him through the door into the carport, together we can probably lift him into the wagon."

"What then?"

"You tell me, Ethan. You're the family genius."

"Why couldn't you call Greg?" My brother is a hot-shot real estate sales guy.

"Greg is in Hong Kong on business."

Here's the thing: How *do* you get rid of a body? Pretend that right now you have a corpse in your house. It's like trying to get rid of a side of beef with nobody knowing. It's hard. "Mom, do you have a carpet you want to get rid of?"

"Why a carpet?"

"The Sikhs are always rolling up the dead bodies of unwilling brides from arranged marriages and tossing them into the Fraser River. Maybe we can do that."

Mom looked disappointed.

"What? What's wrong with that idea?"

"What's wrong is that wherever we put the body it has to *stay* where we put it. I wouldn't want Tim floating to the surface. I think we should bury him."

"We could roll him up inside the carpet *and* bury him."

"Okay. Let's get the carpet from your father's den. I've always hated it. It reminds me of your grandmother."

We went upstairs. Dad used to work for a marine engineering firm. When he was laid off, he got into acting, mostly TV, but lately he'd been copping a few brief non-speaking roles in U.S. theatrical releases. Okay, he gets tiny crappy non-speaking parts in TV commercials where he always seems to be left on the cutting-room floor, as well as gigs as an extra in crowd scenes.

In his den, all of his old ship models and nautical maps had been dumped off the shelves and heaped in a corner in favour of framed headshots—colour and B+W, serious, lighthearted, "The Lover," "The Sad Clown," "Good Cop Gone Bad"— as well as pictures of Dad shaking hands with a galaxy of made-in-Vancouver actors carted up to Canada to max out tax credits: Ben Affleck, Mira Sorvino, Kirk Cameron, Lucy Lawless, Raffi and various Muppets way down the Muppet food chain, like Cookie Monster. There was a new one of him with Uma Thurman. "What was she like to work with?" I asked Mom.

"Apparently a dream. She signed his cast and crew jacket."

Some of Dad's ballroom dancing outfits were draped over an armchair, awaiting dry cleaning.

"What your father sees in that horrid dancing I'll never understand." Mom pointed to a braided rug beneath Dad's desk. "That was a wedding present. It's given me the heebie-jeebies for decades. Is it big enough to hold Tim?"

"I think so."

She bent down. "Lift up the desk, and I'll pull it out from under the legs."

I lifted the desk, and in so doing, toppled a five-hundred-thick pile of headshots of Dad as a Nazi. Mom puffed. "Got it."

We rolled up the rug and lugged it downstairs, where we made a biker-wrap sandwich out of Tim. I dragged him out into the carport—man, was he heavy—and I got oil stains on the carpet.

Mom was holding open the wagon's rear door. "Come on, Ethan, show a little respect."

"You electrocute the guy where my air hockey table used to stand, and you ask me to show some respect?"

"You and your brother never played air hockey after the first Christmas weekend."

"Well, it kind of sucked."

"Well, *I* kind of drove all over town trying to find a place that wasn't sold out of them."

With one big huff, I lifted Tim into the back, but he fell out with an unnerving thump. "Ethan, get him in the car."

I did that, and we backed out of the carport and driveway.

"Okay," Mom said, "let's find a nice big hole."

"Just for the record, Mom, this whole thing is creeping me out."

"Men should never discuss their feelings, Ethan."

"I thought women are supposed to like guys discussing feelings."

"Good God, no."

• • •

It's strange how everything in the world changes the moment your focus becomes extremely specific. *Hmmm . . . is that a good place to bury a body? No, soil's too thin.*

Mom suggested Stanley Park, on the edge of downtown. "If there was ever a place to dump a body, the park is it. At this point in history, there are probably more bones there than soil."

So we drove to Stanley Park, but there were way too many people walking around. We headed back to the North Shore and checked out jogging paths and some of the smaller municipal parks, but even there, people and dogs abounded.

Around six it started getting dark, and I had an idea. "Let's drive up to those monster houses Greg is always selling. We'll put Tim in the foundation of one of the construction sites."

"I don't know . . ."

"The bonus is that we don't have to dig a hole. Instead, we get to fill one in a bit."

"I see your point."

We ended up on the winding treeless roads of West Van's bizarre Canterbury neighbourhood, a rainforest bulldozed to make way for jumbo houses that resembled microwave ovens with cedar shake roofing.

"Who lives in these things?" Mom asked as we drove.

"Greg says it's mostly sports stars and abandoned Asian housewives sitting out their three-year sentences required for citizenship."

"There. Let's put him down there." Mom was pointing at a freshly poured concrete foundation for a house in the twenty-thousand-square-foot range. It had been framed in with two-by-sixes, and from the skeleton I could tell the style would be best described as Sailor Moon's Breezy West Coast Hideaway. The house was on the highest street. There was nobody overlooking us.

Mom's spot selection was good. The basement concrete had been poured and coated with vapour barrier tar. The hole was obviously slated to be backfilled with dirt within a day or two. In it there were a few tatters of tarpaper, a tuft or two of pink insulation and a Wendy's wrapper.

We removed Tim the Biker from the car and ever so casually carried him to the front door area like he was a futon. With a one-two-three, we lobbed him in. We both pretended not to hear the gentle cracking noise.

I said, "Perfect shot. Come on. Let's cover him up."

We entombed Tim using the greyish-orange dirt from the excavation. It went far more quickly than I'd expected, five minutes, maybe.

Mom looked a bit dizzy as we walked back to the car. When we drove away, she sat like a preteen caught shoplifting at Wal-Mart. Her hands were folded in her lap, and her head was down. She sniffled once, twice, and then came the tears, in floods.

"Mom?"

"Ethan, could you pull over?"

I did.

She turned to me, red-eyed. "I didn't tell you everything."

"Oh?"

"I'm telling you because I can't tell your father."

"Tell him what?"

"I quite liked Tim. He was a troubled soul. I thought I could help him."

This was a conversation I wasn't prepared to continue. I said, "Mom, let's turn on the radio. We can discuss this later." I turned on the AM radio, and the music that came on was French. "Mom, you listen to the French station?"

"*Oui*. Sometimes."

From the speakers came the sound of accordions.

"Mom, what's with French music? All the songs have the same title." As we drove home, I composed a mental French song list that went like this:

> *Ça va, ça va*
> *On qui peut*
> *Ma vie*
> *Le Métro, c'est où?*
> *C'est ça*
> *L'amour, c'est bien*
> *Le bon cowboy*
> *De bon Métro*
> *C'est comme ça*
> *J'ai un rêve*
> *Quelle heure est-il?*

*Nous nous allons*
*Dit donc!*
*Chanson des Métros perdus*
*Amour des rêves*
*Où?*
*J'ai mal à la tête*
*Nous sommes perdus (Avez-vous une carte?)*
*J'ai une carte*
*Passé composé*
*Le pamplemousse et la grenouille*
*Le ça*

UnknownSender@UnknownDomain.org

Greetings to you. I am Mr. Macaulay A. Ofurhie from the office of the Department of Petroleum Resources, DPR, Nigeria. I write to solicit your cooperation in the execution of this entreaty.

Without any prejudice to the foregoing, the DPR is the presidium petroleum Inspectorate and directorate of the Nigerian oil and gas industry vested with the following responsibilities: supervising all petroleum industry operations; enforcing safety and environmental regulations and ensuring that those operations conform to national and international industry practices and standards; keeping and updating records on Nigerian petroleum industry operations as well as rendering regular reports on them to Government and relevant Agencies; verifying and processing all applications for payment/debt claims and licenses so as to ensure compliance with laid-down guidelines before making recommendations to Government and relevant Agencies as well as providing estimates and projections for work plans, scheduling methodology, bid documents and to prioritize, distribute and award contracts for the development of oil and gas projects.

To the main purpose of writing you, following a summarized breakdown of the fiscal expenditure by the DPR for the past four years and as reported to the government and relevant agencies, showed that the total project contracts awarded to both local and foreign firms amounted to over five billion US dollars and 52% were awarded to foreign firms/multinationals. The crux of this letter is that along with contracts cleared for payoff is an acclaimed sum of US$38.6million US dollars which has been approved for pay-off by the Federal Ministry of Finance (FMF) alongside with other beneficiaries whose applications are been process. The finance/contract department of the DPR deliberately over-invoiced most of the contracted projected and DPR motivated projects. Consequently in the course of disbursements, the department was been able to accumulate US$38.6million US dollars, as contained in its records and that of the FMF's suspense account with the Debt Reconciliation Committee (DRC). Respective application for payment will not last more than two weeks. Hence, as the Coordinator of this project is to solicit your unalloyed cooperation and assistance to enable us pull out $3.6m into acclaimed foreign beneficiary account owned by your good-self and covered by a foreign company/business name to be used. This business is 100% fool proof, genuine and risk-free. Hence the need for strict and absolute confidentiality till the end is all Important because members of the office the office of the DPR involved in this business are personalities who have attained impeccable track records of probity in the Civil Service of Nigeria and as such are not permitted to operate Foreign Account in discharging their functions as members of the DPR. Furthermore, sharing of this fund after remittance into your provided bank account will be done as follows: 70% for us, 25% for you the account owner and 5% to cover contingencies expenses and to be reimbursed immediately. Confirming your faithfulness to this entreaty and your unalloyed cooperation to consolidate this transaction as proposed to you, please endeavor to reply immediately with your contact/postal address; telephone and fax lines for further briefing.

I thank you for your attention and anticipated co-operation as I am looking forward to hearing from you.

Kind regards,

Mr. M. A. Ofurhie
Office of the Director, Department of Petroleum Resources.

• • •

Back in jPod, Mark accidentally tipped over John Doe's stack of Tom Clancy novels, and it was one of those things that got slightly ugly.

"Look, John, I said I was sorry."

"You should treat books with more reverence."

"You've actually read all of those?"

"Yes. So? What was the last book you read?"

"Book? As in paper and ink and everything?"

"Yes."

"Hmmm . . . it was the manual that came with my microwave oven. I was trying to figure out how to make it tell me the time in the European mode. You know, 18:00 instead of 6:00."

"Could you do it?"

"Yeah, but I used up three sick days nailing it."

"What about fiction?"

"Novels?"

"Yeah."

"Ummmm . . ."

"Just as I thought. You're an emotional blank."

"Oh, *please*."

"Too close for comfort?"

"This is stupid."

Mark went to his desk, but John started heckling him from the other side of the wall baffle. *"Mark's an emotional blaaaaank. Mark's an emotional blaaaaank."*

This was driving me nuts. "Both of you stop it. Neither of you are emotional blanks."

Harrumphs from both cubicles.

"And to prove it," I said, "I'm going to draw up a standardized list that itemizes everything that's special and unique about all of us here in jPod."

"I can't imagine Mark's will be too long," said John.

"Manners, please."

And so I made up a quick template and standardized our personalities on paper. Anything to get out of doing my actual job.

**Living Cartoon Profile No. 1**

**Name:** Casper Jesperson

**Name people actually use:** Cancer Cowboy, or simply Cowboy

**Reason for unusual name people actually use:** Grew up in an agricultural region and was told by well-meaning mother who didn't want him to smoke that the local cowboys were all dying of lung cancer.

**Smokes:** Yes

**Non-work e-name(s):** xtinctionevent@mindlink.com

**Preferred room temperature:** 71°F

**Favourite game:** Doom 3

**Preferred *Simpsons* character:** Duff Man

**Preferred karaoke song:** "Dust in the Wind" by Kansas

**Food group most prevalent within work cubicle:** Skittles, with the green ones removed

**Most disturbing trait:** Is not suicidal, but really enjoys thinking about death, and, to be frank, is actually kind of looking forward to it.

**Living Cartoon Profile No. 2**

**Name:** Brianna Jyang

**Name people actually use:** Bree
**Most evident pathology:** Makes no bones about the fact that she wants to sleep with almost every guy she meets, but only once.
**Does she actually do this?:** We're not sure
**Non-work e-name(s):** boxofpaperclips@hotmail.com
**Preferred room temperature:** 65°F
**Favourite game:** The original PlayStation Tomb Raider
**Preferred *Simpsons* character:** Edna Krabappel
**Preferred karaoke song:** "My Heart Will Go On" by Céline Dion
**Does this song make her mushy?:** Yes
**Does this mean she's a crying drunk?:** Yes
**Food group most prevalent within work cubicle:** A low-fat oat muffin that she eats, one molecule at a time, over the course of an eighteen-hour workday.
**Does this frighten and annoy her co-workers?:** Yes

**Living Cartoon Profile No. 3**

**Name:** John Doe (yes, legally, as of three months ago)

**Birth name:** crow well mountain juniper (all lower case)
**Name people actually use:** John Doe
**Reason for spooky birth name and subsequent selection of John Doe as a real name:** Grew up in a lesbian commune and was home-schooled until the age of twelve. Never saw a TV set until age fifteen. Wants to be statistically normal to counteract his wacko upbringing.
**Non-work e-name(s):** johndoedammit@aol.com
**Preferred room temperature:** 62°F ("I may have grown up in a lesbian commune, but I think we truly are overdependent on climate control systems in our society.")
**Favourite game:** *The Simpsons* Hit & Run
**Preferred *Simpsons* character:** Groundskeeper Willie OR Lard Lad
**Does he watch too much TV, specifically *The Simpsons*, to compensate for his media-free upbringing?:** Yes
**Preferred karaoke song:** None
**Reason for having no preferred karaoke song:** Grew up without pop culture or music: "I just don't get it—but I'm trying, I really am."
**Food group most prevalent within work cubicle:** M&M's (which is based on statistics on items most commonly eaten out of hotel mini-bars).

**Living Cartoon Profile No. 4**


**Name:** Brandon Mark Jackson

**Name people actually use:** Mark
**Reason for boring name people actually use:** Entered jPod
only three weeks ago
**Non-work e-name(s):** bmarkjackson@earthlink.com
**Preferred room temperature:** Haven't yet discussed this, but
I'm guessing 72°F
**Favourite game:** Baldur's Gate
**Preferred *Simpsons* character:** Fast-food guy with cracking
voice OR Moe Szyslak: opposite ends of the food-and-
beverage industry labour cycle
**Preferred karaoke song:** Has yet to show any musical verve
**Food group most prevalent within work cubicle:** None
**Does he think we don't notice this?:** Yes
**Is his office freakishly clean with no evidence whatsoever
of an interior life—not even so much as a snapshot or
anime knick-knackery?:** Yes

**Living Cartoon Profile No. 5**


**Name:** Kaitlin Anna Boyd Joyce

**Name people actually use:** Kaitlin
**Was she at the meeting today with Steve Who Turned Around Toblerone in Two Years?** Yes
**Do we know much about her yet?:** No. She joined jPod yesterday.
**Non-work e-name(s):** C13H20N2O2.HCL@shaw.ca
**Preferred room temperature:** Haven't discussed it, but I'm guessing 72°F
**Favourite game:** Yahoo! Games.com's TextTwist (spied on her)
**Preferred *Simpsons* character:** I'm guessing Lisa
**Preferred karaoke song:** I'm hoping it's one I really like
**Food group most prevalent within work cubicle:** Gum
**Does she notice me?:** To be honest, I think not
**Will I let her see this particular character report?:** No way

**Living Cartoon Profile No. 6**

**Name:** Me

**Name on birth certificate:** Ethan Harrison Jarlewski
**Name people actually use:** Ethan
**Non-work e-name(s):** snacklover@gmail.com
**Preferred room temperature:** 68°F, and I hate hate hate humidity
**Most creative thing ever done:** An old operating system I invented when I was in high school. I called it Mentos.
**Favourite game:** Chrono Trigger on Sony PlayStation, a delectable console RPG with art by Akira Toriyama, sound by Yasunori Mitsuda and Nobuo Uematsu
**Preferred *Simpsons* character:** Kang and Kodos, the aliens
**Preferred karaoke song:** None
**Reason for not having a preferred karaoke song:** I live in fear of karaoke. Even thinking of it in this detached neutral listing format causes me to worry that I might somehow even unintentionally lure karaoke into my life.
**Food group most prevalent within work cubicle:** Kettle Chips with cracked pepper and lime, even though I suspect they give me bad dreams. Went through a Jell-O Pudding Snacks phase last fall, but now can't even look at the stuff.
**Does he consider himself normal?:** I used to, but now I wonder. Or rather, I think I'm still normal, but everyone around me is going random. Now I look at most people like recently lit Roman candles, unsure if they're about to go off, or if they're merely duds.
**Does he enjoy his job?:** The greatest challenge is to have a job without actually doing work, which is really hard to pull off in a company where workspace productivity is measured with just about every conceivable form of metrics.
**Does he take satisfaction in his approach to work?:** Yes

"Ethan, your description of me makes me look like a goof."

"Mark, all I did was collect the data and present it."

Mark was peeved. "Ethan, there has to be more to my life than this."

"Why can't you just be happy as a shallow cartoon glyph of a human like everybody else here?"

"You don't understand—I'm *me*—I have a *soul*."

"Mark, I think you're obsessing on this whole individuality thing. Revel in your averageness the way John Doe does."

On the other side of my wallboard, John Doe gave a muffled, "Amen."

"No. I want to improve my profile now. I demand to be more than just a cartoon character."

"Okay, then, please tell us, what is the single event that most changed you as a person?"

"That's easy. Six years ago I was doing the please-my-parents thing, landing a degree in biological sciences. I had a part-time job in the beetling pit."

"What's that?"

"It's where they take a dead animal and put it into this big stainless steel cone-shaped pit full of starving beetles, and after a few days, there's nothing left except bone-dry bones."

I thought of Tim the Biker's graceless burial. Where are these beetling pits when you need them?

Bree's head was above the wall partition. "You never told me about any beetling pit."

"Bree, by the time we got to your place, we'd only said eleven words."

I said, "Bree, please, I'm doing an interview here. Mark, how was the beetling pit the event that changed you most as a person?"

Mark turned to me. "It was the part of my life that made me realize something had to change in my universe. I was studying biology, as I was saying, to please my parents, and I don't think there's ever been a happy person on earth who chose an education and a job to please their parents. Then, one day, I got notice that the building I lived in was being torn down for condos, so I tried to find a place to live, but I screwed up and didn't find a place in time. When I asked my folks if I could live in the basement, they said *no way*."

"You were a problem child?"

"No. They turned the house into a B & B, and my room was gone."

"What happened then?"

"I was going to crash on a friend's couch, but first I had to put all of my stuff in a U-Store-It place over by the Second Narrows Bridge. It was late on a Friday afternoon, and I was the first client in this new patch of mini-units they'd built. I was glad, because it meant the place was clean, and I didn't have to worry if Jeffrey Dahmer had ever stored his boyfriends in my unit. But then the lights went out, and when I went to check the switch I accidentally clicked shut the big roll-down door; it locked, and because the place was new, they hadn't properly installed the fail-safe unlocking switch. I was stuck in there with no lights. When I tried pounding on the door, there was no one to hear me. It was pretty bad."

I stole a line from my mother: "Boo hoo. What then?"

"I tried to be all Boy Scout-y and positive, but after about nine p.m., I realized I was screwed."

"Can we speed this up?"

"Okay. I was in there for four days without light. The only thing I had to drink was a bottle of Gatorade autographed by John Madden. I had to eat the gum from my sacred collection of twelve factory-sealed boxes of 2003 Upper Deck SP authentic NFL cards, with one autographed and sequentially numbered rookie card per box, including autographed cards from Bart Starr, Donovan McNabb, Jerry Rice and Joe Montana. I was going to use them to fund my retirement."

"How long did the Gatorade last?"

"Almost fifty hours."

"And the gum?"

"Almost seventy-two hours. It was a long weekend."

At this point, all the heads in jPod gophered upwards, making *ooooohhhhhh* sounds.

"Mark," I asked, "so how has that changed you as a human?"

"It's kind of weird."

"We wouldn't *possibly* want to hear something weird, Mark."

"Since then, I need as many edible objects around me as possible."

"Huh?"

"Like my futon. It's from this place in Finland. Cost me $2,500, but the entire futon is edible. They market them to Japanese people who are worried about earthquakes and being trapped alive under rubble."

"Go on."

"My apartment is like Willy Wonka's factory. You can eat my chairs."

"But, Mark, your cubicle is entirely devoid of stuff, let alone edible stuff."

"So it would appear, but you see this stapler?" Mark held up a generic stapler. "It's made of marzipan. I bought it online from this geek shop based in Palo Alto. And these pencils here? Chocolate."

Silence passed over us. We could never look at the world the same way ever again.

"Mark, I think you can safely consider yourself a member of jPod."

• • •

Sidetrack: Cowboy was cleaning out his hard drive and found some old penis enlargement spams he'd saved from 2003. All of us got sentimental for that brief historical moment when a fresh young Internet promised us a better tomorrow with all of the free Viagra, Ambien, Vicodin, OxyContin and enlarged members we were willing to accept.

How come you don't see dildos that are 5 or 6 inches long?

I know you're good looking. You probably have money and a nice car. But I would bet you have one that is small to average size. How do I know? Statistics. On average, men are from 5 to 6.3 inches. And don't tell me you haven't measured it, because every guy does at some point.

I used to be small—so small I'm too embarrassed to even type it. I was like you . . . thinking that it was the love that counted, or that money was all that I needed. How wrong I was! I found that out when my wife of a year packed up her bags and divorced me, yelling as she walked out the door that I was the worst guy she had ever slept with, because my unit was too small to get her off.

Right then and there I decided that I had to do something. But I didn't know where to look. That's when I came across an email telling me that I could gain 3 inches in 3 weeks.

Desperately wanting to try anything, I said to myself "What the heck, it's cheap, and who knows, it might work." It MIGHT work? How about growing 3 inches in only 2 weeks! Now Im the proud owner of an 8.3 inch unit.

Anyway, I just recently saw my ex-wife at our favorite hang out. She told me she still loved me and that she wanted me back. I took her to my house and her eyes almost popped out when I pulled down my pants. Then I told her to get out of my house. As she was walking out the door (crying) she asked me why didn't I want her back, I replied "Baby, I have a huge (actually gigantic) new gun that's loaded with bullets, and its hunting season!"

So, if you like being small (or average), then delete this email. On the other hand if you want to be Better-Than-Average then visit the link below and try it for yourself.

● ● ●

I played this truly evil welcome-to-jPod prank on Kaitlin while she was away from her desk. I popped the M and N keys off her keyboard and switched them. I can't wait to see the mirth and mayhem that ensues.

● ● ●

Okay, so around nine at night I finally got down to work, trawling through Google for data on turtles. Then my father phoned. From the odd background noise, I guessed he was calling from a location shoot.

"Dad, where are you?"

"I'm waythefuck out in Cloverdale."

"Is it a Western? I hear yee-hawing in the background."

"Sort of a Western—it's about ranchers, but they get invaded by aliens."

"What do the aliens do?"

"They inhabit the cattle, but then they get stuck inside them. So the ranchers suddenly discover their cattle are displaying highly intelligent behaviour, and every time the price of beef comes up, the cows go apeshit."

"What's the budget?"

"Crap."

"Why are you calling?"

"Because I want you to come out to the shoot."

Cloverdale is a half-hour drive, but because it's in the Fraser Valley it feels like three hours away. Los Angeles seems closer to me than Cloverdale does. I'm a bad son. I didn't want to make the drive. "Dad, I have to finish scrubbing up some 1980s motherboards I bought on eBay."

"Ethan, I'm in love."

Dad using an expression like "in love" was a wallbuster. "Oh," I said.

"That sounded judgmental."

"Well, this is a pretty weird thing to be hearing. What about Mom?"

"Just come out here and watch the dailies with me."

"Dad, you're an extra in a movie about aliens invading a cattle ranch. Why would you be allowed to watch the dailies?"

"Today I finally got my first speaking part. I thought it'd be a good day to tell you about other changes in my life, too."

I heaved out a lungful of air. "Okay. Tell me where you are."

"I'll pass you along to Sharon here. She's a teamster, and handles anything to do with vehicles."

Sharon's directions were eerie, a mirror image of the two lefts and two rights I took to get to Mom's. I took two rights and two lefts and arrived at Dad's shoot. I parked my car and got shuttled to the trailers. I opened the door to Dad's trailer, expecting to find him in a makeup bib drinking bottled water. Instead, he was French kissing someone who appeared to be Ellen Kovacs, who had been two years behind me in high school.

"Dad?"

It was like a French farce, the two of them separating and trying to appear chaste, smoothing their hair and pulling down their shirts. "Don't worry," I said, "there's no judging going on here."

"Son, this is Ellen."

"Hi, Ellen."

"Ethan, you look just the same as you did in high school."

"You two went to school together?"

"She didn't tell you?"

Dad said, "We're in love. Weird, huh?"

"You know what? You got me on the wrong day. I've actually seen weirder."

Dad still felt the need to justify his love. "Ellen here's in charge of set-dec for this production. She's got a head on her shoulders."

I needed to change the subject. "How's the shoot going?"

Ellen said, "Actually, not too well. We had to do this scene supposedly set in New Mexico, which is impossible to fake in Vancouver, at least on our budget. So we hosed this whole field and ravine with zinc isocyanine, which gives a nice rusty colour, but I don't think the salmon will be hatching in the nearby feeder stream for a few years to come."

"Isn't she talented?" Dad asked.

"Yes, Dad, she certainly is."

Ellen said, "I have to prep for tomorrow. It's a long day's shoot. The mother ship arrives above the ranch."

Dad said, "That's okay. We've got the dailies to watch." He turned to me, "Come on. Let's go check them out."

The lovebirds kissed goodbye, and I followed Dad to another trailer filled with cables and screens. We arrived at an exquisitely bad moment—flubbed shots; a hair trapped in the gate; a failed mike contact. Men in suits sweated vegetable oil as they watched what was, to even the most uninitiated eye, money flittering away into nothing. Dad asked the director, "Matt, can you—"

"You got axed, Jim."

"Huh?"

"Your line is gone."

"Dad, I think we should leave."

As we walked back to the extras' trailer, Dad kept saying, "It was supposed to have been my speaking part."

"Dad, I'll drive you home."

As I gave him a lift, I wondered if there was a more subjective, non-Einsteinian theory of time that could explain how I was able to cram so much weirdness into one day—Steve; turtles; dead bikers; philandering parents. The day felt like two or three days crammed into one. I wondered, if you're an incredibly famous rich person who does more in one day than I do in a month, does your perception of time's passing go slower or faster than it does for me?

Finally I broke the silence to ask Dad what his line in the movie had been.

"Goddam aliens!" he roared with astonishing anger. "Did a good job, didn't I?"

"Dad, I'm the one who's supposed to be looking for approval from *you*."

"We're all adults now, and by the way, we're two people in a car, not one, so let's stay in the commuters-only lane."

"But there's no traffic."

"Think big, Ethan. Your head's always locked in a little cupboard, like boxed-up Christmas decorations in the middle of July. You have to open up your mind about stuff . . ."

During this lecture, I realized Dad was doing something to his shoe. "Dad—are you rubbing a vitamin E capsule on your shoe?"

"So what if I am?"

"Why are you doing that?"

"Keeps the leather alive—vital."

"That is so stupid. What are you doing with a bunch of vitamin E capsules, anyway?"

"I found them in the Fraziers' garbage."

The Fraziers live three doors down from my parents.

"You *what*?!"

"I was trying out my new pedometer, and I saw that the Fraziers had thrown out a perfectly good bottle of vitamin E capsules."

"Dad, I can't believe what I'm hearing. You stole vitamin E from the Fraziers' trash to rub onto your *shoe*?"

"No sense it going to waste."

"I guess not, but doesn't Mom's grow-op clearing God-knows-how-much per year render vitamin E theft kind of silly?"

"We have to save all of that money."

"Why?"

"In case you or Greg is in some other country and needs major surgery. Appendicitis can bankrupt you, especially in the States."

"Dad, I could accept Grandma or Grandpa stealing vitamin E capsules—what with their being members of the Greatest Generation and living through the Depression and all. But you?"

"It wasn't theft! Once trash is on the curb, it belongs to everyone."

"Even in my darkest moment, I would never pilfer vitamins from the neighbours' trash can."

"We like ourselves, don't we?"

"Yes, Dad, we do like ourselves."

Painful silence.

More painful silence.

The effort of not discussing Ellen amplified the silence further. I broke down. "Did they throw out anything else good?"

"An umbrella, a nice black one, with a malacca cane handle and just one of the spokes shot."

"Isn't that something."

We pulled into the driveway. Not twelve hours earlier, I'd dragged Tim the biker into Mom's car.

Suddenly, I felt profoundly tired. I felt like I'd just been tossed into a construction site hole.

I drove home.

• • •

When I arrived in jPod the next morning, I found that my keypad's keys had been rearranged in the following configuration:

**1234D67890**
**QWFRTYUIP**
**A5SHOLEKJG**
**ZXCVBNM**

Kaitlin also won't acknowledge my presence. *Fascinating . . .*

• • •

The first turtle meeting was scheduled for one, and I hadn't yet given it three brain cells worth of thought. I was in denial over the turtle as a concept. Here we have a genuinely non-lame skateboard game for PlayStation, and they add a *turtle* to it? All morning I hung around the cafeteria, pretending to be busy, but actually playing Tetris with my back against the wall. At noon I went upstairs and was sitting down in my cubicle when suddenly I smelled something.

"The Taint!" I yelled.

John Doe's head popped up. He said, "You're right—'tis the Taint!"

My voice was loud enough to escape jPod's remote grotto and reach the cubicles in the main work area. "The Taint! The Taint!" Heads and bodies appeared as if on cue in a Broadway musical: The Taint? *The Taint!*

A minute later the mob zeroed in on Mike, a coder, who sullenly pulled from a drawer beneath his hard drive the crescent-shaped corpse of a partially eaten Quarter Pounder with Cheese and a scraggly bale of cold, dead fries.

"Mike, I can't believe you brought the Taint into our office."

"It's their french fries. They're the only fast-food place that doesn't put that disgusting batter on their fries. I went home to get a disk, and I saw their drive-thru sign and . . . I was weak."

"Silence! Let the shunning begin!"

Mike knew the rules, and he broke them. And so, for the rest of the day, he was shunned by everybody in the company.

Back in jPod, Bree said, "Maybe McDonald's food is the way it is because Ronald is lonely."

"Lonely? He's asexual."

"That doesn't mean he's not lonely. Maybe he needs a cat."

"I bet he's into water sports."

"No, that'd mess up his makeup."

"I think he's probably bi-curious."

"Bi-curious? How can he be bi-curious? By now he's at least fifty."

"He's from a different era. They didn't discuss certain topics back then."

"Well, then, how does he stay so young-looking?"

"Steroids. Botox. Happy Meals."

"But all those kids' birthday parties must leave him pretty haggard."

"I wonder what he'd be like on a date."

"Well, you couldn't really go to a movie with him, because everybody would recognize him. No privacy. It'd be like dating Spider-man."

"Where do you live if you're Ronald McDonald? He must be loaded—Bel Air? I mean, he can't even go out for a coffee without looking like a flashing red light."

"Maybe he takes off his makeup and wears sweats."

"No, I don't think so. If you're Ronald, then part of the whole metaphysical proposition is that you can never 'go civilian.'"

"I agree. On *The Simpsons,* whenever you see Krusty the Clown, even if he's in a Jacuzzi or as a baby, he's always got his full makeup on."

"I bet Ronald drinks."

"All clowns drink. They need to blot out the ravages of terrifying children for a living. I wonder what you say to your parents: 'Mom, Dad—I want to be a clown. I'm going to Clown School, and you can't stop me.'"

"Can you imagine the annual family Christmas card photocopied mail-out? *Dan broke his arm skiing in February, but six weeks in a splint and he's tickety-boo. Laurie got her accreditation and is now a fully qualified dental hygienist. Mark brought shame upon the family after he signed up for the local community college's Clown Program. He says the program will put him into the clown fast track, but he's now dead to us.*"

"I bet Ronald is home as we speak—it's his day off. He's in his bathrobe and staring out the den window at his immaculately maintained front garden. He wonders if it was all worth it—the fame, the money, the fries—and then he has this moment when he realizes that this is all he'll ever be. It shocks him—the purity of the emotion. He has to sit down in an armchair. He reaches over to the bookshelf and, from between a row of comic books, he removes a bottle of Scotch."

"And just then, the Hamburglar walks in wearing a pink nightie."

"We need to find him a mate."

"Let's all write to Ronald to explain why each of us is his ideal mate."

"Who chooses the winner?"

"We'll vote." I went first.

• • •

**Hi Ronald,**

You may or may not remember me. I'm Ethan—you gave away balloons at my seventh birthday party, and my mother says you were able to get the orange drink machine working again with just a paperclip and the wits God gave you.

Ronald, I hear you're looking for a mate. I may not be the best candidate, as I'm straight and, well, too much makeup is always a bit of a turnoff. Maybe you're straight, too. Maybe we're just two lost souls trying to make a go of it in this great big nutty world.

Be all of this as it may, I'm supposed to plead my case. I am nearing thirty, and I make $41,500 a year (Canadian) as a programmer, *but* they've dangled this huge carrot in front of me, telling me that I can become an assistant production assistant if I learn to integrate programming skills with art skills plus skills in managing people. The irony is, assistant production assistants make way less, even though they're higher up the food chain. In any event, this is all to say that I have good prospects as a provider.

Ronald, do you play computer games? I know that the cooking of your french fries is regulated by a special deep-frying computer run by proprietary McDonald's software that beeps once the fries are golden yellow. So I think maybe you're more computer savvy than people give you credit for.

I'm single at the moment, but have had two reasonably longish relationships. Both ended because they simply weren't The One, which is such a corny notion. It always leaves you with a niggling unease that the relationship you're in is merely love's calorie-reduced version. It also would have helped if they cared about my work. It's not like I'm married to my job, but a little "Honey, how was your day?" goes a long way. Speaking of work and relationships, I'm currently more attracted than I acknowledge to Kaitlin, who's new to jPod. She's a programmer and she's . . . just nice to look at. But wait, I'm supposed to be wooing *you*. What else can I add that would make you desire me? Oh, I know—I like both helium and balloons. What a blast it would be to mate with someone who has the entire global helium cartel in his big yellow pockets.

That's about as gay as it gets, Ronald.

Pick me! Pick me!

Ethan

• • •

**Naughty Ronald, you mayonnaise-guzzling bun pig . . .**

It must be hard to live at the top, what with Wendy and Burger King always waiting to knife you in the back. I say to you, smother them in melted cheese while they pray uselessly to their cardiac gods!

I am Bree, and when I was sixteen I worked in a McDonald's in Richmond, BC (which was, BTW, the first non-US McDonald's ever). I was fired because I was never meant to be working in the service industry, which is an elliptical way of saying I dated all the guys on the staff at once, thus triggering a mass-quitting saga. That, and I also reconfigured the french-fry computer to make a ringing doorbell sound instead of beeping, which is how I turned on to technology.

Here's a confession: everyone thinks I sleep with anything with three legs, but the fact is, I don't do it that much, and when I do, it's only to confirm that I don't like it that much—which means I'm maybe into gals instead of guys. That's my challenge for the next year. Are you into gals who like gals? To be honest, I look at your public persona and say, "Okay, Bree, this guy's into Smurfs or something, not women." Or am I wrong? I mean, Ronald, let's face it—what's with you? How do clowns replicate? Do you have parents? A family? Do you believe in God or a political party? After you've taped your TV commercials, do you go back to your toadstool and kick back a box of wine? Part of me is happy to think of you as a mere cartoon, but the more genuine Bree says there has to be something more primal and demanding and blood-and-guts at the centre of it all.

I work in a cubicle farm called jPod with a small handful of geeks. It's called jPod because of a computer glitch that put six people whose last names start with the letter J in the space that was supposed to have been a rock climbing wall, but which got cancelled because it was too twentieth century. Once you're in jPod, there's no escaping. I tried for months, and simply gave up. Kaitlin's new here. She'll try hard to get out for a while, and then she'll simply accept her fate and try to get on with life as best she can.

Oof.

I'm tired and a little bit lonely. What a no-hope statement from a twenty-six-year-old woman. I suppose next it's ten cats and my head in the oven.

Call me.

Your little tease,

X

Bree

●  ●  ●

**Dear Ronald McDonald,**

I'm Mark. I can't believe I'm actually writing this letter, but I talked to this guy downstairs in HR, and he says it's part of the lifestyle here, and I should take part, since it can't hurt me and will help me bond with the others. I'm supposed to ask you (oh God, this is stupid) to choose me over the others to be your mate. And I've been thinking about it, but it's maybe not a good idea we get together, since you seem to kill everything you touch. In all your old commercials, you were romping through french-fry patches with your fellow spokesmascots, but you think I haven't noticed that the french-fry characters vanished a decade ago? Or that nobody's seen that website with JPEGs of the Evil Grimace weighing nine hundred pounds, wearing a diaper and living in a failing mobile home community north of the Mexico-Arizona border? What about Mayor McCheese, unrecognizably bearded and detoxing from pickles in a Las Vegas homeless shelter? Every day, when he prowls the city's alleys, crows and jackdaws bite away at his bun face. How could you allow these creatures to just vanish like that? Don't tell me that it wasn't your decision to make, because I *know* you have clout with the people there. I once saw a video of you golfing with Ray Kroc, so don't go pulling the "No Clout" stunt with me. Maybe you were jealous of those characters sharing your limelight, but I don't think so.

As I'm supposed to be winning your matehood here, I ought to be more cheerful. Okay, here's something: I think it was really brave of you to invest so heavily in purple restaurant fur-niture in the 1970s. You go, clown! Sex would be a problem because, sorry, I'm not into you. Maybe it's a clown issue. Maybe it's me never knowing whose party you've been attending. How about if I offer to be your friend instead?

    Mark

• • •

**Hi Ronald.**

    I'm John Doe, and I think I could help change your life in good ways. I come from a freaky upbringing myself, so I know how it must feel to always be the different one. The thing is, I was stuck being in the family I was in, but what about you? How does it work with clowns—are you born with your face made up? Did you get your mother's red nose and your father's Raggedy Ann hairdo? Is clowning something that is thrust on you at birth? Do other clowns hate you because of your fame and success? Do you have friends?

    Let me be your friend. I'll bring over a loofah and a bottle of Noxzema, and we'll take off your paint. If it turns out that you're really Liv Tyler, we can even make it, too.

    But otherwise, the sex thing? Look, it's not like I have trouble with same-sex relationships—my mother is the biggest raging dyke on the planet, and I love her to death. When I was growing up, she made this big stink about how I had to call her a dyke, and nothing else—even in high school—and because of it I was always being sent home. She really liked that, though, because she relished the fights she had with school staff. It was only after I escaped from home that I discovered, thanks to the miracle of satellite TV, that the real mother I always wanted was, in fact, Lindsay Wagner of *The Bionic*

*Woman*—not as she appeared in her TV series, but rather as she appears in car commercials two decades later: calm and confident; the sort of mother who'd buy you Count Chocula *without even being asked to do so.*

No, I got the scary, crazed dyke mama, *plus*—over the course of seventeen years at home—Joan, Nancy, elan (all lower case), Georgia and Sunn, more often than not overlapping.

So, if there's something you want to tell me, I'm the one with ears. Have you considered gender reassignment procedures? You have to take hormones for years, and then they gradually "regenderize" you. Georgia was regendered.

As for me, I want to look as average as possible. I'm difficult to locate in a crowd because I wear only khakis and a solid-colour buttoned shirt that, scanned in Photoshop and desatu-rated, lies between twenty-five and thirty percent on the grey scale. I keep myself nine pounds overweight and drive a white Taurus, which everyone says looks like a rental car, which makes me happy. I'd never eaten any of your narrow but tasty range of burger-type products until I was seventeen, in the McD's outlet on the other side of town. I ordered a cheese-burger—it was also my first non-vegetarian experience—and it was *wonderful.* I didn't even puke. Thanks for turning me on to cow.

It was actually my love of cow that made me leave home. I kept tasting it in my dreams. My mother had some weird voodoo dream scanner, and she could tell I was being non-vegetarian even while I slept, and come morning it was wheat germ and stern lectures on slaughterhouse procedures. Did you know that a cow enters a meat-processing facility at the top of a seven-storey building and that, as it gets more and more processed, it goes down the building floor by floor? Not only that, but there's a thing in abattoirs called the Chute. Every time they find a diseased lung or something, it goes into one of a succession of seven funnels in the building's centre. By the time you're on the first floor, the Chute is filled with this monsoon of inedible cow remnants, which are then blender-ized into pet food smoothies. I mention this because, here at work, we call our in-house memo system the Chute. So, you see, Ronald, even when you don't think you're giving to society as a whole, you continue to do so—when you cause us to reformulate our personal relationships to carnivorism and the Chain of Meat—a distant cousin of the food chain.

BTW, what's the deal with these salads you're selling now? It kind of rubs me the wrong way. You're about cow, dammit, not leaf. Anyway, send me an email or even phone me. It's area code 604, and the number itself is a seven-digit prime which, when squared, is two digits short of being a factorial. Are you up to that challenge? Let me help *you* become the Power Clown you *know* you can be.

John Doe

• • •

Just before the turtle meeting, I went on eBay and bought a Benelux keyboard. Belgian keyboards are totally from hell. For whatever reason, they scramble the character keys even more randomly than a QWERTY keyboard. Thanks to UPS, it ought to be here the day after tomorrow, and Kaitlin shall meet her match. God, I love the twenty-first century.

I just heard her on the phone with someone in HR, trying to get out of jPod. Good luck.

"What do you mean it's not possible?"

[HR staffer]

"Do you mean not possible now, or not possible *ever*?"

[HR staffer]

"I'm a super-experienced character animator, and I've worked at two other big companies, and none of them would ever have stuck me in this chunk of Siberia with a clump of whacked-out freaks."

[HR staffer]

"Okay, that was harsh, but look at my position."

[HR staffer]

"Call Allan Rothstein. He hired me. There's no way he'd have hired me and then stuck me in jPod."

[HR staffer]

"I know Allan Rothstein is busy, but he wasn't too busy to hire me, so I'm sure you can speak to him and clear this up."

[HR staffer]

"When *does* he get back from the Orlando studio?"

[HR staffer]

"Who else can I speak with?"

[HR staffer]

"They can't *all* be in Orlando. There's a meeting here soon, and *some* of them have to be here for that."

[HR staffer]

"You don't understand. The people in this place you stuck me in perform tasks completely unrelated to mine. I'm a character animator; I have to be with my team."

[HR staffer]

"Oh. How did people ever get out of jPod in the past, then?"

[HR staffer]

"They don't?"

[HR staffer]

"What do you mean, just be quiet and try to make peace with it?"

[HR staffer]

"My last name actually begins with the letter B. I'm Kaitlin Boyd."

[HR staffer]

"Boyd is my stepfather's name. Well, yes, on official forms, it's Joyce."

[HR staffer]

Kaitlin hangs up.

[Sound of phone keypad buttons being pushed.]

"Hello, Allan? It's Kaitlin Joyce calling. Sorry to call your cell number when you're away. But your cell number was on your card, and . . ."

[Allan Rothstein]

"I'm going into a meeting soon, myself, sir."

[Allan Rothstein]

"I'll be quick, then. Your HR people put me in a place called jPod. Can you please call them and have me moved to the team's character-animating pod so that . . ."

[Allan Rothstein]

"What was that noise you just made?"

[Allan Rothstein]

"No. You distinctly said something like, *uh-oh*."

[Allan Rothstein]

"I know you're busy, Allan, and, like you, I want to get to work, but I . . ."

[Allan Rothstein]

"When are you back, then?"

[Allan Rothstein]

"Okay. I'm sorry to have called you on a semi-holiday."

[Allan Rothstein]

"I'll make the best of the situation until then."

[Allan Rothstein]

"Goodbye."

Kaitlin hangs up.

• • •

**Ronald,**

This is Casper Jesperson, a.k.a. the Cancer Cowboy, and I have to ask you, mister, what do you think happens to you after you die? Which is a way of asking, do you believe in something specific, or a warm cosmic glow, followed by the total extinction of your being? Do you go to church? It's hard to imagine you there, no offence, and if you went, you'd probably be thinking about life and death in the Clown Universe, that great balloon-twist in the sky.

I come from a farm community, and when I was maybe seven I went to a party at a friend's place. There was a clown there, juggling navel oranges, and while he was doing it, I went out and looked inside his car by the dog kennel, and there was McDonald's trash all over the floor, front and back, and fifty aluminum beer can empties on the floor of the passenger seat. On the dashboard was a Tom Clancy novel (that's how I turned on to him) with all of the yellow ink sun-faded out of the cover (but not the cyan or magenta), as well as the wet, pulpy stump of a cheap and recently extinguished stogie. There was other crap, too—pizza flyers, a copy of *Oui* magazine opened to a woman sitting spread-eagled, wearing a bandolier of machine gun bullets. It's kind of haunted me my whole life, that car.

So imagine you've just finished scaring kids at a birthday party—you're still in your clown makeup and you get in your car, and maybe it doesn't start right away, so you say *fuck fuck fuck* a few times, which is like a magic phrase that starts it. You pull out of the driveway in reverse, way too quickly, and once you're on the main road you floor it because you have to get to your favourite cocktail lounge to put your birthday party money on a greyhound race. But when you get there, the bar is closed because some pipes burst, and suddenly you can't place your bet, which gives you Clown Rage. You need a drink, but you're a clown, and you can't go into just any bar. Nonetheless, a bet is a bet, so you decide to drive over to the next town and put your money down there. In between the two towns, you stop the car, get out and go to the trunk, where you get your de-clowning makeup remover. Your stomach lurches because you're hungover, and you haven't eaten in a day, and there you are, scraping off the white guck with nothing around you but the sound of the wind whistling over the alfalfa stubble, and maybe a crow on a fence that's curious as to whether your paper towel is edible.

You hear a car approaching, but you pretend you're too busy to look because, from experience, you've learned that making eye contact with adults when you're in clown drag is risky. So your head is in the trunk, and you're scraping away, when without you even knowing what it is, a baseball bat held by a sixteen-year-old kid on meth clubs you on the head and you die. Where do you go from there?

Yours from Planet Earth,

The Cancer Cowboy

• • •

When Mark asked Kaitlin where her letter to Ronald was, she said, "Don't you people have anything better to do with your lives?"

I poked my head up and said, "I can think of no better thing to do."

She said, "Here's what I think. Mark and *you*"—she almost spat out my name—"*Ethan*, are the same person. To read your letters, there's no difference between you, no shred of individuality." (NOTE: I deleted the passage on Kaitlin from my publicly released letter.)

"Well, Kaitlin, if you're such an individual," I shot back, "put your words where your mouth is."

"What a witty comeback. Even John Doe's letter had more edge than yours."

John Doe's head popped up: "Then I have failed. I strive for averageness in everything I do."

"I have an idea," Bree offered. "If Ethan and Mark are so similar, we might as well arbitrarily assign them distinct personality traits. I know—Mark, from here on, you're to be called 'Evil Mark.'"

"Why do I have to be the evil one?"

"Because your email address is so dull—bmarkjackson@earth link.com? We really have to zap your brain with defibrillator paddles to get you up and running."

"If I'm evil, then what's Ethan?"

"Ethan is good."

"This is so 'Spy vs. Spy' arbitrary."

"Which spy did you vote for?"

"The black one."

"There you go. Evil. You are pure evil."

"Just because I didn't root for the white one?"

"It's more complex than that."

Chorus: "Mark is evil! Mark is evil!"

Kaitlin said, "This is so stupid."

I said, "Kaitlin, before you go name-calling, pony up. Send us all a letter to Ronald that says 'Kaitlin,' and only Kaitlin."

"If it gets you off my back, I'll do it."

• • •

It's weird, but every time I visit the Drudge Report website, I'm the fifty-millionth person to visit it, so there must be a software error on their part, because how could they possibly have more than one fifty-millionth visitor? And I can't wait to see what my prize will be.

• • •

Dirk, who's a friend of mine from Hewlett-Packard, sent me photos from his trip to Nagoya, using the Kodak EasyShare photo display system. Using its interface, I felt like I was time-travelling to 1999. I half expected a pop-up window to tell me to submit my mailing address so that they could snail-mail me a 56K floppy. And *then* I got to thinking about it . . . Kodak still *exists*? Even seeing its name makes me feel like I'm at a garage sale. I bet they stopped hiring young people in 1997.

● ● ●

While Kaitlin was writing her letter, my phone rang. "Your father is acting weird around me," Mom said. "Did you tell him about Tim?"

"Of course not."

"Why is he acting so strangely, then?"

"Maybe *you're* the one acting weird, and he's just feeding it back to you."

"I just drove up the hill to make sure Tim's body was still covered up."

"And . . . ?"

"They've already backfilled the area."

"That's a relief."

"I miss him."

"Mom, not here, not now."

"Can I come see you?"

"At *work*?"

"Why are you so surprised?"

"Mom, you never even came to elementary school or high school . . ."

"I always thought you should have a space in the world that was entirely your own."

"I always thought you didn't care."

"Nonsense. What time should I come visit?"

"You can't. I have meetings."

"Meetings? Who are you—Darren Stevens? I'll pop by. It'll be fun."

"Mom—"

She hung up.

• • •

Dad phoned a minute later, his voice kind of distant and calling-from-a-tin-can-y.

"Dad, you sound all funny."

"I'm dying my eyebrows black, so I have to hold the receiver away from me."

"Why?"

"I'm auditioning again."

"What movie this time?"

"Something about a radioactive teddy bear that saves Halloween."

"How do black eyebrows fit in?"

"If I get the part, I get to be a father taking his kid trick-or-treating dressed as Abraham Lincoln."

"So what's up?"

"Your mother is acting weird."

"Maybe *you're* the one acting weird, and she's just feeding it back to you."

"You're not going to mention Ellen, are you?"

"No."

"She's hot, isn't she? Ellen, that is."

"Dad! Do not talk like that to me. She was too young for

*me* to dance with at the Z95 noon-hour Beat Breaks in high school."

"Discussing women makes you feel weird?"

"Discussing women with my father? Yes. It does. Dad, is there anything else? I've got this meeting . . ."

"Gee. You have a job and I don't."

"Dad, let's not go there again."

"Just kidding. You couldn't get me back into an office chair for a million bucks. I should have been an actor all along."

"Dad, I really have to go."

"*Hasta luego,* cubicle boy."

• • •

**Ronald Darling,**

I've just been transferred into a new game development pod, which is truly the pod of the corn. Part of their tribal lore is that I have to write you this degrading letter, which is so stupid, because how many times have you and I already had online sex—three hundred? They don't even think you're real, which pisses me off no end. And I know if I try to discuss our forbidden love, we'll both be mocked and shunned.

All I want to be is in a living room with the lights on low, and the battery in my laptop hot and aroused, with you and me talking smutty across the ether. Tonight I'm yours, and yours always. But Ronald, darling, next time don't let the Hamburglar into the dialogue box. He totally kills the mood. Three-ways are for tramps.

Your McSlut,

Kaitlin

Closed course
Professional driver

*High-Speed CMOS Logic*
*Introduction to Algorithms*
*VHDL Made Easy!*

$$M_1, M_2, M_3 \ldots \infty$$

$$E^3$$

SANFORD    No. 81803

# EXPO

## WHITEBOARD CLEANER

**8 fl. oz. (237 mL)**

**bezierkurv**
**chunkylover53**
**darksideofaplanet**

~~Bwoonhilda~~
**Bwoonnhilde**

# Kill the wabbit

• A 1-terabyte disk for
(get this) only US$699.00!

• • •

Meeting time:

Steve, the guy who turned Toblerone around in two years, tries to be one of the people. He's always hanging around with the cool crowd on a project, and he socializes with them off-hours, so he can say, "Hey, I'm hands-on in the trenches with my team!" of which there are now fifty-six members. As production speeds up, dozens more will pile on as senior management weighs in with all kinds of random, last-minute features. Steve is the only suit in the room and, thanks to Bree's mastery of Google, all of us know it's a $2,200 suit.

"*Be* the turtle!" Steve said.

Nervous titters.

"*Think* like a turtle."

Nervous titters.

"My friends, you *are* the turtle."

Fake contemplative silence peppered with ironic gasps.

"You, over there—" Steve pointed to a world-object texture map artist named Marty Choy, who I worked with two games ago. "When you think turtle, what do you think of?"

Silence. Marty couldn't believe that he, of all people in the room, had been chosen. "Reptile . . ." he said.

"Exactly!"

"Really?"

"Yes, really. Now, you, over there—" Steve pointed to a guy who I think was in either an AI-SE or a Tools SE on hockey titles. "When you think of turtles, what do you think of?"

"Konami's arcade and console games based on the Teenage Mutant Ninja Turtles franchise?"

Steve looked gratified, but then a serious expression came over his face. We were all hoping that the random selection of audience members was over.

"Everybody, I must say before we go any further, that the Teenage Mutant Ninja Turtles characters®, including Raphael®, Michelangelo®, Leonardo®, Donatello®, and April O'Neil® are all registered trademarks of Mirage Studios, and anything we say or do is in no way based on or disparaging of this fine intellectual property."

Dead silence.

"Come on, team—let's talk turtle here. I can't take unless you give."

Someone I couldn't see on the other side of the room volunteered, "Turtle shells don't require many polygons to render. So it won't slow gameplay much."

Another voice said, "That's like Keanu Reeves's black dress/cloak thingy in *The Matrix*."

A different voice yet: "Really?"

"Computers were way slower back then. They used the black cloak to shorten render times."

"Let's get back on track," Steve said.

Kaitlin, going for broke, asked, "Steve, we're at milestone five, and you want to dump a charismatic turtle into an action-sports game? How can you wreck a third-person skateboard game like this? Who's going to play it, Teletubbies?"

Then everyone began to cluster-dump on the turtle idea. Steve remained serene through it all, then held up his hand for silence. "This is all well and good. I encourage vigorous debate and the exchange of ideas—who wouldn't? It's what democracy is based on. I like the fact that all of you are so vocal here this afternoon. But the point of this meeting is that my son Carter loves the turtle character in SimQuest4, and if Carter likes turtles, every kid in the world is going to like turtles. So the fact is, a charismatic turtle character is going to be in the game—that's been decided at the upper levels—so today we take the first steps as a group to flesh out our turtle."

Silence.

"On a constructive front, the game has also been renamed BoardX."

Evil Mark turned purple and shot up his hand. "Why?"

"X says to the world, hip and daring—punk and funk. It tells the world we're not just some average game."

Just then there was a gentle knock on the door. What sort of chowderhead would risk management's ire by intruding in the middle of a grok? The door opened, and in walked Mom.

"Can I help you?" Steve's voice was pleasant.

"Why, yes, I'm looking for my son, Ethan." She spotted me. "Oh hi, dear."

"Mom—?"

Everybody began chanting *EthanEthanEthan* and *Mama's Boy.* I'd have been legally entitled to have a stroke at that point, but I figured, high school was over a decade ago. I stood up and went over to her. How did she get through security? Why wasn't she accompanied by a guard, or wearing a laminated security pass?

Steve said, "Is everything okay, Mrs.—"

"Jarlewski. Carol Jarlewski. Yes, and thank you for asking. I was at home this morning, and I realized that I don't really know much about where Ethan works or what he does. I thought I'd see for myself. Sorry for interrupting your meeting . . ."

"Steve. Steve Lefkowitz."

They shook hands. Mom showed not a twinge of uneasiness at standing before a group of fifty-six geeks. "My! Look at all of you clever young people. What are you doing today?"

Everybody giggled, and Steve, a master of timing, said, "Carol Jarlewski, what do you think of when you think of turtles?"

"Turtles? Well, I think that turtles have to be intelligent creatures, because in evolutionary terms they go back farther than just about every other animal. They're good at surviving. And they're cute, too. Sort of cheeky. My sister and I found one in the pond back when we were kids, and it winked at me. Saucy little things."

Steve looked at all of us. "And you thought turtles weren't hip."

This was now out of my hands—not that it was ever in them.

"Everybody, let's have Carol sit in on the meeting," Steve announced. "Her outsider perspective might add something valuable to our quest." People actually clapped.

And thus Mom took her seat near Steve's podium and spent the next two hours beaming at me and offering the occasional idea, some of which were good. "Those skateboard monsters are always spray-painting everything, including the Edgemont Village SuperValu's walls, and in my opinion they all deserve a few months in jail. But why not make your turtle's shell a surface on which players spray-paint clues? The turtle can't see what's on his back, so one of his goals is to locate reflective surfaces throughout the game, while his competition is trying to wreck those surfaces."

John Doe also lobbed out an idea that stuck. He suggested that a universally appreciated buddy-type personality was that of Jeff Probst—"charismatic host of TV's still-sizzling long-running reality show *Survivor*." I'm not sure if John Doe was kidding, but everybody clapped, and suddenly Steve said, "Hey—this sounds like an idea with legs."

At the end, when I asked Mom if she wanted me to take her on a tour, she said, "That's okay, Ethan. Young Steven here is taking me."

Steve didn't even look at me. His eyes were all on Mom.

I schlumped my way back to the pod.

• • •

Random note from today's meeting:

Fresh New Lucky Charms Marshmallow Shapes . . .

  . . . Masonic emblems
  . . . witch-dunking stools
  . . . stepmothers
  . . . PayPal logos
  . . . anal beads.

God is an Xkb state indicator

God is a Window Maker docked
application

God is a multi-platform Z80
cross-assembler

God is a lightweight XML encoding
library for Java

God is a programmatic API
written in C++

God is Oracle's OCI8 and OCI9 APIs

God is a configuration backup utility

God is Web-based groupware and
collaboration software

God is a graphical editor for drawing
finite state machines

Kaitlin was on the phone again, trying to extract herself from jPod. Cowboy was over by a ventilation unit, having a smoke. One of jPod's quirks is an air intake duct in front of which you can puff away on anything. Hell, you could let off an Exocet missile, and it'd suck everything up and away in a jiffy.

"If that had been my mother who showed up today, she'd have made a big deal of telling people she doesn't shave her armpits," said John Doe.

Bree said, "If that was my mother up there, she'd be asking every guy in the place what his salary was, and what his career prospects were."

Evil Mark said, "If that was my mother up there, she'd be drunk."

Kaitlin slammed down the phone in disgust. She looked over at us and put her face down on her desk.

As we'd all gone through the same responses when we were put into jPod, we felt sorry for Kaitlin. She needed a bit of quiet time.

Respecting her need, we entered work mode. The mood grew nice and quiet as we checked to see what was falling down the Chute. After maybe fifteen minutes, Cowboy piped up, "You know, I'm so sick of cigarette smoking's negative image problems."

There was a chorus of jPod agreement.

He continued, "I have a suggestion. Let's take a minute-long break and blithely pimp for the tobacco industry."

"Okay," Bree said. "But first I could sure use the smooth clear taste of a Marlboro Light."

"Me? I prefer Virginia tobacco. *Mmm*—nothing like a Rothmans to make the afternoon sweeter."

"But you know," said Mark, "I think there's nothing like menthol for a fresh smoking experience."

I asked, "What's the deal with menthol cigarettes? What sort of person smokes regular cigarettes for years and then suddenly says, *Gee, this isn't satisfying enough. I need something more from my tobacco*?"

Bree said, "My mother quit smoking in the 1980s, and then three months later they test-marketed lemon-flavoured cigarettes and she couldn't resist. She's two packs a day now."

I added that if Big Tobacco came up with orange-flavoured cigarettes, I'd probably start smoking.

Bree said, "Chocolate for me."

"I'd like roast beef-flavoured smokes," said John. "Nothing like a touch of cow to perk up a dragging day."

Evil Mark said, "Me, I find that the toasted tobacco flavour of a 100-millimetre-long More helps me to think better."

Bree asked, "More? Are those the skinny brown cigarettes?"

"Yup."

Cowboy said, "Me? I'd like to try one of those lady's cigarettes."

Bree added, "What kind of woman would look at a cigarette and say, *Finally, someone out there is addressing my feminine tobacco needs*?"

"Actually, I did just that last week."

"Cowboy, you're a guy."

"But I wanted to see, you know, what a woman's cigarette might be like."

"How did it taste, then?"

"It made me feel, you know . . . *fresh.*"

•  •  •

As I walked past Evil Mark's cubicle, he moved quickly to get something off his screen.

"Porn?"

"Ha ha. Yeah. Uh. Don't tell anyone."

"That wasn't porn you were looking at. It was something else."

"Ethan, it's none of your business."

"Porn degrades everybody, Mark."

Evil Mark snorted.

"Okay, I was just trying to PC you into coughing up the truth. So what was it you were looking at?"

"Nothing."

"If it was nothing, you wouldn't be overreacting like this."

"I'm not overreacting."

Behind his cubicle wall, John Doe said, "I think he's over-reacting."

"Evil Mark, are you into terrorism or something? Stock scams, maybe? Industrial espionage—passing along confidential in-house documents?"

"Leave me alone, okay?"

"Evil Mark, we're on to you now. We *know* you're up to something."

John Doe added, "We will crush you like a bug when we find out what."

"It was nothing! Just go and feed yourselves on a wide

array of products containing high-fructose corn sugar. *Zheesh.*"

"That wasn't funny, Evil Mark. It sounded fake and hollow. You're terrible at being ironic, and you've been rehearsing that line, haven't you?"

"I am *not* evil."

"People don't get nicknames for nothing, Mark."

Mark was beginning to lose it for real. "Bree arbitrarily chose 'evil' out of nowhere."

"Was it really so arbitrary, Mark?" Bree asked.

"You people are nuts."

"Let's look at the facts: a) boring email name; b) chose the black spy over the white spy in 'Spy vs. Spy'; c) could easily have confessed to having porn on his monitor, but instead chose to pretend it was nothing, *meaning,* it wasn't porn, but something too shameful to let his compassionate pod members in on."

Kaitlin put her head above her wall. "You people are totally fucking crazy. How can you live like this?"

"Like *what,* Kaitlin?" I asked.

"Like people damned forever to a shady armpit of an entertainment empire too cold and indifferent to even try to rescue people from a clerical spreadsheet error that assigns employee seating."

This stopped everything dead.

"Kaitlin"— and you have to remember, this was me, someone with an embryonic crush on her—"I don't think you quite understand the ramifications of being in jPod."

"What's with this whacko jPod shit?"

From all of us: "Oooooooohhhhhhhh . . ."

"She really doesn't get it, does she?"

"Poor girl."

"She still thinks there's hope."

"Just tell me this: How did I end up here, huh?" Kaitlin asked. "Because if I'm here, it means somebody else had to leave."

She'd crossed the line. "We can't talk about that," I said.

"What do you mean, you can't talk about that?"

I headed to the snack machines as the others scampered back to their chairs.

"Augh!" Kaitlin screamed, jumping up onto her desktop, sending her Aeron chair into her hard drive, giving it a good bang. "Stop right now, all you assholes, and tell me what's going on here!"

Bree said, "This is so *Pulp Fiction*."

Cowboy said, "They didn't tell you, huh?"

"No! As far as I can see, nobody tells anyone about anything in this place."

"Well, you're right about that."

Silence.

Kaitlin said, "What? Tell me something. *Anything*!"

"It was helium."

"Excuse me?"

"It was helium. Marc Jacobsen used to have your cubicle."

"You've lost me here."

This was going to be difficult. I said, "Marc was a really nice guy. He was actually a world builder for Xbox games."

"What does he or helium have to do with anything?"

Even Evil Mark had been here long enough to know that this was delicate.

"This isn't the best time and place to be telling you this," I said.

"Telling me WHAT?"

Bree stepped in. "Marc was really sweet, and totally into the games, and really wanted to make people's lives better. And he was the only staffer who was never guilted into coming in on weekends during crunch times, so that shows you how good he was, and how much clout he had."

"Helium? Everybody—*helium*?"

I took over. "Marc was at his sister's birthday party, and he was in charge of party tricks, and so he rented a helium canister from a novelty supply company. He was at the party making twisted balloon animals when he decided to suck back some helium so he could speak in a Donald Duck Munchkin voice."

"*And?*"

"So there were maybe a dozen kids there—eight-year-olds—really easy to entertain. He put his lips onto the helium canister's nozzle and sucked in about a gallon of helium . . ."

"And?"

Silence.

"And?"

"Let Google help us here," said John Doe. "'If the concentration of oxygen falls below eighteen percent in the body, symptoms and signs of asphyxia occur. Helium gas can entirely displace available oxygen. If this continues for even a few seconds, asphyxia and death can occur.' Sure, we all want to sound like Donald Duck—but is it worth the price?"

Kaitlin said, "Uh-oh."

"Exactly. In front of all these kids, Marc keels over, turns blue and dies."

"Oh God. When did this happen?"

"A few months ago."

"And his desk has been empty all this time?"

"That's life. One moment you're mimicking Munchkins, the next, birthday cake is digging its way into your nostrils."

Kaitlin said, "What about Evil Mark? He arrived here only a little while before me. Why didn't he get this Marc guy's old cubicle?"

"Evil Mark? They just came in here one day and installed another cubicle, and then he showed up."

The look on Kaitlin's face said it all. For the first time, it was sinking in that jPod was real, and that she was a part of it, and that there was no escaping her destiny. "I think I'll just sit down now and see what's coming down the Chute," she said.

And with that, jPod fell silent.

Afrikaans
Albanian
Amharic
Arabic
Azerbaijani
Basque
Belarusian
Bengali
Bihari
Björk
Borg
Bosnian
Braille
Breton
Bulgarian
Canadian
Catalan (lisping)
Catalan (no lisping)
Chinese
Cockney
Coleslaw
Croatian
Czech
Danish
Danish (cherry)
Dutch
Elmer Fudd
English (helium)
Esperanto
Estonian
Faroese
Finnish
Fortran
French
French Canadian
Frisian
Galician
Georgian
Greek
Grover
Gujarati
Gym mat
Hebrew

Hindi
Hungarian
Icelandic
Ikea
Indonesian
Interlingua
Irish
Italian
Japanese
Jif
Klingon
Korean
Kyrgyz
Latin
Latvian
Lion King
Lithuanian
Long Island
Lowly Worm
Macaroni
Macedonian
Malay
Maltese
Maltese (on novocaine)
Massachusetts
Müslix
Nepali
Noodle
Norwegian
Nyorsk
Occitan
Ontario
Oriya
Pebbles (Flintstone)
Persian
Pig Latin
Pig Latin (stoned)
Pitcairn
Polish
Portuguese (Brazil)
Portugese (Portugal)
Punjabi
Rastafarian

Romanian
Rotarian
Russian
Sailor Moon
Scooby-Doo
Serbian
Serbo-Croatian
Shoe
Shrink wrap
Sinhalese
Slovak
Slovenian
Snoopy
Spanish
Spice rack
Stepford
Swahili
Swedish
Tagalog
Tamil
Tang
Telugu
Texan
Thai
Tlön
Toast
Turkish
Turkmen
Twizzlers
Ukrainian
Urdu
Uzbek
Vanna White
Vietnamese
Welsh
Welsh rarebit
Xbox
Xena
Xhosa
Yabba Dabba Doo
Yiddish
Zulu

● ● ●

The rest of the afternoon passed without incident, mostly with me going around the building, massaging egos and putting out fires. If I'm ever going to become an assistant production assistant, then this is the way forward.

I got back to jPod around seven, and my message light was blinking, so it had to be Mom or Dad. Dad said, "Ethan, it's five to seven. Call me the moment you get this."

I called him.

"Thank frigging God," Dad said. "Get over here."

"What's going on?"

"Just come, right now."

"Did Mom find out about . . . ?"

"No. Just get over here."

And so I drove to the house. Dad's car was in the carport, and there was a small silver Suzuki Sidekick parked out front, which I assumed belonged to Ellen, as every single woman I've ever met who does set-dec work in film drives one of these things or something similar. I parked behind it, only to see Ellen walk across the lawn towards the creek, naked. Dad opened the door.

"Ethan—help me grab her."

"I'm not touching her, Dad."

"She's high as ten kites."

"It doesn't matter."

Before she fell into the creek and cracked her skull, Dad headed across the grass and lifted her up like a set of heavy golf clubs. "Upsy-daisy." Ellen kept moving her limbs as if she was still walking, which was more than slightly disturbing. He carried her in the front door, yelling over his shoulder, "She went downstairs and took the biggest bud off The Dude. Smoked the whole frigging thing."

"Oh shit. How are you going to explain that to Mom?" Ellen had mutilated Mom's favourite and oldest plant, called The Dude, even though it's a female.

"You tell me. I'm screwed." I followed him down the hall to Greg's old room.

"Ellen and I stopped by to get my Abraham Lincoln hat for my audition, which was set for six o'clock. I gave her a tour of the basement, and then the phone rang, and by the time I got back downstairs—*pow!*—she's baked, and there goes my Abe Lincoln role, stupid bitch. So I laid her down on your brother's bed so I could figure out what to do next, which was when I called you. Next thing, I look out the front window, and she's off sleepwalking towards the Brodies' breakfast nook." Dad was slipping a T-shirt and a pair of sweat bottoms onto Ellen, who was moaning. "Where's your mother?" asked Dad.

"No idea. She came out to visit me at work today."

"She *what*?"

"Exactly. She said she wanted to see where I work."

"Why would she do *that*?"

Just then we heard Mom's car pull into the carport. Dad looked at me. "Ellen's your new girlfriend. End of story." We hightailed it to the kitchen.

From the back door, I heard, "Ethan? Is that you?"

She came into the kitchen. "Oh hi, dear. Didn't get enough of me at work today, huh?"

"I just thought I'd come see how you guys are doing."

Both of them were squinting at me, wondering if I was about to blow their secrets. I glanced at Dad. "I also have a new girlfriend, and I thought I'd introduce her to you."

"A new girlfriend? Finally—the possibility of grandchildren."

"I also have bad news for you, Mom."

" . . . *Oh*?" At this point, bad news could mean many things. "Like what?"

"I showed Ellen your business downstairs, and she picked a bud off The Dude."

"She *what*?"

"It happened before I could say anyth—"

"Ethan, you *know* how I feel about The Dude. And I was trying to get a nice shape back to her after all the clones I made this season." She sat down heavily in a kitchen chair.

Dad said, "Kids. All they do is wreck stuff."

"Where *is* your new girlfriend, dear?"

"She's in Greg's old bedroom."

"Why?"

"She's kind of baked."

"So let me guess, then—she smoked the bud?"

"Kinda."

"Ethan, how *could* you go out with a druggie? Did she steal my earrings, too? Should I check my jewellery to make sure it's all there?"

"You're making too big a deal of this, Mom. It was a first date. Last date, too."

Mom stood up and began removing dinner ingredients from the fridge and freezer. She turned around. "You know what, dear? I don't want to see your girlfriend or know her name. This is your get-out-of-jail-free card. Just pack her up and take her away. I think we've all learned our lesson for the day."

Dad turned to me. "Ungrateful little bastard." He winked. "Come on, I'll help you get her to the car."

Dad and I lugged Ellen out to her car, plunking her in the back seat along with a one-third-empty box of Dad's head-shots, which he made me promise to drop off at his agent's. He wrote down Ellen's address. "Just park it in her garage. When she wakes up, she'll figure things out."

"What about me?"

"Oh, right." He reached into his pocket. "Here's a twenty. Take a cab, but keep the receipt, as I can claim it on taxes."

So I drove Ellen to her condo in Kitsilano, not far from the beach, and put her inside on her bed. I cabbed to pick up my car, then finally got home to my dishevelled but lovable three-storey dump in Chinatown. When I got the door open, a wave of relief flooded me. I could have a long bath and forget turtles and bodies and Steve and Dad and Ellen and . . .

I turned on the light to find maybe twenty stick-thin Chinese people huddled on my floor: men, women and children. I dropped my keys and turned around, only to bump into my brother.

"Greg, what the hell's going on in there?"

"Chill out. They're friends of mine. I just needed a place to put them for a few hours."

"What do you mean, friends? They look like refugees."

"They *are* refugees."

"What the hell are you doing with—refu*gees*? And in my place, too."

"I owe a friend a favour."

"What kind of friend is that?"

"Stop acting like a little girl. They're only here for a few hours, and then they ship out."

"I—" Words failed me. Meanwhile, I looked at the refugees. "Shit, Greg. I gave you a copy of my key for emergencies. Don't get me caught up in your weird business shit. And why aren't you in Hong Kong? Mom said you were in Hong Kong."

"I told them not to touch any surface or object, and trust me, they won't." The refugees looked at Greg in a way that said he was alpha dog, and not to be crossed.

"There, look—they're not even sitting on your furniture."

"What's that smell?"

Greg barked a question in Mandarin, and a woman replied.

"They've been shitting in a cardboard box off the kitchen. They didn't know how the toilet worked."

"Get them out of here now, or I phone the government."

Greg turned frosty on me. "That's not something that's going to happen, Ethan."

"Wait a second. These people aren't really refugees, are they?"

"That depends how you define 'refugee.' And if you mean 'noble fellow world citizens searching for a better life on a new continent'—"

"Greg, you're people-smuggling."

"Keep your voice down. I'm not the one who's people-smuggling. My friend, Kam Fong, is the, uh, businessman here. He messed up a connection, and I owed him one."

"How did they get here?"

"A truck dropped them off six hours ago."

"You're the world's biggest asshole."

"Ethan, it was either that or have my real estate licence revoked. Kam Fong is well connected."

"Kam Fong? Isn't that the name of the guy who played Steve McGarrett's sidekick on *Hawaii Five-0*?"

"It is. Isn't that a gas?"

"Have these people had anything to eat in the past week?"

"What am I—a flight attendant? How should I know?"

"They have to eat something. They're so skinny."

"I'd order pizzas, but all that dairy's not a good idea."

"Where are they from?"

"Fujian Province, northern China."

I went online to search for takeout. Stir-fried clams, lychee nuts, squid with pineapple, prawns, crab, whelks and radishes. "Okay, asshole brother, you're spending ten bucks apiece for dinner for everyone here."

"Ten bucks?"

"Either that, or I call the RCMP."

Greg went to pick up the food, and I orchestrated a hygiene pageant. Two weeks in the hold of a container ship leaves the modern traveller a bit . . . fragrant. I got a conga line going in and out of the shower, and I put their dirty clothing in the washer and gave them my own clothes to wear. The hot water ran out quickly, but nobody seemed to mind. I felt like Elliott from *E.T.* handing out Reese's Pieces.

Greg came back an hour later carrying a Santa's toy sack worth of Chinese food, and he was surprised to see them all in their new duds. "Check out the makeover," he said. "It's like casual Friday at the Asian Studies department of a Midwestern university."

"Just put out the food."

He did, and a feeding frenzy ensued. "Jesus, Ethan, just look at these guys chow down."

"Greg, what or when was the last time these people ate— a dead seagull somewhere off the coast of Guam?"

"Relax."

"How can you be a part of this? It's just—inconceivable you'd get wrapped up in it."

"Don't be so self-righteous. The people in this room probably made the shoes on your feet, the computer you just turned on, the glass in the windows, the light bulb in that lamp, and just about everything else in here. It's okay if these people are across the ocean in a sweatshop working for fifty-nine cents a day, but heaven help us if we have to actually deal with them in real time in our part of the world."

"Your social conscience is making me teary."

"Look, I sell Vancouver condominiums to global pirates from Hong Kong or Taiwan who need a crash pad if China goes ballistic. And tonight it was either bring these folks to your place, or let them starve and shit themselves in a Maersk shipping container over by the Second Narrows. Don't be so pissed off. Here—" He handed me a wad of twenties. "Let them keep your old clothing. You go buy some new stuff."

"I can't take this money." I turned around and gave the pile of twenties to a scrawny young guy wearing my Nine Inch Nails FRAGILITY V. 2.0 tour shirt. "Take one and pass it along." He quickly caught my gist.

The doorbell rang, and everybody stopped as if a DVD's PAUSE had just been hit. Greg answered—it was one of Kam Fong's henchmen. He and Greg had a whispered argument. When it was over, the henchman motioned the Chinese out of the house and into the truck. Aside from the food trash (two dozen completely licked-clean paper plates) and a cardboard box full of shit outside the back kitchen door, it was as if the place had never seen a soul. Greg said, "Okay, then, you're right, this was a pretty big imposition on you. Let me pay you back."

"How?"

He looked around my place. "Ethan, your furniture is total crap. I'll have Kelly from my office send you some pieces left over from our display suites."

"I don't want or need new furniture."

"Don't be stupid. Your furniture is college-grade, and you're pushing thirty. Collectively it spells out L-O-S-E-R."

"My furniture isn't crap. At least my place doesn't look like I ordered the whole thing from a Delta Airlines SkyMall catalogue."

"Gee, that one sure stung. How are Mom and Dad?"

"Busy."

"I'm off."

After I closed the door behind me, I went to the washer and took out the first big load of smuggling-wear—cheesecloth-thin knit shirts too flimsy to buff a car with—profoundly depressing—and I wondered what I was going to wear now.

I put the wet clothes into the dryer, and an hour later, as I removed them, I got to thinking of how you'll sometimes be at a friend's place, and they loan you a jacket or sweater, and how extra-great those garments are to wear because they come with a pre-built aura—and how you even sometimes plan on keeping the sweater or whatever because suddenly it feels so . . . *yours.*

I picked a shirt from the laundry basket of Downy-soft clothes. Voilà! My new look.

Within an hour I was asleep.

• • •

The next day in jPod, Bree and Cowboy saw me in my smuggling-wear. "Dig the threads, Ethan. Begging for spare change at stoplights?"

"It's—a long story. Where's John Doe?"

"He went out last night to tag grain cars with some guys from IT and never came back. Hey, word has it that corporate really loves the idea of the turtle character based on beloved reality TV show host Jeff Probst."

I grabbed an apple granola bar and a banana in the snack room, and then sat down at my desk. I needed to somehow put the day into focus. I decided to research the life and career of Jeff Probst, host of TV's long-running reality TV hit *Survivor,* as well as . . . well, just see for yourself:

Jeff was born on November 4, 1962, and began his career in the early 1990s, bringing us laughter and song as a VH1 vee-jay. From there, Jeff became host of the informative mirthfest that is VH1's *Rock & Roll Jeopardy!,* but only after he'd hosted and made guest appearances on many network TV shows. Yet it was as himself, "Jeff Probst," that Jeff entered our collective hearts as the crusty but fair host of the long-running king of reality shows, *Survivor*. There, Jeff outplayed, outlasted and outwitted all of the naysayers and doom-mongers, and showed us that with pluck, fortitude and a honey bronze tan, one can be both God and the devil, choosing the next soul from the hinterlands to be catapulted into exciting millennium-style fame—and a higher tax bracket!

FUN FACT: Jeff is an accomplished director of art house films. His 2001 thriller, *Finder's Fee,* netted Jeff awards for Best Picture and Best Director at the Seattle International Film Festival. First step Seattle—next stop . . . *the world!*

Bree saw that I was researching Jeff Probst. "Hmmm. I wonder if Jeff Probst has his own specific kryptonite—something that makes him self-destruct."

"What makes Jeff blow up? Bad room service. Or players who quit the game before the game tosses them out."

Bree asked me what my own kryptonite was.

"That's easy—meetings. Yours?"

"Microsoft press releases."

We looked at some JPEGs of Jeff. "If Jeff were a turtle, he'd be on the side of the forces of good, right?"

"Can skateboard games embody morality?"

"I don't think so."

The fluorescent lights flickered for one hundredth of a second, which told us that the render farm a floor up had kicked into operation for the night. "Have you looked in the snack room lately?" I asked.

Bree said, "I never go there. Vegan."

"I forgot. Did you know we have an entire Frigidaire stand-up model dedicated only to condiments and spreads?"

"Huh?"

"Kraft Golden Italian Dressing, gallon-sized, Adams Peanut Butter, HP Sauce, marmalade, Annie's Natural Raspberry Vinaigrette . . ."

"How do you re*member* all that shit?"

"Brain wiring. I've always been able to remember brand names."

"I have this theory about smart people. If you're smart, you're either the only person in your family who's smart, *or* everybody in the family is smart. No in-between."

I considered this. "I think I come from the everybody's smart category. But they don't apply their smarts to . . . *larger picture* pursuits. That includes me."

"My sister works at the World Bank," Bree said. "My older brother's finding a cure for Alzheimer's, and my younger brother played viola at the White House two years ago. They all have trouble with me and gaming."

There was an awkward moment as the two of us considered our lives from a long-term perspective. Then Bree said, "You know, if the company wants to get better work out of the staff, they should follow Jeff's unwritten laws from *Survivor.*"

"Like what?"

"They should starve us. Starved contestants make for better shows, always, so it might make for a more zestful office lifestyle as well. Management could leave bottles of Scotch along the hallways here, like Mario coins. Booze could really loosen us all up. Let's face the truth—drunk people are more fun, and they're much better at telling the truth than sober people."

"And we should be able to vote one person out of the company *every single day,* so that there'd be all these massive intrigues as everybody tries to figure out who's ganging up on who."

"Forget about our office for a second. Do you know what they ought to do on the real *Survivor*? They should forget about the tropics. Make them play in Romania. Romanians will do anything. No more weepy crap about, *We were friends—how could you have abused our friendship?* They'd be slitting each other's throats."

We heard a cat yowl from behind our cubicle wall: Kaitlin. "You people are driving me absolutely fucking *crazy*. All you ever talk about is junk."

I looked over at her—brown hairs Van de Graaffing from her forehead; a pimple she'd been hoping nobody would notice caked in skin product; small, perfect teeth. I was wondering what her kiss would taste like, when she picked up a Clive Cussler novel that everyone in the pod had read, and hucked it at the wall by the air intake.

Bree encouraged her. "You throw that book, Kaitlin! Get it all out!"

She gave another snared-in-the-leg-hold cry, then hurled an N64 development folder from 1998, followed by a hardcover copy of *If They Only Knew,* the 1999 autobiography of World Wrestling Federation sensation Chyna.

After this, she seemed as spent as Mr. Burns handing a shovel to Smithers after throwing a handful of dirt onto a grave, and she spoke in the one-word sentences used by exhausted slaves: "All. I. Want. To. Do. Tonight. Is. Design. A. Realistic. Looking. Waterfall. Ripple. Texture. Is. That. Too. Fucking. Much. To. Ask?"

"I think we should all get back to work," I said.

# a pair of oversize

## green foam latex

# Incredible

# Hulk

## boxing

### gloves

with built-in
Hulk
noises

# All new company passwords must contain at least one character, integer and symbol:

~~happycamper~~

~~happycamper5~~

~~happycamper*~~

happycamper*5 ✔

This fridge belongs to the company.

Anyone using this fridge automatically agrees to obey all rules for fridge usage dictated by the company.

"Usage" is legally defined as "the moment somebody opens the door up until the moment the door is once again shut."

# lens
# urethra
# womb
# tail
# eardrum
# mustard
# bun

pseudorandom number generator

//

**Texture diffuse:**

**DiffuseMap**

**Float amount = 3.0i**

**LightMap**

[ . . . $n_x$, $n_y$, $n_z$, x, y, z, r, g, b . . . ]

• • •

I was about to get to work when I decided that I needed, nay, *deserved* a nap after the previous freaky day, so I crawled under my desk, with a Yellow Pages as a pillow, and conked out for an hour or so. I woke up with my neck feeling cricked and spina bifida-ish. I grabbed an orange juice and went back to my desk. *Ahhhhhh* . . . I have to say, smuggling-wear is actually quite comfy—soft, with no hems or waistbands to dig into the skin.

I began fielding Chute-mail from various levels of producers, and was feeling calm and good, when Gord-O, a senior development director, came rumbling towards jPod. "Ethan, word upstairs is that you're thinking of switching to the production career path."

"It's true."

"Very well, here's the Costco card. I'm going to need you to pick up some DVD-Rs for weekend builds. The Physics SEs want to look at THUG2, so pick up the Xbox version of that. And we're out of Cheerios. Pick us up a couple dozen boxes in a ratio of three boxes of Honey Nut to one box of classic Cheerios."

Such is the life of a young techie dreaming of being a genuine future production assistant: one moment you're trying to round up a selection of C++ fantasy castles to appease an angry fartcatcher in Development, the next you're stuck in traffic with enough Cheerios on the back seat to make the car rattle like maracas going over a speed bump.

En route to Costco, I was phoned by John Doe for details on an upcoming Tetris tournament, but we got sidetracked and ended up discussing work. The big discussion around the office is how to alter BoardX's development cycle to accommodate Jeff the Turtle. "John, this is no Japanese curry-induced bad dream. It's really happening."

"Stop saying that, Ethan!"

Bree then called. "Ethan, did you hear about Adam?"

"No, what?" Adam is senior animator from the company's jock set.

"He got really drunk last night and then went on the treadmill. His anti-chafing nipple tape came off, he freaked, and he ended up whacking his head on a stainless steel bowl filled with bottles of mineral water," Bree said.

"Ow."

"Ten stitches. On the way to the hospital, he started screaming in Jeb's Saab, so Jeb reached into the glove box and got out a can of Solarcaine and started spraying it on Adam's face—which promptly caught on fire from a spark from Jeb's cellphone battery charger. Not a trace of eyebrow left."

"Wow."

"Everybody in his pod is shaving off their eyebrows in sympathy."

# Tetris Challenge
# Tonight, 7:00

# Merlots
# vs.
# Zinfandels

S
Z
T
L
J
Q
bar
square

• • •

My prank Belgian keyboard is in the belly of an Airbus 320 somewhere over the North Polar ice cap, huddled in its little box, wondering if its new owner will love it or not. I've only ever flown across an ocean once, to London with the school band. The entire experience was wasted on me. Mostly I remember that never-ending in-flight information screen that tells passengers how far they've come, and how many miles remain. It's so sloooowwwwwwwwww. Stare at it intently enough and time goes backwards. And do we really need to know that the outside temperature is −59 degrees Fahrenheit? Does this information comfort us with the knowledge that should we crash and somehow survive, death by exposure will be swift and merciful? Also, Celsius conversion seems unnecessary, as around −59, electrons probably crawl to a stop, like Ping-Pong balls on a basement floor. Okay, I know it's 222.6 degrees Kelvin, −50.56 degrees Celsius.

• • •

My phone rang. "Hello, dear."

"Mom. Hi."

"Did you get your girlfriend home okay?"

"Yes. Yeah. Fine."

"She hacked off such a huge chunk of The Dude. It's good to know you've dropped her. You *have* dropped her, haven't you?"

"Uh, yeah."

"You hesitated there for a second. I heard it."

"I was closing windows on my screen."

"Young Steven took me on a tour of the entire facility, you know."

"*Steven?* We call him Steve here."

"Lovely man. He turned Toblerone around in just two years."

"Yes, he did do that."

Silence.

"Ethan, I need your help."

A loaded pause. "Again?"

"My spreadsheets."

Relief. "Okay. Sure."

"Are you free later this afternoon?"

The moment Mom asked if I was free, Gord-O walked into my cubicle and pointed his index finger at me, meaning, *Come talk to me, right now rather than later.* "I can find the time."

"Make sure that time is four o'clock. *Please,* honey?"

"Well . . ."

"I'll make your favourite dessert."

She hung up.

Gord-O asked, "What's with the ragamuffin fashion look?"

"Gord-O. Hi. How can I help you?"

"You get a lot of personal phone calls, Ethan."

"In three years, I've had six personal phone calls, and somehow you're always right there when they happen. Are you stalking me?"

Gord-O ignored me. "The level builders just got a call, and the exec group is on their ass saying they need a better castle model."

"I found maybe four dozen pre-modelled castles, ranging from a molecule-perfect rebuilding of Mad King Ludwig's Bavarian hideaway to a do-it-yourself plywood backyard kit. What do they want?"

Gord-O repeated himself. "The level builders just got a call, and the exec group is on their ass saying they need a better castle model."

"Gotcha. I'll look again." I actually don't mind scouring the Internet, finding stuff. In my brain it doesn't feel like work.

"And, Ethan, next time remember the ratio of Honey Nut to classic Cheerios is three to one."

"They were out of Honey Nut."

"To be merely good enough is to never succeed." With a platitude as his last word, Gord-O left.

I heard Kaitlin's disembodied voice from over the cubicle wall. "Ethan, what exactly is your job description?"

*She speaks.*

"One minute you're supposed to be optimizing code, the next you're bulk shopping for Cheerios. Doesn't this place have free cereal already?"

"Last year Gord-O's team ate too many Cheerios, so Accounting got on their case, and they still ate too many, so then Legal had to draw up a brief outlining the company's free Cheerios policy. Since then, they've had to buy their own."

"And you have to get them?"

"I look upon my job as apprenticeship rather than servitude."

"If you ask me, you're living in Schmucksville."

"Schmucksville?"

"It's a retro reference to 1960s Catskill comedy routines."

"Huh." I tried to think of something witty to say.

Kaitlin asked, "So what *is* the real deal with your ragamuffin look?"

"It's"—how to explain?—"hard to explain."

"You look like Elizabeth Smart's kidnappers."

Her phone rang and I went off in search of more 3-D clip art castles. By three-thirty I was able to squeak out of the building on the pretext of buying Honey Nut Cheerios. Mom was in the kitchen, drinking tea and reading the *Province*. "Hello, dear. You're wearing . . . rags."

"It's the new look."

We went into Dad's den, where Mom had a G4 all set to go. The spreadsheet problem seemed easy to fix. "I think you just have some fields crossed. Which part is giving you the biggest problem?"

"I'm trying to track THC counts, along with the genetic ancestry of the plants."

"I see what it is—genetics are logarithmic, whereas potency counts aren't."

"I'm glad someone here understands it. I'll go get you a nice big piece of double-frosted chocolate devil's food cake."

"I thought you were kidding about that."

"Nothing's too good for my baby boy."

Mom has a pretty good system for tracking the genetic histories of her crops. It involves an alphabetizing scheme wherein each female plant is assigned one upper case letter, which is followed by an upper or lower case letter, depending on whether the plant was a clone or a genetic male/female cross. Td, her favourite, was The Dude, a mutant THC miracle of genetics, and, to be honest, it bugged me, too, that Ellen had given him a pruning.

Mom's plant names reflect her somewhat random TV watching habits. Surrounding The Dude were:

| | |
|---|---|
| CL | Cloris Leachman |
| Ee | Emilio Estevez |
| Fb | Fantasia Barino |
| MK | Mary-Kate Olsen |
| Bb | Bo Bice |
| BbG | former UN secretary-general Boutros Boutros-Ghali |
| LL | the nightingale of Glasgow, "To Sir with Love" songstress Lulu |

• • •

Gord-O saw me walking into jPod.

"Where were you?"

"I was out looking for Honey Nut Cheerios, but Save-On was sold out, too. The guy there said that Martha Stewart used them in a program about homemade energy bars, and they've been out for a week."

"Oh."

*Am I good, or what!*

Everyone in jPod was beavering away, and my entrance generated no enthusiasm.

The phone rang, as I suspected it would: Dad. "My Ellen problem is solved. I gave a producer I know twenty-five grand in cash from my Hummer fund, and he's sending

Ellen to Toronto tomorrow for ten weeks to work on a Hallmark Channel movie."

"That was fast. Hallmark has a channel? The greeting card company?"

"Whoops. I meant Heartland—the chick flick channel."

"Dad, if you want a speaking part in a movie so badly, why don't you find a producer and give him or her some Hummer money, too?"

"That would be cheating. I have to *earn* that speaking role. And by the way, your mother says you're wearing rags."

• • •

Okay, I know I have to address the ragamuffin issue.

Here's the deal: when it comes to duds, I'm really sick of everybody trying to be different from everybody else. In the end, everybody's simply buying their outfits from the same selection of stores at the same mall. I'm also not stupid enough to think that wearing random thrift-store clothing makes me a rebel or an outsider. *Gee, is that a 1997 Chilcotin Rodeo T-shirt you've got on? Wow! Out of 5.5 billion people on the planet, you differentiate yourself from the rest!*

So, when all those smuggled Chinese people had to abandon their clothes at my place, it was like my fashion gift of the gods. Indeed, the gods had handed me a look on a platter. And the thing is, once you establish a look, and once everybody recognizes that look as *your* look, you never have to think about fashion again. It's pig laziness on my part, but so what.

•••

The rest of the evening was quiet.

Turtles.

Jeff.

Deadline.

Efficiency.

Lots of efficiency.

Too much efficiency.

A sense of unease . . . a wave of paranoia.

A slight gust of chilled wind.

Cowboy said, "Do you feel something weird?"

Cap'n Crunch granules of sleep fell from the corners of my eyes into my keyboard, into the seven-key cluster of

**UI**

**HJK**

**NM**

I said, "No."

Cowboy said, "I feel chilled or something."

Kaitlin, surprising us all from behind her cubicle wall, snorted and said (without standing up), "You feel chilled because you have no character. You're a depressing assemblage of pop culture influences and cancelled emotions, driven by the sputtering engine of only the most banal form of capitalism. You spend your life feeling as if you're perpetually on the brink of being obsolete—whether it's labour market obsolescence or cultural unhipness. And it's all catching up with you. You live and die by the development cycle.

You're glamorized drosophila flies, with the company regulating your life cycles at whim. If it isn't a budget-driven eighteen-month game production schedule, it's a five-year hardware obsolescence schedule. Every five years you have to throw away everything you know and learn a whole new set of hardware and software specs, relegating what was once critical to our lives to the cosmic slag heap."

Cowboy considered this. "So, then, what's wrong with that?"

"What's *wrong* with that is that you might just as well be tyrannized cotton-mill workers in rural Massachusetts in the nineteenth century. You might as well be stitching Nikes together in some quasi-corrupt archipelago nation in Asia in return for badly ventilated dorm rooms and $1.95 a day."

Silence.

Loaded silence.

Cowboy said, "Do you have to be so political about it?"

Kaitlin heaved a generic world-weary sigh. "Cowboy, let's look at you—tell us what your character is."

Cowboy fumbled. "Well—"

"I'm listening."

"I think I'm an okay-enough guy."

"Gee. That's fascinating."

"Let me think."

"Take all the time you want."

After thirty pregnant seconds, Cowboy said, "This is stupid. Why should I have to sit here and define who I am?"

"There you have it, Cowboy."

"Have *what*?"

"What you have is the fact that if you don't have a character to begin with, everything and nothing is in character."

"That's really fucking depressing."

"And what if it is?"

"It's like *Melrose Place.*"

"*Melrose?*" said Bree. "That was a hundred years ago."

John Doe got excited. "I watched the whole series on DVD. Remember when the script writers couldn't come up with personalities or characteristics for the characters? They simply made them all go psycho, one by one."

Bree nodded. "It worked, didn't it?"

Evil Mark added, "I liked that show."

I said, "I never watched it. It felt target-marketed."

"Aaron Spelling made so much money with it," said Kaitlin. "But didn't you notice that, when they started, they were all twentysomething slackers looking for meaning in life, living in a motel-like complex with a swimming pool in the centre?"

Bree said, "That's exactly like the characters in Douglas Coupland's 1991 novel, *Generation X.*"

"Exactly."

"So they ripped Coupland off?"

"That's harsh and actionable. But who are we to say?"

"Sounds fishy to me."

"If I were Douglas Coupland, I'd have sued the pants off Aaron Spelling."

"Me, too."

"So would I."

Finally something we all agreed on.

# Lovely pod

jPod は幸せな場所である。jPod
スペースで、また、幸せな彼できる。幸せがありなさい。jPod
がありなさい。

jPod is a happy place!
You can be happy, also, in the jPod space. Be happy. Be jPod.

# *Let's Working!*

私達の落ち着いたオフィスの環境の嬉しい事の大きい変化を見本抽
出しなさい。それらは友人でありたいと思う!
それらはよい時、余りにほしいと思う。

Please sample a large variety of our serene office environment joyful things.
They want to be your friend! They want your good times, too.

jPodding work style は友人を作り、幸せな人生を
楽しむ方法である!

jPodding work style is a way to make friends and enjoy the happy life.

**Zaxxon**
**Manufacturer:** Sega/Gremlin
**Year:** 1982
**Class:** Wide Release
**Genre:** Space
**Type**: Videogame

**Conversion Class:** Sega Zaxxon
**Number of Simultaneous Players:** 1
**Maximum Number of Players:** 2
**Gameplay:** Alternating
**Control Panel Layout:** Single Player Ambidextrous
**Sound:** Amplified Mono (One Channel)

• • •

Kaitlin's dissection of Cowboy's personality made me begin to have doubts about my own personality. Prior to Kaitlin's rant, I thought Cowboy was the quirkiest person I knew. And now he was suddenly just a Lego mini-fig. (Okay, maybe John Doe is the quirkiest person I know.)

But honestly—*do* I have a personality? Do any of us? I scoured my life and saw no overriding purpose, just my love affair with computer games—my old SOL and the 8808s in particular. If nothing else, I was pleased to be able to earn a living within an industry that's increasingly more corporate and bland and soul-killing, but . . . *but* then I got to wondering if I even possessed the ability to fall in love with another human being and . . . I began to feel like such a *module,* especially compared to Kaitlin, who was such a firebrand tonight. I couldn't help but wonder what she's like when she removes all of her brakes.

I was having this crisis of faith while parked outside my Chinatown shack. Then, while attaching The Club, I looked up and saw that the bathroom window upstairs was open, the nylon Union Jack curtain billowing from within. I always keep that window shut (pigeons) and was curious as to what was going on. I put my key in the lock, opened the door, and realized that all of my old furniture was gone. In its place was strange, ornate, gilded, swan-crested, diamond-tufted black and red leather junk—the sort of stuff I'd expect to see in the living room of, say, North Korean president Kim Il Sung. It was disturbing and garish and way too big for my place, like adult furniture in a tree fort. In a corner I saw some boxes that held my flight simulation software, but everything else was new. I wasn't hallucinating—it really *was* my place.

There was a sofa made of curlicued gold wood, upholstered with baloney-coloured fabrics patterned with Chinese mountainscapes. At one end were a matching club chair and a glass coffee table—a lens of blue tinted glass held aloft by worshipful egrets. My framed Offspring poster had been replaced by an oil-painted fantasia of kittens frolicking amidst Louis XIV mirrors and vases filled with blue Himalayan poppies. In what was now the dining room (but what had been the gaming room) sat a glistening black lacquered table with matching chairs for eight. My bedroom and the spare room were similarly decked out.

This was Greg's doing.

Fortunately, his cell number was pencilled onto the kitchen wall, just above a brand new plum-coloured breakfast nook table inlaid with a mother-of-pearl scene depicting Marie Antoinette in her garden throwing lawn darts at poor people.

"Greg."

"Tell me how much you love it!"

"I . . ."

"Yeah?"

" . . . I don't know where to begin."

"Isn't it great? Kam Fong is rewarding your hospitality for helping him with his, um, *shipment*."

"Greg, I told you I've got no interest in dealing with people-smugglers, and I don't want their free furniture."

"Grow up. For the people being smuggled, it's all just one big adventure, and they'll be telling their grandkids about all of your old shitty furniture and your dorky slackersomething clothes."

"Greg . . ."

"And by the way, what's with the Union Jack flag curtain? Only junkies use flags as curtains."

"I . . ."

"Junkies with *lice*, Ethan."

In the background I heard my father shouting, "Who's that?"

"It's Ethan."

"Greg, are you over at Mom and Dad's?"

"I came for dinner here and thought I'd spend the night, too. I'm bagged. By the way, why is there lipstick on my old pillow?"

"It's a long story. What's everybody doing up so late?"

"Dad was on a shoot and came home too stoked to sleep. There's a live feed from the Perth–Fremantle ballroom dancing semifinals coming in, so Dad and I are watching it. You know how he gets during semifinal season."

Dad is a ballroom dancing fanatic. I spent my preteen years being abandoned on the sidelines of dance club floors while dad studied and practised. Mom won't go near a dance floor. I heard a wash of flamenco music. "Where's Mom?"

As if on cue, Mom said, "Greg, is that Ethan?"

"Yup."

She took the phone. "What do you think of your new furniture?"

"It's . . . overwhelming"

"I think your brother is just a dreamboat. And aren't you

lucky his friend, Kam Fong, has such a generous heart and gave you such an amazing array of luxury furniture? You must have done a terrific job helping him redo his accounts and balances spreadsheets."

Words failed me and then re-entered my life. "Yes, I certainly am lucky."

Mom was on to a new topic. "Ethan, I need your help tomorrow. I have to make a collection."

"Mom, I have a job."

"Nonsense. I'll phone young Steven and tell him it's important to me that you take the afternoon off."

"You're still talking with Steve?"

"Of course. I made him a pie today, too. He works so hard, and hard workers need treats every so often."

Mom handed the phone back to Greg. I looked around me and noticed something else. "Greg?"

"What, bro?"

"Everything here is on . . . an angle."

"Oh, *that*. Yeah. Kam brought in his feng shui guy."

"Thanks."

"Ethan, you sound pissed off. This is the last time I ever try to help you out. *Ooh, look at me, I'm an information worker. My job is clean and environmentally friendly and futuristic*—"

"Greg—" Experience has taught me to simply ride out Greg's diatribes until they stop.

"Hey, Ethan, you know the guy who stood in front of the tank in Tiananmen Square? He's the guy who hot-glued the faceplate over the keypad in the phone you're using."

"Greg, I have to go."

He changed his tone. "Hey, speaking of sweatshops and

toxins, I'm flying back to Hong Kong tomorrow. Want anything?"

I thought about this. "Can you pick up an assortment of bootlegged games for me? I've got a bet going with Cowboy that he can't properly detect bootlegs. Just buy a bunch at random. Nothing over two bucks."

"Done."

• • •

Mom's pie worked. The next day I left jPod at noon and passed Steve's Touareg by the main security booth down the hill. He gave me a rehearsed-looking thumbs-up, and that was that.

At Mom's we switched to her K-car wagon and drove out into the Fraser Valley amid a chilly monsoon. I was wearing another outfit cobbled together from smugglees' remnants. Mom took one look at it and said, "Oh, Ethan. You're dressed like a newsie in a Broadway show."

"I told you, it's my new style."

"How am I going to make a collection with you dressed up like a ragamuffin?"

There was a twenty-mile patch of fashion-induced tension before Mom stopped editorializing about my personal style. We were headed to Maple Ridge, a suburb on the city's easternmost extreme—largely built overnight, with overtaxed roads that burped along at a speed best described as digestive. The clouds were so dark it felt like we were night driving. Mom gunned the engine and cut off an impatient Prelude driven by a baby boy with a new driver tag in his rear window.

"Tell me more about this Jeff Probst celebrity. What do you think he's like in real life?"

"Jeff Probst?"

"Yes, Steven has got me intrigued."

"Well, he hosts this show where he's always having to deliver bad news to people. He's like a professional firer they bring in to do mass layoffs. In the first few years of the show, he tried to display empathy, but I've noticed that as he ages and sees more of the world, he's realizing that bad news is a part of life, and that when you have to give it, just say it and get it over with. He's a regular kind of guy, but at the same time, he's not."

"Does he skateboard?"

"Not that I know of."

"Does he wear silly baggy pants and oversized nonsense jewellery?"

"No. Style-wise he's always dressed as if he's about to get into a stolen Cessna on a private tarmac somewhere in central Colombia."

"Who does he look like?"

"Generically handsome—game show-y, but definitely of the twenty-first century. He's a bit too tanned. He'd better watch it, or his skin'll look like caramel popcorn when he's sixty."

"So how does this Jeff Probst fellow's personality convert into a skateboard character who's a friendly turtle?"

"He could maybe be wise and all-knowing like Yoda."

"Who?"

I let it drop, since Mom's curiosity was clearly ebbing. We were entering an older area with uninflated property values and roads last resurfaced in the 1960s. Invisible waves of manure entered the station wagon. I asked, "Is it far?"

"Another few minutes."

"I'm hungry."

"If you can't find something lying around the car, then you can't be very hungry."

I looked in the glove compartment. Mom had stashed some gold-foiled chocolate coins, probably from one of the egg hunts we used to have at Greg's ex-wife's place. I tasted one of them and nearly gagged.

"Mom, how long has this chocolate been in there?"

"A few years, maybe."

"A few *years*?"

"Ethan, everybody knows Easter chocolate lasts forever. If they don't sell it one year, they put it in the warehouse and bring it out again the next year, over and over until it finally sells. By that standard, those coins there are practically new."

I got to thinking about the business at hand. "Mom, one more time, why are we out here in this hillbilly's armpit?"

"Tim's buddy, Lyle, owes me fifty thousand dollars, and won't pay up."

"Okay, that's more than I knew a few minutes ago. Does he know about Tim's, um, *fate*?"

"No. But he found out about Tim and me a few months ago. It caused a rift between them and . . ."

"Wait a second—what do you mean, *found out about Tim and me*?"

"Remove your mind from the gutter. Tim was nice. I felt a closeness with him."

"Don't tell me any more."

"Why not?"

"You're my mother. You're weirding me out."

"Eat another coin."

"So, then, are these guys bikers, too?"

"Connect the dots, Ethan: we're in the middle of nowhere and drugs are involved. Who else is going to live out here?"

The rain wouldn't let up as we turned onto successively dinkier roads, finally coming to a gravel lane.

"We're here," Mom said.

At the turn of the century this had been a farmhouse. It was remote back then, and continued to be remote now.

"Imagine living in Vancouver and managing to miss all the real estate booms," I said.

We knocked at the front door. Inside, a TV was blaring, and a mentally ill dog barked.

"That's Gumdrop," Mom said.

The door opened with a creak.

Mom said, "Hi, Lyle."

"Oh, *you*."

"Yes, me."

"What do you want, Carol?"

"My money, please."

"Who's the guy with you—cradle-robbing again?"

I said, "I'm Ethan. This is my mom."

Lyle shut the door.

I said, "Rude prick."

"Bikers. What do you expect?"

I knocked this time. Mom said, "Lyle. Please come out. Let's discuss this like sensible adults."

Through the door, Lyle told us to fuck off. I heard another

biker laughing above the TV, along with Gumdrop's crazed howling.

Mom knocked. "Lyle, just pay me what's mine, and I'll be out of your hair."

Lyle's friend shouted, "Lyle doesn't have any hair." From behind the door, this witty retort garnered convulsions of laughter.

"They're stoned," I said.

"You know, dear, this reminds me of back when you had your paper route, and on collecting day people would pretend not to be home to avoid you."

"That always drove me nuts. Why didn't people just pay up?"

"I think it's because when you walk up to the door, in the customers' minds, you're like their conscience come to haunt them. Perhaps that's how our biker friends here feel about me."

Just then, a foaming pinkish-white pit bull swooped around a corner of the house and up the front steps and jabbed a justifiably named canine into Mom's shin.

"Mom!"

She pulled a gun from her purse, and one shot later, Gumdrop met his maker. Mom then keeled over and began verbally spazzing, using language about as brutal as is possible for her to use: "Oh shoot! Sugar! Ouch! Oh, Ethan, it hurts! Is that nasty little thing dead? Good."

I kicked Gumdrop's carcass. "You evil little shit. Come to life so we can shoot you again." I turned to Mom. "Let me see your shin."

There was one deep bite that barely missed a varicose vein.

Oddly, my thought was, *Mom has varicose veins?*

"That awful, *awful* dog." Using her good leg, Mom gave Gumdrop a kick, too. Lyle opened the door. He said, "Carol, what the fuck did you do to my dog?"

Mom looked up with an about-to-go-apeshit goggle-eyed stare that I had only ever seen once before, when Greg and I were horsing around the living room and broke her porcelain figurine of Shakespeare knocking on the door of Anne Hathaway's cottage. "Give me my fucking money, you ugly piece of trash."

*Mom swore for real!*

"You crazy bitch, you shot my dog!"

"You dirty little man. Gumdrop punctured my shin bone, and *you* owe Carol Jarlewski fifty grand. Give it to me now."

"Fuck off and die."

I said, "No *you* fuck off and die. Pay up!" Mom fired a shot into the wood floor a whisker away from Lyle's foot. He backed right up.

"Jesus, you're both totally fucking nuts."

Mom and I stormed the house. It reminded me a bit of our grade-three class's gerbil environment—a tossed salad of biker mag porn foldouts, old *TV Guides* and KFC debris drizzled with cat pee. Across the room, Lyle's toasted biker buddy was playing Chrono Trigger on Sony PlayStation, and this is truly shameful of me to report, but I really wanted to go over and join in.

Lyle said, "Andy, Carol's out of her fucking tree."

Mom shouted, "You've made my day unpleasant enough already, Lyle. Give me my money or I'll shoot your foot."

"No."

Mom shot the tip of Lyle's worn black cowboy boot, and he screamed like a girl.

"Lyle, give me my money."

Lyle was keeled over. "Andy, get her the fucking money." He looked at me. "Your family is one sick mess, dude."

Mom fired a warning shot at the ceiling, and a small cauliflower of plaster dust floated downward.

Andy reached into an Ikea Billy bookcase full of sun-faded VHS tapes and removed an Adidas box full of thousand-dollar bundles as Lyle removed his cowboy boot, cursing. Andy counted out fifty of them. "Here. Fifty grand. Now *go*."

Mom became sugar sweet. "Thanks, guys. All you had to do was be nice."

"Meddlesome hag."

Mom shot the ceiling once more and we left.

Out in the car, we did a further inspection of Mom's shin. "I think I'll go to Dr. Tuck and get some stitches."

A few minutes later I said, "Isn't it weird that bikers would have Ikea furniture?"

"Don't talk to me about Ikea furniture. Your father tried assembling an Ikea shelf last year, and it nearly ended our marriage. Look—it's a yard sale over there. Let's stop for a minute."

# Intel® 865PE Chipset-Based

# 865PE Neo2

**Designed for Intel® Pentium® 4 Processors**

**Defender**
**Manufacturer:** Williams
**Year:** 1980
**Class:** Wide Release
**Genre:** Shooter
**Type:** Videogame

**Conversion Class:** Williams
**Number of Simultaneous Players:** 1
**Maximum Number of Players:** 2
**Gameplay:** Alternating
**Control Panel Layout:** Single Player
**Controls:** Joystick: 2-way (up, down) Buttons: 5
**Sound:** Amplified Mono (One Channel)

• • •

When I got back to the pod around three, a FedEx box sat on my desk—Kaitlin's Belgian keypad of the corn. She was away from the pod, so I swapped it with hers. Bree said, "Correct me if I'm wrong, Ethan, but I think you and Miss Thing are sort of sweet on each other."

"She's talked about me?"

"Not directly. But when she makes her exasperated snorts, they're always aimed more at you than the rest of us."

"You think?"

"I *know*."

Cowboy's phone rang and nobody picked it up. I asked, "Where is everybody?"

"Everybody's so bummed out by this charismatic turtle character that they all fled," said Bree, adding, "You know, Ethan, I have an idea how you can torment Kaitlin a bit."

"Really?"

Bree told me her idea—it was genius.

When Kaitlin came back a half-hour later, we were set to put it into operation. I was to pretend I was doing a crossword puzzle and ask Bree for words: "Five-letter word, *UK lineup*."

"Queue."

"That was easy. Okay—four letters, *a festive rum drink, blank-Libre*."

"Cuba."

"Okay, wait, here's a hard one: *Mary Tyler-blank*."

"Say that again?"

"*Mary Tyler-blank*. Five letters."

"Is she a politician or something?"

"I don't know. It sounds familiar."

"Mary-Tyler . . . *Smith*?"

"Maybe she's that old lady they put on the US dollar coin in the 1970s that everybody hated."

"That was Susan B. Anthony."

"Oh. *Mary Tyler-blank.*"

*"Tyler-blank."*

*"Tyler-blank-blank-blank . . ."*

Kaitlin lost it. "Moore! Mary Fucking Tyler Moore," she yelled.

"Let me see—that fits perfectly. Thanks, Kaitlin."

An exasperated grunt.

"Next word, seven letters: *Supercalifragilisticexpiali-blank.*"

"Again?"

*"Supercalifragilisticexpiali-blank."*

"Allocation?"

"Come on, Bree, *try* here."

"I am. What was the first part, again?"

*"Supercalifragilisticexpiali."*

"Then *blank*?"

*"Supercalifragilisticexpiali-blank."*

"Hmmm . . ."

"*Docious,* you morons!" screamed Kaitlin. "Supercalifragilisticexpiali*docious*. It's from *Mary Poppins*."

"Hang on a second, Kaitlin—wait—D-O-C-I-O-U-S. It fits. Thanks." This was fun. I was all set to go onto the next fake clue (*Viva-blank-Vegas*) when I heard a sniffle from Kaitlin's side of the cubicle. I gophered up—she was crying. "Oh man, I'm sorry, Kaitlin. We were just funning you."

"I'm not in a mood to be funned."

I came around to her desk and leaned on it. Bree came over, too. "What's wrong?" she asked.

"I'm hungry. I'm so *hungry.*"

"Then just eat."

"It's not that easy."

I said, "There's penne pesto with free-range chicken on today's cafeteria menu."

"No."

Bree and I swapped maybe-we-went-too-far looks. Bree asked, "So what's going on here?"

"I can't tell you."

"Don't sweat it. No problem."

Bree wagged her head, implying, *Best we leave her alone for the time being.*

I agreed, but first I had to extract the Belgian keyboard. "Kaitlin, sorry, but I did something naughty to your keyboard. I swapped it for this freaky unit."

Kaitlin looked at it. "Cool. A Belgian keyboard."

"You recognize it?"

"My sister works for the EU in Antwerp."

"Oh."

"That's so sweet of you."

"I—"

"No. It's okay."

I went to my cubicle and got her old board. "Here's the real one. For when you want to switch."

"Thanks, Ethan."

I slunk away. Fortunately, Gord-O found me and was able to dump a massive steaming heap of tasks in my lap, relieving me of any time in which to experience remorse. I was considering this steaming pile of tasks when I saw John Doe in the cafeteria, playing Sim City on a wireless. Reprieve! I was able to pre-empt Gord-O's work request with the promise of time well wasted.

"Sim City? That's pretty vanilla, John."

"Is it wrong to play a game that's a proven hit? I only play bestselling games, and never allow myself to become too good, lest I deviate from the norm."

"Okay." I looked at his screen. "Uh . . . John, you're building a city out of body parts." On screen, random body parts glistened alongside traditional buildings. Tunnels passed through feet. Eyeballs formed oil storage tanks.

"Well, yes. I had to tweak the code at least a little bit. The body part patch is floating around in the in-house system if you want to try it." John attached a donkey tail to a fifty-storey building shaped like a human leg from the foot to the knee. "In about fifty years, real-life genetic traits will be as modular as those you're witnessing on my screen. For now we can only dream. See that oil refinery right there? In a few minutes it's going to get a vagina. By the way, I googled Kaitlin, and you'd be surprised at what I found."

"You googled her?"

"Of course I did. Didn't you?"

I'd somehow forgotten to perform this essential task.

"Let's have a peek, shall we?"

A few clicks later, **kaitlin anna boyd joyce** went into the Google request box. A predictable landslide of genealogical links filled the screen.

"Big deal."

"Yes, but what happens if I go back and enter her name again and click the I FEEL LUCKY button."

"Nobody ever clicks that button."

"Maybe they should start." The genealogical mulch came back, but there was a new hit at the top of the page.

"'Dark Stories from the Subway Diet'?"

John said, "Exactly."

He clicked the link, and we were transported to one of hundreds of Subway restaurant fan sites. In it, we saw BEFORE and AFTER photos of Kaitlin—one of her weighing 337 pounds, and the next as the Kaitlin of jPod, weighing at most 105. "Holy crap," I said.

"That's what I thought. Read on, bro."


**Welcome to . . .**
# The Third Rail
**An Unofficial Fan Website for Those Who Enjoy Tasty Sandwiches from Subway!!!**
**07.23.05**
**THIS WEEK: What happens when "THE DIET" goes wrong?**
**TITLE: "To Kaitlin Boyd, it was just a few pieces of cake, but to Subway, it was a violation of a sacred trust."**


I am not a news reporter, so please excuse my mistakes here. For those of you who visit this site regularly (Thank you for visiting!!! Come back next week to see my new graphic overhaul!!!), you will know that Kaitlin Boyd lost over two hundred pounds on the Diet. She was set for fame and wealth—until a neighbour with a Handicam brought a tape to Subway HQ that rocked her world. This former three-hundred-pounder was caught on the fifth month of her diet eating an entire chocolate mud cake on her back stoop. Her lucrative sponsorship contract was cancelled. All Kaitlin has left are bitter memories and a freezer full of complimentary frozen uncooked Parmesan-oregano 12-inch loaves. A little bird told this reporter that Kaitlin likes to thaw and eat these loaves before bedtime while watching reruns of *Who's the Boss?* on a satellite feed from the Turks and Caicos Islands.

THIS WEBSITE ASKS: Was Kaitlin really fired over one lapse with a cake? Surely not!!! A Subway corporate insider (who shall remain nameless!!!) told this reporter, "We're all human, and many of our weight-loss spokesheroes have committed transgressions, but with Ms. Boyd, cake was just the start. That same neighbour also caught Boyd dropping twenty bucks at Popeyes Chicken, and then frittering away an entire afternoon at a Baskin-Robbins. There comes a time when you really have to admit that a line has been drawn in the sand and the line has been crossed. We wish Ms. Boyd the best in her future endeavours."

Frequent visitors to this site know that the Subway Diet is a sacred pact between you and Subway. To honour this pact, I visited Kaitlin's former next-door neighbour in Sunnyvale, California. There, I spoke with exposé creator, Norman Goddard, 31, a nurse. As he told me, "All my friends call me Stormin' Norman!!!" My Sony recorder was acting weird, but here is the general thrust of my conversation with Norman.

**ME:** At what point did you realize that you had to take the law into your own hands and report Ms. Boyd to Subway HQ?

**STORMIN' NORMAN:** That stuck-up scag wouldn't answer any of my phone calls, and I tried calling her every day for a year.

**ME:** What happened then?

**STORMIN' NORMAN:** I sent her a Hickory Farms smoked meat platter selection—one of those ironic gifts. I thought if I sent her flowers, it'd look like I was stalking her or something.

**ME:** What happened next?

**STORMIN' NORMAN:** She came over when I was at work and put the unopened platter on my front stoop. Then the neighbour's labradoodle got into it and then got sick and shat all over the concrete I'd just had power-washed.

**ME:** That's really interesting. Go on.

**STORMIN' NORMAN:** So I went to Michaels crafts store and got some big coloured cardboards and made some signs, which I taped to the side of my house that faces her place. I thought they were kind of nice.

**ME:** What did they say?

**STORMIN' NORMAN:** Let's see . . . One said, IT WAS JUST A GIFT. WHY DO YOU HAVE TO BE SO COLD? Another said, I THINK ABOUT YOU ALL THE TIME. IN A GOOD WAY.

**ME:** Nice enough.

**STORMIN' NORMAN:** Totally. But did she respond to me? No. She went to the cops and tried to get a restraining order, which was so insulting, because all I was trying to do was be nice to a neighbour. And she changed her phone number and got all these locks on the doors.

**ME:** Did she own the place?

**STORMIN' NORMAN:** Rental.

**ME:** What next?

**STORMIN' NORMAN:** She put up tinfoil on all the windows that faced mine.

**ME:** And then?

**STORMIN' NORMAN:** She was having a backyard barbecue with all her geek co-workers, and so I came over with a tray of hamburger patties I spiced and formed all by myself—I even put Saran Wrap on them to keep dust and flies off the meat—and when I walked into her yard, all of these people formed a human chain around her, and she ran inside. Jeez, I mean, I was just trying to be neighbourly.

**ME:** Was there a fight?

**STORMIN' NORMAN:** Nah. We all just yelled a bit. Got it out of our system. And then the cops showed up, so I thought to myself, *Stormin' Norman, maybe it's time you ate a reality sandwich and faced the fact that Kaitlin doesn't like you.* That's when I decided that if I couldn't have her, I'd make sure she noticed me in other ways.

**ME:** Really?

**STORMIN' NORMAN:** Oh yeah. I went to one of those spy shops and spent a fortune and began chronicling every moment of her life. Every single moment.

Unfortunately, website visitors, I lost the rest of the interview, but who says that investigative journalism is dead!!!???

Next week's investigation: What's the top-secret proportion of salt to pepper inside the salt-and-pepper can?

Subway Restaurants is the world's largest submarine sandwich franchise, with more than 24,000 locations in 83 countries. In 2002, the Subway chain surpassed McDonald's in the number of restaurants open in the United States and Canada. Headquartered in Milford, Conn., Subway Restaurants was co-founded by Fred DeLuca and Dr. Peter Buck in 1965. That partnership marked the beginning of a remarkable journey—one that made it possible for thousands of individuals to build and succeed in their own business. Subway Restaurants was named the number one franchise opportunity in all categories by *Entrepreneur* magazine in its Annual Franchise 500 ranking for 2005—for the 13th time in 17 years! For more information about the Subway restaurant chain, visit http://www.subway.com/. Subway® is a registered trademark of Doctor's Associates Inc. (DAI).

ATF
Alcohol, Tobacco and Firearms
AZT
Azidothymidine
BLT
Bacon, Lettuce and Tomato
BSE
Bovine Spongiform Encephalopathy
CIA
Central Intelligence Agency
CMV
Cytomegalovirus
DMZ
Demilitarized Zone
DOA
Dead on Arrival
EEC
European Economic Community
EMP
Electromagnetic Pulse
FBI
Federal Bureau of Investigation
FTP
File Transfer Protocol
GMT
Greenwich Mean Time
GTO
Gran Turismo Omologato
HIV
Human Immunodeficiency Virus
HOV
High Occupancy Vehicle
IMF
International Monetary Fund
IRA
Irish Republican Army
JFK
John Fitzgerald Kennedy
KGB
Komitet Gosudarstvennoi Bezopasnosti
KKK
Ku Klux Klan
LAX
Los Angeles International Airport
LSD
Lysergic Acid Diethylamide
MIA
Missing in Action
MP3
Moving Pictures Experts Group Audio Layer 3
NHK
Nihon Hoso Kyokai TV
NRA
National Rifle Association
NRK
Anarchy

OLE
Object Linking and Embedding
OPD
Officially Pronounced Dead
PFD
Photoshop File Document
PIN
Personal Identification Number
PSA
Prostate-Specific Antigen
PVC
Polyvinyl Chloride
QE2
Queen Elizabeth II
RGB
Red-Green-Blue
RNA
Ribonucleic Acid
SLA
Symbionese Liberation Army
SPF
Sun Protection Factor
SUV
Sport-Utility Vehicle
THC
Tetrahydrocannabinol
TNT
Trinitrotoluene
UPS
United Parcel Service
USD
US Dollar
VCR
Videocassette Recorder
VRE
Vancomycin-Resistant Enterococci
WTC
World Trade Center
WWW
World Wide Web
XML
Extensible Markup Language
XXL
Double Extra Large
XXX
Pornography
YTD
Year to Date
Y3K
The Year 3000
ZIP
Zone Improvement Plan
ZPG
Zero Population Growth

• • •

The next morning I slinked into a BoardX art meeting. Steve, Gord-O and staff from the loftiest links of the corporate food chain were trying to nail the essence of Jeff the Charismatic Turtle, albeit without joy or enthusiasm. Prototype turtle sketches were pinned onto a massive cork wall, all of them goofy and teensploitational: sunglasses, baggy pants and (dear God) a terry cloth sweatband.

"Does Jeff the Turtle follow players around the entire time they manipulate their third person?"

"Almost. Like Watson is to Sherlock Holmes."

"Can you imagine how annoying that would be?"

"Maybe the buddy isn't such a good idea."

Steve more or less squashed what hope remained: "It's going to be a buddy. Players will love it."

"Isn't our turtle supposed to be a bit more studly?"

"Turtles aren't studly by nature."

"What about that turtle they used in the 1950s to pimp the atomic weapons program? He was kind of studly."

"No, he wasn't, and besides, he's dead."

"What?"

"Dead. Hung himself from the side of his posh midtown Manhattan terrarium. Left a note saying he couldn't handle the shame of what he'd done. Wrote it on a piece of Bibb lettuce."

"Can't anyone think of hipper turtles than the Department of Energy's uranium spokesreptile?"

"Spokes*phibian*."

"No one answered my question. Is our turtle studly? Does he have huge pecs?"

"I don't think it's appropriate that a turtle be *hot*."

"Have you ever noticed how they never show the Ninja Turtles' shells if they can avoid it? They're always facing forwards."

"Hey—a thick, rich masculine shell. He could store a tool belt on it."

"If you look, you'll see that the Ninja Turtles' fleshy undersides are always overexposed, and the musculature is too steroidal. It's a reproductive strategy on their part, maybe."

"Are they gay?"

"I told you, Legal said we're *not* allowed to ask that, and besides, turtles are always straight."

"Hang on, we agreed to model the turtle after Jeff Probst, so maybe we could make our turtle wear Banana Republic summerwear. Maybe get a co-licensing deal."

"That could work."

"A tan?"

"I like the tan idea."

"Everybody, do we all like a suntan for our turtle? Let me do a hand count and get it out of the way—okay, suntan it is."

"Can he have more hair?"

"I have one word for you: *mammal*."

"If Donald Duck can have hands, Jeff can have hair. A little brush cut—easy to maintain, and it can take him from the boardroom all the way into a palm-fronded yurt populated with dormant tarantulas."

"No beaches here. Sand gets into skateboard bearings. Game over."

"Is Jeff middle-class?"

"By Jeff, you mean the turtle?"

"Yes. Can we all agree to just call him Jeff?"

"Okay, only so long as the real Jeff Probst never finds out we've been having this discussion."

"Is Jeff middle-class?"

"What you're really asking is, *What's Jeff's story?* What makes Jeff *Jeff*?"

"Yes."

"I think Art did a fine job of depicting Jeff here. Let's look at their ideas and take it from there."

Silence.

"Ideas? Thoughts?"

Silence.

Everyone suddenly remembered they were supposed to look interested. "Is he an adult turtle?"

"No. He's a teenager. Didn't I say that?"

"Where does he live?"

"Players don't need to know that."

"Is he the only turtle in the game?"

"Yes."

"Does he have magic powers?"

"No. He has boarding skill."

"Does he have a weak spot?"

"Yes—being flipped onto his back and left to die in the sun, or to have his innards ripped out by rogue weasels."

"Please," Steve said. "I believe in joshing around as much as the next guy, but let's all be serious. We have to get Jeff locked in by tomorrow."

"Jeff's not going to sing or do rap songs, is he?"

"We'll cross that bridge when we get there."

• • •

Three hours later Steve walked into jPod while I was procrastinating by downloading car crash images from a gore site in the Czech Republic.

"Steve. Uh, hi. You must be lost. What part of the building do you need to get to?"

"Here is fine."

"Oh."

"Your mother's a nice woman, Ethan."

"Well, yes."

"You're a lucky fellow."

"Thanks, Steve."

"She's got a good sense of humour. And when she talks to you, it's like you're the only person in the universe."

"Steve, I think I left my car in the parking lot." I stood up to go.

"Don't be in such a hurry. So, uh . . ." Steve began buying time. "Your brother sells real estate, right?"

"Sort of." I explained Greg's specialty.

"You think he'd sell me a place?"

"It's your money, Steve."

I gave Greg's information to Steve, and he left. I sat down, turned to look at my screen and then had a blinding headache. It was time to go home—eight o'clock—the earliest I'd left since the last game shipped.

Upon arriving at my stylish Chinatown shack, I walked in

the door to see that all my new furniture was gone, and my original furniture hadn't come back. *Fuck*. I phoned Greg, but realized he was on Cathay Pacific 889, headed to Hong Kong. I phoned Mom.

"Ethan, you didn't even like the furniture."

"That's not the point. There's nothing in my place. Nothing."

"If you had a girlfriend, there'd be more possessions."

"You told me to dump my girlfriend."

"She was a mess. Good riddance. Greg said you really made that generous Chinese businessman angry."

"Who?"

"The one whose furniture you made fun of. Kam Fong."

"I didn't mock it. It's just not *me*."

"*Me*? Someone lavishes you with opulent furniture, and you simply dismiss it as '*Not me*'?"

"Okay, I didn't re*ject* it. I merely grudgingly accepted it."

"Which in Chinese culture is like piercing the heart with a freshly sharpened oyster shucker."

Silence.

"Ethan, I'm not supposed to tell you, but you might as well know. Kam Fong was hurt by your rejection of his gift."

"He doesn't even know me."

"He knew you well enough to give you over fifty thousand dollars worth of premium lacquered maple furniture. Here I am trying to breathe a bit of life into my old side table with Krylon spray paint, while *you*, Mister *Trading Spaces*, turn your nose up at a windfall from heaven."

"I can't believe we're having this discussion."

"All I'm saying is that he's probably not the sort of person you should tick off. Be nice to him when visits you."

"What—he's going to be coming here?"

"Of course he is. He wants to hear from you in person why you snubbed him."

"When is he coming?"

"When did you get home?"

"A few minutes ago."

"I imagine he'll be there any time now."

"What?"

I hear a large purring rumble outside the kitchen window. "Shit. That'll be him."

"Just don't tick him off any more. He's an important person who can do wonders for your career."

"In videogames?"

"Offer him something to drink the moment he walks in. If my business with the Asians has taught me anything, it's the power of a drink the first time you meet them."

I heard a knock at the door, and when I opened it, I found a chauffeur in an outfit imported from a 1930s drawing-room comedy. "Hello?"

"You're Mister Ethan?"

"Yes."

"Please wait. Mister Fong will be with you in a moment."

The car was parked at the foot of the stairs, a manly black brute of a machine, of unidentifiable manufacture and era. Pre-capitalist Red China? India? Munstermobile? A minute passed while the driver conferred through the car's rear passenger window slit. I was expecting Kam Fong to resemble that knife-throwing guy in a bowler hat from *Goldfinger;* instead, when he climbed out of the car, he was a guy a bit older than me—friendly-looking and decked out in Kidrobot chic with a shattered hairdo, wearing a set of fawnskin Puma reissued runners worth five hundred bucks—which is to say he looked like most of the kids at work who do low level coding, the job that lands them the biggest salary and perks. "You're Ethan?"

"Yes."

"I'm Kam."

We shook hands.

"Hi. Uh, do you want to come in for a drink?" I was wearing garments traded with his most recent cargo shipment, but if he noticed, he didn't show it. He also seemed to be unfazed by the absence of any furniture.

"Why don't we go somewhere else?"

Insert a funeral dirge here.

"Uh—it's been a long day. I think I just want to crash."

"No. Come on. What—like I'm going to hurt you? Don't be crazy. You're Greg's brother."

Nervous laughter.

"I never meet people who say no to me. I'm a bit curious to see what sort of person Greg's brother might be."

"I didn't say no to your furniture, I . . ." *I don't want to put an oyster shucker through your heart.* "Okay. Sure. Let's go."

We got into his car. "Look, about the furniture, I don't know what Greg told you, but—"

"Let's not talk about that. Not now."

"Where are we going?"

"A club I like. You know, I once visited someone out in the building where you work. Out in Burnaby."

That was odd. "Really?"

"Yes. I had to, er . . . *influence* somebody."

"Somebody up high?"

"No. At the bottom of your food chain. In quality assurance."

"Oh, Q/A. Everybody tortures the guys in Q/A. It's like being hazed for a living. But you're pretty high up the ladder—why would you bother with some kid in Q/A?"

"His father transferred ownership of several loads of, um, *cargo* into his name without asking me first."

"Wait a sec—if his family is so hoity-toity, why does he bother working at all, let alone in Q/A?"

"He enjoys bug testing."

"*Get paid to play videogames!* It's how they sucker staff into working there every time."

The car purred towards Kerrisdale. I'd always wanted to visit one of the neighbourhood's fabled Chinese nightclubs, where white ghosts like me are never permitted. Sadly, after a few minutes of small talk, we pulled up to a derelict medical-dental office building from the 1950s; my visions of pyramids built of champagne flutes, and costly drinks paid for by someone else, vanished.

"Here?" I asked.

"Yes. Let's go in."

So we entered a cool lobby, lit by a single fluorescent tube, the walls resonating with countless dental tortures of yore. We passed through oversized cherrywood doors, and then down a hallway to another pair of doors. I said, "You know why videogames make you wait for doors and gates to open between levels?"

"No, why?"

"The computer's buying time while it generates the new worlds behind them."

"Is that funny?"

"It wasn't supposed to be."

"I have no sense of humour."

"Huh?"

"No. I really don't. I pretend to laugh when I know someone's said something that, from experience, I know is supposed to be funny. To people with no sense of humour, laughing is a very ugly noise. Like my grandfather coughing up a throat-squid."

"Come on. You must find *something* funny—"

"No. Medically, legally, I have no sense of humour. It's a rare variety of autism. It doesn't even have a name."

More doors.

"Really?"

"It's a fact."

I heard sociable noises behind the final door. "What's in there?" I asked.

Kam jumped and turned to me while pulling something out of his rear pocket. "Freeze, asshole!"

I just about had a stroke.

"Gotcha," said Kam. "Come on in. This is a place I like to visit when I'm in town."

Kam Fong opened the door, and we walked into the middle of a ballroom dance club. He clapped his hands and a table with chairs appeared. "Cocktail?"

This was one of those moments when I remember saying to myself in a calm, clinically detached manner, *Ethan, you should simply go with the flow.*

"A whisky sour."

"Two whisky sours."

We were surrounded by women dressed as Carmelitas and men dressed like bi-curious toreadors. As I'd grown up in this sort of space, I felt quite at home. I decided to push the furniture issue. "Kam, look, about your furniture—it's just that Greg never asked me, and—"

"Ethan!"

I turned around. "Dad?" He was dressed in his favourite Casanova outfit, a toreador's cap rakishly adhered to his skull.

"Ethan, I never thought I'd see you in a ballroom dance club of your own volition."

"Actually, me neither."

"You're wearing your ragamuffin clothing. Aren't you getting too old for fashion statements?"

"It's not just a fashion. It's a—never mind. Dad, this is Kam Fong."

I introduced him as someone Greg does business with.

Dad shook hands. "Real estate?"

"No."

"Hey, but aren't you the guy who gave Ethan all that great furniture? That was really nice of you."

"Thank you."

"Ethan, why the hell couldn't you just enjoy the furniture and shut the fuck up? Christ, Mr. Fong, I have to apologize for Ethan."

"Apologies accepted. You're quite a dancer, Mr. Jarlewski."

"Latin and modern. Not professional, mind you, but I nearly got a bronze in the 1999 Snowball Classic."

"The IDSF Open to the World Standard?"

"That's the one."

"You're *that* Jim Jarlewski!"

"That's me."

"This is so exciting! Please, join us for a drink. Ethan, your father is *the* Jim Jarlewski. Greg never mentioned it."

"Gee."

At the far reaches of my twenties, once again I was a ballroom-dance-club orphan. Dad and Kam Fong began talking shop and drinking heavily, while blousy women in their forties, radiating imminent divorce and sexual despondency, tried to get their attention. At one point, Dad laughed at something, and, in response, Kam Fong delivered a grim flak of ersatz chuckles. He says he doesn't have a sense of humour, but maybe it's just a pose.

"Ethan, isn't this guy the greatest?" Dad was smitten with Kam's gangster charm.

"Sure is, Dad."

"Enough talk, Kam Fong. Now we must dance!"

The two of them reached out their hands, and each grabbed nearby Pinot Gris-soaked floozies—it was a dance-off.

If I didn't know better, it would have looked like Dad and Kam Fong were falling in love. However, I'd seen my father battle like this before, and knew it was no different than two ruffed grouse fluffing their feathers in competition for a hen's attention. When their dance-off ended, clapping drowned the room. They returned to our little table, flush with pheromones and the leftover traces of their respective partners' perfumes.

"I think I'll be going now," I said. "We're conceptually rejigging a new skateboard game to incorporate a charismatic turtle who follows the player throughout the game like a Dr. Watson, offering ongoing banter while logging gameplay statistics."

If Kam Fong had had a reason for taking me to his club, his male bonding with Dad had long since obliterated it. He was drunk, and obviously mellow. He said, "My people will try to find you some furniture more suitable to your obviously picky taste."

The music kicked into the Razormaid remix of "Copacabana," and Dad and Kam Fong were back on the floor. I cabbed back to my place, where I slept on the floor after drinking a NeoCitran made with hot tap water. I hoped that God would shake my Etch-a-Sketch clean overnight.

# *Bruce Lee vinyl action figure*

## $55.95

BeeKing and BugBoy
Ah Gum and Ah Aun
Blue Brother Sunni
Grey Brother Raini
Anti-Potato Wheel
Odajima Hitoshi
Da Team Bronx
RC-911 figure
Balzac in Red
Potato Wheel
BJ Hammer
King Green
CosMouse
Scarygirl
Cloudi
Shiori

*Grind the molten bucket*

• • •

I found Bree, Cowboy, Evil Mark and John Doe in the cafeteria, feeding on cannelloni stuffed with confit of duck and wild rice. Evil Mark, obviously at the end of another rant, announced, "We're all clones."

"Huh?"

"Look at us. We're just clones working for the man."

"Oof. Take *that,* Dilbert."

"Working for the *man*?" Bree said. "Are you serious?"

"I was trying for ironic."

"You're always making these ironic comments that don't quite work."

"I think we're going to have to add 'humourless' to 'evil' in your nickname. But do tell us, why exactly are we clones?"

"Because we all really *do* dress like junior IT clones."

"Huh?"

"Blue or black denim pants—unless you're a senior and over thirty-five, after which point you spot-weld khakis to your lower torso for life."

"Go on."

"Dark-coloured long-sleeved outdoor-wear shirts—blue or black preferred. Haven't you noticed how nobody ever allows their forearms to be exposed here?"

We looked around, and Evil Mark was right. "Spooky."

Cowboy asked, "Does anybody here at the table speak a dead language?"

"COBOL?"

"No. Greek or Latin."

"Some. Why?"

"What's fear of exposed forearms?"

"Popeyedactylophobia."

Bree said, "Long-sleeved dark-coloured shirts conceal both obesity and scrawniness. They double as pajamas."

I said, "Stop, I can't take any more of this identity crap."

"That's easy for you to say," said John Doe, "now that you have a distinct fashion style with your refugee chic. Anyway"—he and Cowboy stood up to leave—"it's time we hit the malls."

"Is it Tuesday already?"

"'Tis."

Tuesday is new shoe day, and Cowboy and John Doe are shoeheads—cool new sneakers reduce them to drooling Homer Simpsons in a blink. As for Evil Mark, he went off to buy ammonium persulphate to etch his motherboards at home. I must also note that calling Mark 'evil' may have started off as an arbitrary label, but now we're wondering if he really *does* make scary shit in his spare time.

Bree asked me, "How's the Kaitlin agenda going?"

"It's not. I think she could be worried I'm stalking her and she'll have to relive all that crazed next-door-neighbour nightmare shit again through me."

"Please. Have you tried talking to her?"

"No. I haven't even made eye contact with her since I read the Subway site. Have you?"

"No."

I was restless but couldn't figure out a good way to shirk my workload. I went online to see if there were any sneak previews of the new *Angel*—Wednesday is actually new comics day, but sometimes you can track down a tidbit the day before. I heard Kaitlin come into the pod space, and taking Bree's advice, I looked up to say hi, but my face collapsed—she was carrying a box of Krispy Kremes and a bag of the dreaded Taint.

"Hi, Ethan."

"Um, hi, Kaitlin." This would have been an optimum moment for her to offer me a donut, but she didn't. I got an instant message from Bree:

**Oh.**

**My.**

**God.**

**She's going to**

**eat herself**

**to death.**

Neither Bree nor I had the heart to announce a Taint-shunning. We settled down to work.

• • •

The good news is that BoardX will be keeping a large number of its pre-turtle skating environments, including a massive shopping mall level in which players score points for trashing the place. But given the suckiness of Jeff's character, it's hard to imagine players will still get to raise hell.

Personal dialogues with Jeff keep running in my brain . . .

"Gee, player. That was a super-duper wheelie."

"Thanks, Jeff. Now fuck off."

"No can do, player. You're stuck with me."

"No, I'm not. I have the option to play without you."

"Not for the first three levels you don't, and even then, my friend, my likeness and name will be embedded in all gaming levels: billboards, signage, windows and street names. Your boss, Steve, has ensured that my presence will be pervasive."

"There must be a way to kill you."

"Sorry, player, but no."

In my mind, Jeff was on his back, a drill press approaching his tender underbelly from above.

"Excuse me, player," the turtle said, "but did you just have a degenerate thought picture in your head?"

"Me?"

"You wouldn't hurt Jeff, would you?"

"No."

"I don't believe you."

"Then don't."

"I'm going to tell Steve about you."

"You do that."

"Ethan?"

"*Whuh . . . ?*"

"Ethan, wake up."

I opened my eyes: *Steve.* "Oh. Steve. Hi."

"I can see that was a doozy of a nightmare you were having."

He stood there staring at me.

"Steve, is there something I can help you with?"

"No. Nothing. Just thought I'd pop by."

"Okay . . ."

"How's BoardX going?"

"It's one smoking game, Steve."

"It is. And Jeff is going to be a big hit. I can feel it."

I looked at my screen: "Look! An email's come down the Chute! I'm going to have to answer this one, Steve. See you later?"

"Righty-o, pardner."

• • •

Comics day came and went. Another shoe day came and went. And another comics day followed that—the typical production and consumption cycles that help us survive our dismal, meaningless little lives.

Starting with that first Krispy Kreme box, Kaitlin's been collecting all her fast-food packaging and arranging it into a big stack. She takes cardboard and other greasy items to the bathroom, where (Bree tells me) she treats them with alcohol and another chemical that makes them ungreasy.

I'm still too freaked out to talk to her. When she comes in with ever more massive quantities of food, the five of us keep our heads bowed as we listen to the endless rumpling of bags and wrappers and clamshell containers and straws hiccupping their way in and out of plastic lids. She's like an alien luxuriously chewing away on a cocooned earthling. It gives us fear.

# Doritos

**Rollitos**
**Nacho Cheesier!**

Bite-Size Tortilla Snacks

JL 19
6 053 14027
09:51

Product enlarged to show texture

## 300 g

Amount Per Serving

| | |
|---|---|
| Calories: | 150 |
| Total Fat: | 12% RDA |
| Saturated + trans fats: | 8% RDA |
| Cholesterol: | 0% RDA |
| Sodium: | 8% RDA |
| Total Carbohydrate: | 6% RDA |
| Dietary Fiber: | 5% RDA |
| Vitamin A: | 2% RDA |
| Vitamin C: | 0% RDA |
| Calcium: | 0% RDA |
| Iron: | 2% RDA |
| | |
| Sugar: | less than 1 g |
| Protein: | 2 g |

Ingredients: corn, vegetable oil (contains one or more of the following: corn, soybean, or sunflower oil), salt, monoglyceride, cheddar cheese (cultured milk, salt, enzymes), whey, monosodium glutamate, buttermilk solids, Romano cheese from cow's milk (cultured pasteurized partskim milk, salt, enzymes), tomato powder, whey protein concentrate, onion powder, partially hydrogenated soybean oil, disodium phosphate, lactose, natural and artificial flavor, garlic powder, dextrose, sugar, citric acid, spice, lactic acid, sodium caseinate, artificial color (including Yellow 6), disodium inosinate, disodium guanylate and non fat milk solids.

CONTAINS MILK INGREDIENTS.

made with non-hydrogenated oil

o 60410 10 03997 2

• • •

I won the third floor's intramural Tetris competition, which took place in the conference room this afternoon—a canister of liquid nitrogen! So afterwards we scoured the office for flash-freezables.

Effects of liquid nitrogen on office items:

| | |
|---|---|
| Half a tuna sandwich | Shattered like chalk |
| Souvenir vintage *Diff'rent Strokes* pocket calculator | Kept working |
| Paper (20-lb bond) | No discernable effect |
| Half-eaten donut from Kaitlin's trash | Crumbled |
| Philodendron leaf | Went potato-chippy |
| Fat Bastard figurine | Paint flecked off |
| Tip of John Doe's ring finger | Lost all sensation |

After a while we ran out of possibilities, so we went down and flash-froze puddles by the soccer field, and for the rest of the day everyone talked about Ice-9 from Kurt Vonnegut's *Cat's Cradle*. Anything that lowers productivity is fine by me.

• • •

I caught Evil Mark licking his stapler.

• • •

In order to keep my podmates' minds off the insect-like sounds of Kaitlin's rustling food packaging, I made up a template and challenged them each to use five hundred words or less to sell themselves as if they were on eBay.

# All-purpose IT Worker & Stud. "Cancer Cowboy." One only. Cool in a Steve McQueen Kind of Way.

**Item number:** 7471313007
**Current bid:** US $6.66 (Reserve not met)
**Time left:** We're doomed
**Start time:** Apr-11-76 17:19:35 PDT
**Ends:** At any moment, PDT
**History:** 19 bids
**High bidder:** time_wastr (1)
**Item location:** Burnaby, BC
Canada/Suburbia
**Ships to:** Worldwide
**Seller:** maudlin_drinker

## Description
You are bidding on the fully functional IT worker "Cancer Cowboy," serial number: CASPER JAMES JESPERSON. 28 years old. Some scarring. What you see in the photo is what you get. Not responsible for congenital health issues or bastard children who may or may not appear on owner's doorstep.

Cowboy has been extensively reconditioned by a recently vacated ex-girlfriend, and has had a NEW wardrobe installed by overpriced designer boutiques that give you cappuccinos while you shop. Cowboy's hair has also been beautifully reconditioned by a pair of nail scissors, half a bottle of tequila and persistent self-esteem issues.

IT workers the world over know of Cancer Cowboy's manly prowess. Pilot your way through his many levels and bonus rounds, dodging STDs and provincial in-office cigarette smoking regulations. For double-gun firepower, acquire liquor, cleverly mixed CD song sets and antibiotics.

Most sellers will not tell you what I'm telling you because they want you to believe their product is "mint" and will never break. That's obviously impossible.

**Click on picture to enlarge what is already large**
**Supersize picture**
**Shipping and payment details**

Soul-sucking cubicle > Aging > Babydoll > PVC > Body stockings > Thigh highs

# L@@K WOW!!!!!
# Mega-Rare Tech Ho
# Complete w/ Stalled Career

| | |
|---|---|
| **Item number:** | 000111000111 |
| **Current bid:** | US $9.95 (Reserve not met) |
| **Time left:** | According to parents, spinsterhood shortly |
| **Start time:** | Apr-22-80 |
| **Ends:** | Seemingly never |
| **History:** | 0 bids |
| **Item location:** | Coquitlam, BC |
| | Canada/Suburbia/Everywhere/Nowhere/Global |
| **Ships to:** | Preferably Tokyo |
| **Seller:** | brasspole (0) |

## Description

This auction is for Bree Jyang, who has fallen into the depressingly predictable yet still sexy Bettie Page look/thing/whatever.

**Bree** is 64 inches tall and has jointed arms and legs and a moveable head. Her hair is long, black and rooted, and her makeup is flawless, complete with mole on left cheek.

**Bree** also sometimes wears a large sombrero hat, a style that was brought back into the limelight when *The Rocketeer* was released, starring Jennifer Connelly and Timothy Dalton.

**Bree** is wearing a gold silk-look crop top with a daring neckline and black and gold shoulder straps; her 7 1/2-inch heels are *so* Dita Von Teese.

**Bree's** inner life is one of burlesque, complete with singers and saucy strippers, including famed female impersonator Vickie Lynn. In her mind, Bree has even made a guest appearance in the greatest stripper movie of all time, *Varietease*.

**Bree** was born on April 22, 1980, in Nanaimo, BC, where she was known as Dark Queen of Bondage. Okay, not really, but she knew what she liked at an early age. In 2002 she was discovered by her parents to have not enough concern for her future, so she was shipped to one of 400 videogame design schools in Vancouver, where it turned out she not only had a flair for game design, but was also but a mere gentle puff of a rotating nipple tassel away from four local strip clubs.

**Bree** is awaiting your interest. She has just changed her outfit and is now wearing a fabulous "Bow" bustier by Bali, style #8211, c. 1940s, with a black satin torso. The cups are stunning and have black sheer-illusion lace with the famous "circle stitch" for that sizzling sweater-girl bullet-bra look. The size on tag reads 36D and will fit up to a 38" bust. Bree would like to know what you are wearing, too.

If **Bree** is something you've been looking for, don't let this pass you by! **BUY BREE NOW AND SAVE! CHECK OUT MY OTHER AUCTIONS! SHOP EASILY BY THUMBNAIL PICTURE GALLERIES!**

# 2005 All-Star Winner Mark Jackson

**Item number:** 4522041813 (generated with pseudorandom # generator)
**Current bid:** 23 Zlotys (made that up)
**Time left:** Hours ago (not very funny)
**Start time:** Now (ditto)
**Ends:** When it ends
**History:** 0 bids
**High bidder:** 0 bids
**Item location:** North Vancouver, BC, Canada
**Ships to:** You (ha ha ha witty)
**Seller:** prefersblackspy

## *Buy it now!*

**Description**
You are bidding on a comprehensive LOT OF CHARACTER TRAITS
made from premium DNA and SPECIFIC CULTURAL CIRCUM-
STANCES: MARK JACKSON IS A TECH MONEY BONANZA CON-
TENDER, THREE-D CODER AND HARDWARE DESIGNER to name
a few. This lot is also LOADED WITH FEATURES: PERSEVERANCE,
AMBITION, A 3.9 COLLEGE GPA and, if I listen to my shithead cubicle
neighbours, EVIL.

CODING LANGUAGES (C++, SOFTIMAGE) ABILITY TO BENCH
PRESS 250, ENCYCLOPEDIC KNOWLEDGE OF NFL, CFL & NBA
STATS, 4% BODY FAT, NATURALLY ENDOWED WITH EPIC GREEK
MUSCLES (SIDES OF STOMACH). Currently KILLING TIME UNTIL
MY SECRET HARDWARE IDEAS ARE PATENTED AND MADE
GLOBAL. YOU LOOK AT RICH PEOPLE AND THEIR PICTURES AND
WONDER, WHY IS THAT PERSON RICH AND NOT ME? THERE'S
NO ANSWER TO THIS, EXCEPT TO SAY THAT I AM GOING TO BE
RICH.

Other GOOD VALUES appear in abundance in this lot, and exceed the
best 2005 tech employees now being offered on eBay. Everything you
see will be included w/ no surprises.

# Sensible Value for Typical Fellow

**Item number:**   1234567890
**Current bid:**   US $99.99 (Reserve not met)
**Time left:**   74.5 years minus current age
**Start time:**   June-06-77
**Ends:**   When the time comes
**History:**   Average amount
**Item location:**   Vancouver, BC
**Ships to:**   Anytown
**Seller:**   bellcurve (0)

## Description

John Doe comes with no scary Web links or disturbing images stashed in the bowels of his computer. Not one. What few cuts and dings exist are exposed for all to see, as is his small bald spot. John Doe is clean and sensible, but can also be stylish if enough advance notice is given. To be this good a deal, John has had to be stored in a garage for an awfully long time.

John Doe is excellent for families and clean normal living. Yes, John Doe has all the features that are a must-have in today's hectic world.

Dude > XBox > Wolverine > Open source

# Ethan Jarlewski

**Item number:**    Second-born of two sons
**Current bid:**      C $41,500 per year (Reserve not met)
**Time left:**         After age 30 will probably become bitter
**Start time:**       Now
**History:**           0 bids
**Item location:**    Vancouver, BC
**Ships to:**        Anywhere
**Seller:**           IAMU&URME

**Feedback Score: 1,000**
**Positive Feedback: 1,000%**

**Description**
Ethan was developed in a cool, dry, non-smoking home and was
released in 1976. His body movements are disarmingly realistic, and
his voice feature often works when connected to a compatible play
set.

Ethan is a hard-to-find item, especially in this condition, Good to Very
Good or better. He has no tan and his acne ended four years ago. All
wiring and plumbing is in good order. No manual is included, but his
operation is highly intuitive. WARNING: Ethan does not respond well
when people try to change him. Highest bidder takes him as is, NO
REFUNDS.

Ethan remains highly annoyed by the Sprite™ ad campaign from the
late 1990s and early 2000s, even though that campaign is over. "Obey
Your Thirst"—what kind of idiotic slogan is that? "Gee, I'm thirsty, but
I'd better not drink anything, because that would mean obeying my
thirst." Ethan is also annoyed by the Audi campaign that says, "Never
Follow." Frankly, Ethan is annoyed with all of these dumb campaigns
that indoctrinate millions of people into thinking they're tough-guy free
spirits when, in fact, there's probably much to be said for following and,
in any event, the food chain isn't structured to encompass millions of
non-followers. So you end up with a population of frustrated, brink-of-
bitterness cranks.

Like anyone, Ethan Jarlewski enjoys a good game. Of the following
true or false questions, only one is true. Choose which one and win an
insider's discount and free shipping with real bubble-pack, not crumpled paper. Ethan is yours for the having—bid with confidence!

| T | F | Ethan secretly enjoys checking into low-rent motels and dressing up in a Sir Lancelot costume. |
|---|---|---|
| T | F | Ethan was a regular guest on the popular 1980s police drama *Cagney & Lacey.* |
| T | F | Ethan has a double recessive genetic anomaly that allows him to photosynthesize chlorophyll. |
| T | F | Ethan is able to make toilets flush clockwise in both the northern and southern hemispheres. |
| T | F | In a few minutes Ethan is going to pretend he doesn't like singing karaoke, but he really does like it, and with just a minimum of coaxing will steal hearts and souls with his own sound stylings of Neil Diamond's "Cracklin' Rosie." |
| T | F | Ethan's secret buyer name on eBay is DungeonLad, and he can almost always be found bidding on memorabilia related to the life and career of Charlotte Rae, better known as Mrs. Garrett from TV's enduring family comedy *The Facts of Life.* |
| T | F | Ethan secretly wishes life were simpler and he could sell lemonade from a card table at the end of his street. |

• • •

Dad phoned while I was trying to beat Super Metroid on a PC SNES emulator (in under an hour and ten, with no more than 50% items).

"Ethan, come out to the set and spend time with me."

"Dad, it's eleven p.m. I'm still at work. What's wrong?"

"Is it so much to ask that you come cheer up your old man?"

"Dad, hanging out on sets is boring. They're even more boring than ballrooms. Learn how to knit."

"The food here sucks."

"Dad, are you even listening to me?"

"And the actress in this dog of a movie is vegan, so everybody else has to be one, too."

"Unions allow that?"

"Ethan, I really need you here."

"Is it Ellen?"

"No."

"What is it, then?"

"I said it was nothing. I just want to see you."

"I'm going to hang up if you don't tell me what's going on."

"Oh, all right. It's Kam Fong."

"He's messing with your life?"

"Yeah."

"How? Why?"

"He got . . . a speaking part on this movie."

"*What?*"

"What a prick, huh?"

"He's not even an actor. How did he get a speaking part?"

"Well, you know, since that night at the club, we've become pretty good friends, so I invited him out here to visit the set. I was taking him from the crew parking lot to the cameras, when he stepped in a puddle and dirtied his precious booties. He went mental in Mandarin, and the director heard him. *How authentic!* he shrieked, and *bingo.* Kam Fong is Mister moo-goo-gai-pan-Charlie-Chan-me-so-horny Asian actor guy, and I'm still a generic asshole who gets blown up at the start of act one."

"Being blown up is pretty good. At least for a few seconds the audience is focused entirely on you."

"This big woof-woof of a movie is a gorefest. Nobody's going to notice me."

"Hey wait—a vegan actress is doing a movie with so much violence?"

"I know—weird, huh?"

I couldn't keep Dad sidetracked for long.

"All those years in voice training and method and work-shops, and this shit-for-brains steps in a puddle, and he's already drawing blueprints for his personal trailer."

"Dad, mellow out. It's a small speaking part. Big deal."

*Sniffle.*

"Dad, are you crying?"

"Am I a jerk-off of a father to call his son in a time of need?"

"Okay, okay, I'm coming. Where are you?"

As I was driving out to Dad's shoot, Mom called my cell. "Ethan?"

"Hi, Mom."

"Where are you?"

"In the car. I'm heading out to see Dad on the set."

"Why?"

"He called me up—he's bummed because Kam Fong got a speaking part in his movie."

"What's the deal with your father and this new best friend of his, Mr. Kung Fu? They're on the phone all day, talking about ballroom dancing."

"Mom, Kam Fong's head of a Chinese people-smuggling syndicate. He doesn't have time to be Dad's secret gay lover."

"He's your father's gay lover?"

"No. But he loves ballroom dancing, and you don't."

"Ethan, you know how boring that ballroom world is."

"Yeah, but Dad loves it."

"All those divorcees dressed like fourteen-year-old figure skaters."

"Well, now he finally has a friend to discuss it with."

Silence.

"Mom?"

Silence again.

"Mom—are you jealous?"

"Me? No. Why should I be jealous? My husband is merely spending all his waking moments with a man who probably has five bolero jackets at the dry cleaners, and a dozen fruit-flavoured lip smackers concealed in an ostrich-feather clutch purse."

"Mom, what are you doing up at"—I looked at the dash clock—"eleven-thirty?"

"I can't sleep."

"How come?"

"Oh, nothing."

I let it go and said good night—it was too late in the day to investigate Mom's interior world, too.

At the set, I found Dad and Kam Fong practising ballroom dance steps with invisible partners.

So much for Dad being miserable.

"Hi, guys."

"We're rehearsing a variation on the East Coast Swing. Ready, Kam?"

"Ready."

As a duo, they began to move, and in my head I remembered all the colour-commentary dance notations I'd had to learn while growing up . . .

. . . *backaway*

. . . *she turns*

. . . *he turns*

. . . *tuck-in release*

. . . *basic step in open position*

. . . *underarm turn in open position*

. . . *change of places*

. . . *crossover turn in open position*

. . . *behind the back changes*

. . . *flirtation*

. . . *close.*

"I hear you got a speaking part, Kam Fong," I said when they stopped. "Congratulations."

"I never thought of being in films before."

"What's your character?"

"I play a Chinese gang kingpin. The guy who was supposed to be playing it had an allergic reaction to erythromycin. He's dead."

"It's your big break."

"You said it."

Dad didn't like this conversation. He cut it short. "Ethan, I have to go out to Port Coquitlam on an errand. Come with me."

"Errand?"

"Yeah. The guy who helps your mother and me get bootleg satellite TV signals has gone to the Yucatan. We need to get a software patch for the satellite card from his brother. He lives way out in the boonies."

"What's the hurry?"

"Your mother wants to catch a *Sex and the City* marathon tomorrow, and I like to watch *Band of Brothers* in the mornings. It gives me a lift for the rest of the day."

"Dad, just buy a satellite card. What's the big deal?"

"Pay full price, when I can get one for almost nothing? Talk about throwing money away."

"You North American young people spend money like crazy," added Kam.

"He practically *lives* in restaurants," Dad said, nodding in my direction, "and last year he bought a fridge and paid retail."

"Fool."

"You dragged me out here just so you could have some company in the car?"

"Yes."

What the hell. "Oh, all right."

Dad's car was being detailed by a gofer, while my car had been hemmed in by a trailer, so we borrowed Kam's two-ton smuggling-mobile. Our destination? A mildewed dump of a shack owned by some yokel named Clem. It bordered the slope of a Port Coquitlam forest recently scraped clean to make way for a subdivision. The trunks of the few trees that remained resembled telephone poles.

Clem opened the door like an ElfQuest troll about to hand us a curse and a talisman. He motioned us inside, where all of the walls were made of heavily varnished logs seasoned by decades of nicotine. I spotted a bookshelf filled with Mel Gibson tapes and DVDs, and three flatulent German shepherd/lab crosses that evidently enjoyed the house's sauna-like atmosphere. Clem noticed me looking and said, "Mel is God. I think I've got your satellite card in the dining room. Don't mind the clutter." I scrutinized the walls—pictures of Clem's days as a longshoreman mingled with framed inspirational Alcoholics Anonymous plaques. There was a newspaper clipping of Clem holding a sockeye in the 1963 *Sun* Salmon Derby that had faded away almost to nothing. When Clem gave Dad the new card, we bolted for the truck. Once inside, we started laughing. Dad laid rubber, and I was glad the evening was coming to a close.

The dashboard beeped. Dad looked down. "We're low on gas."

"There's a Mohawk station down the hill."

While Dad was filling up the truck, I went to the station's mini-mart to stock up on Slim Jims. At the cash I glanced out at the pumps and saw Lyle from the biker house filling up his hog—*crap*.

The clerk asked if everything was okay, and I said, "Yeah, yeah."

A large delivery vehicle pulled in, giving me enough cover to scramble to our truck. Dad asked, "What's wrong with you?"

"That guy on the bike."

"What about him?"

"Mom and I went to collect a few days ago."

"And?"

"His pit bull chomped Mom's leg, and she fired a few shots, and it was kind of a, um, mess."

"Pit bull? Your mother told me it was a gardening wound—kneeling on a rake."

Dad kept his cool while paying the cashier just ahead of Lyle, but once back in the truck, he announced, "Nobody's dog attacks my wife. Let's nail the bastard."

I had no idea what Dad's plan was, but we pulled out from the pumps ahead of Lyle. "Dad, what are you—?"

I heard Lyle's hog approaching us from behind. Once we were around the corner and out of sight of the gas station, Lyle gunned his throttle to pass us. Dad veered sharply into the other lane, walloping the bike, sending Lyle flying out into the roadside weeds. The hog somehow managed to get snagged beneath the truck.

"Dad! Holy shit! The bike's stuck." The metallic scraping reminded me of trash cans being dragged down the driveway. "Are you going to stop or what?"

"In a second."

Sparks from the bike flared in the rear-view mirror. "Awesome light show," I said.

A quarter-mile down the road, Dad stopped the truck, then reversed it a bit to dislodge the hog. Then he said, "Get out, son, and open the back. We're putting it in."

"Why?"

"So our dog breeder pal can walk home."

As I got out, I heard Lyle screaming at us from back up the road. I looked his way, but he didn't seem to be running. I opened the back hatch.

Dad said, "Grab the front wheel. On the count of three we toss it into the back. One. Two. *Three*—" The bike was heavier than I thought it would be.

"Dad, this thing weighs a ton."

"Let's get some help then."

Dad shouted, "移动您的懒惰身体，傻瓜!" and from the deepest recesses of the truck emerged a half-dozen Chinese people.

"Dad?"

Dad shouted, "移动您的懒惰身体，傻瓜!" and the boat people hoisted the bike into the back. Dad closed the door. "Let's go."

"What does 移动您的懒惰身体，傻瓜 mean?"

"Kam says it all the time into his cellphone. It means *move your ass.*"

# EWTN Europe
## WAM/America's Kidz Network
## Dish Music—New Orleans Jazz

# Daystar

## Nickelodeon/Nick at Nite (East)

# Fox Kids Italia

## CD-Contemporary Jazz Flavors

# TV Martí

# America's Store

# Future TV USA

## Dish Music—Piano & Guitar Encore

# ESPN Now

## Hallmark Channel Mexico

# SatMex 5

# Almavisión
# Sky Link TV
## BBC America
# QVC UK

### Naples Fort Myers Greyhound Park
California Community Colleges Satellite Network
## Prison TV Network

**C-SPAN2**

**Total Living Network**

**MTV China**

**Praise TV**

# JCTV

# GRTV 2

# NASA TV

**TBN Philippines**

# FamilyNet

**INSP—The Inspiration Network**

**Bloomberg TV Asia-Pacific**

**Bloomberg TV Deutschland**

. . .

I made Dad stop at a 7-Eleven and we bought chocolate bars, bottled water and orange juice for the people in the back. As we neared the production's trailers, my cell rang. It was Cowboy.

"Ethan, man, I'm losing it."

"Losing *what*?"

"You've got to help me, man."

"Where are you?"

"I'm in North Van."

"What happened?"

"I was in a fourgy with these three BMX chicks I met last weekend, and it was a dream come true, and then this one chick puts on a Raggedy Ann wig and a red foam nose, and says, *Look at me, I'm Ronald McDonald,* and I freaked."

I hopped out and made a *gotta go* hand gesture to Dad. "You freaked over a *wig*?"

"You don't understand. We wrote all those crazy-assed letters to Ronald, and he somehow got registered in my subconscious as the devil. It was like I could already see the cheesy Hi8 video of a four-way, and instead of hair, Ronald's ass had red yarn sticking out of it."

"Uh-huh. And makeup all over the sheets."

"Don't mock my freak-out."

"Are you on anything tonight?"

Silence.

"Cowboy, *are* you?"

"I got pretty 'tussed up beforehand."

"Cowboy, you know you can't drink cough syrup.

Robitussin takes you to the dark side every time. It's your kryptonite."

"But these chicks were all doing it, and I had to look cool in front of them."

"Cowboy, if these naked chicks were jumping off a cliff, would you jump after them?"

"Sure."

I thought about that for a second.

He said, "Man, it was so freaky. It was like Ronald could look into my eyes and see the part of me that's dying."

"Where are you specifically?"

"In the Denny's on Marine Drive."

"Did you manage to dress before you fled?"

"Sort of. I didn't have time for underwear, and I left my favourite Doritos baseball cap behind."

"I'll be there in fifteen minutes."

I got into my own car. There's nothing like driving on an empty freeway to clear the mind. How often have I rescued Cowboy from his sex/death freak-outs? Too many times. I really had to lay down the law this time, and I was practising my speech as I pulled into the parking lot.

I found him hunched in a booth, a coffee in front of him. "Okay, Cowboy—three BMX chicks? Please. What's the real story?"

"You don't believe me?"

"No. Girls rarely enter bike culture. If they do, they're fully mated. Who were you really with?"

"I can't believe you don't believe me."

"You're boring me."

"All right, all right. They were skanks."

"I *knew* it. Where'd you meet?"

"At a coffee place on Marine Drive. They were at the next table and buzzed out on 'tuss, and we made eye contact and—it just kind of happened. I mean, Ethan, nobody *plans* a four-way."

We ordered Grand Slams and when the food arrived, we picked at our scrambled eggs half-heartedly. Finally Cowboy said he was feeling better and apologized for having roped me into his el skanko lifestyle. It was four-thirty a.m. when we left the Denny's.

In the back seat of my car was a pile of kitchen things I'd promised to return to Mom. As I was near the old house, I decided to drop them right then. I drove up the hill, pulled into my parents' street, and there, parked in front of their hedge, was a Touareg with a box sitting on top of it wrapped in gold paper with a big silk bow. The driver's door was open, and as I slowly drove past I saw Steve at the wheel. I stopped and got out. Steve was shaving in the rear-view mirror.

"Oh. Ethan. Hi. Uh. How are you?"

"Steve, why are you shaving at the end of my parents' driveway at 4:45 in the morning?"

"It's not what it looks like."

"Which would be what?"

"Your mother's a fine woman, Ethan."

"And?"

"I think I'm in love."

That shut me up.

"I know she's fifteen years older than me, but I can't stop thinking about her."

"Steve, she's married to my *dad*. And you're going to give

her a present at 4:45 in the morning? What kind of a loser are you?"

"I was going to wait until six."

"Steve, why don't you go home right now, and I'll forget this ever happened."

"I need to talk about her a bit. Let me do that. There's nobody in my life I can do that with, and it's killing me."

"I thought you were married."

"Divorced."

"Okay, here's the deal: you get to talk about my mother for five minutes, but no sex stuff. In return, I get to ask you privileged questions about BoardX."

"Deal."

"I go first. Why are you wrecking a potentially massive and successful game with this pathetic turtle idea?"

"Who says it's pathetic?"

"Cough up some truth, or I'm not going to discuss Mom with you. You know the turtle's a crappy idea. Something's up."

"My kid likes turtles."

"I know that. So what?"

"I don't have visitation rights."

"Why not?"

"I won't talk about that."

"So you're sticking a turtle in our game in order to communicate with your son?"

"Yes."

"Do you know how many man-years go into making a game? How much heart and soul? You'd fuck that over to send a personal message to your kid?"

"I would. Jeff is worth it."

"Jeff? I thought you told us his name is Carter."

"I fibbed."

We heard the first bird tweets of the day.

"Steve," I said, "send your kid a fruit basket. A birthday card. An FTD bouquet of gerbera daisies, but *don't* doom our game to oblivion because you can't get your fathering act together."

"Your feelings are valid, Ethan, but my therapist warned me that if I don't go through with the Jeff character, I could easily enter a shame spiral from which I might never return."

"That's it. I'm leaving."

"Ethan? It's my turn to talk about your mother. A deal's a deal."

"Okay, but remember, she's married to my father and they've been together forever, so you know right from the start that any hope you might have for a relationship is doomed."

"I do."

I looked at my watch. "One, two, three, *go.*"

"Where to begin? Well, she made me a pie. It was blueberry, and when she gave it to me, its smell mixed with her perfume and it made me feel—"

"Stop. Getting too personal."

"And she even brought a cloth napkin, not a paper one . . ."

"Deal's off. I can't do this."

I abandoned him there, half-shaved and moony.

• • •

The sun was rising—a glowing apricot washed by pink clouds. Lions Gate Bridge was empty and the ducks in Lost Lagoon were chattering away. Closer to home, the junkie needles and gum wrappers on the streets twinkled like Mario sprites.

My phone rang just as I was passing the vegetable stalls setting up for the day on Keefer Street: Bree.

"Ethan, do you have a minute?"

"Bree, it's almost six in the morning—why are you calling?"

"Don't play the time card stunt with me. You know we're not like other people."

"Is everything okay?"

"Yes. No."

"Where are you?"

"jPod."

"And?"

"Ethan, I feel so old."

This isn't the first time I've had this call from Bree. "So?"

"It's different for girls than it is for boys."

"How?"

"Because we have a finite number of eggs, Ethan. It's not like we generate a billion new ones every time we get off."

"Are you pregnant?"

"I wish. No, strike that—no, I *don't* wish. I have no idea."

"Let me pull over to the side of the road." I did. "When was the last time you got some sleep?"

"Two days ago."

"Go home and sleep, then."

"Sleep is overrated. Everyone thinks that just because you have a nap, your life is fixed."

"Bree, did the whole city just take the same drug? *Everybody* in my life is going random all over the place."

"Like who?"

"My dad—and probably my mother. And Cowboy had another sex/death bottoming-out. He was the filling in a skank sandwich in North Van. Triple-decker. One of them put on a Ronald McDonald wig, and he flipped out."

"No way."

"It's true."

"Was he 'tussed up?"

"Yeah."

"He's got to stay away from that stuff. Why was a skank wearing a Ronald McDonald wig?"

"Strictly speaking, it was a Raggedy Ann wig."

Vitamin G: *gossip.* I could tell Bree was feeling a bit better, but I was suddenly racked by a wave of sleepiness and told Bree I had to hang up. Inasmuch as a car can limp, I limped home, back to my crappy furniture, which had magically reappeared a few weeks ago.

However, when I got there, I saw five profoundly expensive cars parked outside my place—a Bentley, a Lotus and three Italian somethings. I parked behind them, and as I got out of my car, I heard loud music and the sounds of cats in great pain. At my front door stood a gym goon wearing a headset.

"You're Ethan? Go in."

"Gee, thanks."

Taped to the door was a laser-printed sheet of 8½ x 11 paper:

The transition from the early morning sunlight into the mysteriously darkened house made me squint. Projected onto my living-room wall was a soft-lens film shot of fluttering cherry petals. In front of it stood a stout little fireplug of a Chinese guy singing a cat-wailing version of "Maniac." He was obviously tanked. Arranged around him in a semicircle were maybe a dozen other Chinese guys, including Kam Fong.

Mr. Fireplug finished his tune, and the others clapped loudly and sarcastically. Kam looked over at me. In Chinese, he said to the guys in the room,

" 這是我告訴您的那個輸家。我們演奏以他的頭腦和刺激他入唱一首可笑歌曲一首可笑歌曲 "

("This is that loser I was telling you about. Let's play with his mind and goad him into singing a ridiculous song.")

Everybody clapped and invited me over to try some of their paint-stripper sake, served by three pretty young women in hot pants and top hats. Then one of the guys stood up and began singing the Psychedelic Furs classic "Love My Way," against a backdrop of the neon-lit alleys of Tokyo.

"Kam, what's all this about?"

"These are guys I went to school with. We're having a blast."

"Why are you in my house?"

"We needed a place with an atmosphere of poverty to

remind us of the old days. Come on and drink with us. Get hammered."

"Kam, it's morning."

"Not in Hong Kong." He clapped his hands, and one of the servers brought a Scotch and soda. Before I had a chance to wave my hands and say no, Kam and his buddies made a toast that appeared to be to me. What the heck—I drank it—and, three drinks later, I was catapulted into that fetid pit of ritualized humiliation called karaoke.

Kam clapped his hands, and the male technician running the karaoke machine giggled as he put on, yes, Bonnie Tyler's "Total Eclipse of the Heart." I was doomed.

What is the science behind humiliation? Does it generate a special molecule of adrenaline? Does your blood recognize what's happening and take different paths through your body in response? And why does the inside of your mouth turn to lint and your ears begin to burn?

I looked behind me: dandelions fluffed across a Swiss meadow. A lark flittered from a branch out into a blue sky draped with marshmallow clouds as the first few notes of the song's tinkling dirge haunted my living room. I was totally fucked—which, of course, made great entertainment for Kam's drunken buddies. I tried to put down the mike thirty seconds in, but Kam slammed his glass on the table in a manner that let me know it would be disadvantageous to do so.

I suppose I blacked out after that point. I remember the music dying down and opening my eyes to see everybody—servers and tech guy included—cramped with laughter. Needless to say, the technician filmed the whole thing.

Suddenly it was ten a.m. I went upstairs to my bedroom, which was being used as the party's coatroom. I considered sleeping on the floor again, above the raucous chattering below, then went back downstairs. I went into the kitchen and grabbed a box of Chinese donuts made with bean paste, then got into my car and drove directly to work. The only person in jPod was Kaitlin. She said, "Caught your performance. Kam did a live webcast."

"I—" I handed her the box of donuts. "I brought these for you. By the way, I really like you."

She looked at them as if I'd just handed her a dismantled carburetor.

"Please. Just eat them," I said. "I'm tired right now. I'm going to nap under my desk."

I was on the cusp of sleep when Kaitlin moved my chair away and bent down to speak to me. "You know, the whole Subway website thing was a hoax."

*"What?"*

"I just wanted to fuck with all of you. I've been a size 2 my entire life. I eat like a pig, and nothing sticks."

"But how did they get that photo of you? You weighed, like, 337 pounds!"

"That's my sister. She got the family's lard gene."

"But—"

"Ethan, be quiet. I saw you at that conference my first week here—your momma walked in and you were really nice to her, and then here, this morning, you give me donuts, which means you're not trying to change me or anything— that you can handle me being me, even if that means eating myself to death."

I looked up and was suddenly, irrationally, pleased there was no gum tucked under the desk's front lip.

Kaitlin said, "I'm going to see *Princess Mononoke* tonight at the Ridge—and you're coming with me."

I nodded yes.

"Good." She gave me a kiss. "I'll keep people away so you can sleep. I'll wake you up at seven."

"Thanks."

"Good night, Ethan."

"Good night, Kaitlin."

# Yummy Dainty Sheer-Lace Sexy Adult Sissy Girly-Girl

**Item number:**    100000000000000

**This auction has ended.**

| | |
|---|---|
| **History:** | 1 bid |
| **High bidder:** | luckydog (1) |
| **Item location:** | Burnaby, BC |
| | Canada |

## Description

Kaitlin is oh . . . . . . . . . . soooooooooo HOT. This is the daintiest girl ever made! So pretty and simple. No reserve bid.

**Leadership and the One-Minute Manager . . .**

*Increasing*

# Effectiveness

*through*

# Situational Leadership®

*nice
parking,
asshole*

# NHF

**Nu-Sport Health & Fitness**

# Ultra-RX

**Bio-engineered Meal Alternative
Natural Belgian Chocolate Flavor**

# 1.51 kg

**Contains ion-exchanged whey protein concentrate**

INDIANA                    KANSAS

# NCAA

## *FINAL FOUR*

# 2002 • ATLANTA

**The Georgia Dome
Atlanta, Georgia
March 30th & April 1st**

**TOYOTA**
**Panasonic**
**BASF**
**Bayer**
**American Airlines**
**Pan Am**
**Lufthansa**
**northAmerican**
**Bell**South
**Aeroméxico**
**AGFA**
**Hapag-Lloyd**
**Prudential**
**xa**nax

# Bankers Box®

Econo/Stor® 789

# Altered Rules

# No Penalties

The way you deal with money is learned behaviour you get from your father. If he was superstitious about money, you will be, too. If he saved money, then you'll also save money. Was he a bastard? Were you ever really sure what your allowance was? Decades later, does your father have any clue about the jobs you had during high school? Reading the newspaper too closely during coffee breaks will make upper management question your loyalty. Who knows why. Do you deserve a raise? Maybe you don't. Be that as it may, asking for a raise is uncomfortable and intimidating. Does your job have perks? Free toner cartridges don't constitute perks. Nor does a good parking stall, or a liberal dress policy. Does a compressed work week fill you with a tingly sensation? Or perhaps flextime or telecommuting days? You deserve success—and now you can have it—and go to hell, too. You deserve the success you desire. You also deserve happiness, irritable bowel syndrome, personal fulfillment, a bad haircut and an abundance of crap from Pottery Barn. Catchy ring tones, search engines and supermarket customer loyalty programs are emerging as the engine of the new global economy. Who'd have thought? People started getting incredibly fat almost exactly the same week that Coke changed its formula. Coincidence? All project managers are asked to update their project information using the corresponding colour code for each project phase and add quality control drawing review periods accordingly. How many putty-coloured appliances do you own, including peripherals? Customer satisfaction survey results: yeehaw! I used to stay with a job only until I'd learned just about as much as I could from it. After that, it was all downhill. I'd show up at noon. I'd take naps under my desk. I was quite brazen in my attempts to get fired. I look back now and wonder, well, why didn't I simply quit? Just to let you all know, the filtered water reservoir at the fourth floor kitchen sink has been serviced and you can once again enjoy a tall, cool, refreshing drink of clear, clean, fast-pouring $H_2$-oh! Brenda. Too much free time is certainly a monkey's paw in disguise, isn't it? Most of us can't handle a structureless life. A clever way to make money on the job is to gamble . . . bet your boss that you will meet or exceed a target! Oh God, how depressing. Is this what life has come to? Thank you for continuing to hold. Here at American Airlines we believe in alchemy. Do not change visibility settings in either the "Overall," "Partial" or "Sector" views. Only change settings in the "Working" views. Retiring in the Caribbean is a form of death. Do you ever listen to success tapes? Have you ever sat in the ballroom of the city's third-largest hotel with four hundred people wearing bad shoes? Get out of debt. Build wealth. Gain confidence. Enhance self-esteem. Develop leadership skills. Chew gum. Fester while you curse nature for not having made you charismatic. Yachts are boring. Do you have hidden mental abilities? You have three new messages. Statistically, your hidden mental abilities are far more likely to be dormant pathologies just waiting to explode: schizophrenia, delusional thinking, memory loss or various subcategories of autism. Your subconscious mind isn't some kind of adventure-packed "Land of the Lost" that you can visit in safety and comfort and then leave any time you want to. It's expensive and difficult, and your discoveries, if any, might simply be dull. People who have a seductive handshake have really worked on it. They might be good in bed, too. You're being judged at all times. Don't take sides. Remain emotionally uninvolved. Have a stroke. Most anger is justifiable. Secretly destroy the lives of bullies. Jeff, the hour you spent with me last Tuesday morning on the phone changed me entirely, from a cowering servant of fear and anxiety into a free and happy human being, but it only lasted a few hours, and now I want—*need*—more of what you have. Jeff, be my friend. Let me buy your whole series of tapes. If you can control your emotions, chances are you don't have too many. Fear is nature's way of making sure too many people don't get everything they want, hence stripping the planet of raw materials too quickly. People who go to seminars and come away from them thinking they no longer have fears are a real nuisance until you find out how their old fears have reconfigured themselves. Sometimes that never happens, and they get to float to the grave thinking they're groovy. Seminar people are a pain in the ass. In a pinch, it's always easiest just to blame your parents. Your parents' mistakes are your get-out-of-jail-free card. Rejoice! Some people are only interested in people who are in pain. They seem helpful, but there's a name for these people: vampires. *But I care about you! I really do!* No. All you care about is sucking up desperate energy during crises. Are you addicted to failure? Who writes this shit? Only damaged people want good things to happen to them through visualization. They want something for nothing. It's not a tough call. Losers attract losers. Please recycle your old phone book by stacking it opposite the freight elevator. This action is currently prohibited. Beautiful people only like to have sex with beautiful people. Pretending you're passionate about something you're not really passionate about is just plain depressing, and people can smell it a mile away. Having a nice, loving family might, in the end, just not be enough. You have to face that. People will always choose more money over more sex. There may be a part of you that feels you don't deserve to have money. Loser. Some people get to have lots of money, and you don't hold it against them, but some people get even a bit of money, and man, do you hate their guts. If it hasn't happened by now, it's probably not going to happen. If the previous sentence made you angry, then it's easy to understand why countries undergo political revolutions. Doing nothing is fun. Has anyone seen a spare calculator floating around? Mine has gone missing from my desk. Try the new #10 Trade Size Poly-Klear single-window envelopes with privacy tint. I promise I'll answer your emails. I promise to overdeliver on all my promises. Sometimes failure isn't an opportunity in disguise; it's just you. If you don't feel like you're in the know, you most likely aren't. Are you disgruntled or merely gruntled? This stackable chair's smooth rolling casters allow for easy mobility. From the conference room to the workstations, from lobbies to training areas, this chair is ready for the fast lane. Maybe you can help me. Like you, I'm a professional here. I love networking with fellow professionals. Maybe there's a way we can help each other. Let's go for coffee sometime. Do you have an actual skill? Let me get this straight: you're using the company server to download a pirated German-language screening version of *Mrs. Doubtfire,* starring Robin Williams? Have a happy birthday, Kelly! The next year is going to be terrific! Lordy, Lordy, Kelly's Forty! Signed, your cellmate, Darryl. Hi, Kelly, it's all downhill from here, kiddo. Fran. It's quite easy to tell which text has been typed by someone living in the Indian subcontinent because they all too frequently forget to put spaces after periods or commas. Whenever people say, "So, what are you waiting for?" what they're really saying is, "Hand over your cash while you're still in a semi-hypnotized state." Boost your career to a new height. This mailbox is full; please try again later. Sell more products. Be a corporate fartcatcher. Some people like to begin sentences with the word "frankly," and this is very annoying. Ask these people, "Hey, does this mean everything you say that doesn't have 'frankly' in front of it is bullshit?" Hey, Mr. IT Smartass. Your cleaning staff despises you. You know that in your heart, but you smile and say good night anyway. Is there anything in the world more annoyingly creepy than an unspoken dress code? Personality-wise, does your office have "one of everything"? Use any of the following three words in the coffee room and just watch the mess that results: dissolute; peregrination; zaibatsu. Tits. All I think about is tits, forty hours a week, and that's above and beyond the amount of time I spend thinking about them on my own time. Hello. Adware and Spyware have been added to your computer. Allow us to do a scan so that we can protect you. Simply click here. Blame is great! It's fun to make life hard for newcomers. Skipping meetings makes you look cool. Five minutes of missed work per day adds up to one day per year, so find joy in shaving the minutes off like crazy every day—it's like a time-release slow-acting holiday drug. It's awfully darned sexy to see someone get piss drunk at lunchtime. Assume one active affair per every 32.5 staffers. Don must have some kind of sickness, as he can't stay away from your overgrown larva-infested snatch, you cow. Free NASCAR and NHL box seats? I'm your bitch. Even the Japanese have finally abandoned as pointless the notion of corporate loyalty. Go, Team Members, Go! What's the difference between a venerated senior staff member and a lifer? Chances are you feel superior to almost everyone you work with—however, they probably feel the same way about you. What a shitty world. Unbeatable firewalls! Install your own PBX! Everyone is roughly 33.5 years old in their heads. People with bad fingernails probably drink too much. Relentlessly perky women often have deeply rooted fertility issues. Ageism and rankism are great because they make for such good gossip when abused. It can be really fun to go down with the ship. Four-line phone with speaker-phone, only $89.99. There was this one guy I worked with, Ian, who got a DUI for his third time, and he lost his driver's licence. It was weird because he had this sort-of "gee-whiz" aura that always sur-rounded him, like a holy man, and people started assuming all these crazy mystical things about him. I Wuv Hugs. Thanks for leaving melted cheddar all over the microwave's bottom, dickwad. No iPods or Walkmans or any other similar devices permitted. I'd like to speak with a real human being, please. Ever since the new no-smoking bylaws passed, it's like I don't know Craig any more. He spends all his breaks smoking outside the ground-floor lobby with his new smoking buddies, like we're not good enough or risqué enough for him. I secretly don't mind Kyle's lame backrubs. AutoReply: Out of Office. I'm away until the 27th. If you have urgent business, please contact my assistant, Sandy, at ext. 238. There's nothing cute or funny or lovable about being cheap. It's ugly, and people really hate seeing cheapness in operation. If you think being frugal makes you look sensible, just stop right now and hope your friends come back to you.

**Part Two**
Steve's Grand Adventure

## Four Months Later

A Volkswagen Touareg belonging to a missing Vancouver man, Steven Lefkowitz, has been found in the woods near Buntzen Lake. The RCMP aren't speculating as to Lefkowitz's whereabouts, but foul play is suspected. Anyone who might have information relevant to the disappearance is urged to contact his or her local RCMP detachment.

*Canadian Press*

The big drama is that Steve has gone missing. Nobody saw him around the office for a few days, and the newspapers said cops found his Touareg with its door open beside a lake in the Fraser Valley. We all figured Steve was dead, and we also felt slightly guilty for having wished him to be so for all those months. BoardX is a mess, and Steve has made it look like anybody's fault but his. God, he's good.

The afternoon the RCMP found Steve's car, we were having a soul-crushing meeting in which we hammered out the next phase of the BoardX production schedule. The good news is that months of marketing studies have convinced the company that the whole Jeff the Turtle thing is an unappealing idea. This was presented at today's production meeting.

Here's my theory about meetings and life: the three things you can't fake are erections, competence and creativity. That's why meetings become toxic—they put uncreative people in a situation in which they have to be something they can never be. And the more effort they put into concealing their inabilities, the more toxic the meeting becomes. One of the most common creativity-faking tactics is when someone puts their hands in the prayer position and conceals their mouth while they nod at you and say, "Hmmmmm. Interesting." If pressed, they'll add, "I'll have to get back to you on that." Then they don't say anything else.

The uncreative people who run a meeting say such things as, *Does anybody here have something to say about Ethan's idea?* The ensuing silence makes even a good idea look stupid.

Or they'll say, *That's an interesting idea, but let's focus on matters at hand.*

Many people think that the best way to make meetings tolerable is to walk into the room and fire away with lots of ideas to get juices flowing. Such ideas goad uncreative colleagues into building more elaborate strategies to conceal their lack of creativity. You think you're giving away all this great material, but all you're really doing is generating fear and envy.

In a way, the best meetings are the ones where nobody is creative and nobody has any ideas about anything. People sit around, stare at their notepads, and then, after a plausible amount of time has passed, everyone leaves. Everybody's happy because nothing was demanded of them, and nobody was made to look bad in front of the others.

Knowing all of this doesn't make meetings any less numbing, but at least now you know why they're numbing.

In general, if you have been stupid enough to venture a new and possibly good idea during a meeting, you may as well kiss it goodbye. On the other hand, you might as well enjoy the behaviour of your co-workers as they try to attach their names to your idea, while at the same time distancing themselves from it. Co-workers will generate an email trail of bland musings that can function as good evidence or bad evidence.

Hi, Ethan—interesting idea you reminded Glenn about—racking up the CPUs in a Kendall formation may just work. Let's maybe talk about it some time. Did Sheila get you those upgrade cards like I asked?

The above email 1) took almost no work to do; 2) leaves a connective trail to you and your idea; and 3) gives the illusion of friendship and caring.

After I had my moment of grand insight about creativity

and meetings, Bree looked at me and said, "Ethan, you've done something—I can see it in your face. Are you on drugs?"

"*Moi?* No."

"Bullshit. You suddenly look peaceful. That's not possible in a situation like this. What gives?"

"Whatever do you mean?"

Bree BlackBerried Cowboy. **Ethan is looking far 2 peaceful all of a sudden. Cowboy, did U giv him some Robitussin?**

**Nope. I'm trying 2 clean out my system. He DOES look suspiciously at peace.**

It was fun watching everybody squirm.

• • •

Peaceful as I was with my new theory about meetings, I still had to flee the boardroom about an hour before that one ended—I started getting that itching-from-the-inside feeling, like ants were collecting bread crumbs around my cranium—and the ants were growing bigger and angrier.

Kaitlin thinks I'm claustrophobic, but that's not true—I love elevators and small cars. What I *don't* like is being exposed to unfiltered social contact, like at parties or meetings, when just anyone can talk to you with no other reason than that you happen to be there. She and I discussed this after the meeting.

"Ethan, I think you have mild autism."

"What?"

"You have to admit, half the people who work here are

mildly autistic: poor social skills, the ability to obsess on any-thing numerical or repetitive, the odd outfits, the paranoia and the sense of continually being judged and measured. Autistics almost always can't stand being touched or approached by other people."

"Then what do you make of our sex life?"

"Good point. Strike that—autistics often can't stand being touched by *strangers*. Also, Ethan, you spend way too much time playing Manhunt, which is the goriest game of all time. It signals your detachment from humanity."

"Players of Resident Evil: DC might disagree with you. Or The Suffering."

"Ethan, watching you play Manhunt is like watching a steak being carved at Benihana."

"It's only pretend gore."

"With characters customized to resemble people here at work?"

I changed the subject. "Evil Mark was being slightly secre-tive at the meeting."

"I saw that. What was he doing?"

"I craned my neck and checked it out—he was practis-ing new signatures."

"*What?*"

"I know. Grown-ups don't do that." I tried to remember when I came up with my own signature, but all that came to me were flickering images of killing time in high school English classes. I asked Kaitlin if she remembered inventing hers.

"Absolutely. I used to have loopy teenage-girl handwrit-ing—the kind that scares away guys—but late in high school

I went tagging with friends from the school's smoking area and got radicalized. That's why my signature looks like a tag. And why my handwriting's illegible."

"I can't believe people still write anything any more. I grew up expecting machines to do all of that for us, and I think we're actually close to that point."

"I hope. And I wish they'd hurry up with language translating machines, too. I'd like to visit Europe, but I always think about the language issue and say, *Maybe next year.*"

I was about to make yet another Cheerios run for Gord-O when Kaitlin called me over to her screen. "Check out what just came down the Chute . . ." She was looking at blueprints for a machine that resembled a piece of gym equipment. "It says here that autistics are calmed down by the sensation of pressure on their skin from non-living sources, such as heavy blankets and, apparently, these hugging machines."

"So?"

"So I'm going to build one here in jPod and let it be used for the communal good. We could be the world's first tech company with its own hug machine."

• • •

Steve remained vanished, and we were all still unsure if that was good or bad. We scoured the Toblerone website for clues, but all we got was hungry. That, and we found out that Kraft Foods owns Toblerone. Cowboy also discovered in one of Toblerone's many chat rooms that Campbell Soup owns Godiva Chocolates. We are disillusioned. Our Wonka daydreams have died.

I keep on receiving spams where they've put random words inside the body copy to trick anti-spam programs into thinking it's a real letter. There has to be some other form of coded message in operation here.

clams evil garage clowns bogey lie saran in depart wait celery drooling puncture at bartend the pronto thought luxurious of earthmoving ripping arabesque at hypodermic your orchid lazy carrion human recriminatory flesh never bulkhead mock eleventh my rifleman clown thermal rage wan or gorse my octopus darklings airlift will cozy torment eightfold your aphasic spawn revelatory until collard your montage sun irresistible burns frog supernova sterile

• • •

Bree told me this great story. She was assigned to show around a visiting middleware consultant from France. Nobody was sure if he was gay or not. His name is Serge Duclos—which is sort of funny in itself, because in high school, the fictional guy in my French textbook was Serge Duclos. Everyone my age in my school district has this same Serge Duclos guy in their heads, forever asking where the Métro is.

"It turns out Serge isn't gay," Bree said, "so we had a bit of a fling, and he spent a few nights at my place. Then he really started to get on my nerves. Fortunately, his boss flew in, and he had to move back into his hotel—just in the nick of time.

"So I came home from work, and there was a beautiful cashmere shawl inside a FedEx envelope on my front stoop. I thought, *Shit, now I'm going to have to get him something, too.*

"And then I read the note attached to the sweater, and it turns out he's staying here longer because he has to implement his middleware into the company pipeline. Aargh!

"I asked my dad for a gift suggestion. He's a urologist, and people give him stuff all the time. He handed me a bottle of red wine a patient had given him. It seemed kind of lame as a gift, but it was better than nothing.

"So I gave him the wine, and his face dissolved and he just wept.

"He said, *You could have given me platinum cufflinks or a new car, and I would have thought it was a vulgar North American gesture, but this*— he cradled the bottle like it was a newborn—*This magnificent bottle of 1970 Chateau Latour Bordeaux—I'm speechless.*

"The moment he was gone, I looked online, and it turns out the wine was worth seven hundred bucks. Shriek! When we met the next day, he treated me like a classy *layyyyyy*dy, which no one's ever done before. Everything I say to the man is wise, and everything I do is chic. And now I'm falling in love with him, and it's all because of that bottle of wine."

• • •

On the way home yesterday I stopped at a Ricky's Pancake Hut for a cheeseburger, fries and Coke. It's not what I usually order, but for a short while I wanted to pretend I was living inside an Archie comic—don't we all feel like that at some time or other?

When my food arrived, the Coke glass had a slogan on the side in cheerful fake-1950s lettering:

# Coca-Cola
# Free Will!

I thought to myself, *Wow, it's great that Coca-Cola is now sponsoring independent thinking at the most grassroots of levels. Maybe global corporations aren't evil at all. Maybe they represent the future of knowledge and the transmission of culture to future civilizations. Maybe I've been too hard on them all these years!*

I looked more closely at the glass, and realized it didn't actually say Free Will!, but rather, Free *Fill!* I asked the waitress what that meant, and she said I could drink as much Coke as I wanted on that one drink order.

I told John Doe, who had an interesting thought. "I used to yearn for Coke when I was growing up in the lesbian commune. And I yearned to try Pepsi as well. I thought that being a cola virgin was a great opportunity to offer the definitive taste test. So I snuck out and walked to the bait shop, which was maybe three miles from home, and bought a Coke. They didn't have Pepsi, so I brought the Coke home and hid it in the backyard beneath a stump beside the communal talking circle, and the next week I was able to hitch into town, and I found a Pepsi and brought it home. I snuck out into a birch glade, opened them up and had this big woo moment when I tasted them."

"And?" We were all curious to find out which was better.

"They both tasted like crap."

"But wasn't one better than the other?"

"Does cat shit taste better than dog shit? The weird thing was that neither of them tasted as sweet as I'd anticipated. So that afternoon, when my mother was going into town to do her monthly 'Look, I don't shave my armpits' challenge to the locals, I went along and snuck into a diner and stole sugar and NutraSweet packets. When we got home, I took two glasses and a spoon into the glade and added sugar to what was left of the two colas."

"What happened?"

"The weird thing is, *nothing* happened."

"Huh?"

"It doesn't matter how much sugar or aspartame you add to a Coke or Pepsi, it can't get any sweeter than it already is. That's their secret formula. It's not some secret ingredient — which, by the way, would have to be registered with federal food and drug administrations, so let's scotch that little urban legend about Secret Ingredient X7—it's that their beverages are already supersaturated with sweeteners."

• • •

The RCMP interviewed everyone on the BoardX team about Steve. Did we notice anything odd before he disappeared? I decided not to mention what had happened months ago—finding Steve at the bottom of my parents' driveway at 4:45 in the morning with a huge gift on top of his car. But I began to wonder if . . . no. No way. Not possible. No.

• • •

I was reading my old *Inuyasha* comics on the campus soccer field, trying to renegotiate my relationship with this particular manga franchise. I don't know if I did. Maybe it's an age thing, but it suddenly dawned on me that, in general, I'm really sick of crystals and jewels and swords and rings that have woo-woo magic powers. I mean . . . it's really not at all different from being at a beach and throwing sticks to your dog. *Master, oh master, which stick possesses the magic power of "it" that makes me want to chase that one stick and no other? . . . Until, of course, you choose another stick and that stick becomes "it."*

Jewels and rings are basically nothing more than the human equivalent of a stick being "it." It's hokey: *Gee, the ring is mine. I have all the power.*

It's also lazy. Instead of learning skills and knowledge, characters merely have to obtain the magic token. *Gee, here I thought I was just a statistically average John Doe, and suddenly it turns out that I'm not—I own THE RING! I AM THE CENTRE OF THE UNIVERSE!*

I was feeling pretty pleased with myself about this little observation until I misplaced the copper Haida bracelet Kaitlin had given me for my birthday. Boy, did the fireworks fly. Guess who was sleeping on the floor until he remembered leaving the bracelet in the basement on top of the box the new furnace filter came in. Now I can appreciate what it must have been like for Frodo, carrying that ring around.

# New Rebel Strategy!

*Against the terrifying might of the Imperial forces, the Rebels must constantly devise new and more ingenious methods of combatting their relentless foes . . .*

## Suddenly . . . Starfire!

BLAMMM! WHOOSH! PA-TOOMMM! The Rebel base is under attack! Young warriors dart back and forth as titanic warships of the Imperial Alliance begin a devastating frontal assault!

## "But, Sir, I—Mmh . . . Mffh . . ."

An impatient Han Solo decides to set out on his own to rescue Luke. When faithful droid Threepio voices some concern, Solo cuts the conversation with one decisive gesture.

## Examined: Luke's Tauntaun

At the Rebel base, a surgeon droid examines the carcass of Luke's Tauntaun, the latest victim of the mysterious ice creature known as the Wampa.

## Surgeon Droid™

Tending the critically ill Luke Skywalker in the rejuvenation chamber is a surgeon droid, Too-Onebee, one of many such droids designed to nurse ailing humans back to health.

## General Rieekan™

A man of exceptional intelligence and military skill. He is the perfect choice to lead the Rebel Alliance against the untold evils of the Empire.

● ● ●

Everyone was invited to my place to watch an episode of a Hong Kong TV program called *White Ghost*—a weekly show in which they present North American people doing crazy embarrassing shit. It was my night to appear—they were going to show the webcast clip of me singing "Total Eclipse of the Heart." It went viral, and pretty well every human being on the planet with a high-speed connection has seen it a dozen times. But at least on *White Ghost* I was up for a prize, and frankly, dammit, I deserved it and wanted to win. (Please note that I'm now at peace with the karaoke issue, and have learned to be gracious when the subject of that unmentionably demonic song by premier Welsh song vixen, Bonnie Tyler, arises.)

All of jPod was in my living room.

"Any news about Steve yet?"

"Nothing."

"Pass me another Zima."

"Why are we drinking Zima? It's beyond irony. It's not funny or anything. It's just gross. Why not just serve us jugs of Hitler's piss instead?"

"Drinking Zima is something Douglas Coupland would make a character do."

"To what end?"

"It'd be a device that would allow him to locate the characters in time and a specific sort of culture."

"Is that all we are—*Zima* drinkers? Zima is so nineties."

Mom and Dad came in the door just then. The cops had busted the guy who sold Dad bootleg satellite computer cards, so they had to come to my place to watch the show on my own *paid for* satellite system.

Mom said, "Look at all you clever young people."

Dad was jolly, too. "It's good to hang out with the folks who are going to be wiping spit off my bib a few years down the road. Ethan, are you ever going to stop wearing those ragamuffin clothes? Is Kam Fong here yet?"

"He went to get more Zima. He lives for it, and he can't find it in Hong Kong."

Everyone chimed in, "So *that's* why we're drinking it."

"You got it."

Mom asked, "Are you excited to see your episode, dear?"

I said, "The producers didn't tell me much."

"Is young Steven still missing?"

"Yup."

"Hmmm."

Okay, I'm not stupid. But how do you ask your mother what she might have done to the guy? *Hi, Mom, I know that every guy who gets sweet on you ends up in a grim situation, but could we put all of that aside for a second?*

Dad asked, "How's Kam working out?"

"Actually, not too badly. I'm surprised. Best roommate I ever had."

Here's what happened: Kam screwed up and accidentally put not just smuggled people but a smuggler into a Nedlloyd freight container. They spent eight days lolling about the Pacific with almost no food, water, light or sanitation. Kam had to hide out at my place for a few weeks until things calmed down. He was philosophical about the mistake: "I had to give the bastard a freebie on that particular shipment, *and* I also had to buy a McMansion for his mother in West Van, one bordering the golf course. Of course, the mother's gaga and could live in a Maytag box for all she cares."

In any event, Kam ended up staying with us in Chinatown—the poverty nostalgia factor—and Kaitlin and I couldn't be happier. He makes no noise at all when he's home, and the fridge is bursting with tons of free food, renewed daily.

Greg walked in with Kam. "Zima for all!" He threw everybody a bottle, and since Kam can sometimes get snarky towards people who don't appreciate his generosity (p.s. all of Kam's shiny Chinese furniture reappeared the day he moved in), bottles were listlessly accepted and opened. "Isn't this stuff great?" Kam insisted.

Evil Mark led the chorus. "Woohoo!"

John Doe surprised us. "I actually know a few facts about Zima."

"Why on *earth* would you?"

"From my efforts to figure out what normal guys ate and drank. I thought Zima was it for a while, so I researched it. Zima was developed in the early 1990s, during our culture's love affair with clear products. Remember Crystal Pepsi? And Ivory Liquid Clear? I'm glad I was around for that craze, which was my first exposure to mass consumer culture. Anyway, the Coors Brewing Company developed Zima as a beer alternative. The word means 'winter' in Russian. It was supposed to be cool and fresh, lacking the bitterness of hops, or vodka's high-alcohol punch. It went national in 1994. It's a niche beverage with no real competition, and—this will surprise you—it's drunk mostly by men in their early twenties. Mock it as you will, but Zima is fresh and sassy and here to stay."

Kam said, "I read in an in-flight magazine once that members of Generation X like to drink Zima."

John Doe said, "*Ahhh* . . . yes . . . Generation *X*."

Everyone looked awkward, as if Angela Lansbury's aging collie dog had noiselessly passed wind.

"What did I say? Why is everyone so quiet suddenly?"

I said, "Let's change the subject to something better."

Then, in one of life's great coincidental moments, a Zima commercial appeared on TV, and we all shrieked.

• • •

Years ago I read in a psychology book about this experiment in which people were asked to spit into a saucer and then drink back the spit—still warm from their mouths. Most people couldn't do it, because the moment spit leaves your body, it's not *you* any more. That's what it's like seeing yourself on TV—it's like drinking your own spit. It's not nice. I was bracing myself for this sensation when, just before the show started, the local network affiliate inserted a news teaser between commercials:

> The RCMP have new evidence in the case of missing man Steve Lefkowitz—tune in to the evening news after . . .

My mother and Kam Fong exchanged a glance that lasted a microsecond too long. Nobody noticed it but me.

The show's introductory music began. Beneath the music was a jump-cut montage of morbidly obese people with bad hair, skin, teeth and posture driving cars off bridges, catching on fire, walking into lampposts—that kind of stuff. Meanwhile, Dad, clueless as always, didn't realize that what we were seeing was the actual show.

He demonstrated this by picking up the remote and pushing one of its buttons, making the TV blare out shrieking blue fuzz.

"Dad, whatthe*fuck* do you think you're doing?" Greg shouted.

"I only wanted to see if tonight's *Law & Order* is a rerun or not."

"Put it back to where it was. Our show just started!"

"How was I to know?" Dad fiddled with the remote. "I can't find the right button. It's a different satellite system than mine."

"How useless can you possibly be? Ethan, put the channel back on before the show starts again."

Dad somehow managed to push another button, and the TV volume blasted like 150 freight cars loaded with plywood shunting in hot weather. "Jesus, Dad, what button did you push?" Greg shouted.

"Be quiet. Your brother and I are trying to fix this."

"I am not, because you won't let me," I said.

"Where did I put my glasses?"

"Dad, give me the remote."

"Ethan, *no.* I can fix this."

Everyone in the room was trying to conceal their inner glee at witnessing my family enter major fuck-up mode. Any of my podmates could have solved the fracas with the remote with three brain cells, but no way were they about to engage in this mess.

Seconds ticked by. Mom said, "Jim, you're always doing this. You won't simply admit you can't see the buttons. Ethan, take the remote away from your father."

Dad dropped the remote. It hit the tabletop and shattered, sending its batteries cartwheeling between Kaitlin's legs, and then into the coat closet by the front door.

"You've damaged Ethan's coffee table," Mom cried.

Greg shouted, "Dad, you're a total fuck-up. The show's started, and we're missing it."

"Greg, it's not my fault."

"It is-fucking-*too* your fault."

"Ethan's system is Mickey Mouse." Dad went over to the TV and touched one of those little black knobs beneath the screen that nobody ever touches. Big mistake: we got a choppy satellite porn channel with heaving, thrusting, pulsating, thwomping and gushing. The noise that accompanied it was like shattering glass. It was shocking. Greg went to shoo Dad away and bashed his shin on the sharp edge of the coffee table and started screaming *shitshitshitSHIT*.

I got mad. "Dad, get away from the TV set."

"I'm not going anywhere until your brother apologizes to me."

"Greg, just apologize to Dad, okay?"

"Like hell I will. Do you know how hard Kam and I worked to get you on that show? And numbnuts here just waltzes in and fucks up the system by pushing the one button in the whole fucking universe that makes the TV self-destruct."

"I was only trying to see if *Law & Order* was a rerun or not tonight."

"Wait a second, Dad," I said. "*Law & Order* is on right after *White Ghost* . . ."

"Yeah, so?"

"You mean to say that the moment *White Ghost* ended you were going to hog the TV to yourself and watch *Law & Order* with no regard whatsoever for the nine other people in the room?"

"What's your problem?"

I lost it. "That is so fucking rude! You came into my house already planning to zap to another show the moment this one ends?"

"Ethan, watch your mouth," Mom said.

There was a green and purple fellatial funfest on the screen, and suddenly the sound became perfect. We could hear slurping, glurping and god-knows-what slapping against all forms of membrane. Dad said, "Turn that off, right now."

Greg said, "No *way* is Dad getting off the hook by unplugging the set. He's going to have to fix his mess first."

Dad turned it off. My ears felt cool and relieved.

Mom moaned, "A great big gouge in the middle of Ethan's table."

"My shin's bleeding all over the place!" And it was true—Greg's wound was pulsing away in Monty Python splendour. My podmates discreetly pulled away from him.

"Oh, Greg," Mom said. "First the table, and now you're spraying blood all over the beautiful carpeting."

Dad went to get his coat, but Greg plugged the TV back in. "You're not leaving until you clean up the mess you made."

I said, "It's my house, Greg. *I'll* decide."

"Well, you agree with me, right?"

"Of course I do. Dad, you're not leaving here until you fix what you screwed up."

Mom decided to rescue Dad, and used her silent-but-deadly voice. "We're leaving. You're awful, all of you. We're leaving." She stormed out the door, and Dad followed her. Greg limped off to the bathroom in pursuit of a Band-Aid or a tourniquet or a cauterizing tool.

The room was suddenly appallingly quiet.

Kaitlin said, "I keep forgetting that your family runs on Microsoft software."

Evil Mark walked over to the TV and touched one button, just as my segment on *White Ghost* was ending to thundering audience applause. I ended up finishing second to some guy in Arizona who was juggling five kittens, but then, when they threw in the sixth kitten, it went horribly wrong.

• • •

Bree was at her desk and briefly forgot to mute her audio, so we all heard a few seconds of that old Morrissey song, "Everyday Is Like Sunday." This set Kaitlin off. "That song always puts me in a crappy mood because Sundays are actually the worst day of the week. Nobody's answering the phones or dressed properly or doing anything productive. If I ruled the world, every day would be a Thursday."

"Huh?"

"Look at it this way: Mondays suck because you're resent-ful that you can't sleep in, and it's also the day on which sixty percent of life-sucking meetings occur. Tuesdays suck because the week has four more workdays left; you hate your-self and the world because you're trapped in this wage-slave hamster wheel called life. Wednesdays are bad because you realize around noon that the work week is half over, but the fact that you're viewing your life in this manner means that you're nothing more or less than the third panel of that old, unfunny comic strip *Cathy,* where she realizes she's a fat lonely spinster and her hair flies out and she makes the *auggh-hhhhh!* noise. Fridays are bad because you feel like a rat wait-ing for a food pellet to come down the chute, the food pellet being the weekend. Saturdays are okay, but only barely. And Sundays, as mentioned before, are like the day that time for-got, when nothing happens and when, perversely, you start wishing for Monday again. So give me a week of Thursdays any time. Everyone's in a good mood, people actually get stuff done, and a glint of Saturday puts a sparkle in your step."

• • •

I just realized that us jPodders are becoming quite different from other workers here. Our quirks are increasing, while non-jPodders seem to be more and more . . . *normal.* I real-ized that other employees our age have hobbies, legally wed-ded mates and, more eerily, *children.* Instead of pulling all-nighters, they leave the premises, ride a bike, eat wholesome food, discuss non-work-related activities, have a nap and then return to work the next day . . . *not that same night!* Older staffers don't even bother coming in on weekends. Where is the sleep-crazed, Pepsi-fuelled one-point-oh tech environment that can only be created by having no green vegetables, no sex and no life?

Cowboy said, "I miss the greed of the 1990s bubble."

John Doe said, "I miss the possibility of unearned wealth."

Bree said, "I miss the possibility of doing something Apple, something one-point-oh."

Evil Mark said, "I miss people having Hot Wheels tracks set up in their cubicles." (Evil Mark is nostalgic for a stint he did at ILM in the Bay Area two years ago.)

Gord-O walked into the pod. "You can't miss the nineties, because you weren't there. They were great. Too bad you screwed-up twits missed out on the party."

I asked, "What was it like—all that money out there just waiting to rain down on you?"

"It wasn't merely *all that money,* Ethan. It was a Fort-Knox-is-hemorrhaging cash geyser. But forget that. This is the Wretched Decade, and here in the Wretched Decade, you drive to Costco to buy Honey Nut Cheerios for my team and me. Oh, and while you're at it, I need six Stouffer's breaded white-meat chicken filet dinners with mashed potatoes. They put a microwave in our coffee station, and I want to try it out."

Welcome to my life.

Hello,

We are Exchange Company in Russia. We find for a partner in USA for work, we need persons of America or companies which can accept bank wires on your bank accounts.

Our clients are in USA everyday buy big amounts of E-gold money (e-gold.com), they then send you big amount to your bank account, you receive cash and send western union to us, we deposit client e-gold money.

For this work you be the receiver of 10% of amount (amount starts from 3000 F up to 7000 F per 1 transication)

If you are interested Reply BACK, we will provide more details.

FULL INSTRUCTION ON: http://westernexchange.smnetworking.biz/intro.exe
EMAIL TO REPLY: exchange@smnetworking.biz

Thank you!

• • •

Three days ago I had to drive John Doe to his house in South Van so he could pick up some car keys, and in his kitchen I was looking around, and there was a jumbo four-slice toaster.

"Jesus, John—four slices—are you on breakfast duty at Rikers?"

"Is it so wrong to like toast?"

"I guess not."

His living room looked like a Radisson Suites hotel room in somewhere blank like Des Plaines, Illinois. "John, have you considered maybe taping up a poster or something?"

"Yes, but I decided not to. I like the room's air of calculated neutrality. And poster colours might fade in the sunlight."

"That's possibly the most depressing thing I've ever heard."

"Nonsense. Hey, look at these—" From beneath the kitchen counter he pulled out a yellow plastic dairy crate filled with arcade game motherboards from the late 1980s, all of them wrapped in bubble-pack. He'd converted some crap Ikea furniture into a full-scale, ergonomically correct arcade game simulator. We ended up spending the entire afternoon playing Konami's The Simpsons Power Test, which was primitive but cool. We both agreed we couldn't watch the superearly *Simpsons* episodes where the voices are wrong—especially Homer's—and the line quality is thin and slightly scary.

• • •

The day after I visited John's house, I dropped Bree off at her place because her car was in the shop. Right outside her window was this huge exhaust vent from a fried chicken restaurant, spewing oily particulates at her apartment.

"Bree—what the hell *is* that thing? How can you live with it?"

"Oh, that."

"Yes, *that.*"

"I call it the trans-fatty acid vapour funnel."

"It doesn't scare the crap out of you? The smell doesn't keep you up at night?"

"I grew up with frying-chicken smell. My father the urologist also ran an illicit gambling parlour, and my mom made snacks until five a.m. every night. I find it comforting."

Who am I to argue?

• • •

I just sat through possibly the longest meeting I've ever been in, and possibly the dullest. Let me go through the four hours point by point. Okay, I'm kidding—I wouldn't have sent my worst enemy to today's meeting. The upshot is that, now that Steve is gone, a political battle has given rise to Steve's replacement: *Alistair.* Today Alistair told us our new mandate for BoardX: "Its new title is SpriteQuest. SpriteQuest is a warm, heartfelt journey into magical and fantastic lands, where our hero, Prince Amulon, allows children to rediscover life's joys as he teaches us all to laugh and dream again."

Something died inside us as we heard this proclamation.

Senior management, though, interpreted the ensuing silence as tacit agreement.

Alistair carried on. "We decided that a skateboard was too constraining a vehicle for storytelling. If we convert the skateboard into Prince Amulon's magic carpet, on which kids can ride along, we can create more options for learning and growth for the players."

*Learning? Growth?*

Kaitlin raised her hand.

Alistair short-circuited her query. "I can read your mind, and let me answer your question. We all felt that Jeff the Turtle might ultimately be interpreted as too derivative of the TMNT franchise. We want to be industry leaders, and SpriteQuest will take us all to a new place—a place of excitement and challenge. While Jeff the Turtle is, unfortunately, no longer with us, his mesh, utilities and properties will live on as we repurpose him into Prince Amulon—a bold twist that will create many more opportunities to explore him as a character. How does Prince Amulon *think*? What are his *motivations*? What *drives* him through the game? With just a few extra polygons, we ought to be able to convert BoardX's inner-city environment frameworks into dungeons. Ditto the rest of the game. Think magic. Think challenge. Think *possibilities*! And now I think it would be appropriate to have a minute of silence in memory of Steve, wherever he may be."

After the meeting ended, we shuffled, zombie-like, back to jPod. Fortunately, I had to make Gord-O's Cheerios run, which allowed me to space out for a few hours in traffic.

I've come to the conclusion that documents are thirty-four percent more boring when presented in the Courier font. Please see the following examples:

| | |
|---|---|
| Message validation | `Message validation` |
| Mods to upcoming builds | `Mods to upcoming builds` |
| New version release schedule | `New version release schedule` |
| XML namespaces | `XML namespaces` |
| Implementation tutorial | `Implementation tutorial` |
| Walkthrough glitch | `Walkthrough glitch` |
| XML serialization | `XML serialization` |
| Event logging | `Event logging` |
| Miscoupling | `Miscoupling` |
| Unstable Refresh | `Unstable Refresh` |
| Broken builds | `Broken builds` |
| Dropped code | `Dropped code` |

I showed the above list to Kaitlin, and she berated me. "In order for something to become boring, it has to be interesting to begin with," she said. Thus, I present Kaitlin's list:

| | |
|---|---|
| brain lice | `brain lice` |
| cream of hitchhiker soup | `cream of hitchhiker soup` |
| sun-bloated babysitter | `sun-bloated babysitter` |
| fistfuckers in Spain | `fistfuckers in Spain` |
| see the monster's penis? | `see the monster's penis?` |
| lean, fit and willing | `lean, fit and willing` |

sorority sleepover
baby oil & rope

sorority sleepover
baby oil & rope

• • •

I went to get some skin tone at Tanfastic, and was lying in the sunbed, enjoying its dull lavender hum, when somebody in the bed one room over put on Bonnie Tyler's "Total Eclipse of the Heart" at full volume. My six minutes instantly began to feel like three hundred.

• • •

We just invented a cubicle game called Baffle. It's a hot potato clone. Everyone sits in his or her cubicle as we toss a loaded stapler over the fabric wall baffles between us. You never know who's going to throw it to whom, and you'd be surprised at how much fun it is. For technical reasons, the game made us assign a code name to each disassemblable fabric-covered wall baffle in the pod. We decided to assign them non-specific food flavours:

Regular
Original
Classic
Alpine
Ranch
Frost
Extreme
Fresh

# Arctic
# Blast

• • •

Okay, I'm procrastinating about the meeting's fallout.

• • •

Okay . . .

When I got back to the pod after Gord-O's Cheerios run, Kaitlin was gone. Bree said she had gone to my parents' place. "Your mom needed help harvesting."

"Oh jeez, I forgot."

"Ethan, you did *not* forget. I can tell because you just used your fake voice. How come you're not there helping her?"

"Because my mother makes a huge pot of curry every time she harvests—it's to cover up the pot smell—and the curry smells even worse."

"Oh."

"What did you mean, my 'fake' voice?"

"The voice you use when you're not telling the truth. We talk about it all the time. Cowboy does a really good impression of it. You're a terrible liar."

"Where is everybody?"

"We're all in denial. Cowboy went to sniff magic markers and watch planes land at the airport, and John Doe's out having his weekly mouse-brown hair tinting."

"Evil Mark?"

"Some bug tester downstairs has some NFL cards he wants to buy for his collection."

"So why are you still here?"

"I played Freecell for two hours. Now I'm off to a downtown wine-tasting seminar. Zinfandels."

"You're still determined to be chic for Mr. French Guy?"

"Absolutely."

"Do you feel like discussing SpriteQuest?"

"Not yet."

"I know what you mean."

Bree left. I was considering the sixty-seven unopened emails at the end of the Chute when the phone rang: Kaitlin. "Ethan, can you come over here?"

"Kaitlin, you know how I feel about that curry smell—"

"Your mom isn't making a curry this time, and besides, this is about something else. I found something."

"What?"

"I can't say. Come over."

When I got to my parents' place, Mom was dithering about in the front hallway, wearing a safari suit. "Hi, dear. Glad you could find the time to help out."

"Mom, what's with the outfit? You look like the host of a faltering Japanese game show."

"Well, dear, I suppose one might say the same about your ragamuffin outfits, but *some* people have manners. Kaitlin's downstairs separating and sorting buds for me. Could you go help her?"

"Sure."

"I'm making spaghetti tonight, not curry."

"Praise the Lord."

Downstairs, Kaitlin whispered, "Can she hear us?"

"What's going on?"

I sat down and started to pluck seeds from the buds and trim out the stalky bits.

"An hour ago I cut myself, so I went upstairs to get a Band-Aid from the guest bathroom drawer."

"And?"

"I found Steve's tie in the drawer, along with some guest soaps."

"His tie?"

"You know the one—the 'I'm kooky' tie with little penguins wearing sunglasses on it."

"Uh-oh."

"Ethan, I'm looking at your face, and I *know* there's something you're not telling me. Spill."

I looked across the room to make sure I'd have enough time to shut up if Mom came down. "I think Steve and my mom were having a fling," I whispered.

*"What!"* Kaitlin shrieked.

*"Shhhh!"*

"No way. Your mother's at least fifteen years older than him."

"Your point being? My mother's always been a major guy magnet. Oh God, it feels so weird talking about her like this."

"Like she has sex? Grow up. But with *Steve*?"

"Imagine how I feel. A few months ago, I came by the house to drop off some magazines at four in the morning, and he was at the bottom of the driveway, shaving with an electric razor."

*"Yughh."*

During the awkward silence that fell, we shucked seeds into a steel salad bowl.

Kaitlin said, "Do you think there's a connection between your mom and Steve's, you know, Steve's disappearance?"

"I doubt it," I said, trying hard not to use my easily detected fake/lying voice.

"What should we do?"

"No idea."

Mom was chopping mushrooms when I walked into the kitchen. She seemed cheerful. "Mushrooms have come a long way from those beige buttons I ate growing up. Shiitake, inoki and morels—such flavour."

"Mom, I was in the guest bathroom looking for a Band-Aid and found Steve's penguin tie in the drawer."

Mom put down her knife. "*Did* you?"

"Yes, I did."

Mom picked up the knife and began chopping mushrooms again. "Well, he's not dead, if that's what you're wondering."

"If he's not dead, where is he?"

"Keep your voice down. Kaitlin might hear."

"Do you know where he is?"

"No, Ethan, I don't know where he is, but Kam Fong *did* say he wouldn't kill him."

"*Kam Fong?*"

"Shush! Yes, Kam Fong. Such a nice man."

"How does Steve connect to Kam Fong?"

"Pour me a vodka tonic and I'll tell you. Make it a double. Slice of lime—a circular slice, not a wedge."

"I think I'll pour one for myself, too."

"No you don't. You and Kaitlin will be using the scales

tonight, and I want to make sure you get the numbers right."

So I mixed Mom a drink and pulled up a bar stool while she sliced and diced.

"You have to understand that I liked young Steven, but I was never in love with him."

"Gee. I feel much better already."

"Hand me my drink." She took a big gulp. "I know that gulp didn't look too good, but truth be told, I do feel a bit bad about what happened."

"What happened?"

"I'm getting to that. You have to realize that Steven was in love with me."

"That doesn't surprise me."

"Are you being facetious?" Mom stared at me. "A girl can't control who will and who won't fall in love with her, Ethan. And sometimes, when a nuisance person falls in love with you, it can be awfully . . . awkward."

"How?"

"In the case of young Steven, he was always phoning and waiting for your father to leave so he could come around. It was awful."

That still didn't explain Steve's tie in the soap drawer in the guest bathroom. "And?"

"I just wanted Steven to leave me alone. So I called Kam Fong." Mom stared at me uneasily. "Why do you care about young Steven, by the way? I thought he was making your life miserable."

"He was, but now that he's gone, we've ended up with something much worse than him."

"I thought you might be happy to have him out of your hair."

"What did Kam Fong do with him?"

"I made him promise that he wouldn't kill him."

"How humane."

"Shush. You'll just have to ask Kam yourself. I can't ask him because it'll look as if I don't trust him—and if you *do* ask him, make sure he knows that it's *you* who wants to find Steven, not me."

"Done."

"Dinner will be ready in ninety minutes," said Mom. "Oh, I forgot—your father may have landed a speaking role in an SUV commercial. He's so excited."

I went downstairs again. Kaitlin asked, "Well?"

"I'm not sure."

"You think there's a connection?"

"I just don't know."

"How did the tie end up here?"

"She didn't say."

"Ethan, you're using your fake voice."

*Shit.*

"No, I'm not."

"And you're even lying about using your fake voice."

*Crap.*

"Ethan, I'm going to let this one go because it's family, and family stuff is always weird, but don't think I'm going to forget any of this."

"Kaitlin—" I looked at her. I love every molecule of her body. "That is really nice of you." I looked down at the task at hand. "I really just want to turn off my brain. Let's groom this pot and veg for a little bit."

Kaitlin sighed. "I wish my parents took such good care of their grow-op. My mom's lazy about tracking genetics. Her plants are the foliage equivalents of Cletus the Slack-Jawed Yokel. And my dad's electrical wiring is like that scene in *Poltergeist* where the evil bedroom is trying to suck the little girl into another dimension. When you turn on the light, you clench your toes, tighten your sphincter and wait for a different universe to suck you up."

• • •

Dinner went off without a hitch, although when I had to use the guest bathroom, Steve's tie was gone. Dad was stoked about his potential speaking part. "For once I get to be the asshole driving the shiny silver climate-killer down a mountain road that's been sprayed with a firehose by set-dec."

"What's your line in the commercial?"

"'Smooth, smooth, smooth.' Do you want me to demonstrate my various possible readings?"

"Go for it, Dad."

"Here's the one I think is best, but you listen and you tell me. Smooth, smooth, *smooooooooth*. What do you think?"

"Do a few more."

"Of course. *Smooooooth, smooooooooth, smoooooooooooooth*."

Kaitlin said, "I like that one."

"Really? Did you like the way I lengthened the *oooooooooooo* sound?"

"It was good."

Imagine an hour more of this and you have dinner. Afterwards, we weighed Mom's crop and bagged it. Back at my place, around midnight, Kaitlin and I found Kam Fong leaving with a suitcase. He was moving out.

"Kam—no—we'll miss you." We really would.

"I'm not going far. Your brother just found me this great house in West Van—up on the hill. A bargain, too—the owner got nailed for shipping sugar pills to American seniors who thought they were buying Gleevec and OxyContin. Got it for peanuts. It's got a commanding city view, two karaoke rooms and it's been feng-shuied by a Grand Master." This was about as excited as Kam gets.

Kaitlin asked if Kam would have bought it if it hadn't been feng-shuied.

"Of course. Feng shui's one of those mumbo-jumbo Chinese things people expect Chinese people to get all serious about. It's total crap, but I use it all the time to haggle for lower prices. In any event, come to my housewarming the night after tomorrow. And Ethan, be prepared to sing along to Madonna's 'Vogue.'"

"Mother of God, no."

"Host chooses the tunes. Bye, kids."

• • •

Kaitlin's first meeting in the morning was about the repurposing of BoardX's characters. "I suppose I don't mind doing yet one more anime-style project, but Jesus, anime's like the gaming equivalent of those $8.95 white plastic stacking chairs from Wal-Mart. Sure, they work, but they've also slaughtered every other chair on the market. It's a category killer."

John Doe said, "Anime performed a vital Darwinian function. In the early 1990s the animation world was becoming shockingly lazy. As an art form, animation was dying. Anime offered new hope to young storytellers and animators. Competition and new ideas are good. Imagine a world in which there was only Coke, and no Pepsi. Coke would get lazy, wouldn't it? It'd become arrogant, and with total control of the world's cola nut production, it could raise the price of a tasty beverage to extortionate levels. They could mess with the formula—they could put cinnamon in it. Floor sweepings. Dirt."

Bree said, "I thought you didn't like Coke."

"Not specifically. But I like the idea that people can compete with it."

Cowboy said, "Wait a second—cola nuts? They actually grow them? I thought cola flavouring was entirely synthetic."

"The cola nut I refer to is *Cola acuminata,* which is no longer grown for that use. Modern cola flavouring is a petrochemical derivative. You can buy cola nuts in powdered form."

Kaitlin said, "Let's make our own Coke, right here in jPod."

John Doe said, "What an excellent idea, but please, for legal reasons, let's not call it Coke. Let's call it a cola-flavoured beverage. At the count of three, everybody google. First person to locate a place that sells cola powder and then make an online purchase gets the Halo 2 game I won as the door prize in last week's Tetris Challenge. One, two, three— *google*!"

Evil Mark was fastest. He found a pound of powdered cola

for $10.98 from some hippie place in Iowa. John Doe said, "Congratulations, but you haven't officially won until I see a paper printout of your sale confirmation." The air was electric, because Cowboy was just then finalizing a sale. Mark, in a moment of brain death, entered a SAVE AS key command, and Cowboy ended up winning.

• • •

Back to SpriteQuest. For now, Cowboy, Evil Mark and John Doe are part of the team that assigns attributes to 3-D objects—making sure metals dent, stone crumbles, glass shatters and so forth. The three of them are also part of a squad whose mission is to reconfigure the skateboarding universe into a fantasy universe.

Me? I carry on fetching Honey Nut Cheerios for Gord-O. The big surprise was Bree, who showed up for work today with a wedge-cut hairdo and a navy blue business suit. Kaitlin said, "Bree, you look like a saleslady at a Liz Claiborne factory outlet store circa 1993."

"*Merde*. I was trying to look French. And I might as well tell you guys now, I've decided to try cracking upper management. I have to look the part."

"Why is it, if a guy wants to enter management, all he has to do is declare the fact," Kaitlin asked, "while if a woman wants to do it, she has to dress like a linebacker in drag?"

John Doe: "It's the way of the world, Kaitlin."

I must say, the entire morning was the most demoralized and dispirited I can remember. Around noon I was in the cafeteria, trying some prosciutto and melon, when this guy named Alec came in. I worked with him a few years back, and we got to talking about an Easter egg in this old Atari 2600 game, where the programmer hid his name in a secret room. If you were in the know, or if you got the right zines, you could enter the room, and you got to see his signature just floating in the air in 3-D. The image has always haunted me.

The thing about Alec is that he has no indoor voice—instead of speaking to you, he broadcasts. Many people in gaming are like this. It's just one more form of human behaviour that's being reclassified as an offshoot of autism. Kaitlin can't finish her hugging machine soon enough.

In spite of his too-loud voice, Alec had a good point. "It's all about authorship. We work so hard on these games, but it's like our voices don't matter. That guy from the Atari 2600 game had to make himself count."

On the spot, I renewed my earlier vow to sabotage the game—except now I wasn't sabotaging BoardX with a turtle, I was sabotaging SpriteQuest with Prince Amulon.

• • •

John Doe ordered up a 50/50 regular/decaf from the floor's new and swanky watch-while-I-make-it-from-freshly-ground-beans machine. Evil Mark saw him do this and asked, "John, how can you drink half-and-half crap?"

"It's like trying to reconcile wave-particle duality," John Doe replied. "You can't taste the caffeinated brew at the same time you taste the decaf—or vice versa. You can only taste one or the other. So it's like two beverages in one."

"I've never thought of it that way before."

"You shouldn't be so quick to judge, Mark."

Bree was right there: "John, I think you're binarizing a complex taste situation. I don't think it's that simplistic."

"Bree, is it wrong to try to make some sense of this chaotic world?"

As a joke, I asked Bree if she was taking coffee-tasting lessons, and it turns out she *is*. "The French take their coffee seriously, but I'm still trying to get past the café-au-lait-in-the-morning issue," she confessed. "It tastes like something a cartoon character would drink. Imagine Secret Squirrel getting up at five-thirty a.m., fighting a wicked macadamia hangover, groping for something, anything, to make the pain go away—and he reaches for a café au lait. I think I need to study this a bit more."

• • •

Evil Mark stood up in the middle of the afternoon and said, "I'm about to hand out sheets listing the 8,363 prime numbers between 10,000 and 100,000. Embedded in this list of numbers is one non-prime. First person to find that non-prime number wins my *Family Guy* promotional sixteen-ounce beer cozy."

In less than five minutes I won.

FUN FACT: any even number can be made by adding together two primes.

• • •

```
10007  10009  10037  10039  10061  10067  10069  10079  10091
10093  10099  10103  10111  10133  10139  10141  10151  10159
10163  10169  10177  10181  10193  10211  10223  10243  10247
10253  10259  10267  10271  10273  10289  10301  10303  10313
10321  10331  10333  10337  10343  10357  10369  10391  10399
10427  10429  10433  10453  10457  10459  10463  10477  10487
10499  10501  10513  10529  10531  10559  10567  10589  10597
10601  10607  10613  10627  10631  10639  10651  10657  10663
10667  10687  10691  10709  10711  10723  10729  10733  10739
10753  10771  10781  10789  10799  10831  10837  10847  10853
10859  10861  10867  10883  10889  10891  10903  10909  10937
10939  10949  10957  10973  10979  10987  10993  11003  11027
11047  11057  11059  11069  11071  11083  11087  11093  11113
11117  11119  11131  11149  11159  11161  11171  11173  11177
11197  11213  11239  11243  11251  11257  11261  11273  11279
11287  11299  11311  11317  11321  11329  11351  11353  11369
11383  11393  11399  11411  11423  11437  11443  11447  11467
11471  11483  11489  11491  11497  11503  11519  11527  11549
11551  11579  11587  11593  11597  11617  11621  11633  11657
11677  11681  11689  11699  11701  11717  11719  11731  11743
11777  11779  11783  11789  11801  11807  11813  11821  11827
11831  11833  11839  11863  11867  11887  11897  11903  11909
11923  11927  11933  11939  11941  11953  11959  11969  11971
11981  11987  12007  12011  12037  12041  12043  12049  12071
12073  12097  12101  12107  12109  12113  12119  12143  12149
12157  12161  12163  12197  12203  12211  12227  12239  12241
12251  12253  12263  12269  12277  12281  12289  12301  12323
12329  12343  12347  12373  12377  12379  12391  12401  12409
12413  12421  12433  12437  12451  12457  12473  12479  12487
12491  12497  12503  12511  12517  12527  12539  12541  12547
12553  12569  12577  12583  12589  12601  12611  12613  12619
12637  12641  12647  12653  12659  12671  12689  12697  12703
12713  12721  12739  12743  12757  12763  12781  12791  12799
12809  12821  12823  12829  12841  12853  12889  12893  12899
12907  12911  12917  12919  12923  12941  12953  12959  12967
12973  12979  12983  13001  13003  13007  13009  13033  13037
13043  13049  13063  13093  13099  13103  13109  13121  13127
13147  13151  13159  13163  13171  13177  13183  13187  13217
13219  13229  13241  13249  13259  13267  13291  13297  13309
13313  13327  13331  13337  13339  13367  13381  13397  13399
13411  13417  13421  13441  13451  13457  13463  13469  13477
```

13487 13499 13513 13523 13537 13553 13567 13577 13591
13597 13613 13619 13627 13633 13649 13669 13679 13681
13687 13691 13693 13697 13709 13711 13721 13723 13729
13751 13757 13759 13763 13781 13789 13799 13807 13829
13831 13841 13859 13873 13877 13879 13883 13901 13903
13907 13913 13921 13931 13933 13963 13967 13997 13999
14009 14011 14029 14033 14051 14057 14071 14081 14083
14087 14107 14143 14149 14153 14159 14173 14177 14197
14207 14221 14243 14249 14251 14281 14293 14303 14321
14323 14327 14341 14347 14369 14387 14389 14401 14407
14411 14419 14423 14431 14437 14447 14449 14461 14479
14489 14503 14519 14533 14537 14543 14549 14551 14557
14561 14563 14591 14593 14621 14627 14629 14633 14639
14653 14657 14669 14683 14699 14713 14717 14723 14731
14737 14741 14747 14753 14759 14767 14771 14779 14783
14797 14813 14821 14827 14831 14843 14851 14867 14869
14879 14887 14891 14897 14923 14929 14939 14947 14951
14957 14969 14983 15013 15017 15031 15053 15061 15073
15077 15083 15091 15101 15107 15121 15131 15137 15139
15149 15161 15173 15187 15193 15199 15217 15227 15233
15241 15259 15263 15269 15271 15277 15287 15289 15299
15307 15313 15319 15329 15331 15349 15359 15361 15373
15377 15383 15391 15401 15413 15427 15439 15443 15451
15461 15467 15473 15493 15497 15511 15527 15541 15551
15559 15569 15581 15583 15601 15607 15619 15629 15641
15643 15647 15649 15661 15667 15671 15679 15683 15727
15731 15733 15737 15739 15749 15761 15767 15773 15787
15791 15797 15803 15809 15817 15823 15859 15877 15881
15887 15889 15901 15907 15913 15919 15923 15937 15959
15971 15973 15991 16001 16007 16033 16057 16061 16063
16067 16069 16073 16087 16091 16097 16103 16111 16127
16139 16141 16183 16187 16189 16193 16217 16223 16229
16231 16249 16253 16267 16273 16301 16319 16333 16339
16349 16361 16363 16369 16381 16411 16417 16421 16427
16433 16447 16451 16453 16477 16481 16487 16493 16519
16529 16547 16553 16561 16567 16573 16603 16607 16619
16631 16633 16649 16651 16657 16661 16673 16691 16693
16699 16703 16729 16741 16747 16759 16763 16787 16811
16823 16829 16831 16843 16871 16879 16883 16889 16901
16903 16921 16927 16931 16937 16943 16963 16979 16981
16987 16993 17011 17021 17027 17029 17033 17041 17047

17053 17077 17093 17099 17107 17117 17123 17137 17159
17167 17183 17189 17191 17203 17207 17209 17231 17239
17257 17291 17293 17299 17317 17321 17327 17333 17341
17351 17359 17377 17383 17387 17389 17393 17401 17417
17419 17431 17443 17449 17467 17471 17477 17483 17489
17491 17497 17509 17519 17539 17551 17569 17573 17579
17581 17597 17599 17609 17623 17627 17657 17659 17669
17681 17683 17707 17713 17729 17737 17747 17749 17761
17783 17789 17791 17807 17827 17837 17839 17851 17863
17881 17891 17903 17909 17911 17921 17923 17929 17939
17957 17959 17971 17977 17981 17987 17989 18013 18041
18043 18047 18049 18059 18061 18077 18089 18097 18119
18121 18127 18131 18133 18143 18149 18169 18181 18191
18199 18211 18217 18223 18229 18233 18251 18253 18257
18269 18287 18289 18301 18307 18311 18313 18329 18341
18353 18367 18371 18379 18397 18401 18413 18427 18433
18439 18443 18451 18457 18461 18481 18493 18503 18517
18521 18523 18539 18541 18553 18583 18587 18593 18617
18637 18661 18671 18679 18691 18701 18713 18719 18731
18743 18749 18757 18773 18787 18793 18797 18803 18839
18859 18869 18899 18911 18913 18917 18919 18947 18959
18973 18979 19001 19009 19013 19031 19037 19051 19069
19073 19079 19081 19087 19121 19139 19141 19157 19163
19181 19183 19207 19211 19213 19219 19231 19237 19249
19259 19267 19273 19289 19301 19309 19319 19333 19373
19379 19381 19387 19391 19403 19417 19421 19423 19427
19429 19433 19441 19447 19457 19463 19469 19471 19477
19483 19489 19501 19507 19531 19541 19543 19553 19559
19571 19577 19583 19597 19603 19609 19661 19681 19687
19697 19699 19709 19717 19727 19739 19751 19753 19759
19763 19777 19793 19801 19813 19819 19841 19843 19853
19861 19867 19889 19891 19913 19919 19927 19937 19949
19961 19963 19973 19979 19991 19993 19997 20011 20021
20023 20029 20047 20051 20063 20071 20089 20101 20107
20113 20117 20123 20129 20143 20147 20149 20161 20173
20177 20183 20201 20219 20231 20233 20249 20261 20269
20287 20297 20323 20327 20333 20341 20347 20353 20357
20359 20369 20389 20393 20399 20407 20411 20431 20441
20443 20477 20479 20483 20507 20509 20521 20533 20543
20549 20551 20563 20593 20599 20611 20627 20639 20641
20663 20681 20693 20707 20717 20719 20731 20743 20747

20749 20753 20759 20771 20773 20789 20807 20809 20849
20857 20873 20879 20887 20897 20899 20903 20921 20929
20939 20947 20959 20963 20981 20983 21001 21011 21013
21017 21019 21023 21031 21059 21061 21067 21089 21101
21107 21121 21139 21143 21149 21157 21163 21169 21179
21187 21191 21193 21211 21221 21227 21247 21269 21277
21283 21313 21317 21319 21323 21341 21347 21377 21379
21383 21391 21397 21401 21407 21419 21433 21467 21481
21487 21491 21493 21499 21503 21517 21521 21523 21529
21557 21559 21563 21569 21577 21587 21589 21599 21601
21611 21613 21617 21647 21649 21661 21673 21683 21701
21713 21727 21737 21739 21751 21757 21767 21773 21787
21799 21803 21817 21821 21839 21841 21851 21859 21863
21871 21881 21893 21911 21929 21937 21943 21961 21977
21991 21997 22003 22013 22027 22031 22037 22039 22051
22063 22067 22073 22079 22091 22093 22109 22111 22123
22129 22133 22147 22153 22157 22159 22171 22189 22193
22229 22247 22259 22271 22273 22277 22279 22283 22291
22303 22307 22343 22349 22367 22369 22381 22391 22397
22409 22433 22441 22447 22453 22469 22481 22483 22501
22511 22531 22541 22543 22549 22567 22571 22573 22613
22619 22621 22637 22639 22643 22651 22669 22679 22691
22697 22699 22709 22717 22721 22727 22739 22741 22751
22769 22777 22783 22787 22807 22811 22817 22853 22859
22861 22871 22877 22901 22907 22921 22937 22943 22961
22963 22973 22993 23003 23011 23017 23021 23027 23029
23039 23041 23053 23057 23059 23063 23071 23081 23087
23099 23117 23131 23143 23159 23167 23173 23189 23197
23201 23203 23209 23227 23251 23269 23279 23291 23293
23297 23311 23321 23327 23333 23339 23357 23369 23371
23399 23417 23431 23447 23459 23473 23497 23509 23531
23537 23539 23549 23557 23561 23563 23567 23581 23593
23599 23603 23609 23623 23627 23629 23633 23663 23669
23671 23677 23687 23689 23719 23741 23743 23747 23753
23761 23767 23773 23789 23801 23813 23819 23827 23831
23833 23857 23869 23873 23879 23887 23893 23899 23909
23911 23917 23929 23957 23971 23977 23981 23993 24001
24007 24019 24023 24029 24043 24049 24061 24071 24077
24083 24091 24097 24103 24107 24109 24113 24121 24133
24137 24151 24169 24179 24181 24197 24203 24223 24229
24239 24247 24251 24281 24317 24329 24337 24359 24371

24373 24379 24391 24407 24413 24419 24421 24439 24443
24469 24473 24481 24499 24509 24517 24527 24533 24547
24551 24571 24593 24611 24623 24631 24659 24671 24677
24683 24691 24697 24709 24733 24749 24763 24767 24781
24793 24799 24809 24821 24841 24847 24851 24859 24877
24889 24907 24917 24919 24923 24943 24953 24967 24971
24977 24979 24989 25013 25031 25033 25037 25057 25073
25087 25097 25111 25117 25121 25127 25147 25153 25163
25169 25171 25183 25189 25219 25229 25237 25243 25247
25253 25261 25301 25303 25307 25309 25321 25339 25343
25349 25357 25367 25373 25391 25409 25411 25423 25439
25447 25453 25457 25463 25469 25471 25523 25537 25541
25561 25577 25579 25583 25589 25601 25603 25609 25621
25633 25639 25643 25657 25667 25673 25679 25693 25703
25717 25733 25741 25747 25759 25763 25771 25793 25799
25801 25819 25841 25847 25849 25867 25873 25889 25903
25913 25919 25931 25933 25939 25943 25951 25969 25981
25997 25999 26003 26017 26021 26029 26041 26053 26083
26099 26107 26111 26113 26119 26141 26153 26161 26171
26177 26183 26189 26203 26209 26227 26237 26249 26251
26261 26263 26267 26293 26297 26309 26317 26321 26339
26347 26357 26371 26387 26393 26399 26407 26417 26423
26431 26437 26449 26459 26479 26489 26497 26501 26513
26539 26557 26561 26573 26591 26597 26627 26633 26641
26647 26669 26681 26683 26687 26693 26699 26701 26711
26713 26717 26723 26729 26731 26737 26759 26777 26783
26801 26813 26821 26833 26839 26849 26861 26863 26879
26881 26891 26893 26903 26921 26927 26947 26951 26953
26959 26981 26987 26993 27011 27017 27031 27043 27059
27061 27067 27073 27077 27091 27103 27107 27109 27127
27143 27179 27191 27197 27211 27239 27241 27253 27259
27271 27277 27281 27283 27299 27329 27337 27361 27367
27397 27407 27409 27427 27431 27437 27449 27457 27479
27481 27487 27509 27527 27529 27539 27541 27551 27581
27583 27611 27617 27631 27647 27653 27673 27689 27691
27697 27701 27733 27737 27739 27743 27749 27751 27763
27767 27773 27779 27791 27793 27799 27803 27809 27817
27823 27827 27847 27851 27883 27893 27901 27917 27919
27941 27943 27947 27953 27961 27967 27983 27997 28001
28019 28027 28031 28051 28057 28069 28081 28087 28097
28099 28109 28111 28123 28151 28163 28181 28183 28201

28211 28219 28229 28277 28279 28283 28289 28297 28307
28309 28319 28349 28351 28387 28393 28403 28409 28411
28429 28433 28439 28447 28463 28477 28493 28499 28513
28517 28537 28541 28547 28549 28559 28571 28573 28579
28591 28597 28603 28607 28619 28621 28627 28631 28643
28649 28657 28661 28663 28669 28687 28697 28703 28711
28723 28729 28751 28753 28759 28771 28789 28793 28807
28813 28817 28837 28843 28859 28867 28871 28879 28901
28909 28921 28927 28933 28949 28961 28979 29009 29017
29021 29023 29027 29033 29059 29063 29077 29101 29123
29129 29131 29137 29147 29153 29167 29173 29179 29191
29201 29207 29209 29221 29231 29243 29251 29269 29287
29297 29303 29311 29327 29333 29339 29347 29363 29383
29387 29389 29399 29401 29411 29423 29429 29437 29443
29453 29473 29483 29501 29527 29531 29537 29567 29569
29573 29581 29587 29599 29611 29629 29633 29641 29663
29669 29671 29683 29717 29723 29741 29753 29759 29761
29789 29803 29819 29833 29837 29851 29863 29867 29873
29879 29881 29917 29921 29927 29947 29959 29983 29989
30011 30013 30029 30047 30059 30071 30089 30091 30097
30103 30109 30113 30119 30133 30137 30139 30161 30169
30181 30187 30197 30203 30211 30223 30241 30253 30259
30269 30271 30293 30307 30313 30319 30323 30341 30347
30367 30389 30391 30403 30427 30431 30449 30467 30469
30491 30493 30497 30509 30517 30529 30539 30553 30557
30559 30577 30593 30631 30637 30643 30649 30661 30671
30677 30689 30697 30703 30707 30713 30727 30757 30763
30773 30781 30803 30809 30817 30829 30839 30841 30851
30853 30859 30869 30871 30881 30893 30911 30931 30937
30941 30949 30971 30977 30983 31013 31019 31033 31039
31051 31063 31069 31079 31081 31091 31121 31123 31139
31147 31151 31153 31159 31177 31181 31183 31189 31193
31219 31223 31231 31237 31247 31249 31253 31259 31267
31271 31277 31307 31319 31321 31327 31333 31337 31357
31379 31387 31391 31393 31397 31469 31477 31481 31489
31511 31513 31517 31531 31541 31543 31547 31567 31573
31583 31601 31607 31627 31643 31649 31657 31663 31667
31687 31699 31721 31723 31727 31729 31741 31751 31769
31771 31793 31799 31817 31847 31849 31859 31873 31883
31891 31907 31957 31963 31973 31981 31991 32003 32009
32027 32029 32051 32057 32059 32063 32069 32077 32083

32089 32099 32117 32119 32141 32143 32159 32173 32183
32189 32191 32203 32213 32233 32237 32251 32257 32261
32297 32299 32303 32309 32321 32323 32327 32341 32353
32359 32363 32369 32371 32377 32381 32401 32411 32413
32423 32429 32441 32443 32467 32479 32491 32497 32503
32507 32531 32533 32537 32561 32563 32569 32573 32579
32587 32603 32609 32611 32621 32633 32647 32653 32687
32693 32707 32713 32717 32719 32749 32771 32779 32783
32789 32797 32801 32803 32831 32833 32839 32843 32869
32887 32909 32911 32917 32933 32939 32941 32957 32969
32971 32983 32987 32993 32999 33013 33023 33029 33037
33049 33053 33071 33073 33083 33091 33107 33113 33119
33149 33151 33161 33179 33181 33191 33199 33203 33211
33223 33247 33287 33289 33301 33311 33317 33329 33331
33343 33347 33349 33353 33359 33377 33391 33403 33409
33413 33427 33457 33461 33469 33479 33487 33493 33503
33521 33529 33533 33547 33563 33569 33577 33581 33587
33589 33599 33601 33613 33617 33619 33623 33629 33637
33641 33647 33679 33703 33713 33721 33739 33749 33751
33757 33767 33769 33773 33791 33797 33809 33811 33827
33829 33851 33857 33863 33871 33889 33893 33911 33923
33931 33937 33941 33961 33967 33997 34019 34031 34033
34039 34057 34061 34123 34127 34129 34141 34147 34157
34159 34171 34183 34211 34213 34217 34231 34253 34259
34261 34267 34273 34283 34297 34301 34303 34313 34319
34327 34337 34351 34361 34367 34369 34381 34403 34421
34429 34439 34457 34469 34471 34483 34487 34499 34501
34511 34513 34519 34537 34543 34549 34583 34589 34591
34603 34607 34613 34631 34649 34651 34667 34673 34679
34687 34693 34703 34721 34729 34739 34747 34757 34759
34763 34781 34807 34819 34841 34843 34847 34849 34871
34877 34883 34897 34913 34919 34939 34949 34961 34963
34981 35023 35027 35051 35053 35059 35069 35081 35083
35089 35099 35107 35111 35117 35129 35141 35149 35153
35159 35171 35201 35221 35227 35251 35257 35267 35279
35281 35291 35311 35317 35323 35327 35339 35353 35363
35381 35393 35401 35407 35419 35423 35437 35447 35449
35461 35491 35507 35509 35521 35527 35531 35533 35537
35543 35569 35573 35591 35593 35597 35603 35617 35671
35677 35729 35731 35747 35753 35759 35771 35797 35801
35803 35809 35831 35837 35839 35851 35863 35869 35879

35897 35899 35911 35923 35933 35951 35963 35969 35977
35983 35993 35999 36007 36011 36013 36017 36037 36061
36067 36073 36083 36097 36107 36109 36131 36137 36151
36161 36187 36191 36209 36217 36229 36241 36251 36263
36269 36277 36293 36299 36307 36313 36319 36341 36343
36353 36373 36383 36389 36433 36451 36457 36467 36469
36473 36479 36493 36497 36523 36527 36529 36541 36551
36559 36563 36571 36583 36587 36599 36607 36629 36637
36643 36653 36671 36677 36683 36691 36697 36709 36713
36721 36739 36749 36761 36767 36779 36781 36787 36791
36793 36809 36821 36833 36847 36857 36871 36877 36887
36899 36901 36913 36919 36923 36929 36931 36943 36947
36973 36979 36997 37003 37013 37019 37021 37039 37049
37057 37061 37087 37097 37117 37123 37139 37159 37171
37181 37189 37199 37201 37217 37223 37243 37253 37273
37277 37307 37309 37313 37321 37337 37339 37357 37361
37363 37369 37379 37397 37409 37423 37441 37447 37463
37483 37489 37493 37501 37507 37511 37517 37529 37537
37547 37549 37561 37567 37571 37573 37579 37589 37591
37607 37619 37633 37643 37649 37657 37663 37691 37693
37699 37717 37747 37781 37783 37799 37811 37813 37831
37847 37853 37861 37871 37879 37889 37897 37907 37951
37957 37963 37967 37987 37991 37993 37997 38011 38039
38047 38053 38069 38083 38113 38119 38149 38153 38167
38177 38183 38189 38197 38201 38219 38231 38237 38239
38261 38273 38281 38287 38299 38303 38317 38321 38327
38329 38333 38351 38371 38377 38393 38431 38447 38449
38453 38459 38461 38501 38543 38557 38561 38567 38569
38593 38603 38609 38611 38629 38639 38651 38653 38669
38671 38677 38693 38699 38707 38711 38713 38723 38729
38737 38747 38749 38767 38783 38791 38803 38821 38833
38839 38851 38861 38867 38873 38891 38903 38917 38921
38923 38933 38953 38959 38971 38977 38993 39019 39023
39041 39043 39047 39079 39089 39097 39103 39107 39113
39119 39133 39139 39157 39161 39163 39181 39191 39199
39209 39217 39227 39229 39233 39239 39241 39251 39293
39301 39313 39317 39323 39341 39343 39359 39367 39371
39373 39383 39397 39409 39419 39439 39443 39451 39461
39499 39503 39509 39511 39521 39541 39551 39563 39569
39581 39607 39619 39623 39631 39659 39667 39671 39679
39703 39709 39719 39727 39733 39749 39761 39769 39779

39791 39799 39821 39827 39829 39839 39841 39847 39857
39863 39869 39877 39883 39887 39901 39929 39937 39953
39971 39979 39983 39989 40009 40013 40031 40037 40039
40063 40087 40093 40099 40111 40123 40127 40129 40151
40153 40163 40169 40177 40189 40193 40213 40231 40237
40241 40253 40277 40283 40289 40343 40351 40357 40361
40387 40423 40427 40429 40433 40459 40471 40483 40487
40493 40499 40507 40519 40529 40531 40543 40559 40577
40583 40591 40597 40609 40627 40637 40639 40693 40697
40699 40709 40739 40751 40759 40763 40771 40787 40801
40813 40819 40823 40829 40841 40847 40849 40853 40867
40879 40883 40897 40903 40927 40933 40939 40949 40961
40973 40993 41011 41017 41023 41039 41047 41051 41057
41077 41081 41113 41117 41131 41141 41143 41149 41161
41177 41179 41183 41189 41201 41203 41213 41221 41227
41231 41233 41243 41257 41263 41269 41281 41299 41333
41341 41351 41357 41381 41387 41389 41399 41411 41413
41443 41453 41467 41479 41491 41507 41513 41519 41521
41539 41543 41549 41579 41593 41597 41603 41609 41611
41617 41621 41627 41641 41647 41651 41659 41669 41681
41687 41719 41729 41737 41759 41761 41771 41777 41801
41809 41813 41843 41849 41851 41863 41879 41887 41893
41897 41903 41911 41927 41941 41947 41953 41957 41959
41969 41981 41983 41999 42013 42017 42019 42023 42043
42061 42071 42073 42083 42089 42101 42131 42139 42157
42169 42179 42181 42187 42193 42197 42209 42221 42223
42227 42239 42257 42281 42283 42293 42299 42307 42323
42331 42337 42349 42359 42373 42379 42391 42397 42403
42407 42409 42433 42437 42443 42451 42457 42461 42463
42467 42473 42487 42491 42499 42509 42533 42557 42569
42571 42577 42589 42611 42641 42643 42649 42667 42677
42683 42689 42697 42701 42703 42709 42719 42727 42737
42743 42751 42767 42773 42787 42793 42797 42821 42829
42839 42841 42853 42859 42863 42899 42901 42923 42929
42937 42943 42953 42961 42967 42979 42989 43003 43013
43019 43037 43049 43051 43063 43067 43093 43103 43117
43133 43151 43159 43177 43189 43201 43207 43223 43237
43261 43271 43283 43291 43313 43319 43321 43331 43391
43397 43399 43403 43411 43427 43441 43451 43457 43481
43487 43499 43517 43541 43543 43573 43577 43579 43591
43597 43607 43609 43613 43627 43633 43649 43651 43661

43669 43691 43711 43717 43721 43753 43759 43777 43781
43783 43787 43789 43793 43801 43853 43867 43889 43891
43913 43933 43943 43951 43961 43963 43969 43973 43987
43991 43997 44017 44021 44027 44029 44041 44053 44059
44071 44087 44089 44101 44111 44119 44123 44129 44131
44159 44171 44179 44189 44201 44203 44207 44221 44249
44257 44263 44267 44269 44273 44279 44281 44293 44351
44357 44371 44381 44383 44389 44417 44449 44453 44483
44491 44497 44501 44507 44519 44531 44533 44537 44543
44549 44563 44579 44587 44617 44621 44623 44633 44641
44647 44651 44657 44683 44687 44699 44701 44711 44729
44741 44753 44771 44773 44777 44789 44797 44809 44819
44839 44843 44851 44867 44879 44887 44893 44909 44917
44927 44939 44953 44959 44963 44971 44983 44987 45007
45013 45053 45061 45077 45083 45119 45121 45127 45131
45137 45139 45161 45179 45181 45191 45197 45233 45247
45259 45263 45281 45289 45293 45307 45317 45319 45329
45337 45341 45343 45361 45377 45389 45403 45413 45427
45433 45439 45481 45491 45497 45503 45523 45533 45541
45553 45557 45569 45587 45589 45599 45613 45631 45641
45659 45667 45673 45677 45691 45697 45707 45737 45751
45757 45763 45767 45779 45817 45821 45823 45827 45833
45841 45853 45863 45869 45887 45893 45943 45949 45953
45959 45971 45979 45989 46021 46027 46049 46051 46061
46073 46091 46093 46099 46103 46133 46141 46147 46153
46171 46181 46183 46187 46199 46219 46229 46237 46261
46271 46273 46279 46301 46307 46309 46327 46337 46349
46351 46381 46399 46411 46439 46441 46447 46451 46457
46471 46477 46489 46499 46507 46511 46523 46549 46559
46567 46573 46589 46591 46601 46619 46633 46639 46643
46649 46663 46679 46681 46687 46691 46703 46723 46727
46747 46751 46757 46769 46771 46807 46811 46817 46819
46829 46831 46853 46861 46867 46877 46889 46901 46919
46933 46957 46993 46997 47017 47041 47051 47057 47059
47087 47093 47111 47119 47123 47129 47137 47143 47147
47149 47161 47189 47207 47221 47237 47251 47269 47279
47287 47293 47297 47303 47309 47317 47339 47351 47353
47363 47381 47387 47389 47407 47417 47419 47431 47441
47459 47491 47497 47501 47507 47513 47521 47527 47533
47543 47563 47569 47581 47591 47599 47609 47623 47629
47639 47653 47657 47659 47681 47699 47701 47711 47713

47717 47737 47741 47743 47777 47779 47791 47797 47807
47809 47819 47837 47843 47857 47869 47881 47903 47911
47917 47933 47939 47947 47951 47963 47969 47977 47981
48017 48023 48029 48049 48073 48079 48091 48109 48119
48121 48131 48157 48163 48179 48187 48193 48197 48221
48239 48247 48259 48271 48281 48299 48311 48313 48337
48341 48353 48371 48383 48397 48407 48409 48413 48437
48449 48463 48473 48479 48481 48487 48491 48497 48523
48527 48533 48539 48541 48563 48571 48589 48593 48611
48619 48623 48647 48649 48661 48673 48677 48679 48731
48733 48751 48757 48761 48767 48779 48781 48787 48799
48809 48817 48821 48823 48847 48857 48859 48869 48871
48883 48889 48907 48947 48953 48973 48989 48991 49003
49009 49019 49031 49033 49037 49043 49057 49069 49081
49103 49109 49117 49121 49123 49139 49157 49169 49171
49177 49193 49199 49201 49207 49211 49223 49253 49261
49277 49279 49297 49307 49331 49333 49339 49363 49367
49369 49391 49393 49409 49411 49417 49429 49433 49451
49459 49463 49477 49481 49499 49523 49529 49531 49537
49547 49549 49559 49597 49603 49613 49627 49633 49639
49663 49667 49669 49681 49697 49711 49727 49739 49741
49747 49757 49783 49787 49789 49801 49807 49811 49823
49831 49843 49853 49871 49877 49891 49919 49921 49927
49937 49939 49943 49957 49991 49993 49999 50021 50023
50033 50047 50051 50053 50069 50077 50087 50093 50101
50111 50119 50123 50129 50131 50147 50153 50159 50177
50207 50221 50227 50231 50261 50263 50273 50287 50291
50311 50321 50329 50333 50341 50359 50363 50377 50383
50387 50411 50417 50423 50441 50459 50461 50497 50503
50513 50527 50539 50543 50549 50551 50581 50587 50591
50593 50599 50627 50647 50651 50671 50683 50707 50723
50741 50753 50767 50773 50777 50789 50821 50833 50839
50849 50857 50867 50873 50891 50893 50909 50923 50929
50951 50957 50969 50971 50989 50993 51001 51031 51043
51047 51059 51061 51071 51109 51131 51133 51137 51151
51157 51169 51193 51197 51199 51203 51217 51229 51239
51241 51257 51263 51283 51287 51307 51329 51341 51343
51347 51349 51361 51383 51407 51413 51419 51421 51427
51431 51437 51439 51449 51461 51473 51479 51481 51487
51503 51511 51517 51521 51539 51551 51563 51577 51581
51593 51599 51607 51613 51631 51637 51647 51659 51673

51679 51683 51691 51713 51719 51721 51749 51767 51769
51787 51797 51803 51817 51827 51829 51839 51853 51859
51869 51871 51893 51899 51907 51913 51929 51941 51949
51971 51973 51977 51991 52009 52021 52027 52051 52057
52067 52069 52081 52103 52121 52127 52147 52153 52163
52177 52181 52183 52189 52201 52223 52237 52249 52253
52259 52267 52289 52291 52301 52313 52321 52361 52363
52369 52379 52387 52391 52433 52453 52457 52489 52501
52511 52517 52529 52541 52543 52553 52561 52567 52571
52579 52583 52609 52627 52631 52639 52667 52673 52691
52697 52709 52711 52721 52727 52733 52747 52757 52769
52783 52807 52813 52817 52837 52859 52861 52879 52883
52889 52901 52903 52919 52937 52951 52957 52963 52967
52973 52981 52999 53003 53017 53047 53051 53069 53077
53087 53089 53093 53101 53113 53117 53129 53147 53149
53161 53171 53173 53189 53197 53201 53231 53233 53239
53267 53269 53279 53281 53299 53309 53323 53327 53353
53359 53377 53381 53401 53407 53411 53419 53437 53441
53453 53479 53503 53507 53527 53549 53551 53569 53591
53593 53597 53609 53611 53617 53623 53629 53633 53639
53653 53657 53681 53693 53699 53717 53719 53731 53759
53773 53777 53783 53791 53813 53819 53831 53849 53857
53861 53881 53887 53891 53897 53899 53917 53923 53927
53939 53951 53959 53987 53993 54001 54011 54013 54037
54049 54059 54083 54091 54101 54121 54133 54139 54151
54163 54167 54181 54193 54217 54251 54269 54277 54287
54293 54311 54319 54323 54331 54347 54361 54367 54371
54377 54401 54403 54409 54413 54419 54421 54437 54443
54449 54469 54493 54497 54499 54503 54517 54521 54539
54541 54547 54559 54563 54577 54581 54583 54601 54617
54623 54629 54631 54647 54667 54673 54679 54709 54713
54721 54727 54751 54767 54773 54779 54787 54799 54829
54833 54851 54869 54877 54881 54907 54917 54919 54941
54949 54959 54973 54979 54983 55001 55009 55021 55049
55051 55057 55061 55073 55079 55103 55109 55117 55127
55147 55163 55171 55201 55207 55213 55217 55219 55229
55243 55249 55259 55291 55313 55331 55333 55337 55339
55343 55351 55373 55381 55399 55411 55439 55441 55457
55469 55487 55501 55511 55529 55541 55547 55579 55589
55603 55609 55619 55621 55631 55633 55639 55661 55663
55667 55673 55681 55691 55697 55711 55717 55721 55733

55763 55787 55793 55799 55807 55813 55817 55819 55823
55829 55837 55843 55849 55871 55889 55897 55901 55903
55921 55927 55931 55933 55949 55967 55987 55997 56003
56009 56039 56041 56053 56081 56087 56093 56099 56101
56113 56123 56131 56149 56167 56171 56179 56197 56207
56209 56237 56239 56249 56263 56267 56269 56299 56311
56333 56359 56369 56377 56383 56393 56401 56417 56431
56437 56443 56453 56467 56473 56477 56479 56489 56501
56503 56509 56519 56527 56531 56533 56543 56569 56591
56597 56599 56611 56629 56633 56659 56663 56671 56681
56687 56701 56711 56713 56731 56737 56747 56767 56773
56779 56783 56807 56809 56813 56821 56827 56843 56857
56873 56891 56893 56897 56909 56911 56921 56923 56929
56941 56951 56957 56963 56983 56989 56993 56999 57037
57041 57047 57059 57073 57077 57089 57097 57107 57119
57131 57139 57143 57149 57163 57173 57179 57191 57193
57203 57221 57223 57241 57251 57259 57269 57271 57283
57287 57301 57329 57331 57347 57349 57367 57373 57383
57389 57397 57413 57427 57457 57467 57487 57493 57503
57527 57529 57557 57559 57571 57587 57593 57601 57637
57641 57649 57653 57667 57679 57689 57697 57709 57713
57719 57727 57731 57737 57751 57773 57781 57787 57791
57793 57803 57809 57829 57839 57847 57853 57859 57881
57899 57901 57917 57923 57943 57947 57973 57977 57991
58013 58027 58031 58043 58049 58057 58061 58067 58073
58099 58109 58111 58129 58147 58151 58153 58169 58171
58189 58193 58199 58207 58211 58217 58229 58231 58237
58243 58271 58309 58313 58321 58337 58363 58367 58369
58379 58391 58393 58403 58411 58417 58427 58439 58441
58451 58453 58477 58481 58511 58537 58543 58549 58567
58573 58579 58601 58603 58613 58631 58657 58661 58679
58687 58693 58699 58711 58727 58733 58741 58757 58763
58771 58787 58789 58831 58889 58897 58901 58907 58909
58913 58921 58937 58943 58963 58967 58979 58991 58997
59009 59011 59021 59023 59029 59051 59053 59063 59069
59077 59083 59093 59107 59113 59119 59123 59141 59149
59159 59167 59183 59197 59207 59209 59219 59221 59233
59239 59243 59263 59273 59281 59333 59341 59351 59357
59359 59369 59377 59387 59393 59399 59407 59417 59419
59441 59443 59447 59453 59467 59471 59473 59497 59509
59513 59539 59557 59561 59567 59581 59611 59617 59621

59627 59629 59651 59659 59663 59669 59671 59693 59699
59707 59723 59729 59743 59747 59753 59771 59779 59791
59797 59809 59833 59863 59879 59887 59921 59929 59951
59957 59971 59981 59999 60013 60017 60029 60037 60041
60077 60083 60089 60091 60101 60103 60107 60127 60133
60139 60149 60161 60167 60169 60209 60217 60223 60251
60257 60259 60271 60289 60293 60317 60331 60337 60343
60353 60373 60383 60397 60413 60427 60443 60449 60457
60493 60497 60509 60521 60527 60539 60589 60601 60607
60611 60617 60623 60631 60637 60647 60649 60659 60661
60679 60689 60703 60719 60727 60733 60737 60757 60761
60763 60773 60779 60793 60811 60821 60859 60869 60887
60889 60899 60901 60913 60917 60919 60923 60937 60943
60953 60961 61001 61007 61027 61031 61043 61051 61057
61091 61099 61121 61129 61141 61151 61153 61169 61211
61223 61231 61253 61261 61283 61291 61297 61331 61333
61339 61343 61357 61363 61379 61381 61403 61409 61417
61441 61463 61469 61471 61483 61487 61493 61507 61511
61519 61543 61547 61553 61559 61561 61583 61603 61609
61613 61627 61631 61637 61643 61651 61657 61667 61673
61681 61687 61703 61717 61723 61729 61751 61757 61781
61813 61819 61837 61843 61861 61871 61879 61909 61927
61933 61949 61961 61967 61979 61981 61987 61991 62003
62011 62017 62039 62047 62053 62057 62071 62081 62099
62119 62129 62131 62137 62141 62143 62171 62189 62191
62201 62207 62213 62219 62233 62273 62297 62299 62303
62311 62323 62327 62347 62351 62383 62401 62417 62423
62459 62467 62473 62477 62483 62497 62501 62507 62533
62539 62549 62563 62581 62591 62597 62603 62617 62627
62633 62639 62653 62659 62683 62687 62701 62723 62731
62743 62753 62761 62773 62791 62801 62819 62827 62851
62861 62869 62873 62897 62903 62921 62927 62929 62939
62969 62971 62981 62983 62987 62989 63029 63031 63059
63067 63073 63079 63097 63103 63113 63127 63131 63149
63179 63197 63199 63211 63241 63247 63277 63281 63299
63311 63313 63317 63331 63337 63347 63353 63361 63367
63377 63389 63391 63397 63409 63419 63421 63439 63443
63463 63467 63473 63487 63493 63499 63521 63527 63533
63541 63559 63577 63587 63589 63599 63601 63607 63611
63617 63629 63647 63649 63659 63667 63671 63689 63691
63697 63703 63709 63719 63727 63737 63743 63761 63773

63781 63793 63799 63803 63809 63823 63839 63841 63853
63857 63863 63901 63907 63913 63929 63949 63977 63997
64007 64013 64019 64033 64037 64063 64067 64081 64091
64109 64123 64151 64153 64157 64171 64187 64189 64217
64223 64231 64237 64271 64279 64283 64301 64303 64319
64327 64333 64373 64381 64399 64403 64433 64439 64451
64453 64483 64489 64499 64513 64553 64567 64577 64579
64591 64601 64609 64613 64621 64627 64633 64661 64663
64667 64679 64693 64709 64717 64747 64763 64781 64783
64793 64811 64817 64849 64853 64871 64877 64879 64891
64901 64919 64921 64927 64937 64951 64969 64997 65003
65011 65027 65029 65033 65053 65063 65071 65089 65099
65101 65111 65119 65123 65129 65141 65147 65167 65171
65173 65179 65183 65203 65213 65239 65257 65267 65269
65287 65293 65309 65323 65327 65353 65357 65371 65381
65393 65407 65413 65419 65423 65437 65447 65449 65479
65497 65519 65521 65537 65539 65543 65551 65557 65563
65579 65581 65587 65599 65609 65617 65629 65633 65647
65651 65657 65677 65687 65699 65701 65707 65713 65717
65719 65729 65731 65761 65777 65789 65809 65827 65831
65837 65839 65843 65851 65867 65881 65899 65921 65927
65929 65951 65957 65963 65981 65983 65993 66029 66037
66041 66047 66067 66071 66083 66089 66103 66107 66109
66137 66161 66169 66173 66179 66191 66221 66239 66271
66293 66301 66337 66343 66347 66359 66361 66373 66377
66383 66403 66413 66431 66449 66457 66463 66467 66491
66499 66509 66523 66529 66533 66541 66553 66569 66571
66587 66593 66601 66617 66629 66643 66653 66683 66697
66701 66713 66721 66733 66739 66749 66751 66763 66791
66797 66809 66821 66841 66851 66853 66863 66877 66883
66889 66919 66923 66931 66943 66947 66949 66959 66973
66977 67003 67021 67033 67043 67049 67057 67061 67073
67079 67103 67121 67129 67139 67141 67153 67157 67169
67181 67187 67189 67211 67213 67217 67219 67231 67247
67261 67271 67273 67289 67307 67339 67343 67349 67369
67391 67399 67409 67411 67421 67427 67429 67433 67447
67453 67477 67481 67489 67493 67499 67511 67523 67531
67537 67547 67559 67567 67577 67579 67589 67601 67607
67619 67631 67651 67679 67699 67709 67723 67733 67741
67751 67757 67759 67763 67777 67783 67789 67801 67807
67819 67829 67843 67853 67867 67883 67891 67901 67927

67931 67933 67939 67943 67957 67961 67967 67979 67987
67993 68023 68041 68053 68059 68071 68087 68099 68111
68113 68141 68147 68161 68171 68207 68209 68213 68219
68227 68239 68261 68279 68281 68311 68329 68351 68371
68389 68399 68437 68443 68447 68449 68473 68477 68483
68489 68491 68501 68507 68521 68531 68539 68543 68567
68581 68597 68611 68633 68639 68659 68669 68683 68687
68699 68711 68713 68729 68737 68743 68749 68767 68771
68777 68791 68813 68819 68821 68863 68879 68881 68891
68897 68899 68903 68909 68917 68927 68947 68963 68993
69001 69011 69019 69029 69031 69061 69067 69073 69109
69119 69127 69143 69149 69151 69163 69191 69193 69197
69203 69221 69233 69239 69247 69257 69259 69263 69313
69317 69337 69341 69371 69379 69383 69389 69401 69403
69427 69431 69439 69457 69463 69467 69473 69481 69491
69493 69497 69499 69539 69557 69593 69623 69653 69661
69677 69691 69697 69709 69737 69739 69761 69763 69767
69779 69809 69821 69827 69829 69833 69847 69857 69859
69877 69899 69911 69929 69931 69941 69959 69991 69997
70001 70003 70009 70019 70039 70051 70061 70067 70079
70099 70111 70117 70121 70123 70139 70141 70157 70163
70177 70181 70183 70199 70201 70207 70223 70229 70237
70241 70249 70271 70289 70297 70309 70313 70321 70327
70351 70373 70379 70381 70393 70423 70429 70439 70451
70457 70459 70481 70487 70489 70501 70507 70529 70537
70549 70571 70573 70583 70589 70607 70619 70621 70627
70639 70657 70663 70667 70687 70709 70717 70729 70753
70769 70783 70793 70823 70841 70843 70849 70853 70867
70877 70879 70891 70901 70913 70919 70921 70937 70949
70951 70957 70969 70979 70981 70991 70997 70999 71011
71023 71039 71059 71069 71081 71089 71119 71129 71143
71147 71153 71161 71167 71171 71191 71209 71233 71237
71249 71257 71261 71263 71287 71293 71317 71327 71329
71333 71339 71341 71347 71353 71359 71363 71387 71389
71399 71411 71413 71419 71429 71437 71443 71453 71471
71473 71479 71483 71503 71527 71537 71549 71551 71563
71569 71593 71597 71633 71647 71663 71671 71693 71699
71707 71711 71713 71719 71741 71761 71777 71789 71807
71809 71821 71837 71843 71849 71861 71867 71879 71881
71887 71899 71909 71917 71933 71941 71947 71963 71971
71983 71987 71993 71999 72019 72031 72043 72047 72053

72073 72077 72089 72091 72101 72103 72109 72139 72161
72167 72169 72173 72211 72221 72223 72227 72229 72251
72253 72269 72271 72277 72287 72307 72313 72337 72341
72353 72367 72379 72383 72421 72431 72461 72467 72469
72481 72493 72497 72503 72533 72547 72551 72559 72577
72613 72617 72623 72643 72647 72649 72661 72671 72673
72679 72689 72701 72707 72719 72727 72733 72739 72763
72767 72797 72817 72823 72859 72869 72871 72883 72889
72893 72901 72907 72911 72923 72931 72937 72949 72953
72959 72973 72977 72997 73009 73013 73019 73037 73039
73043 73061 73063 73079 73091 73121 73127 73133 73141
73181 73189 73237 73243 73259 73277 73291 73303 73309
73327 73331 73351 73361 73363 73369 73379 73387 73417
73421 73433 73453 73459 73471 73477 73483 73517 73523
73529 73547 73553 73561 73571 73583 73589 73597 73607
73609 73613 73637 73643 73651 73673 73679 73681 73693
73699 73709 73721 73727 73751 73757 73771 73783 73819
73823 73847 73849 73859 73867 73877 73883 73897 73907
73939 73943 73951 73961 73973 73999 74017 74021 74027
74047 74051 74071 74077 74093 74099 74101 74131 74143
74149 74159 74161 74167 74177 74189 74197 74201 74203
74209 74219 74231 74257 74279 74287 74293 74297 74311
74317 74323 74353 74357 74363 74377 74381 74383 74411
74413 74419 74441 74449 74453 74471 74489 74507 74509
74521 74527 74531 74551 74561 74567 74573 74587 74597
74609 74611 74623 74653 74687 74699 74707 74713 74717
74719 74729 74731 74747 74759 74761 74771 74779 74797
74821 74827 74831 74843 74857 74861 74869 74873 74887
74891 74897 74903 74923 74929 74933 74941 74959 75011
75013 75017 75029 75037 75041 75079 75083 75109 75133
75149 75161 75167 75169 75181 75193 75209 75211 75217
75223 75227 75239 75253 75269 75277 75289 75307 75323
75329 75337 75347 75353 75367 75377 75389 75391 75401
75403 75407 75431 75437 75479 75503 75511 75521 75527
75533 75539 75541 75553 75557 75571 75577 75583 75611
75617 75619 75629 75641 75653 75659 75679 75683 75689
75703 75707 75709 75721 75731 75743 75767 75773 75781
75787 75793 75797 75821 75833 75853 75869 75883 75913
75931 75937 75941 75967 75979 75983 75989 75991 75997
76001 76003 76031 76039 76079 76081 76091 76099 76103
76123 76129 76147 76157 76159 76163 76207 76213 76231

76243 76249 76253 76259 76261 76283 76289 76303 76333
76343 76367 76369 76379 76387 76403 76421 76423 76441
76463 76471 76481 76487 76493 76507 76511 76519 76537
76541 76543 76561 76579 76597 76603 76607 76631 76649
76651 76667 76673 76679 76697 76717 76733 76753 76757
76771 76777 76781 76801 76819 76829 76831 76837 76847
76871 76873 76883 76907 76913 76919 76943 76949 76961
76963 76991 77003 77017 77023 77029 77041 77047 77069
77081 77093 77101 77137 77141 77153 77167 77171 77191
77201 77213 77237 77239 77243 77249 77261 77263 77267
77269 77279 77291 77317 77323 77339 77347 77351 77359
77369 77377 77383 77417 77419 77431 77447 77471 77477
77479 77489 77491 77509 77513 77521 77527 77543 77549
77551 77557 77563 77569 77573 77587 77591 77611 77617
77621 77641 77647 77659 77681 77687 77689 77699 77711
77713 77719 77723 77731 77743 77747 77761 77773 77783
77797 77801 77813 77839 77849 77863 77867 77893 77899
77929 77933 77951 77969 77977 77983 77999 78007 78017
78031 78041 78049 78059 78079 78101 78121 78137 78139
78157 78163 78167 78173 78179 78191 78193 78203 78229
78233 78241 78259 78277 78283 78301 78307 78311 78317
78341 78347 78367 78401 78427 78437 78439 78467 78479
78487 78497 78509 78511 78517 78539 78541 78553 78569
78571 78577 78583 78593 78607 78623 78643 78649 78653
78691 78697 78707 78713 78721 78737 78779 78781 78787
78791 78797 78803 78809 78823 78839 78853 78857 78877
78887 78889 78893 78901 78919 78929 78941 78977 78979
78989 79031 79039 79043 79063 79087 79103 79111 79133
79139 79147 79151 79153 79159 79181 79187 79193 79201
79229 79231 79241 79259 79273 79279 79283 79301 79309
79319 79333 79337 79349 79357 79367 79379 79393 79397
79399 79411 79423 79427 79433 79451 79481 79493 79531
79537 79549 79559 79561 79579 79589 79601 79609 79613
79621 79627 79631 79633 79657 79669 79687 79691 79693
79697 79699 79757 79769 79777 79801 79811 79813 79817
79823 79829 79841 79843 79847 79861 79867 79873 79889
79901 79903 79907 79939 79943 79967 79973 79979 79987
79997 79999 80021 80039 80051 80071 80077 80107 80111
80141 80147 80149 80153 80167 80173 80177 80191 80207
80209 80221 80231 80233 80239 80251 80263 80273 80279
80287 80309 80317 80329 80341 80347 80363 80369 80387

80407 80429 80447 80449 80471 80473 80489 80491 80513
80527 80537 80557 80567 80599 80603 80611 80621 80627
80629 80651 80657 80669 80671 80677 80681 80683 80687
80701 80713 80737 80747 80749 80761 80777 80779 80783
80789 80803 80809 80819 80831 80833 80849 80863 80897
80909 80911 80917 80923 80929 80933 80953 80963 80989
81001 81013 81017 81019 81023 81031 81041 81043 81047
81049 81071 81077 81083 81097 81101 81119 81131 81157
81163 81173 81181 81197 81199 81203 81223 81233 81239
81281 81283 81293 81299 81307 81331 81343 81349 81353
81359 81371 81373 81401 81409 81421 81439 81457 81463
81509 81517 81527 81533 81547 81551 81553 81559 81563
81569 81611 81619 81629 81637 81647 81649 81667 81671
81677 81689 81701 81703 81707 81727 81737 81749 81761
81769 81773 81799 81817 81839 81847 81853 81869 81883
81899 81901 81919 81929 81931 81937 81943 81953 81967
81971 81973 82003 82007 82009 82013 82021 82031 82037
82039 82051 82067 82073 82129 82139 82141 82153 82163
82171 82183 82189 82193 82207 82217 82219 82223 82231
82237 82241 82261 82267 82279 82301 82307 82339 82349
82351 82361 82373 82387 82393 82421 82457 82463 82469
82471 82483 82487 82493 82499 82507 82529 82531 82549
82559 82561 82567 82571 82591 82601 82609 82613 82619
82633 82651 82657 82699 82721 82723 82727 82729 82757
82759 82763 82781 82787 82793 82799 82811 82813 82837
82847 82883 82889 82891 82903 82913 82939 82963 82981
82997 83003 83009 83023 83047 83059 83063 83071 83077
83089 83093 83101 83117 83137 83177 83203 83207 83219
83221 83227 83231 83233 83243 83257 83267 83269 83273
83299 83311 83339 83341 83357 83383 83389 83399 83401
83407 83417 83423 83431 83437 83443 83449 83459 83471
83477 83497 83537 83557 83561 83563 83579 83591 83597
83609 83617 83621 83639 83641 83653 83663 83689 83701
83717 83719 83737 83761 83773 83777 83791 83813 83833
83843 83857 83869 83873 83891 83903 83911 83921 83933
83939 83969 83983 83987 84011 84017 84047 84053 84059
84061 84067 84089 84121 84127 84131 84137 84143 84163
84179 84181 84191 84199 84211 84221 84223 84229 84239
84247 84263 84299 84307 84313 84317 84319 84347 84349
84377 84389 84391 84401 84407 84421 84431 84437 84443
84449 84457 84463 84467 84481 84499 84503 84509 84521

84523 84533 84551 84559 84589 84629 84631 84649 84653
84659 84673 84691 84697 84701 84713 84719 84731 84737
84751 84761 84787 84793 84809 84811 84827 84857 84859
84869 84871 84913 84919 84947 84961 84967 84977 84979
84991 85009 85021 85027 85037 85049 85061 85081 85087
85091 85093 85103 85109 85121 85133 85147 85159 85193
85199 85201 85213 85223 85229 85237 85243 85247 85259
85297 85303 85313 85331 85333 85361 85363 85369 85381
85411 85427 85429 85439 85447 85451 85453 85469 85487
85513 85517 85523 85531 85549 85571 85577 85597 85601
85607 85619 85621 85627 85639 85643 85661 85667 85669
85691 85703 85711 85717 85733 85751 85781 85793 85817
85819 85829 85831 85837 85843 85847 85853 85889 85903
85909 85931 85933 85991 85999 86011 86017 86027 86029
86069 86077 86083 86111 86113 86117 86131 86137 86143
86161 86171 86179 86183 86197 86201 86209 86239 86243
86249 86257 86263 86269 86287 86291 86293 86297 86311
86323 86341 86351 86353 86357 86369 86371 86381 86389
86399 86413 86423 86441 86453 86461 86467 86477 86491
86501 86509 86531 86533 86539 86561 86573 86579 86587
86599 86627 86629 86677 86689 86693 86711 86719 86729
86743 86753 86767 86771 86783 86813 86837 86843 86851
86857 86861 86869 86923 86927 86929 86939 86951 86959
86969 86981 86993 87011 87013 87037 87041 87049 87071
87083 87103 87107 87119 87121 87133 87149 87151 87179
87181 87187 87211 87221 87223 87251 87253 87257 87277
87281 87293 87299 87313 87317 87323 87337 87359 87383
87403 87407 87421 87427 87433 87443 87473 87481 87491
87509 87511 87517 87523 87539 87541 87547 87553 87557
87559 87583 87587 87589 87613 87623 87629 87631 87641
87643 87649 87671 87679 87683 87691 87697 87701 87719
87721 87739 87743 87751 87767 87793 87797 87803 87811
87833 87853 87869 87877 87881 87887 87911 87917 87931
87943 87959 87961 87973 87977 87991 88001 88003 88007
88019 88037 88069 88079 88093 88117 88129 88169 88177
88211 88223 88237 88241 88259 88261 88289 88301 88321
88327 88337 88339 88379 88397 88411 88423 88427 88463
88469 88471 88493 88499 88513 88523 88547 88589 88591
88607 88609 88643 88651 88657 88661 88663 88667 88681
88721 88729 88741 88747 88771 88789 88793 88799 88801
88807 88811 88813 88817 88819 88843 88853 88861 88867

88873 88883 88897 88903 88919 88937 88951 88969 88993
88997 89003 89009 89017 89021 89041 89051 89057 89069
89071 89083 89087 89101 89107 89113 89119 89123 89137
89153 89189 89203 89209 89213 89227 89231 89237 89261
89269 89273 89293 89303 89317 89329 89363 89371 89381
89387 89393 89399 89413 89417 89431 89443 89449 89459
89477 89491 89501 89513 89519 89521 89527 89533 89561
89563 89567 89591 89597 89599 89603 89611 89627 89633
89653 89657 89659 89669 89671 89681 89689 89753 89759
89767 89779 89783 89797 89809 89819 89821 89833 89839
89849 89867 89891 89897 89899 89909 89917 89923 89939
89959 89963 89977 89983 89989 90001 90007 90011 90017
90019 90023 90031 90053 90059 90067 90071 90073 90089
90107 90121 90127 90149 90163 90173 90187 90191 90197
90199 90203 90217 90227 90239 90247 90263 90271 90281
90289 90313 90353 90359 90371 90373 90379 90397 90401
90403 90407 90437 90439 90469 90473 90481 90499 90511
90523 90527 90529 90533 90547 90583 90599 90617 90619
90631 90641 90647 90659 90677 90679 90697 90703 90709
90731 90749 90787 90793 90803 90821 90823 90833 90841
90847 90863 90887 90901 90907 90911 90917 90931 90947
90971 90977 90989 90997 91009 91019 91033 91079 91081
91097 91099 91121 91127 91129 91139 91141 91151 91153
91159 91163 91183 91193 91199 91229 91237 91243 91249
91253 91283 91291 91297 91303 91309 91331 91367 91369
91373 91381 91387 91393 91397 91411 91423 91433 91453
91457 91459 91463 91493 91499 91513 91529 91541 91571
91573 91577 91583 91591 91621 91631 91639 91673 91691
91703 91711 91733 91753 91757 91771 91781 91801 91807
91811 91813 91823 91837 91841 91867 91873 91909 91921
91939 91943 91951 91957 91961 91967 91969 91997 92003
92009 92033 92041 92051 92077 92083 92107 92111 92119
92143 92153 92173 92177 92179 92189 92203 92219 92221
92227 92233 92237 92243 92251 92269 92297 92311 92317
92333 92347 92353 92357 92363 92369 92377 92381 92383
92387 92399 92401 92413 92419 92431 92459 92461 92467
92479 92489 92503 92507 92551 92557 92567 92569 92581
92593 92623 92627 92639 92641 92647 92657 92669 92671
92681 92683 92693 92699 92707 92717 92723 92737 92753
92761 92767 92779 92789 92791 92801 92809 92821 92831
92849 92857 92861 92863 92867 92893 92899 92921 92927

```
92941 92951 92957 92959 92987 92993 93001 93047 93053
93059 93077 93083 93089 93097 93103 93113 93131 93133
93139 93151 93169 93179 93187 93199 93229 93239 93241
93251 93253 93257 93263 93281 93283 93287 93307 93319
93323 93329 93337 93371 93377 93383 93407 93419 93427
93463 93479 93481 93487 93491 93493 93497 93503 93523
93529 93553 93557 93559 93563 93581 93601 93607 93629
93637 93683 93701 93703 93719 93739 93761 93763 93787
93809 93811 93827 93851 93871 93887 93889 93893 93901
93911 93913 93923 93937 93941 93949 93967 93971 93979
93983 93997 94007 94009 94033 94049 94057 94063 94079
94099 94109 94111 94117 94121 94151 94153 94169 94201
94207 94219 94229 94253 94261 94273 94291 94307 94309
94321 94327 94331 94343 94349 94351 94379 94397 94399
94421 94427 94433 94439 94441 94447 94463 94477 94483
94513 94529 94531 94541 94543 94547 94559 94561 94573
94583 94597 94603 94613 94621 94649 94651 94687 94693
94709 94723 94727 94747 94771 94777 94781 94789 94793
94811 94819 94823 94837 94841 94847 94849 94873 94889
94903 94907 94933 94949 94951 94961 94993 94999 95003
95009 95021 95027 95063 95071 95083 95087 95089 95093
95101 95107 95111 95131 95143 95153 95177 95189 95191
95203 95213 95219 95231 95233 95239 95257 95261 95267
95273 95279 95287 95311 95317 95327 95339 95369 95383
95393 95401 95413 95419 95429 95441 95443 95461 95467
95471 95479 95483 95507 95527 95531 95539 95549 95561
95569 95581 95597 95603 95617 95621 95629 95633 95651
95701 95707 95713 95717 95723 95731 95737 95747 95773
95783 95789 95791 95801 95803 95813 95819 95857 95869
95873 95881 95891 95911 95917 95923 95929 95947 95957
95959 95971 95987 95989 96001 96013 96017 96043 96053
96059 96079 96097 96137 96149 96157 96167 96179 96181
96199 96211 96221 96223 96233 96259 96263 96269 96281
96289 96293 96323 96329 96331 96337 96353 96377 96401
96419 96431 96443 96451 96457 96461 96469 96479 96487
96493 96497 96517 96527 96553 96557 96581 96587 96589
96601 96643 96661 96667 96671 96697 96703 96731 96737
96739 96749 96757 96763 96769 96779 96787 96797 96799
96821 96823 96827 96847 96851 96857 96893 96907 96911
96931 96953 96959 96973 96979 96989 96997 97001 97003
97007 97021 97039 97073 97081 97103 97117 97127 97151
```

97157 97159 97169 97171 97177 97187 97213 97231 97241
97259 97283 97301 97303 97327 97367 97369 97373 97379
97381 97387 97397 97423 97429 97441 97453 97459 97463
97499 97501 97511 97523 97547 97549 97553 97561 97571
97577 97579 97583 97607 97609 97613 97649 97651 97673
97687 97711 97729 97771 97777 97787 97789 97813 97829
97841 97843 97847 97849 97859 97861 97871 97879 97883
97919 97927 97931 97943 97961 97967 97973 97987 98009
98011 98017 98041 98047 98057 98081 98101 98123 98129
98143 98179 98207 98213 98221 98227 98251 98257 98269
98297 98299 98317 98321 98323 98327 98347 98369 98377
98387 98389 98407 98411 98419 98429 98443 98453 98459
98467 98473 98479 98491 98507 98519 98533 98543 98561
98563 98573 98597 98621 98627 98639 98641 98663 98669
98689 98711 98713 98717 98729 98731 98737 98773 98779
98801 98807 98809 98837 98849 98867 98869 98873 98887
98893 98897 98899 98909 98911 98927 98929 98939 98947
98953 98963 98981 98993 98999 99013 99017 99023 99041
99053 99079 99083 99089 99103 99109 99119 99131 99133
99137 99139 99149 99173 99181 99191 99223 99233 99241
99251 99257 99259 99277 99289 99317 99347 99349 99367
99371 99377 99391 99397 99401 99409 99431 99439 99469
99487 99497 99523 99527 99529 99551 99559 99563 99571
99577 99581 99607 99611 99623 99643 99661 99667 99679
99689 99707 99709 99713 99719 99721 99733 99761 99767
99787 99793 99809 99817 99823 99829 99833 99839 99859
99871 99877 99881 99901 99907 99923 99929 99961 99971
99989 99991

• • •

When I taped the prime numbers to my cubicle wall and looked at them from a distance, I could see darker and lighter patches within the body of the text that formed interesting shapes and patterns. I bet if I took the time to format the numbers correctly, I could see some sort of hitherto never-before-noticed magical numerical pattern that would allow me to solve the formula for generating prime numbers once and for all. I mentioned this to Cowboy. All he said was, "Maybe, but what if it turns out that the numbers form a kind of Magic Eye image, and when your brain resolves it, you see a goat walking on its hind legs, drinking from a horn full of blood?"

Scotch *that* idea.

• • •

Bree, in her new plan to crack upper management, has decided to can the French stuff and start speaking with a British accent. "It's a proven fact that women with British accents climb corporate ladders much more quickly in North America than those of us who speak with a shopping mall accent."

• • •

The night of Kam Fong's housewarming I was in a testy mood. I'd been inside my head all day—some days that just happens. You get lost doing just one task, and suddenly you look up and it's dark out, but you still don't want to leave your headspace, and then Kaitlin comes up behind you with a 150 KHz marine emergency blow horn and lets off one big parp that has you shitting out your eyes, ears and nostrils, and when you turn around, you discover that your evil co-workers were videoing the entire prank, and you get furious and you scream for everybody to fuck off and die. *Aw shucks, it was only a joke,* but the fact remains that because of that one loud parp you'll never be able to parse C++ code again because you fried those dendrites that dictate logic patterns, and in a flash you see yourself as a future object of pity, forced to work at a TacoTime outlet, feeding disrespectful larvae of the middle classes while taking soiled orange PVC trash bags out to the back alley, where you see a grease stor-age drum and wistfully remember that earlier, more charmed portion of your life when you once knew the chemicals and procedures necessary to convert restaurant grease into clean-burning planet-friendly ethanol, and that was just one of the many feats your brain was capable of, back before the parp-ing, back before people whispered when they saw you walk-ing their way, hoping they wouldn't have to make small talk with you, back before they dumbed themselves down to the verbal level of Pebbles Flintstone to make you understand them.

"Jesus, Ethan, it was just a practical joke," Kaitlin said, as we drove to Kam's housewarming.

"You're not the one who can't do long division any more."

"Get over it. What's the address number again?"

"1388. It ought to be up around this corner."

And it was: a stuccoed candy pink gargoyled fantasia land

designed by a committee of fourteen-year-old girls, a handful of Smurfs and whoever creates carpeted claw-scratching environments for cats. It did have a stunning view of the city, Vancouver Island, the Olympic Peninsula and Mount Baker. Most importantly, flanking the front doors were a pair of New Zealand tree ferns of a type even I knew were expensive and finicky. Underneath the tree fern on the right, beneath leftover Tyvek sheets, pink insulation scraps, several scoops of clay and a foot of mushroom manure soil, rested the body of Tim the biker.

I was hesitant to knock. Kaitlin looked in the front window. To the muffled sounds of "Boogie Woogie Bugle Boy," Dad was dancing with a chair, and Kam Fong was dancing with a ski. Now *she* was the speechless one.

"They're chairjacking," I explained.

*"What?"*

"It's a ballroom dancing exercise. You have to dance with an inanimate object and imbue it with the sense that the object is alive. It's hard to do. Dad rents Disney cartoons all the time to see how teapots and flying carpets express themselves."

Kaitlin was re-evaluating my possible use as genetic material for any future child of hers. She rang the doorbell, and Kam Fong seamlessly opened it and returned to the main room for the song's climax. Then he bowed and said, "Am I not grand?"

Dad said, "You're an hour early."

Kam said, "Not to worry, I can put them both to work. Come to the kitchen."

"Hey, we're supposed to be guests here."

"And I was supposed to have housekeepers until I fired them this afternoon."

"Why?" Kaitlin asked.

"I caught them eating."

Kam waved around a kitchen in which hundreds of hors d'oeuvres sat half finished. "Here. Make some canapés. Jim and I have to practise."

We stood at the counter and tried to figure out what to make, but we couldn't think of what to do with all the cheeses and vegetables. We went to the Dell beside the phone and put the word "canapé" into Google Images. This generated a predictable deluge of porn, as well as some retro 1950s canapé photos.

"Do we have radishes?" Kaitlin asked.

"Yes, but nobody likes radishes."

"I know. Has anybody in the history of humanity ever sat down one day and said to themselves, *You know, I'd like nothing more right now than to eat a crisp yummy radish?*"

We lurked for a while in a radish chat room. Snoozeville.

Kaitlin continued her rant. "Carrots coast through life. If they were any colour other than orange, they'd be extinct by now." She adopted her carrot voice: "*Hi, I'm a carrot and have a bland nothing flavour, but because I'm attractive and because I'm just about the only orange vegetable that can be eaten in raw form, you keep me in your kitchen. I mock you for your weakness.*"

"Look at the canapé sofas." Kaitlin and I quickly learned that a canapé sofa is a sofa designed to seat two people.

"Boring."

Two clicks later we ended up on the Cunnilingus Web Ring.

"Ethan, I want to go home. This is the worst housewarming ever."

Just then Mom, showing no sign that she remembered Tim decomposing mere feet away, walked in and said, "Canapés! What fun!" Tying her apron, she said, "You know how boring I find ballroom dancing. It's a side of him I've never understood." With a paring knife she began whittling radishes into rosebuds. "He and Kam Fong are entered in a competition called 'Canteen.'"

"Canteen? What's it about?"

"'The Greatest Generation Goes to War—A Ballroom Tribute.'" Yet again, "Boogie Woogie Bugle Boy" pulsed from the living room.

Kaitlin said, "I'm so sick of that 'Greatest Generation' crap. We finally drive a silver nail through the heart of Generation X, only to have this new monster rear its head. And I'm *soooooooooo* sick of Tom Hanks looking earnest all the time. They should make a Tom Hanks movie where Tom kills off Greatest Generation figureheads one by one."

Bree arrived on cue: "And then he starts killing other generations. He becomes this supernova of hate—all he wants to do is destroy."

"He starts killing the surviving members of the Sex Pistols."

"Hate clings to him like a rich, lathery shampoo. His lungs secrete it like anthrax foam."

Mom lost it. "Stop it! All of you! Tom Hanks is a fine actor who would never hurt anybody. At least not onscreen."

I thought, *Hey, didn't Tom Hanks mow down half of Chicago in Road to Perdition?* Well, whatever.

"You young people stop your prattling and help me out here. Kaitlin and Bree, peel these cucumbers. Ethan, fill me in on your secret plan to sabotage the videogame you're working on now."

"*What!* Who told you about it?"

"Your friend Mark."

"You were talking to Mark?"

"He's getting me some bootleg gardening software, and he told me that you've begun collectively designing a secret slasher character named Ronald, a birthday clown who lives in a secret lair within SpriteQuest."

"He told you about Ronald?"

"He did."

I'll spare the world Mom's translation. Basically, we're concealing the coding files used to generate Ronald inside a folder called MOAT WATER TEXTURES that nobody's particularly in charge of nor interested in. There's going to be a switch inside the configuration files that allows a player with the secret password to go from one mode to another, including Ronald's Lair of Death, releasing him on a spree of carnage and terror within the SpriteQuest realm. But because this secret file can be found and unlocked by a debugger, the jPod development team needs to covertly insert Ronald into the game's coding during the final stage—after the debugging is done. Just before the master gold disk is shipped to the factory, Bree has to have an affair with the FedEx deliveryman. She'll demand that her FedEx boyfriend give her the disk before it goes on the plane. Ronald's complete files will be inserted into the game at this final moment.

Mom asked, "Bree, what if the FedEx delivery guy is a gal?"

"Well, there's a first time for everything."

Mom asked, "Bree, why are you speaking with an English accent?"

"To speed up my career."

"A sensible decision. English women are so bossy-sounding, and they love giving orders. Men are too lazy to bother fighting back. That Thatcher woman really knew how to crack the whip."

Other guests started arriving, most of them ballroom dancers or thugs. Over the next four hours, smokers lit up outside by the glistening fronds of the New Zealand tree fern above Tim's grave. I popped out, if only to convince myself that Tim's bony forearms weren't punching their way out of the topsoil like in the final scene of *Carrie*. I then wondered if some future civilization would ever dig up Tim's bones and wonder what his life was like, or if his last cheeseburger would remain mummified within his gut. About half of the smokers were on their cellphones. Kaitlin came out, ready to go home. She said, "Remember how, back in 1990, if you used a cellphone in public you looked like a total asshole? We're all assholes now."

Dad came out with John Doe and Cowboy. I asked them what they were doing, and Dad said they were headed down to the rail yard to tag grain cars.

"*Dad!* John and Cowboy are too old to be doing that, let alone you."

"I'm getting in character for a role I'm playing."

"What role is that?"

"It's for a bank commercial. I have to roll my eyes when young hip-hoppy people come in to open savings accounts."

"For that you have to go tagging?"

"If I'm supposed to hate the little fuckers, I might as well have a fresh memory in my head to make me do so. It's method. Why are you always so harsh with me about my craft?"

He's still traumatized because his speaking role was axed from the SUV commercial. He needs a bit of joy in his life.

"Just go," I said.

After Dad left, Mom came out to the front step area outside the main doorway.

"What a lovely home. Kam is so lucky to live here."

She went back inside.

• • •

Part of my job in subverting SpriteQuest is to provide Ronald's creation myth—his backstory that tells players how he ended up in his secret lair, dedicated to mayhem. Here it is:

Ronald was attending his one-billionth birthday party in a suburban basement, handing out little cups of orange drink to churlish brats. He looked up the stairs briefly and saw the kids' mothers in the kitchen, drinking martinis and making jokes at his expense. He abandoned the kids to confront them. "If you've got something to say, then say it to my face." The mothers giggled. I mean, this was a living Pez dispenser suddenly in their faces.

"Relax. We were just having fun."

"Fun is my business, lady. I know fun. Those cracks you were making aren't fun. There's a sensitive soul beneath this greasepaint."

"Were you born with all of that shit on?"

Another mother asked, "What do you do when you get home—leave your makeup on and eat TV dinners and make prank phone calls?"

"As a licensed mascot for a multinational corporation, nondisclosure agreements prevent me from telling you what I do in a non-commercial situation."

"Chickenshit. I bet you eat at Wendy's."

Ronald stuck out his finger and pointed into her face. "Wendy is a *whore*."

As this conversation took place in an American house inhabited by Americans, lots of guns were handy. One of the mothers—let's call her Alpha-Mom—reached into her knitting basket and withdrew a .44. She couldn't believe it—she was turned on by her ability to choose whether the clown lived or died. She pointed it at Ronald. "Okay, clownywowny, time for you to go."

Ronald said, "No way. Not until you apologize."

"For what?"

"For mocking clowns."

One of the mothers was about to dial 911, but the gun mother said, "Sheila, no. Not until we have some fun." She motioned to the others. "Nell, lock the kids in the basement." She turned to Ronald. "Okay, bun boy. Strip."

"Huh?"

"You heard me. Strip. We all want to see what's under all that yellow fabric."

One of the mothers whacked him behind the knees with a folded-up aluminum mini-scooter and he fell to the kitchen floor.

"Strip. Now. Or we'll get really ugly."

Ronald was surrounded by six mothers brandishing knives, collapsed folding chairs, guns and one heavy table lamp. One of mothers whacked Ronald on the lower back, and the others pulled her back. Alpha-Mom said, "Not just yet, Katie." She looked down at Ronald, and there was no mercy in her eyes. "Start with those bright red, overly large novelty clown booties. One, two. Bang bang."

Ronald obeyed, and as he did, he realized he was turned on. It was a new sensation that both frightened and pleased him. Through his red and white striped socks, he could feel the cool, dry, recently washed floor tiles. In submission, he handed over his boots to Alpha-Mom.

"Good. Now the socks. Did you phone Waldo and borrow them?"

Ronald removed his socks. The air cooled his toes. Nakedness was going to be a treat. He started to remove his yellow gloves.

"Did I say you could remove your gloves?"

"No."

The women cackled. Alpha-Mom said, "Now for a big ticket item—*overalls*."

The women started betting against each other: *Boxers or briefs? Painted-on underwear or a smooth, bulby nub like a doll?*

Ronald unzipped the three-foot-long zipper down his front. A strap fell from each shoulder. He wanted to laugh, but he knew that if he did, it would kill the mood.

Alpha-Mom was huffy. "*That's* underwear? It looks like an adult diaper. Now take off the gloves."

Ronald obeyed. He was now down to his shirt and diaper-like undergarment.

"The shirt goes, clown. Do it quick."

From the basement, Ronald heard the children's piercing sugared-up voices. He felt freer than he had ever felt before.

"Hey, wait a second—you've never taken your clothes off before, have you?" Alpha-Mom said.

"Part of being a corporate spokesmascot is that I can only remove my clothing if commanded. And nobody's ever asked before."

Alpha-Mom: "So you've never looked *down there?*"

"No."

Alpha-Mom said, "Time you did."

The room was almost religiously charged, as if the women—and Ronald—were to glimpse the contents of the Ark for the first time. Ronald was fumbling with the garment's fastening system when an escaped child suddenly entered the room, scaring the mothers. The .44 went off by accident, hitting Ronald in the upper arm. Blood sprayed everywhere. "You crazy fucked-up bitch, what the hell do you think you've done?" Another escaped child entered the room and began screaming. Katie moved to shush the kids out of the room, but slipped in a pool of clown blood, cracking the back of her skull on a sharply tiled corner of the decorative, retro, Cape Cod fireplace. A vermouth bottle shattered.

Ronald looked. "Holy shit, she's dead." He could even see brains.

The children screamed even more. Nell said, "Get them out of here."

Ronald's grease-painted torso was speckled with beads of blood.

Alpha-Mom was freaked. "Shit, shit, *shit*. What are we going to do?" She tossed Ronald his clothes. "Put these on. Now."

"But I never had a chance to look inside my undergarment . . ."

Sheila said, "Shut up and dress." She looked at the other mothers. "Here's what happened—the clown did it. That's our story. He tried to molest me, and I had to protect myself. You were all here. You saw it."

Ronald knew he was fucked. He also knew he had maybe ninety seconds before the police cruisers arrived, and so, half-dressed, carrying his stained clothes, he ran into the living room, where a Legend of Zelda game was on pause. Ronald dove into the screen, and the glass closed up behind him. And he's been trapped inside games ever since . . .

. . . And now he's out for revenge.

• • •

For the past few weeks, Bree has had ten Scrabble games piled on her desk; some weekend, her plan is to glue their letter tiles onto her bathroom mouldings. "What a depressing Spinsters of Tomorrow craft project, huh? But it'll look so cute."

Suddenly—*ping!*—all of us were playing Scrabble, making the stupidest words. It turned out that Bree had removed nearly all the E's and S's from the letter bag—har, har, har—and some T's as well. We got her to put them back and we played again and made pretty good words. The best was mine: "tsetse," as in tsetse fly.

Afterwards, Bree said, "As a special treat, I've printed out a list of the 972 three-letter words allowed in Scrabble, *but* I've added one non-regulation word to the list. First person who finds it wins a jumbo-sized Toblerone chocolate bar."

"Why do you have a jumbo Toblerone bar? Nobody ever buys them."

"I wanted to see what it was that Steve was working on when he rescued that company, and dammit, maybe he's on to something. They're good."

Mark added, "Toblerone's not just for mini-bars any more." No one said anything. He still hasn't learned how to be ironic.

Herewith Bree's list. Let it be noted that Microsoft Word's spell-check rejects most of them—so, then, how real *are* these words?

| | | | | | | | |
|---|---|---|---|---|---|---|---|
| AAH | AAL | AAS | ABA | ABO | ABS | ABY | ACE |
| ACT | ADD | ADO | ADS | ADZ | AFF | AFT | AGA |
| AGE | AGO | AHA | AID | AIL | AIM | AIN | AIR |
| AIS | AIT | ALA | ALB | ALE | ALL | ALP | ALS |
| ALT | AMA | AMI | AMP | AMU | ANA | AND | ANE |
| ANI | ANT | ANY | APE | APT | ARB | ARC | ARE |
| ARF | ARK | ARM | ARS | ART | ASH | ASK | ASP |
| ASS | ATE | ATT | AUK | AVA | AVE | AVO | AWA |
| AWE | AWL | AWN | AXE | AYE | AYS | AZO | BAA |
| BAD | BAG | BAH | BAL | BAM | BAN | BAP | BAR |
| BAS | BAT | BAY | BED | BEE | BEG | BEL | BEN |
| BET | BEY | BIB | BID | BIG | BIN | BIO | BIS |
| BIT | BIZ | BOA | BOB | BOD | BOG | BOO | BOP |
| BOS | BOT | BOW | BOX | BOY | BRA | BRO | BRR |

| | | | | | | | |
|---|---|---|---|---|---|---|---|
| BUB | BUD | BUG | BUM | BUN | BUR | BUS | BUT |
| BUY | BYE | BYS | CAB | CAD | CAM | CAN | CAP |
| CAR | CAT | CAW | CAY | CEE | CEL | CEP | CHI |
| CIS | COB | COD | COG | COL | CON | COO | COP |
| COR | COS | COT | COW | COX | COY | COZ | CRY |
| CUB | CUD | CUE | CUM | CUP | CUR | CUT | CWM |
| DAB | DAD | DAG | DAH | DAK | DAL | DAM | DAP |
| DAW | DAY | DEB | DEE | DEL | DEN | DEV | DEW |
| DEX | DEY | DIB | DID | DIE | DIG | DIM | DIN |
| DIP | DIS | DIT | DOC | DOE | DOG | DOL | DOM |
| DON | DOR | DOS | DOT | DOW | DRY | DUB | DUD |
| DUE | DUG | DUI | DUN | DUO | DUP | DYE | EAR |
| EAT | EAU | EBB | ECU | EDH | EEL | EFF | EFS |
| EFT | EGG | EGO | EKE | ELD | ELF | ELK | ELL |
| ELM | ELS | EME | EMF | EMS | EMU | END | ENG |
| ENS | EON | ERA | ERE | ERG | ERN | ERR | ERS |
| ESS | ETA | ETH | EVE | EWE | EYE | FAD | FAG |
| FAN | FAR | FAS | FAT | FAX | FAY | FED | FEE |
| FEH | FEM | FEN | FER | FET | FEU | FEW | FEY |
| FEZ | FIB | FID | FIE | FIG | FIL | FIN | FIR |
| FIT | FIX | FIZ | FLU | FLY | FOB | FOE | FOG |
| FOH | FON | FOP | FOR | FOU | FOX | FOY | FRO |
| FRY | FUB | FUD | FUG | FUN | FUR | GAB | GAD |
| GAE | GAG | GAL | GAM | GAN | GAP | GAR | GAS |
| GAT | GAY | GED | GEE | GEL | GEM | GEN | GET |
| GEY | GHI | GIB | GID | GIE | GIG | GIN | GIP |
| GIT | GNU | GOA | GOB | GOD | GOO | GOR | GOT |
| GOX | GOY | GUL | GUM | GUN | GUT | GUV | GUY |
| GYM | GYP | HAD | HAE | HAG | HAH | HAJ | HAM |
| HAO | HAP | HAS | HAT | HAW | HAY | HEH | HEM |

| | | | | | | | |
|---|---|---|---|---|---|---|---|
| HEN | HEP | HER | HES | HET | HEW | HEX | HEY |
| HIC | HID | HIE | HIM | HIN | HIP | HIS | HIT |
| HMM | HOB | HOD | HOE | HOG | HON | HOP | HOT |
| HOW | HOY | HUB | HUE | HUG | HUH | HUM | HUN |
| HUP | HUT | HYP | ICE | ICH | ICK | ICY | IDS |
| IFF | IFS | ILK | ILL | IMP | INK | INN | INS |
| ION | IRE | IRK | ISM | ITS | IVY | JAB | JAG |
| JAM | JAR | JAW | JAY | JEE | JET | JEU | JEW |
| JIB | JIG | JIN | JOB | JOE | JOG | JOT | JOW |
| JOY | JUG | JUN | JUS | JUT | KAB | KAE | KAF |
| KAS | KAT | KAY | KEA | KEF | KEG | KEN | KEP |
| KEX | KEY | KHI | KID | KIF | KIN | KIP | KIR |
| KIT | KOA | KOB | KOI | KOP | KOR | KOS | KUE |
| LAB | LAC | LAD | LAG | LAM | LAP | LAR | LAS |
| LAT | LAV | LAW | LAX | LAY | LEA | LED | LEE |
| LEG | LEI | LEK | LET | LEU | LEV | LEX | LEY |
| LEZ | LIB | LID | LIE | LIN | LIP | LIS | LIT |
| LOB | LOG | LOO | LOP | LOT | LOW | LOX | LUG |
| LUM | LUV | LUX | LYE | MAC | MAD | MAE | MAG |
| MAN | MAP | MAR | MAS | MAT | MAW | MAX | MAY |
| MED | MEL | MEM | MEN | MET | MEW | MHO | MIB |
| MID | MIG | MIL | MIM | MIR | MIS | MIX | MOA |
| MOB | MOC | MOD | MOG | MOL | MOM | MON | MOO |
| MOP | MOR | MOS | MOT | MOW | MUD | MUG | MUM |
| MUN | MUS | MUT | NAB | NAE | NAG | NAH | NAM |
| NAN | NAP | NAW | NAY | NEB | NEE | NET | NEW |
| NIB | NIL | NIM | NIP | NIT | NIX | NOA | NOB |
| NOD | NOG | NOH | NOM | NOO | NOR | NOS | NOT |
| NOW | NTH | NUB | NUN | NUS | NUT | OAF | OAK |
| OAR | OAT | OBE | OBI | OCA | ODD | ODE | ODS |

| | | | | | | | |
|---|---|---|---|---|---|---|---|
| OES | OFF | OFT | OHM | OHO | OHS | OIL | OKA |
| OKE | OLD | OLE | OMS | ONE | ONS | OOH | OOT |
| OPE | OPS | OPT | ORA | ORB | ORC | ORE | ORS |
| ORT | OSE | OUD | OUR | OUT | OVA | OWE | OWL |
| OWN | OXO | OXY | PAC | PAD | PAH | PAL | PAM |
| PAN | PAP | PAR | PAS | PAT | PAW | PAX | PAY |
| PEA | PEC | PED | PEE | PEG | PEH | PEN | PEP |
| PER | PES | PET | PEW | PHI | PHT | PIA | PIC |
| PIE | PIG | PIN | PIP | PIS | PIT | PIU | PIX |
| PLY | POD | POH | POI | POL | POM | POP | POT |
| POW | POX | PRO | PRY | PSI | PUB | PUD | PUG |
| PUL | PUN | PUP | PUR | PUS | PUT | PYA | PYE |
| PYX | QAT | QUA | RAD | RAG | RAH | RAJ | RAM |
| RAN | RAP | RAS | RAT | RAW | RAX | RAY | REB |
| REC | RED | REE | REF | REG | REI | REM | REP |
| RES | RET | REV | REX | RHO | RIA | RIB | RID |
| RIF | RIG | RIM | RIN | RIP | ROB | ROC | ROD |
| ROE | ROM | ROT | ROW | RUB | RUE | RUG | RUM |
| RUN | RUT | RYA | RYE | SAB | SAC | SAD | SAE |
| SAG | SAL | SAP | SAT | SAU | SAW | SAX | SAY |
| SEA | SEC | SEE | SEG | SEI | SEL | SEN | SER |
| SET | SEW | SEX | SHA | SHE | SHH | SHY | SIB |
| SIC | SIM | SIN | SIP | SIR | SIS | SIT | SIX |
| SKA | SKI | SKY | SLY | SOB | SOD | SOL | SON |
| SOP | SOS | SOT | SOU | SOW | SOX | SOY | SPA |
| SPY | SRI | STY | SUB | SUE | SUM | SUN | SUP |
| SUQ | SYN | TAB | TAD | TAE | TAG | TAJ | TAM |
| TAN | TAO | TAP | TAR | TAS | TAT | TAU | TAV |
| TAW | TAX | TEA | TED | TEE | TEG | TEL | TEN |
| TET | TEW | THE | THO | THY | TIC | TIE | TIL |

TIN TIP TIS TIT TOD TOE TOG TOM
TON TOO TOP TOR TOT TOW TOY TRY
TSK TUB TUG TUI TUN TUP TUT TUX
TWA TWO TYE UDO UGH UKE ULU UMM
UMP UNS UPO UPS URB URD URN USE
UTA UTS VAC VAN VAR VAS VAT VAU
VAV VAW VEE VEG VET VEX VIA VIE
VIG VIM VIS VOE VOW VOX VUG WAB
WAD WAE WAG WAN WAP WAR WAS WAT
WAW WAX WAY WEB WED WEE WEN WET
WHA WHO WHY WIG WIN WIS WIT WIZ
WOE WOG WOK WON WOO WOP WOS WOT
WOW WRY WUD WYE WYN XIS YAH YAK
YAM YAP YAR YAW YAY YEA YEH YEN
YEP YES YET YEW YID YIN YIP YOB
YOD YOK YOM YON YOU YOW YUK YUM
YUP ZAG ZAP ZAX ZED ZEE ZEK ZIG
ZIN ZIP ZIT ZOA ZOO

N N N N N N
N N N N N N
N N N N N N
N N N N N N
N N N N N N
N N N N N N
N N N N N N

L L L L L L
L L C C L L N
L L C L L L N
L L N N L L N
N N N N N N N
N N N N N N N
N N N N N N N

T T T T T T
T C T T T C T
C C C C C C
T C C C C T
T T T C T T T
T T T T T T T
T T T T T T T

• • •

A few days later I caused a sensation in jPod: "Everybody listen up. At the count of three, write me a list on a topic of your own choosing. You've got five minutes. The best list wins . . ." at which point I held up the trophy " . . . this six-inch Japanese kewpie doll complete with working squeak. This doll is the spokesmascot of Japan's most beloved mayonnaise company. I bought it off eBay because I thought it was cool and that when I put it on my desk my life would be somehow better—but, well, this hasn't proven to be the case. Are you ready? Get set . . . One . . . two . . . three . . . *Go!* "

**Bree:**

**Things my new French boyfriend does that are making me begin to wonder about him**

1)
Tucks his sweaters into his pants.

2)
Eats Play-Doh fragments.

3)
Wears yellow-lensed Fendi eyeglasses that make him resemble a repeat sex offender.

4)
Sold all of his Fred Perry shirts on eBay because I told him
they make him look pregnant (he should have
given them to charity).

5)
Refuses to capitalize the letter "I" when writing about
himself in emails.

6)
Is a selfish and incoherent lover.

**Cowboy:**

## Faggy colour names (alphabetized)

bisque
cerise
chartreuse
conch
cornflower
corn silk
fern
goldenrod
honeydew
leather
lichen
lox
mica
moccasin
opal

plum

saddle brown

shiraz

snow

thistle

yolk

**John Doe:**

## Why buying lottery tickets is simply wrong

### 1)
Would you ever go into a lottery booth and buy a 6/49 with the following numbers: 1, 2, 3, 4, 5, 6 and a bonus of 7? Of course you wouldn't. But that number has just as ludicrously small a chance of winning as do some idiotic numbers you pulled out of the air.

### 2)
When you buy lottery tickets, your lifestyle elevator travels only down. Buy enough tickets over a long period of time and, before you realize it, you'll find yourself living in a listing mobile home. Its linoleum kitchenette counters will be constellated with crystal meth pipe burns. Its throw cushions will be caked in DNA best left unexplored. There will be a Domino's pizza boy bound and gagged beneath the main living area beside the cinder blocks.

### 3)
Oh, for God's sake, how many more reasons do you need?

**Kaitlin:**

### Things Ethan doesn't know I know about him

1)

Three weeks ago he was suntanning on the back stoop using an old Supertramp double album covered in tin foil to concentrate the rays onto his face.

2)

He knows the technically correct word for the act of playing music using the rims of wine glasses.

3)

He has dextrous toes and uses them to pick socks off the bedroom floor when he thinks I'm still sleeping.

**Evil Mark:**

### Starch discs from around the world

pizza
naan
pancakes
tortillas
waffles
crepes
communion wafers

Bree won.

About once every three years I get a craving for a Coca-Cola, and only a Coca-Cola—no cheeseburgers or fries. Shortly after Bree won, I had my triennial craving. I went to the kitchen area to get a can, and on a table beneath a stacked totem of plastic coffee creamers was an abandoned car magazine open to a spread on the Volkswagen Touareg's fuel economy. This got me thinking about Steve and his abandoned car and Mom and Kam Fong and all. I thought, "Oh well," and took my Coke back to my desk, and when I did, John and Evil Mark were arguing about Coke versus Pepsi. John was convinced that Coke has a valid reason for being the top cola, that, "Even though we're haggling about the difference between catshit and dogshit, Coke is technically more delicious." To prove it, he pulled out mini-bar cola consumption statistics that showed Coke to be number one. *Mini-bars*—and of course, mini-bars mean Toblerone, the signature mini-bar snack of all time—another Steve indicator. So I tried getting on with my work, but then I heard Cowboy pacifying some fartcatcher from the facilities department who claimed they'd found cigarette butts in an air filter and thought the butts might be coming from jPod. Cowboy was doing his thirtieth Sudoku of the day and was feeding the facilities people the rich, nourishing crap they deserved. He ended it all with "Okey-diddily-dokey" . . . just like Ned Flanders—and so yet again I was reminded of Steve. My conscience began getting the worst of me.

*Well, at least he's not dead.*

Oh God. I felt so guilty. So in the mid-afternoon I drove

over to Kam Fong's. How strange that all you have to do sometimes to meet somebody is walk up to their house and ring a doorbell, and magically they appear as if from nowhere.

With x-ray eyes I saw the maggots scouring Tim's corpse in pursuit of Tim Jerky.

Kam opened the door. "Ethan."

"Hi, Kam."

He was covered with maybe a hundred acupuncture needles.

"Sorry to interrupt your session."

"No worry. What's up? Come in."

Kam's acupuncturist was futzing about with the contents of his suitcase and wasn't introduced to me.

"Kam, I need to find Steve."

He didn't blink as he back-hopped onto the acupuncture table. "I thought he was a jerk and was ruining your skateboard game. Why are you asking me about him?"

"Believe it or not, we need him at the company to override a recent decision to make our new game even stupider. Mom told me that you—"

"Yes?"

"That you helped her out on the Steve issue."

"He's not dead or anything."

"That's what she said."

More needles went into Kam's calves. I couldn't look, and Kam said, "Ethan, stop being such a pussy. Acupuncture's one of the few Chinese things that actually works. Unlike feng shui."

Tim's nearby carcass amplified my unease. Kam asked, "How badly do you want to see Steve, then?"

Good question. "Well, I think Steve might be just powerful enough to reverse the company's decision on the latest botch-up with the game. And I feel kind of rotten hearing that he's . . ."

"That he's what?"

"Ummm . . . being *detained* somewhere."

"He was hassling your mother."

"Mom can take care of herself just fine. Can you tell me if he's okay or not?"

"He's not in pain, if that's what you mean."

"That's a good start."

"And he's now happy in his own way."

Coming from Kam, this suggested the most gruesome of fates. "Just tell me where he is, and I'll go get him—no questions asked. I doubt he's going to hassle Mom any more."

"Give me a week or so to figure out a thing or two."

"Thanks."

• • •

While I waited for Kam to get back to me, in jPod we carried on with the generating of Ronald's Lair. We're doing the most basic levels of coding, which is kind of boring, and we also had to do it on top of our regular jobs—and our regular jobs are made even worse because of eye candy. Just when you think you're meeting a schedule, your team has to generate weekly eye candy for marketing so that they don't think the project's tanking, and thus allow it to live until the next milestone. On the good side, so much ill will and torture surrounds the SpriteQuest project in-house that we can get away with doing amazingly little and yet still give the illusion of being team players. Mostly this means walking around, acting pumped and saying things like "Man, this is going to be one rocking game!" with a straight face, thus inflating the egos of superiors while creating a protective bulletproof coating of enthusiasm. It's so easy it's scary. Even for me, with my fake voice. It's all so stupid that the fake/real part of my brain doesn't tickle even the slightest bit.

• • •

I've noticed that, as we ramp up on our game-building skills and generalized knowledge about Ronald, we're googling every ten minutes. The problem is, after a week of intense googling, we've started to burn out on knowing the answer to everything. God must feel that way all the time. I think people in the year 2020 are going to be nostalgic for the sensation of feeling clueless.

• • •

A small cold passed through the pod, and we suffered a seventeen percent health loss, even though we zinc'ed up like crazy. And Cowboy kept saying, "Remember everybody: limb-specific gunshot damage" to the point where we felt slightly spooked.

Amid all of this, Bree was moping out of concern that, in her quest to make a corporate success of herself, she might become unattractive to her French beau. John Doe told Bree that if she were artier she'd be more of a catch for her

French paramour. As a result, Bree has canned the business attire in favour of an all-black look. To take this new lifestyle philosophy further, she and John ended up driving to Brentwood Mall to do performance art. Bree walked down the main atrium area, shaving her neck with an electric razor, and met John Doe, who applied lipstick in the middle of a crowded restaurant. I tried to imagine the public's response and John's counter-response: "Is it so wrong for a man to wear MAC Brick-O-La? Are your gender ideas that limited?" Afterwards he said, "Maybe it's just my dykey upbringing, but lipstick really does taste gross. How do you women do it?"

He inspired Kaitlin to confess: "Sometimes I get too lazy to wear makeup. To compensate for it, I simply dress like a slut."

• • •

Cowboy's signed on to a site called chokingforit.com, where people all across the city put in their name, a photo of their body, their address and a numerical rating from one to ten of how horny they are. Depending on how entries mesh, Cowboy simply vanishes for seventy-five minutes and then comes back saying nothing. I've gotten so used to this kind of behaviour with Cowboy that it no longer registers. The upside for me is that his trysts now happen during the day, so he never has to be rescued after ODing on Robitussin.

Also: Evil Mark is an evil genius, and Ronald's Lair's core code could never exist without him. But he also has yet to adorn the walls of his cubicle, which is really spooky. It just is. And the other day I secretly ate one of his novelty lemon-flavoured Post-its. It was really quite tasty. Tangy—with a hint of dust.

• • •

The next day the big drama was that John cast a spell on Evil Mark after Evil Mark ate a packet of Handi-Snacks John had left on his desk. Like anything weird in life, it began small and escalated.

"Evil Mark, did you eat my Handi-Snacks?"

"You mean that small plastic tray of shitty crackers that comes with a blob of cheese spread you can dip the crackers into?"

"Yes. Exactly."

"I did."

John got up. "You didn't ask for permission. You *know* how seriously I take my snacking rituals."

"John, it was only a fucking plastic tublet with some crackers and a cheese-like orange substance. Big deal. I'll get you another one."

"Big deal? That was my *snack*, Mark. And now it's not, because you ate it."

"I'll get you another one. I'll even let you eat my stapler if it makes you feel better."

"I don't want to eat your stapler, and I don't want another Handi-Snacks. That's not my point. You took it without asking, and then you act like private property is meaningless."

"You're overreacting."

John Doe said, "Apologize." John was getting fierce. I began to wonder if this would erupt into cubicle rage.

"I don't like the way you're saying that."

"It was my property, Mark. And you just stole it like you were some global corporation absorbing a small African nation into its balance sheet. Evil Mark, I am officially casting a spell on you." John waved his hand in a circle and then threw invisible gnome dandruff at Mark. "I hereby strip you of the ability to perceive cartoons."

"What the hell does that mean?"

"Just what I said. Until you apologize for what you did, your eyes may look at cartoons, and your ears may listen to them, but they will make no sense to you. Cartoons will be nothing more to you than abstract shapes bouncing about to garbled noises."

"That's so stupid, John."

"Is it really? You won't think so when you come crawling to me, begging to be able to apprehend cartoons again."

"This is fucked up. I'm going back to work."

"You do that."

We could *hear* John simmering.

• • •

I have to say, it's a blast making SpriteQuest as we simultaneously secretly sabotage it. It reminds me of when I was a kid and I'd felt-pen doors and windows onto Ritz Cracker boxes and then set fire to them while providing colour commentary. *Oh no, the wedding party of fifty and the junior lacrosse team on the seventh floor are trapped! Somebody forgot to replace the smoke detector batteries!*

Every time we do something to make SpriteQuest "sparkle" (Management's term), such as building an interesting mesh frame for a turret, we build leaks and vulnerabilities into that turret so that Ronald can use them as a means of generating carnage.

Gord-O has been so impressed by the jPod enthusiasm level that he's taken me off Cheerios duty and has grudgingly had to admit that I'm assistant production assistant material after all.

• • •

A week later, out of nowhere, Cowboy said, "Isn't time weird? I'm already forgetting about Steve."

Time to go back to Kam and his exclusive alpine hideaway. I rang the bell and the acupuncturist opened the door and nodded me inside. In the living room, a sweatshop-like crew of six women, seated at folding bingo-hall tables, were busily weighing and bagging white powder that came from a Road-Runner-cartoon FREE-BIRDSEED-like mound in the centre of the floor.

"Kam."

"Ethan."

Kam had an Ikea desk set up in the corner, and he paused a game of AmmuNation. "AmmuNation!" I said. "All right! What do you think of it?"

"It's the best. It allows me to park my evil in one place so I can be a better person in the real world."

"That's thoughtful of you."

The sound of little scales clicking and the rustling of

ziplock bags amplified the silence. Kam said, "You're here about Steve."

"Yup."

"You're in luck. I heard this morning that he's fine. Do you want to go get him?"

"Sure. Where is he?"

"China."

"*What?*"

"Too late. You said you'd go. You can't back out now."

"What's he doing in China?"

"Having the experience of a lifetime. He'll thank me for it."

"I don't have the money to go to China."

"Relax." He reached into a desk drawer and removed a wad of twenties. "Done. Do you need a passport? I can get one made for you in a few minutes."

"No. I got one three years ago for my trip to Mexico."

"I'll put you on a China Airlines flight tonight. You'd better pack, and for God's sake, don't wear any of your dorky outfits. You wouldn't believe what my . . ."—he looked over at the women—" . . . *helpers* have been saying about you in Chinese. Go to a fucking Gap and stock up."

"I don't know anything about China."

"I'll take care of all that. I'll courier the ticket to your office, and there'll be people helping you all over the place in Shanghai. Just be at the gate and ready to go."

A woman across the room made a hissing sound.

Kam, returning to his game, said, "Who says I'm not a kind soul?"

• • •

Late that afternoon Kaitlin and I combed the net for basic information about China, and somehow we ended up yet again on the Cunnilingus Web Ring. Kaitlin said, "What a weird coincidence. I should go out and buy a lottery ticket."

"How come?"

"Any time you have a coincidence happen to you, it means you've entered a luck warp—for the next short while everything you do will be touched by it."

John Doe gave a snort from behind his cubicle wall and left it at that.

"Kaitlin, you know what? Let's stop this search for info. I'm simply going to show up for the plane, like when you go see a movie without having seen the trailer."

"Good idea."

I went home, looked at my clothing from the Kam Fong point of view and then went out to a Gap. I stocked up on new duds and packed. I'm not proud to say it, but when I looked at my new waffle-knit T's, my washable merino wool sweaters, my groovy herringbone blazers, my unpleated olive khakis and my low-ironing stress-free shirts, it made me feel, you know . . . *freshhhhh.*

• • •

A lumber delivery for Kaitlin's hugging machine arrived just as Kam's car came to get me. When I kissed her goodbye, she smelled like a house under construction.

At the airport, it turned out Kam had booked me into first class—*woohoo!*

It was a brilliant early evening, with magic light beaming in through the windows of the silent, thick-carpeted first-class lounge. I sipped Veuve Clicquot and surveyed the airport, appreciating its wonderful made-of-Lego quality—high-tech brightly coloured ramps and cones and poles and carts and movable stairways. Walking onto the plane, I felt like I was entering the world of Lego in a way I hadn't since I was eleven.

The flight took off without any complications, and I lolled in my sprawling 180-degree reclining seat, wishing I could live in a house that was just like a first-class cabin.

But then, while I was trying to decide which of many sumptuous meals to order, I looked over to the seat opposite mine, and I couldn't believe my eyes—it was Douglas Coupland in 3K. What a bringdown. I saw that he was tapping some sort of crap into a laptop, and suddenly I wasn't hungry any more. I ordered tri-coloured penne pasta with Italian funghi in a lemongrass reduction and spent an hour optimizing my laptop's animation pipeline, but my heart wasn't in it. So I ordered a Scotch because it seemed like a first-classy drink to order, and tried to choose which Hitchcock classic to watch on the in-flight video service—but I couldn't help obsessing about Coupland. What bad luck that he was on this flight. And what *was* he typing? I may never have flown in first class before, but I do know it's the one place on earth where you shouldn't be working. I figured that if I went to the bathroom and walked back past him, I could get a clear glimpse of what he was working on. My eyesight is good.

In any event, after my fake pee, I walked quietly down to where Coupland was sitting, and on his laptop was a photo of that guy standing in front of the tank at Tiananmen Square.

A flight attendant passed by with a load of hot perfumed towels, and I reached for one, but I fumbled and it landed on Coupland's left arm.

"Sorry about that."

"No problem." He handed it back to me.

"Hey, aren't you Douglas Coupland?"

"Uh, yes. That's me."

"I've read all your books. I think they're great." *Oh God, I just soiled myself.*

"Oh, well, uh, thank you."

Awkward silence.

More awkward silence.

I said, "I'm Ethan. So you're off to China, huh?" *Did I really say something that dorky?*

"For a few days."

"A special project?"

"Yes. It's a piece for *Wired* magazine."

*Wired? How 1996.* "Really?"

"It's about this new design trend coming out of China. Well, technically it's not simply China—it's the PRC—the People's Republic of China."

*Boring.* "Fascinating."

"It's called 'designer prisoner-of-conscience labour.'"

"Huh?"

"Manufacturers locate people famous for political activism, and then they have that person make something and sell it as a value-added good."

"I don't get it."

"This guy here on the screen—" Coupland turned up his laptop to show me the JPEG of the Chinese guy in

Tiananmen Square. "Know what he's doing now? He's working out this co-sponsor deal with Verizon Wireless and Pizza Hut. He'll be attaching faceplates to a series of cellphones that come with Pizza Hut promotional meals. They're trying really hard to get that cheese-inside-the-crust idea going but it's just not catching on."

"My brother told me about that!"

"Cool. And on this trip I'll also be visiting Aung San Suu Kyi."

"Who?"

"She's that woman from Burma who won the Nobel Peace Prize a few years back."

"Oh right."

"She's negotiating a deal with Wal-Mart. She's going to be manning the pressure-moulding machine that stamps out white plastic stacking chairs."

"How would you know the chairs were hers and not somebody else's?"

"Each chair would come with a frameable hand-signed certificate of authenticity."

"That's a lot of certificates to sign."

"No kidding. Wal-Mart is two percent of China's GDP. I think these chairs would have to be limited edition, though. Prizes for Wal-Mart cardholders who shop above a certain amount per year."

"Wow." Dinners were being served. "Talk to you later."

"Sure."

After my penne I got a bit too tipsy on Scotches and began cycling through the video screen's programs. Let me say something right now: I speak neither Japanese nor Mandarin, but I *do* know that Japanese TV is really cool to watch and Chinese TV is appalling. Even on a plane, they show factory tours. After maybe my tenth visit to a microchip factory, I fell asleep for a bit.

When I woke up, I was a bit fuzzy but feeling expansive— me, a world traveller! I remembered Bree in the coffee room once, talking about Coupland's books as I was waiting for some soup to heat. She said that Coupland said that unless your life was a story it had no meaning, that you might as well be kelp or bacteria. I wondered if Coupland knew the answer. He certainly owes me for that time we had to read one of his books in my third year at university.

His eyes went a bit wary when he saw me coming.

"So, Mister Coupland. This friend of mine said that you said that unless your life is like something in a story there's no point in being alive, that you're basically no more important than kelp."

"But kelp *is* important."

"That's not what I meant. See, I think that . . ." Locating the words was harder than I'd estimated.

"What's your name again?"

"Ethan."

"Ethan, why are you going to China?"

"I've got to go pick somebody up."

"Who's that?"

"Steve."

"Who's Steve?"

And suddenly it all came spewing out of me—Mom, Steve, Dad, Kam, Kaitlin, Bree—everybody and everything. I have to hand it to myself: I think I told my story well.

Coupland seemed to be pretty enthusiastic while I was talking—he even took notes!—and asked lots of questions. And then, at the end of all this, Lord forgive me, I asked him whether he could write a mini-story about me and my life.

"I don't know if that's such a good—"

"No, do it. It'd be fun."

"Okay. Bring me your laptop."

I set him up with Word, then went back to my seat to order one last Scotch. Suddenly it was hours later, the sun was blazing in the windows and all the passengers were chugging bottled water, applying moisturizing balms and doing stretches. The by-now familiar pertussive hackings of older Chinese nationals kept me from going back for a snooze cycle. And then . . . thorn by thorn, my chat with Coupland came back to me. I cringed and looked his way; he was obliviously making cellphone calls (in mid-flight) while stuffing a stolen flotation vest into his carry-on baggage. Sociopathic shit. My laptop was in the magazine pouch in front of me.

Just then the plane did a slight lurch, and I couldn't even look out the window while we landed. My bloodstream felt fetid, like time-expired dairy products. I waited until everybody else was off the plane, then two annoyed flight attendants bunted me towards the gate.

Sandra Alves, Joe Ault, Vinod Balakrishnan, Jason Bartell, Scott Byer, Jeff Chien, Scott Cohen, Andrew Cover, Chris Cox, Karen Gauthier, Todor Georgiev, Mark Hamburg, Jerry Harris, Dave Howe, Thomas Knoll, Sarah Kong, Mike Leavy, Tai Luxon, Seetharaman Narayanan, Sean Parent, Marc Pawliger, John Penn II, Dave Rau, Tom Ruark, Cris Rys, Michael Scarafone, Stephanie Schaefer, Del Schneider, Sau Tam, Gwyn Weisberg, Russell Williams, Matt Wormley, John Worthington, Rick Wulff

*Nicole-Kidman.net: Your #1 Resource for ALL THINGS Nicole Kidman . . .*

• • •

There was a Word file from Douglas Coupland on my laptop's desktop. It said,

Ethan, thanks for telling me about your life and everything. It's intriguing. There's probably even a book there. You were also probably drunker than you think, and so you told me personal stuff that may or may not have been true, but most of which is shocking and actionable. More to the point, you let a total stranger have full, unguarded access to your *laptop*? Are you a fucking idiot? What were you thinking? I trawled through your emails (snooze) and porn stashes (cheerleaders? How vanilla) and Google cookies (potpourri gift baskets?) and . . . I'm appalled. Absolutely appalled. You come across smart, but then you do stupid shit like this. Does being upgraded to first class screw you up this much? I have no idea. So maybe you really *want* to be caught doing all the weird stuff you do. Fuck, I feel like Lisa Simpson giving you an on-the-spot quickie analysis but . . . are you a moron? How damaged are you?

You live in a world that is amoral and fascinating—but I also know your life is everyday fare for Vancouverites, so there's no judgment that way. But, for the love of God, grow up. Or read something outside your normal sphere or use what few savings you have ($23,400.06, if your files are correct) and go to a college or university and rebuild your hard drive.

This is weird diagnostic shit coming from a stranger, but, Ethan, you're on a one-way course to utter fuckedupedness. I'm not suggesting you stop— but I am saying *wake up.*

                                                              Doug

What an asshole.

                            • • •

Immigration procedures were essentially non-existent. Kam had arranged for a driver to pick me up, and we wormed our way through the traffic on a dull grey Asian morning. My first impression was that there wasn't a square inch of land that wasn't being used to grow defeated-looking crops of spinachy plants. The city was an endless Sim-like blend of shacks, bikes, more bikes and still more bikes, tour buses, black-windowed Mercedes-Benzes and gaunt people smoking and standing around in front of concrete apartment buildings, most of which looked like they were built out of grey playing cards and seemed seismically unequipped, dreaming of the day gravity would take them back to Mama. And the air! Okay, imagine that you've built a bonfire of telephone poles—the ones dripping with creosote— and throw in a fax machine, a photocopier, some asbestos stacking chairs and a roasting chicken. That pretty much sums up the air quality, though it changes moment by moment depending on where you go. Turn a corner and—

*thwack!*—different items are thrown into the flames: a load of running shoes, four thousand plastic bags, hog carcasses and a Dumpster of barbershop floor sweepings. And it's thick—a few blocks down the street, buildings vanish like in a fog effect in a memory-impaired videogame from the early 1990s. And it's humid, and I *hate* humidity.

What a relief to check in to my hotel—all five stars of it—and fall down on my bed's cool sheets.

*Just twenty-four hours ago I was schlepping about my cubicle, and now I'm on the other side of the planet—on a mission, no less.*

I opened my luggage to get a fresh shirt, but when I pulled back the black nylon flap, I saw that my clothes had been replaced with about forty pounds of white powder. I—

Words failed me.

I phoned Kam—I had no idea what time it was in Vancouver, and I didn't care.

"Hello?"

"You asshole! I could have ended up in prison for this."

"Stop snivelling. You made it through okay."

"Where the hell are all my new clothes?"

"Go to a Gap. They're the same everywhere."

"And what do I do with all this . . . *stuff*?"

"Store it with the concierge, and relax, okay? Order a cheese platter and a hooker. Go stroll the Bund."

"When do I get Steve?"

"My driver will pick you up at eight a.m. tomorrow."

• • •

It was late afternoon and sleep was pointless. I tried going online, but the Ethernet feed was dead. When I called the concierge, he said, "It's the Great Firewall of China. Nothing you can do. Shall I send you up some green tea?"

I showered and walked out into Shanghai proper, once called the Whore of Asia, now called the Pearl of Asia, though it might just as well be called the Tire Fire of Asia. It's like shopping inside an active ball barbecue.

At a Gap I bought the exact same things I had bought before the trip (at a third of the price), then I wandered the streets a bit. I tried to find the bootleg videogame district but failed. Beside a pork-on-a-stick booth, I bought a bootleg DVD of outtakes and bloopers from the making of *Schindler's List*.

The crowds began to irk me. Everyone in the city spits and coughs and wheezes. People jostle you everywhere. The Chinese notion of private space has no connection to my own, and I tried not to be irked, but then I got paranoid about my kidneys going missing. I went back to the hotel and ordered room service, breathed fresh hotel-room air and watched CNN Asia. The weather report was so odd. There's a map of maybe half the planet on the screen, and the weather woman says, "Let's see what's happening in the 'Stans'"—meaning Pakistan, Tajikistan, Afghanistan. She made it sound like, "Let's see what my close personal friends, all named Stanley, are up to."

Around midnight I went downstairs and poked my head out the front doors. Onto the cosmic tire fire, the Chinese had recently tossed a boxcar load of leaded enamel paint, a hopper of pesticides and some rendering plant scraps. I ended up falling asleep watching the *Schindler's List* bloopers DVD.

Slept like a dog.

I woke up at seven a.m. on an alpha wave high. Jet lag? Not for me, Ethan Jarlewski, citizen of the world. I had coffee and a breakfast plate that featured a selection of fruit geometrically cut and arranged to create the feel of a Zen garden. Clothed in my new Gap duds, I waited for my driver down in the foyer. He showed up precisely on time in a crisply pressed outfit like Batman's butler, Alfred. I asked where we were going, and the driver said, "Not to worry. We're taking good care of you." It quickly became clear to me that we were headed *away* from the city.

After an hour the superstructures of Shanghai were gone, and we were in a semi-industrialized ghostscape of worker housing, rice paddies, shacks, monochrome grey office buildings—actually, everything on the outskirts of a Chinese city is grey. All you'd need to portray the place is an HB pencil, and then dip your brush in a spittoon.

We stopped at a tea shop for a break. A TV bolted onto the ceiling blared out factory tours at full volume while a trio of women looked at me with profound suspicion. One of them had a frog in a plastic bag, hopping on the ground at her feet.

We drove for maybe another three hours, and I began to feel unnerved. "How much farther?" I asked.

"By your North American standards? Not far at all."

"How far would you say, then?"

"We'll be there soon."

An hour later we pulled up to a three-storey cinderblock hotel that stood sentry over several thousand acres of rice paddies. Just over the crest of a naked hill, four smokestacks belched out the remains of deep-fried neurotoxins and the ground-up dust of a million or so non-stick cooking pans.

"You are to wait here, Mr. Jarlewski."

"For how long?"

"Not too long. Have a tea. I'll be out in the car."

I ordered a tea in the lobby and watched as the driver started up the car and pulled away. Uh-oh.

Over the next several hours I ordered a few more glasses of tea, and then had to use the toilet. After much gesturing and an eight-yuan tip, I was directed to a dilapidated wooden unisex shack, where I ended up crouched over the bowl with a shoe firmly placed on each side of the seat. Sanitation was an issue. Fortunately, I had a packet of Kleenex with me.

I made a mental note: *keep buying Kleenex.*

Around sundown a busload of factory workers singing in unison pulled up to the hotel, and a woman holding up a yellow flag got out of the bus, blew a whistle and herded the workers into the restaurant, where they ate a meal built of chicken feet, mystery dumplings and glasses of a beverage from a box labelled HAPPY LOQUAT.

Thirty minutes later, a whistle blew and everybody shuffled back to the bus. The woman with the yellow flag looked at her passenger manifest, looked at me and motioned for me to come. I said, "No, I think you've got the wrong person," but she showed me a piece of paper that had the following written on it:

确切三十分钟以后,口哨吹了和大家被拖曳回到公共汽车,但另一方面妇女与黄旗看她乘客明显,看我和行动为我去对此。EthanJarlewski我说,"没有,我认为您有错误人员,但她显示了我有以下被写对此的一张纸。

Having no desire to spend my night sleeping beside the unisex shack, I got on the bus. The workers had been loaded to allow a three-row gap between them and my poxed Western self. I was suddenly dead tired. I stretched out on the first row of seats and was lulled to sleep by the sound of the sputtering diesel engine.

Sometime in the night we crossed a mountain range, and at six a.m., we stopped at a roadside canteen for a breakfast of green tea, a pasty semi-sweet nodule the size of a fist and an orange. I tried asking the driver for a map, but no go.

Around noon we entered one of those industrial instant cities they write about fawningly in business magazines as the core of *China—the New Asian Tiger!* A massive sign the size of Dodger Stadium's Jumbotron told me in English:

## WELCOME TO SPECIAL ECONOMIC ZONE

# SEZ

*We Love Shopping World*

The city, SEZ, was huge and obviously brand new, but otherwise as bleak and soot-covered and numbing as the rest of urban China. There were maybe twenty thousand bikes for every car, but the cars were Audis and Porsches and Jaguars. Imagine driving a luxury sports car in China in 1965—the brain can't even process the thought properly. In modern China? It's the new dream. I thought back to my grade-six science project on ecology; I'd known that the moment

China discovered cars and craved gasoline, it was curtains for the planet. SEZ confirmed it.

We pulled up outside a concrete building—five storeys with no signage—and I was escorted to a separate entrance from the rest of the bus passengers. After intense haggling between the desk clerk and the woman with the yellow flag (and the handover of a plastic bag filled with yuan), I was given a key and shown to a second-floor room. It was essentially a zero-security jail cell: a single bed, no TV, a chair, a mirror and a penitentiary-style bathroom down the hall. I sat on my bed and was about to have a good cry when I noticed a box on the small bedside table. It contained a Toblerone chocolate bar and a message from Kam, which said, *Isn't travel glamorous? p.s., look under the bed.*

I looked and found a suitcase with my Vancouver clothes in it. I experienced a burst of happiness and then fell asleep.

# 购物

Shopping

# 乏味

Boredom

# 色情

Pornography

# 整容外科

Cosmetic surgery

# 旅游业

Tourism

互联网浏览

Internet browsing

# 电视

TV

···

*Whistle.*
*Ethan was awakened by the sound of a whistle.*
*Shrill whistle, shrill whistle . . .*
*Whistle! You awaken me with your scornful shriek.*
*Why are you so angry, little whistle?*
*Pain.*

Well, so much for poetry, but that's how I woke up. Miss Yellow Flag gave everybody her signature wake-up call just a few moments after a clinically depressed dawn tried to cut through the new day's capitalist mist. New on the daily fire? Fifty thousand feet of orange rubber extension cords, a box-car of recently exterminated Norway rats and a stadium-load of high-sulphur coal cut with acetone.

Carrying my black nylon Samsonite suitcase onto the bus, I was thrown a seed-riddled orange. A cautionary stare from Miss Yellow Flag told me, *So much as one complaint from you, buster, and you're off the bus, whereupon you'll be promptly kidnapped and sold into buggery, and your suitcase will end up on eBay. As for your clothing? I will steal it.*

I tried to put a good face on it. We drove and drove for several hours, the view never changing from one eye opening to the next: everything grey, save for the greys, which were black. Then, out of nowhere, we pulled up to a factory that was belching out toluene, rubber tires, floor sweepings and styrene plastics. More whistles followed, and my fellow bus passengers were escorted into a low building the size of several high school gyms. I was escorted into an office area—my arrival caused no sensation whatsoever. In fact, I simply sat in a chair for an hour or so until an old guy, his face ravaged by six decades of yo-yoing ideologies, motioned for me to follow him. In sign language I mimed, "Should I leave my suitcase here?" He motioned a most definite "no."

I followed him into the factory's bowels, the fist-like stench of industrial solvents robbing my brain, dendrite by dendrite, of the ability to make Scrabble words longer than four letters. My eyes watered, but through the fog of tears I saw that the factory was making Nikes. Well, actually, not real Nikes—*fake* Nikes. After a quarter-mile or so I found Steve.

"Steve!"

"Hi, Ethan." Steve was padlocked onto a mattress-sized cutting device that punched insoles out of large sheets of waffled polyfoam.

"What the hell are you doing here, Steve?"

"Making shoes. How are you, Ethan?"

"I'm shitty, thank you. How long have you been here?"

"Months."

Here Steve was, apparently clam happy, making fake Nikes on one of hell's more ghastly rungs.

"If you're wondering why I'm in such a good mood, it's because I just had my fix."

"What?"

"Heroin. It's great. Makes life feel good 24/7."

"Since when do you use heroin?"

"Kam got me addicted to it before he put me to work here on the line."

"—!"

"Don't feel sorry for me. I like it here. And besides, I can't leave, because otherwise I wouldn't get my fix. You know how far we are from Shanghai, and even then, how does someone buy drugs in a country where drugs theoretically don't exist?"

"—!"

"It's actually fun being here. Excuse me a sec—" A sheet of waffled foam emerged from a ceiling chute, and Steve positioned it and then punched out 288 soles.

"As I was saying, I like it here. Why don't you put down your baggage and help me for a while?"

The old guy shrugged and looked at his watch. Clearly, Steve and I had to leave quickly.

"Steve, I came here to get you. You have to come with me."

"That's kind of you, but you can see my predicament."

"I've got smack galore back in the hotel in Shanghai. This old guy wants us to leave right now. He's got instructions. Steve—?"

Steve was tearing up. "Steve? Are you okay?"

"I'm going to miss it here. All my new comrades, too."

"You're joking."

"At least here you know where you stand."

Steve's replacement worker arrived, accompanied by a foreman who removed his padlocked chain. With one shrill of (what else) a whistle, he booted Steve off the line.

"Steve, they don't want you here any more. You're free. Let's go."

He looked miserable.

The two of us followed Old Guy back to the office, where a car awaited us. Thank God.

Just then an alarm went off in the factory.

• • •

The Associated Press
Updated: 12:54 p.m.

BEIJING—China confirmed two more cases of a new and powerful SARS-like virus on Saturday. The World Health Organization urged further testing to ensure the diagnosis was correct. The new cases were a 37-year-old dentist and a 20-year-old seamstress, the official Xiangxinhua News Agency reported. The seamstress had worked at a factory canteen in the northern Chinese city of Quang Zhouxing, which served civet cats banned by the government after the 2003 SARS outbreak.

This new strain has been tentatively called Cat-Related SARS, or CSARS, and the total number of CSARS deaths in the past week stands at 11.

The government of the province of Guangdong, where SARS first emerged in 2003, said in a statement that "the clinical symptoms and results of laboratory tests and x-ray tests were in line with a diagnosis standard recommended by the U.S. Centers for Disease Control for SARS."

In order to prevent confusion, the 2003 strain of SARS that appeared in China and Toronto is now being called "SARS Classic."

• • •

The driver fled without us. Steve and I were ushered into a large, drippingly humid hall beside the factory, where a gentleman used a Charlie Brown PA system to relate the news of CSARS to maybe six hundred shoemaking workers. I may not speak Mandarin, but I do know that the moment Mr. Megaphone said the following words—

"請不要恐慌。一切將是美好的。沒有立即危險。安靜地請回到您的工作安置。"

("Please don't panic. Everything will be fine. There is no immediate danger. Please quietly return to your work positions.")

—the crowd exploded in all directions, fleeing like Muppets, abandoning the factory. Inside of two minutes the hall was empty, save for me, Steve and the lunkhead who had given the Don't Panic speech. We asked him if he spoke English, and he did—just enough to tell us in Chinese-restaurant English, "Very bad disease. Almost instant death. Much pain." This was followed by a gesture that indicated exploding eardrums.

Then he, too, abandoned us.

"Ethan," Steve said, "how am I going get my next fix?"

"We've been caught in the middle of a modern-day plague in the middle of nowhere, and you want a fix?"

"That pretty much sums it up. A fix is a fix."

We found a blue felt pen in the emptied main office. On the flip side of an industrial slogan poster, Steve drew a large hypodermic needle to convey his need. Somehow, his drawing style made the needle look terrifying, like a syringe Nazis would use to inject truth serum into your veins.

"Steve, that's a pretty nasty-looking rig. Can't you soften it up a bit?"

"It *is* kind of harsh. Here—" He drew daisies all around it, softening the message. The thing was, there was nobody to see the sign, save for some octogenarian shufflers looking for debris left behind by panicking workers. The shoe-moulding machines were all asleep, and across the floor, banks of lights were switching themselves off with noisy *boonk* sounds. The factory without noise was beautiful.

"Steve, chances are they kept your heroin near the station you were working at. Let's check it out."

At Steve's workstation, we rummaged about the first-aid kit and supply boxes, and hit pay dirt almost immediately. "Bingo!" He found a bag of H and a twenty-four-pack of clean rigs behind a case of carbonated lychee soda bottles.

"Life is sweet."

As there seemed to be no ride in our future, we walked for two depressing miles to Steve's dorm building. As we trudged, Steve asked, "Does anybody miss me back home?"

"Steve, to be honest, no."

He looked at me pointedly. "*Anyone?*"

"You mean Mom? No, she doesn't."

"Huh. I didn't think so. How's the game going?"

"BoardX? It's not. It got killed by management. It's called SpriteQuest now."

He stopped. "They killed my game?"

"No. They repurposed it. They're recycling as much of the

functionality as they can, but Jeff is dead and has been rein-carnated as Prince Amulon."

"Dear God."

When we got to Steve's dorm, his ex-co-workers had bar-ricaded the doors with jumbo concrete ashtrays. They assumed that Steve was, if not the harbinger of CSARS, bad luck. His few personal effects came flying down from a sixth-floor window into an azalea bush. His toothbrush cut into the soil like a javelin.

"I thought they were my friends," he said.

"Steve, just be grateful they were even willing to touch your personal effects. Where are we going to sleep tonight?"

"The factory."

"—!"

"Ethan, it'll be fun."

And so we trudged back to spend the night camped out on the two couches in the shoe factory's front office. We scrounged tea and sultana raisin cookies that were in a box on top of somebody's desk. Then, across the room, I noticed something that made me think I was hallucinat-ing—a computer monitor displaying a working Internet connection.

• • •

**From Kaitlin . . .**

Hi, Ethan, you glamorous world traveller. How is your Xanadu Hotel? We're so jealous of you. I'm not wearing makeup today, and I'm dressed like a slut, and all the guys in motion capture are ogling me. Am I making you jealous?

The big news here is that John Doe's cartoon curse on Mark is working, and Mark is really losing it. There was a particularly explicit (and hence funny) *Itchy & Scratchy* MPEG circulating yesterday, and everyone was in stitches. Mark was sweating and turning white. We thought he was faking it, but no.

What else . . . lunch in the cafeteria was braised lamb shanks with rabbit profiteroles, so all the vegetarians staged an hour-long hunger strike that was totally pathetic . . .

• • •

**From Cowboy . . .**

Hey, Dude. Gord-O tried to get me to do a Cheerios run for him. What balls, huh? What else is new? I'm adding an ACDelco automotive cigarette lighter to my PC so that I can bring fire into the pod (and also my Bluetooth GPS). It's this neat little subroutine that . . .

• • •

**From John Doe . . .**

Ethan, are you aware that there is nothing green anywhere in or around your desk? Do you think you might be either partially colour-blind or perhaps genetically encoded so as to dislike green? What would be the Darwinian advantage to such a quirk?

• • •

**From Evil Mark . . .**

Everybody's probably telling you I'm crazy and can't understand cartoons, but it's not that simple . . .

• • •

**From Mom . . .**

Hi, dear. I hope your trip is going well, and I hope you have
found young Steven in good spirits. Kam tells me he's been
doing some important business work over there! Kam is so generous. You're lucky to know him. Please promise me you won't
spend too much money on those appalling sneakers that make
you look like a hoodlum. Honestly, if you'd just put your money
into a savings account . . .

• • •

**From Dad . . .**

That pesky bitch Ellen is back from Toronto and keeps calling my cellphone. What am I going to do about her? I think I'll
ask Kam to help. He's such a can-do sort of guy. Also,
Canteen is next week. Promise you'll show up, and no excuses
like you've given me the past five years running. It's important
to Kam and me that you show your support.

• • •

Sending mail was impossible because of the QWERTY-hostile
Chinese keypads. Clicking on REPLY didn't work, and having
an Internet connection was so precious that we didn't want
to dick around with too many key commands. On the plus

side, Steve's company account was still operative. He cruised through many months of cc's that guided him step by step through the gutting of BoardX and the rise of SpriteQuest. When he logged off, he said, "Ethan, hand me my rig."

Then we looked to the right, where we saw hundreds of car keys on a rack, each one numbered.

Under a setting sun, we sped off in what we hoped was the direction of Shanghai, in a top-of-the-line Feng Shui 3000 combination grain harvester/off-road vehicle. Fifteen minutes later we ran out of gas in the middle of nowhere.

With no food.

With no water.

Night had fallen, and we were out on the road, trying to decide what to do next, when a showroom-condition black GMC Yukon with high beams on approached us and slowed down. It had Washington State plates, and at the wheel was . . . *Douglas Coupland*?

"Ethan Jarlewski? What the hell are you doing out here?"

"What the hell are *you* doing here?"

"I'm taking photographs of abandoned factories as an art project. Like I need to explain myself to you."

"Where'd you get that car?"

"I suspect it was probably a sweet-sixteen present for the daughter of the guy who runs the pesticide distillery three valleys away from here." Coupland looked at Steve. "Would that be *Steve*?"

Steve said hi.

"Okay. I guess I'll be going, then." Coupland clicked his automatic window roll-up button.

"Doug!"

*"What?"*

"Get us out of here."

Coupland snorted. Steve asked, "How did you get into this zone? There's a quarantine."

"Haven't you guys learned yet that the global economy is fuelled almost exclusively by American hundred-dollar bills?"

"*Doug*. Take us back to Shanghai. *Please.*"

"Why should I do that? I've got my next two days all planned."

"We're trapped. We're fucked. We have no idea what to do."

Coupland rubbed his chin. "What will you give me if I drive you back?"

I looked at Steve and we shrugged. "A few hundred bucks."

"Grow up. Give me something real."

Steve and I were stumped.

Coupland said, "I knew you were a fuck-up, Ethan. Tell you what, if I get you guys back to Shanghai, then you have to give me your laptop computer, period. No erasing anything."

"What?"

"That's it, game boy. Give me your life."

"That's evil."

"Take it or leave it."

"But you've already gone through it."

"I barely scratched its surface. Do we have a deal?"

"Okay. Sure."

"Look me in the eyes and say it like you *mean* it."

I looked into Coupland's cold eyes; it was like looking into wells filled with drowned toddlers. "Okay. I promise."

"Hop in. And remember this, Ethan, *I own you now.*"

We drove away.

. . . pause

. . . waiting to respawn

Outside of videogames, how many games do you play by yourself? Here's a question: did people in the past masturbate more than they do now—or is self-pleasuring a biological constant? A wicked CPU can never replace the artificial intelligence provided by human beings—or can it? Just in case you were in doubt, other people can secretly tell everything about the way you feel. Hi. I'm a definitive gridiron videogame experience! Hi. I'm an expansion pack. Hi. Let me tell you, I would have *never* played Grand Theft Auto: San Andreas had I known that it harboured pornographic content or comely sluts who tempt you. What's this? Another year, another fifty dollars? Is it really worth it? You know, when you dream at night, your brain doesn't use your eyes to see. When you play videogames, your brain plays sports without using your body. Does this make you feel free, or does this make you feel like a prisoner of your meat? That buzz you're always hearing is everybody having sex. Dungeon master. Pimp. Prince. Crack ho. Why do games always want good to triumph over evil? Sometimes it's good training to fight for the dark side. If you're trying to quit drugs, who do you seek out, an ex-addict or Ned Flanders? You know what? When you read a book, you're totally lost in your own private world, and society says that's a good and wonderful thing. But if you play a game by yourself, it's this weird, fucked-up, socially damaging activity. What sort of narrow-minded moron propagates this lie? When your grandfather plays solitaire, is he isolating himself? Get a grip, people. Amateur. Anal. Asians. Babes. Big clits. Big cocks. Big tits. Blacks. Nothing I feel is real. Gaming isn't storytelling. Don't be so sentimental. Gaming is about killing your prey. It's about you killing me, or us killing them. All online activity is monitored. Attempts to bypass security are grounds for legal action. I look forward to a day when everybody who lives in sweatshop equatorial nations has the disposable income to choose from the fine array of games and gaming systems our society creates. Lock and load! The differences between you and the others are almost non-existent. The human body is one of the sickest and most foul things we can possibly view. I think that people who savour looking at nude bodies are pervs and molesters—we ought to lock them away and chuck the key. I love touching a game—you know what I mean? When your reptile brain and your CPU become one. Hey, if unplayable crap is such unplayable crap, why does it keep getting made? Last night I had this dream where Mario was a greeter at Wal-Mart and it really fucked me up. No matter what they say, to the gaming companies it all boils down to one dollar per hour of gameplay. It's a constant. Blondes. Bondage. Brunettes. Butts. Celebrities. Cumshots. If you crave tits, schlong, snatch or getting it on, you're a godless, amoral monster who will burn in hell. Online gaming makes me feel empty and powerful. And online gaming also makes me feel that the world is a conquerable place, not a globally warmed degraded shithole. Kill the killers. Hi. I'm Xbox and 360 negative. Other people are boring. Entering a game space and running like hell isn't my idea of a good time. Do you like anonymous sex? Sometimes the story wrecks the game. Instead of getting fun, you only get blather. Come on, just stop it. There's a lot to be said for ignoring the main quest line. Sometimes we all just want to drive a cab or get a blowjob in GTA: SA. Life is good. Life sucks. Pen-and-paper RPG gamers are too into the story. They're escaping reality in a lazy way. Books are too non-interactive. Come on, just give us a cheat code . . . wait—it's called reading the last page so you don't have to read the whole thing. I like flaunting my eighties geek credentials. I hate guys who flaunt their eighties geek credentials. To me they just seem old. Thinking you're immortal is the same as being immortal. I eat sugary crap all day long, and at my pathetically young age I've stopped tucking in my shirt because my stomach sags out over my waistband. It makes me look like a bad source of genetic material. Dating. Dildo. Drunk girls. Escorts. Farm sex. Feet. It pisses me off that advertisers lump me in with extreme sports people, but at the same time it's okay because people will think I'm more fit than I really am. You may not post new threads. You may not post replies. You may not post attachments. You may not edit your posts. VB code is On. User Name. Remember Me? Password. I noticed this thing— no matter how smoothly you walk, your head always bobs side to side, just a little bit, whereas in games, the smooth, bobless motion generates a strange and omniscient sensation that is more primal than we're willing to admit. This next one is the first song on our new album. It just came out this week, and the song is called "Pocky." In my neighbourhood, all the teenage boys are dying because they're driving their cars using videogame physics instead of real-world physics. They turn too quickly and change lanes too quickly. They don't understand traction or centripetal force. And they're dropping like flies. Puzzles aren't stories. Games that incorporate sex skills as a payoff are embarrassing. Hey, you asked for it! *It may be easy for me, but it's hard as hell for Joe Gamer.* Fuck machines. Gay. Gloryhole. Group sex. Hairy. Hand jobs. Hardcore. Housewives. Indians. Ever since I got addicted to ElfQuest, I've stopped dreaming at night. It's scaring me. I'll choose God mode over Normal mode every time. Non-linear stories? Multiple endings? No loading times? It's called life on earth. I have yet to shoot my load too early. Thread. Tools. Search this thread. Show printable version. Email this page.

All flaming, trolling and off-topic debates will be removed from these threads. All childish banter will be closed or deleted from now on. A troll is a user who posts solely for the purpose of provoking arguments and flamefests. Feeling unique isn't the same as being unique. Trolls typically offer little in terms of useful debate. Hey, girls. Hey, boys. Superstar deejays . . . here we go! A flame is an argument in which one user verbally attacks another using conflicting opinions. Once users begin arguing like children, insulting each other as they do, we have what can be considered a flame war. Individual girls. Interracial. Rate this thread! I'm too old to give a shit about what's hot under the Christmas tree this year. Just stop overpricing everything. Stop bundling your units. Stop being SKU-driven greedheads. Stop scroogeing me. And while we're at it, please stop putting quotes from Nietzsche at the end of your emails. Five years ago you were laughing your guts out over *American Pie 2*. What—suddenly you've magically turned into Noam Chomsky? You think you're special, but you're still just an embryo. Latinas. Legs. Lesbians. Live sex cams. Mature. Midgets. They made you a moron. A potential H-bomb. Natural tits. I sometimes wonder who's really writing those reviews out there. I have this friend, Gail, whose job was to generate fake websites about nine months in advance of a big game or movie so that when media sloths went to "research" their articles, they simply regurgitated what the studio wanted them to. You know, everyone talks about games like they're oxygen or food, and we'll die without them. What a load of sludge. They didn't exist twenty years ago. They're blank. They add nothing to the world. It drives me nuts when people say, "Gamers are developing hand-eye coordination skills that will help them in future situations, like when flying a military jet." Stop defending gaming. It doesn't want it or need it. I never finish any of my games. There's a big pile of them beside the TV. I'm too stupid to throw them out, and too bored to play them. I deserve whatever life throws at me. I know what Castlevania is, and that sort of scares me. LMFAO. To pray for a killer is to be a killer. Hi. I'm selectively backwards compatible. After playing Halo 2 for three hours, I went out and mowed down a Red Cross blood bank, raped anything with a pulse and trashed the local mall. Then I toasted the gods of destruction with a goblet of blood stolen from a Girl Guide's body. Old men and teens. Panties. Pantyhose. Peeing. You know that psychiatric question where they ask you, "If you could push a secret button and kill someone you hated, and nobody else on earth would ever know, would you push it?" I would. Every single time. And to look at me, you'd never know it. Console makers have feelings, too. No they don't. They're monsters. There's always some asshole who brings back the latest thing from Tokyo, isn't there? Your urges are the dark side of God. Every console, every hand-held device is like a language or a dialect. The brain was designed to know only maybe five or six languages, tops. Even those linguistic freaks from Holland max out at five languages. So choose and love your game systems with care. Anything can be a weapon. After your teens, it's kind of loser-ish to be discussing corporate pricing strategies for games. You are an individual with free will. Either buy it or don't buy it. Shaved. Small tits. Smoking. Squirting. Don't discuss Sony like it's a great big benevolent cartoon character who lives next door to Astro Boy. Like any company, Sony is comprised of individuals who are fearful for their jobs on a daily basis, and who make lame decisions based pretty much on fear and conforming to social norms—but then, that's every corporation on earth, so don't single out one specific corporation as lovable and cute. They're all evil and greedy. They're all sort of in the moral middle ground, where good and bad cancel each other out, so there's nothing really there—which is, in it's own way, far darker than any paranoid or patriarchal theory of Sony. Time = torture. After playing Tony Hawk's Pro Skater, I went outside and rode my board down the handrail outside the civic library. I'm a quad now. "Her name is Rio, and she dances on the sand." In the end, it's the Chinese gamer who'll dictate the business. Learn Mandarin. Look, it's just one more button to push to make something happen. All things considered, you're still an ass clown. Gamers aren't consumers. They're gamers, but they also enjoy looking up the stock price of Sony on Yahoo! Finance. Everybody saw you cheat. Trannies. Uniforms. Wrestling women. New Cheats! It doesn't matter how good games get, heaven will always be an arcade full of arcade games to me. MMOG 2K6 SFX PS2 MSRP. God approves of the market-share battle between Coke and Pepsi. Hurry, you thick-fingered trolls! Two-Edge has captured Ekuar! Why didn't you stupid Wolfriders send Petalwing back to us? They have tasted troll blood . . . they smell fear, and the prey is old and easy! Runes. Wizard. Immortal. Fucktoy. Your inner sickness is visible to others. They're only flattering your consumer ego by telling you you're unique. The hotter the elves, the worse the game. You can't kill people who are already dead. Even on my Athlon XP 2600+ with a GeForce4 Ti4800, I stuttered a few times when zoomed all the way out and in a heated battle. Nature made more of you than is necessary. Gameplay: 2 of 5. Graphics: 4 of 5. Sound: 3 of 5. Two characters in the same game sharing the same voice is kind of suspicious. Meekness is a strategy for losers. Contains one or more of the following: sunflower oil, salt, trisodium phosphate, cultured milk, salt, agar, whey and disodium glutamate. Disco mode. Flame mode. Hoverboard mode. Sim mode. Super Blood mode. People confuse children with angels: make it work for you. You asked for it.

**Part Three**
Breakfast Is for Losers

<u>**Five Months Later**</u>

Kwantlen College Learning Annex
Course 3072-A

**Assignment:** Write about What You Know
. . . and the People You Know

**"All Rise and Pray to the
Hug Machine"**
*Meeting Today's New Tech Worker*

by Kaitlin Anna Boyd Joyce

After having worked at my current tech firm for the larger part of a year, I have come to the conclusion that my co-workers aren't so much idiots as they are fellow citizens in the thrall of various modes of persistent low-grade autism.

The clinical definition is that they are suffering from mild versions of "pervasive development disorders" or "sensory integration dysfunctions." Asperger's syndrome is one variant that has recently garnered much media hype. People with this sort of condition are known as "high functioning" autistics because they can more or less operate in the day-to-day world. Some people like to think of high-functioning autism as a trendy disease. Wrong. It is not a disease, it's a condition. Most high-functioning autistics resent being talked down to and value their condition. It is not a badge of victimhood for them—it is merely who they are.

Perhaps the broadest way of understanding the world of the high-functioning autistic is to treat all stimuli that impact on the human body not as sensory input but as information bombardment. Most people are able to sift out the day's excess information without ever thinking about it, but to the tech worker exhibiting autistic—okay, let's just say the word: *geek*—to most geeks, a hug is not a hug, it's the physical equivalent of holding a novelty marine foghorn up to the ear and blasting it directly into the central nervous system. When you hug a geek, you're overloading them in a manner they find intolerable. They feel and express shock and revulsion when touched.

Here's a personal example. Low-grade autistics have problems with sensory input, sound being a biggie. My boyfriend, Ethan, is a seemingly average NT (neurotypical), and yet he exhibits a specific autistic variant called hyper-acuity. He has a small, specific band of sound frequencies that make him go mental. If I'm in the bathroom with the door closed and Ethan is in the living room watching a Wrestling Entertainment marathon with the volume set on high, all I have to do is clip one of my toenails with a small generic nail clipper and his entire cerebral system shuts down. He screams at me for making "that awful fucking noise." Likewise, Ethan cannot fall asleep if the Braun eight-cup coffeemaker on the floor below us is turned on because, according to him, it makes a specific brain-spiking click every forty-five seconds. I have pulled a chair up to the coffee maker and sat with my ear pressed right up to it. I have yet to hear such a noise. The fact remains that Ethan screams at me to *turnitthefuckoff* every forty-five seconds.

Here is another example. My cubicle mate John Doe (yes, that is his legal name—a long story) is a complete geek. He finds an immense sense of relief in performing small specific tasks that cumulatively lead to something larger—a textbook prerequisite of the previously mentioned condition called Asperger's syndrome. John is ideally suited to the coding universe, where tens of thousands of lines of numbingly dull code string together to make a hockey puck shoot and score with thrilling real-time physics.

I, too, am a geek and have my own set of autism-related problems. I have a mild version of facial blindness, prosopagnosia. It's hard for me to remember faces and names, and I have trouble telling when someone is either happy or sad. It's not something I'm too thrilled about.

It turns out that most people suffer from prosopagnosia to some degree. Who out there past the age of twenty-five can get through an entire party without faking a name or two? The entire Dale Carnegie method of Winning Friends and Influencing People boils down to ways of mechanically training yourself past facial blindness. It appalls me that people will like and respect you for no other reason than that you give the illusion of remembering their name. Is that all we are in the end—vain lumps of DNA flattered by the cheesiest of mnemonic devices?

More examples will follow. What is important here is at least to become comfortable with the increasingly more apparent scientific fact that what we describe as "character" and "personality" are not so much spiritual or cosmic states of being, but rather, an overall effect created by clusters of overlapping brain dysfunctions.

Witness the universally understood archetype of the class clown. Is he funny and lovable, or is he farther along the personality spectrum of disinhibition? In the middle of the spectrum you have the bulk of society. Move a bit to the left and you find people who are "talkative" or "funny." Move a bit more to the left and there's the class clown. Move along farther and you find a personality who "doesn't know when to shut up." Farther still is someone who talks to himself, or perhaps someone with Tourette's syndrome, which is merely one dimension of disinhibition. Perhaps at the farthest reaches of disinhibition we have the babbling idiot.

Very well. Now then, let's go back to the centre and move a little the other way. We find a person who is "quiet." Then we find people who are "shy." Moving ever rightward, we encounter the "aloof," then the "loners" and then the "spooky." At the far right we have the Unabomber frothing away inside his geographically secluded shack.

My point here is that autistic mini-traits exist within the general population, and that microautism seems to favour people in tech and computer industries.

Here's a much simpler example of geeks and neural processing malfunctions: Has anybody experienced a geek environment in which said geeks wear perfume or deodorant? Chances are no. While advanced microautistics are more commonly men than women, both share a marked dislike of scent. My co-worker Bree was trying to impress this snobby French guy, and she wore a stinky Parisian floral fart perfume to work. She was chased out of the work area with crumpled-up balls of paper and anti-Gallic invective. Likewise, my geek co-workers are unable to process the smell of McDonald's food, and call it the Taint. The worst odour of all is the smell of butter-flavoured microwaved popcorn wafting out of the coffee room. Despite the unspoken ban on said substance, a co-worker nicknamed "Cowboy" popped a bag one Friday afternoon only to return to his desk to find all of his possessions removed. He quickly returned the bag to the kitchen, where he incarcerated it inside three ziplock bags. When he returned to his desk, all of his possessions had reappeared, as if by magic.

Another interesting autistic scenario in my life is one shared by two people I know—Kam, a businessman, and Steve, a marketing executive. Steve and Kam have, in a genuine medical and biological sense of the phrase, no sense of humour. Yes, that's right, they live in a world without laughter. Science tells us that humourlessness is just another offshoot of autism, a type of social disengagement that ultimately ends in a shutdown life.

Likewise, I'd argue that boring people aren't boring—they're hampered by microautism, the clinical term being "lack of social or emotional reciprocity." In a clever twist of fate, when Steve started working at my company, he spoke almost entirely in cutesy cloying management jargon peppered with self-help poop. However, for complex reasons, Steve ended up as a heroin addict. In becoming an addict, Steve acquired both a sense of humour and irony. Steve no longer uses stereotyped and repetitive language. He's fun to have around but, for reasons I can't go into here, has to keep his new personality hidden from most of the people at work.

My co-worker Bree exhibits another form of microautism. Her autism is the lack of social or emotional reciprocity she exhibits in her relentless pursuit of sexual encounters. This isn't just a trashy cable-TV urban sluttery—Bree loses all social engagement skills after she's bagged a shag. Ironically, her way of stopping this microautistic behaviour is through an age-inappropriate relationship with her guy from France, who's maybe forty.

I am not a complainer. I believe that if you identify a problem you should also try to fix that problem. So, for extra credit on this assignment, I have built a hugging machine.

What is a hugging machine? It is an ungainly device made of plywood, two-by-fours and two crib mattresses that's used to apply pressure to the entire body without the sensory overload of being hugged by another human being. It is an affordable, comfortable, non-sexual means of calming a person, and is designed to allow your typical geek to get more productivity from his or her days.

• • •

After almost half a year of stalling, Kaitlin finally finished her hug machine. We were bustling about jPod, installing the final few bolts in preparation for its campus christening party. The last-minute pressure made Kaitlin needy.

"What if nobody comes?"

"Kaitlin, relax. The party will be mobbed."

"What if people come but don't like the machine?"

"Kaitlin, this is a game design company."

"Or what if they want to come, but they don't think they can handle the social pressure of being seen using a hug machine?" Kaitlin has become convinced that everybody in the tech industry is autistic to some degree. It's her new cause.

"Relax."

As an added bonus, after being held by Agriculture Canada for inspection for umpteen months, Cowboy's shipment of dried cola nut powder arrived from the US. He'd perfected a formula for "jCola" and was excited about debuting his creation alongside the hug machine. He'd rented a 1960s beverage machine like something from a roller rink, and the uncarbonated brew looked really, well . . . *refreshing*, swishing away inside the machine's colourless Plexi dome.

"Cowboy, just give me a taste."

"No way. Not until everyone's here and we toast the success of the hug machine."

Was there excitement in the air? No. But a party was much needed after the hours we'd been logging on SpriteQuest.

I spent the morning generating texture mapping for soot, powder burns, blood stains and some awesome particle effects for Ronald's Lair—this on top of my regular job. I pretty much live at work now.

At five we sat around waiting for guests to show up. Who was first to arrive? Mom, who was accidentally invited through the overzealous use of email lists on Cowboy's part. Mom had actually been on her best behaviour in the months following my China trip. I think she's feeling a bit guilty for having Steve sold into slavery, and we still haven't totally mended that fence.

"Hello, dear," she said. "Always nice to come visit your workplace. That ventilation duct over there looks awfully strong. I think I'll go light up a cigarette."

"We cranked up the ventilator just so partygoers can smoke."

"You're a thoughtful child."

Sure enough, come five o'clock, geeks began to arrive and mill about, but Cowboy refused to give sneak previews of jCola until six, so people had to fetch their own beverages from the cafeteria machines. This bothered John Doe. "Cowboy, I may not be a member of Van Halen, but I do know one must serve drinks at a party. Therefore I am going to hand out my private stock of Zima." He produced a twenty-four-pack from beneath his desk. "Yes, Zima—a bold, tasty treat with a spark of arctic freshness. But did you—" John stopped dead and turned a monochrome grey.

"Are you okay?" Kaitlin asked.

"Oh, my dear God."

We turned around to see what he was staring at. It appeared to be a highway construction worker: faded denim, a sun-ravaged face, short black hair and a stocky build, bounding straight towards us. The construction worker barked like a bull walrus protecting his harem. "crow! There's a penis infestation happening here in this ridiculous building!"

"Hi, Mom."

*John Doe's mother!*

"So *this* is where you work." She glowered at the pod. "I see just one woman here. What's your name?"

"Kaitlin."

"Kaitlin, how can you possibly work in a space where there's not even one other woman and the possibility of synchronizing ovulation cycles?"

"Legally, the men's and women's rooms have to be the same size. So it's actually quite nice. And my friend Bree works here, too."

"Wait! I see another female over there smoking."

Kaitlin said, "That's Ethan's mother. Ethan works with your son, too."

"crow," barked his mother, "I need you to introduce me to your comrades."

"Um, Mom, this is Ethan, Ethan's mother, Kaitlin, Cowboy, Evil Mark. Everybody, this is my mother, freedom."

Without asking, all of us knew that "freedom" was not capitalized.

I said, "John never told us his family called him crow."

"It is his name. But I respect his right and need as a male to generate a name that supports his masculinity in the cheerless environment of technology."

Cowboy snorted.

freedom cut him a withering glance. "You must be the male slut," she said. She looked at the jCola machine. "What's this—you have your own sugar-water facility here?"

"It's our own brand of cola." I could hear the pride in Cowboy's voice.

"Of all the corporate cysts and welts on the planet, you choose to mimic Coca-Cola?"

Cowboy surprised us. "It's actually a form of subversion," he said. "I located an organic cruelty-free source of cola nut powder, and the sugar came from a Zimbabwe sugar-making facility endorsed by the UN."

"That's still cash cropping."

"One step at a time, freedom."

"Amen," came a male voice from behind me: Kam Fong. A more potentially disastrous clash of personalities was hard to imagine.

freedom asked, "Do you work here, too?"

"Not at all."

"crow, introduce us."

"Mom, this is Kam Fong. Kam Fong, this is my mother."

"Kam, what do you do?"

"I work with the Chinese government to ensure that as many male babies are born as possible. We take the unwanted girl babies, dry them out, and then grind them into a powder, which we mix with latex paints to make anti-skid coating for the military's helipads."

freedom squinted hard at Kam, and then announced, "Finally! A true radical spirit here in this psychic morgue you call jPod."

Kam pulled out cigars. "Smoke?"

"Love to. Anything to help Cuba."

Kam and freedom went over to the ventilation duct and chewed the fat like old school friends. From snippets I could tell they were discussing hydroponics. Their unlikely but cheerful meshing of personalities was a jolt—so much so that when I finally realized my mother was talking to me, I found I'd completely gapped out. "Sorry, Mom, what were you saying?"

"What an amazing woman. So strong. So confident. So manly yet female at the same time. So forceful."

I should have removed Mom from the party at that moment, but alas, it was too late. Mom was infatuated.

A few minutes later Cowboy went off to get Styrofoam cups from the coffee room, and Kam Fong put a quarter-pound of medicinal-grade cocaine into the jCola, where it dissolved beautifully. "You losers might as well get the real thing," he said.

Cowboy came back and poured a glass for everybody, and Kaitlin stood up to give a brief inaugural speech. Her hug machine looked like a cross between an incline bench and an industrial loom.

Kaitlin said, "I'd like you all to know that this hug machine is for everybody in the company, and any time you need to use it, come right in. I've covered the hugging pads with removable terry cloth cozies, which I promise I'll wash twice a week. Remember, you're not walking diseases in need of correction. You're confident industry professionals who lead rich, rewarding lives and who don't need to prove anything to anybody."

freedom led a salvo of applause.

Kaitlin looked at John Doe. "John, would you like to be the first to try the hug machine?"

"Yes, please."

"Very well. In you go."

John sat on the little chair portion and then pulled a lever, which activated the two baby crib mattresses. With equal pressure applied from both sides to his torso, John appeared to be in bliss. "I want to live inside this machine."

Kaitlin said, "This hug machine is now launched." She raised her glass: "To the hug machine!"

The medicinal beverages took maybe fifteen seconds to kick in. A boom box was produced and people began to dance—well, okay, they moved their bodies quickly and in an odd manner.

Steve came in. "Techies are *dancing*?"

"I know," I said.

"How did *that* happen?"

"They're high as kites. Kam dumped a quarter-pound of premium coke into Mark's jCola."

"Any left?"

"All gone."

"Shit. Well, maybe it'll improve their productivity."

"I suspect they'll all start developing amazing ideas for new games, but they'll pass out around three a.m. The next morning it'll turn out that all they wrote down was the natural logarithm of yesterday's Jumble puzzle."

"I need to score real bad," said Steve. "Can you drive me downtown?"

Steve lost his driver's licence a week after we got back from China. "Steve, why don't you just kick your habit? I feel like I'm back doing Gord-O's Cheerios runs. At least at Costco I can park my car reasonably safely."

"Don't knock smack if you haven't tried it."

"Why can't you buy it in bulk?"

"Ethan, if it was bulk, how could I keep it fresh? Good fresh smack is like good lettuce or fresh meat. Look—here comes Kam."

"Hi, boys."

Since he got back, Steve has decided to like Kam. Why? Because without Kam, Steve would never have discovered smack, and without smack, he would have been trapped inside his old personality forever. ("Ethan, do you think I enjoyed being Ned Flanders every diddily-day of the week? Fuck diddily-uck *no*. Every fibre of my being wanted to napalm the dry-erase boards, but instead I'd stand there smiling at pie charts, discussing how much of the budget we should allot for dried cranberries for the goodie bags at the Orlando staff retreat."

"Dried cranberries—you mean Craisins?"

"Yes, Craisins.")

"Kam, can you give Steve some smack so I can get on with work here?" I said.

"Ethan, I promised your mother I wouldn't interfere with Steve's life any more."

"Then let's just go downtown and get it over with," I said.

In the car Steve had a jones and was rubbing his hands all over his body and shivering. "Steve, can you maybe keep your hands still? You're freaking me out, and you're flaking all over the upholstery. I just vacuumed it."

"Kam is right. You really are middle-class."

"You guys talk about me in those terms?"

"Sure."

I let it drop. "Which corner today?" Shopping for heroin with Steve is like choosing the right deli. I looked around; I'd never seen so many people looking for fixes.

"I forgot," Steve said, "it's Welfare Wednesday."

The alleys were a maze of graffitied brick, soiled Dumpsters and lame, dispirited pigeons atop crumbled pavement glazed with algae blooms. I could hear plastic mini bleach bottles popping under the car's wheels. Then I spotted three relatively together people, who looked like they had day jobs and fixed addresses, scoring from a shrunken-apple-headed hippie. They looked relatively jolly, and Steve said, "There."

I never would have believed how normal some smack users can be. (*This is my coffee break. I have to get back and install the new Norton AntiVirus patch.*) It turned out our hippie saleslady was named Tina, and she was handing out free lotto tickets with every purchase. Steve commended her. "You should move up the food chain a bit. You're too good to be doing one-to-ones."

"You think so?"

"I sure do."

"I've been thinking about it. But most of the time all I

really want is to supply my own habit and maybe get some donuts and a new nightgown with no cigarette burns."

"Tina, you can aim higher than that."

"Mister, you're the wind beneath my wings."

• • •

Much news when I returned from the smack run. First off, Cowboy went nuts after three glasses of jCola and hooked up with some fine young lady using his pseudonym on choking-forit.com. They arranged to meet in the Denny's beside the building where his sister lives, and then in walked his sister, and it turned out that, yes, he'd arranged to get together *with* his sister. He's sworn off sex forever. He's never made that promise before.

"It felt like that dream you get where your dick falls off and you put it back into place like it was a plastic dildo, except it was . . ." He drifted off.

"Except it was *what*?" Podoids always demand the full story.

"Except it was like looking at myself, except I had tits and female plumbing and . . ."

"And?"

"I don't want to talk about it any more."

And then John Doe told me that he and Kam Fong were involved in some kind of business deal with Douglas Coupland.

"*What*?"

"Just what I told you. Hardware. LED screens, that's all I can say. It's what he was doing in China when he was there with you."

"He said he was there to take pretentious arty-farty photos."

"For God's sake, Ethan, wake up. He's a novelist. He lies for a living. And besides, Kam's always right about business. I've invested some money in the project already."

"*What?*"

"Me, too," said Bree.

"Anyone *else?*"

Everybody, including Kaitlin, raised their hands. "I don't believe this. Why didn't anyone tell me?"

Kaitlin said, "He came here last week. You were out looking at the new Nikes at Brentwood Mall when Doug dropped by."

"He came in here?"

"He's a really great guy."

*This isn't happening.* "Tell me, what is this screen project he's doing?"

"We can't tell you."

"What do you mean you can't tell me?"

"We can't. We signed nondisclosure agreements."

I looked at Kaitlin. "Why didn't *you* tell me?"

"I didn't think you liked the guy. Besides, you know how stringent NDAs are."

"But you and I live together and have sex several times a week."

"You make it sound so romantic."

The phone rang and I grabbed it. "Hello?"

"Hi, dear."

"Hi, Mom."

"That was a fun party earlier this evening. How nice to

see you introverts having a dab of happiness in your lives."

"Yeah. I guess so."

"Ethan, what is it I'm hearing in your voice?"

"I'm just pissed at everybody here. They've all invested in one of Kam Fong's schemes—with Douglas Coupland, no less—and nobody told me about it."

"The screen project?"

"That's it. Don't tell me you've invested, too?"

"Sorry, dear, but I did. It's a smart idea."

"Can you tell me about it, then?"

"I had to sign a nondisclosure form. So did your father."

*"What?"*

"Fair's fair, dear. And besides, I don't think I'd be comfortable if Kam Fong knew I'd violated my nondisclosure agreement."

She had a point.

"Okay, so what's up?"

"I was wondering if you could ask your friend there for his mother's phone number."

"John?"

"That's him. I'd like to speak with his mother, freedom."

Whatever Mom was up to, it didn't bode well for freedom's future. I paused too long, and this made Mom suspicious.

"Ethan? What's going on?"

"It's nothing, Mom."

"I just don't know how I gave birth to such a suspicious son. All I want to do is ask freedom about a new boron phosphate fertilizer she's imported from Vietnam. It's raising her crop yield remarkably."

I handed the phone to John Doe and went off to the coffee room to fume. I could feel clown rage welling up inside me and knew it was time to go back to my work.

‰»¥∏§¿£≈‡O

●○æ■□·♦√◆❖◆⊠□§

:O

)⑧collapsing Korean department store

궤멸 백화점

**Assignment:** Interview Someone
You Think You Already Know

**"Hi, I'm Steve"**

by Kaitlin Anna Boyd Joyce

**Steve Lefkowitz, forty-five,** is project director of a game I'm working on called SpriteQuest. Recently Steve had a remarkable but not unpleasant change in personality . . . but why tell you when you can meet Steve for yourself?

**Kaitlin:**
Steve, when I arrived at the company I thought you were a sexless prig.

**Steve:**
I think that was the general impression I gave everybody. There was a part of me that knew things were all wrong in my life. But in order to repress that emotion, I'd do things like wear sweaters draped over my shoulders with the arms twisted together. I didn't want to be who I was.

**Kaitlin:**
Where were you before coming to work here?

**Steve:**

I was at Toblerone.

**Kaitlin:**

You mean those European triangular chocolate bars that most North Americans associate with hotel mini-bars?

**Steve:**

You nailed it. It was as if Toblerone had been typecast and couldn't get any new roles outside of hotels. So I revamped its image. We had to "think outside the mini-bar."

**Kaitlin:**

That's a stupid joke.

**Steve:**

Tell me about it. But that joke was my life for two years. Not like there was much else going on.

**Kaitlin:**

Is there a Mrs. Lefkowitz?

**Steve:**

Once. Briefly. I usually scared women away by date number three—even the hard-core husband chasers. I was hard to be around. In my spare time I'd do things like go into your sock drawer and reorganize it so that it made better use of the space.

**Kaitlin:**
Yuck.

**Steve:**
The sock drawer was what usually ended things.

**Kaitlin:**
Don't you have a kid?

**Steve:**
He and his mother are back east. We never got married. I
was a one-hit wonder in the kid department.

**Kaitlin:**
Let me get this back to work. Tell me about Toblerone.

**Steve:**
I'm one of the world's few experts on mini-bars.

**Kaitlin:**
Tell me something about mini-bars I probably don't know.

**Steve:**
Here's a good one about hotel rooms in general. Most
hotels have an armoire-type thing where they stash the TV
set. Next time you go into your hotel room, stand up on a
chair and look on top of the armoire.

**Kaitlin:**
Why?

**Steve:**

When people are checking out of a room, it's where they dump stuff they don't want to take with them, but which they can't throw away in case the maid finds it. Stuff that could get them arrested or cause them shame.

**Kaitlin:**

Like what?

**Steve:**

Really harsh porn. Pot. Pills. Coins. Touristy things that people gave them that they don't really want. It accumulates from one year to the next. In a Portland hotel I once found a pile of Italian lire, three copies of *Screw* and a $200 photography book inscribed *To Dennis—without you I could never have conceived this book, let alone had the courage to see it to its completion. I owe you everything, Diane.*

**Kaitlin:**

Sounds like Diane needed a reality sandwich.

**Steve:**

The Dianes of this world usually get hosed, don't they?

**Kaitlin:**

It's a law of the universe. But back to mini bars and your Toblerone victory. You took them from near bankruptcy and made them a global victor in the hazelnut–milk chocolate category. I found a picture of you on the cover of *PLU Magazine.*

**Steve:**

Yeah. Everyone expected me to try to coast on my laurels. Maybe I'd go in and revamp the cashew sector. But I wanted a fresh challenge. That's why I decided to go into producing games.

**Kaitlin:**

You play them?

**Steve:**

Good God, no. They're as boring as dirt. The little brats who obsess about them make me sick with worry for the future of the species.

**Kaitlin:**

So why—

**Steve:**

Marketers like to believe that their skills are fully translatable into any other product group. Gaming seemed like a natural challenge.

**Kaitlin:**

Once you were hired, you took a skateboard game that was happily chugging along and changed it into a skateboard game with a turtle as the star.

**Steve:**
Shitty idea, huh? I'm not creative, and yet I felt a need to maintain the illusion of being creative. I wrecked your skateboard game. Sorry about that.

**Kaitlin:**
At least you're honest. But, Steve, the reason for this interview is to ask you about your recent personality change.

**Steve:**
Pretty freaky, isn't it?

**Kaitlin:**
To say the least. What happened?

**Steve:**
Well, I had a crush on a woman, and I think I was a bit of a pest around her.

**Kaitlin:**
Stalking?

**Steve:**
Not quite. But I was a real nuisance, and she had to do something to get me out of her hair. So one morning I got in my car to go to work, and a guy got in the passenger side—fake moustache and the works—and he had a gun. He said we had to drive out of the city, so we did. I was actually feeling really good, because at least something interesting was happening in my life. You'd think I'd be scared,

but no. So we went into the valley. We stopped, and he told me to get out, and I did, and then he handcuffed me, and there was some other guy there with a panel van. They told me to get in, and then they injected me with something. Heroin, I found out later.

**Kaitlin:**
Really?

**Steve:**
Oh, yeah. And it was great. It made being kidnapped seem like an in-flight movie.

**Kaitlin:**
What next?

**Steve:**
The van drove for an hour, and then I could smell salt air, and the van drove onto something floating—a dock or a boat—and the heroin made me kind of woozy. I heard a lot of clanking and thumping, and then it became pretty evident that we were sailing somewhere. A freighter.

**Kaitlin:**
Afraid?

**Steve:**
No way. They kept shooting me up. I wasn't sure if I was dead or alive, but the whole episode was great.

**Kaitlin:**
We have to speed this up.

**Steve:**
A few days later we were in China. They put me in the back of some kind of bus, and I could see everything clearly. Have you ever been to China? No? Well, it's interesting but so polluted and grey and—

**Kaitlin:**
So I've heard.

**Steve:**
Before you know it, I was chained to a machine that stamped out the soles of imitation Nikes, 288 in one go. I got room and board and as much smack as I wanted.

**Kaitlin:**
You weren't freaked out?

**Steve:**
I wasn't even aware I was alive. It wasn't heaven and it wasn't hell. It was interesting.

**Kaitlin:**
Did working there teach you anything about human rights violations and the politics of sweatshopping?

**Steve:**

That's a politically correct kind of question a bit late in the game, Kaitlin.

**Kaitlin:**

I know, but I had to ask it or they'd probably kick me out of this English class I'm in.

**Steve:**

Now *that's* thinking like a true executive.

**Kaitlin:**

Thanks. But, Steve, you still didn't answer the question.

**Steve:**

I didn't learn anything about human rights, but later I did learn about how much my personality changed on smack. When I got back to Vancouver, I realized I was no longer a prisoner of that part of my brain that made me such a generic corporate suckhole. I found that I no longer cared about much of anything—and that I could say whatever I wanted whenever I wanted. It was great.

**Kaitlin:**

You're not reverting back to the old Steve, are you?

**Steve:**

Not as long as I have my daily arm snack.

**Kaitlin:**

Have you since pestered the woman you had a crush on?

**Steve:**

I bumped into her once at a party. The magic is gone, but I'm fond of her.

**Kaitlin:**

And they gave you your old job back, right?

**Steve:**

When I got back home, I was a news story for the first few days. That gave me a forty-eight- to seventy-two-hour pity window, which I totally milked, and they rehired me.

**Kaitlin:**

You can't milk a window.

**Steve:**

?

**Kaitlin:**

Well, this is an English assignment, and you mixed a metaphor. Back to you—how has this big personality change influenced your work?

**Steve:**

While I was gone, they came in and killed the turtle game and repurposed it as an uninspired fantasy game. I may not be creative, but the turtle was my idea and they fucked with it.

**Kaitlin:**
So . . . ?

**Steve:**
I'm working covertly with a team of talented young people to embed a Trojan horse serial killer into the fantasy game.

**Kaitlin:**
I forgot to ask—you still act like the old Steve when you're at work, right?

**Steve:**
Only inasmuch as it allows me to wreck that particular game. It's wonderful pretending to be the old me for nefarious aims.

**Kaitlin:**
Thanks for taking the time to talk to me today, Steve.

**Steve:**
My pleasure, Kaitlin.

• • •

"Ethan."
    "Hey, Dad. What's up?"
    "Your mother's new friend is here, and she's driving me up the wall."
    Cautiously: "New friend?"
    "Christ, she looks like Fred Flintstone's fetus."

*freedom.* "Okay. What are they doing?"

"They're down in the basement, talking about fertilizers. She started talking about semen and fertilization and vulva this and vulva that. I had to get out of there."

Best to change the subject. "How's the new dance routine going?"

"I think I may be too old for ballroom dancing."

"Too old?" Dad placed seventh out of sixty in Canteen (an endless night for all of us). He lost points for not having a light enough touch. Kam came in second. I fully expect the first-place winner to vanish some night while walking the dog. I said, "You're never too old to dance, Dad . . . and you're never too old to dream."

"That's the stupidest thing I've ever heard you say. Were you saying that with irony or for real?"

"Irony?"

"Don't play dumb. I read the paper like anyone else, Ethan. I've read about Generation K and your need to distance yourself from the world by using irony."

"Okay, I *was* being ironic."

"I knew it. By the way, I hear you blew your chance to get in on the Coupland guy's stock offering."

"I was only gone for forty-five minutes."

"Snooze and lose. Your mother and I are going to be *so* rich because of it. I thought you and he were friends."

"It's more complicated than that. Maybe I should give him a call."

"I hear he doesn't like phones, and never answers them."

"How on earth would you know that?"

"Everyone knows that."

"Do you have his number?"

Pause.

"Dad?"

"You can't tell him I gave it to you."

"Why not?"

"Just don't." Dad gave me the number.

"I'm going to phone him right now."

"You do that." There was another pause. "Jesus, they're coming upstairs. I have to go."

*Click.*

. . .

I called Doug.

"Hello?"

"Hi—Doug? It's Ethan."

"Ethannnnnnn . . . . . . . . . ?"

"*China* Ethan."

"Oh yeah. Right. How did you get my number?"

"You gave it to me in Shanghai."

"I did not. I never give out my number. And I never answer the phone. The only reason I picked up this time is because I have an interview scheduled with the *Sydney Morning Herald*. Why are you calling?"

"Doug, can I, uh—"

"Can you *what*?"

"Can I maybe buy into your business plan?"

"Ethan, are you dim? No. It's not like a lemonade stand where you just come over and put down your nickel. Besides, you had your chance, and you were out at

Brentwood Mall, shopping for shoes, of all things. Richly ironic, I have to say."

"Can you at least tell me what your idea is?"

"You want to buy into something, but you don't even know what it is?"

I decided to channel John Doe here: "Is that so wrong?"

"You're a moron. By the way, I've already gotten an advance for the novel I'm going to write based on the contents of your laptop."

"You're a sick fuck."

"I seem to remember a lonely little lamb lost in the remote wastes of industrialized China. *Doug! Doug! Help us! Help us! We have to get out of here!* Face it, Ethan, if it hadn't been for me, you'd be dead by now, so don't play woe-is-me. A call is coming in right now, and it's Australia. I have to go."

"Could you maybe—"

*Click.*

• • •

I asked Kaitlin about irony, and it turns out that only twenty percent of human beings have a sense of irony—which means that eighty percent of the world takes everything at face value. I can't imagine anything worse than that. Okay, maybe I can, but imagine reading the morning newspaper and believing it all to be true on some level.

Brrrrr
Shudder
Shake
Milkshake
McDonald's milkshake
Chalk?
Brain freeze
Milk products
Nestlé
Mineral-deficient baby formula
Switzerland
Corporations
Globalization
Milkshakes everywhere
Even India
Dairy products
Cows
Confusion
Ancestors
Apu from the Kwik-E-Mart
Donuts
The Fox Network
Five thousand channels
Heather Locklear
Healthy, shimmering hair
Computer-generated hair
Pixar cartoon frames in a render farm
First weekend box office
DVD sales
Home entertainment systems

Karaoke
Fear of Karaoke
Abandoning the party
Driving
Shitty old car
Rain
Car commercials
Money
Never enough
Coupland's business thing with Kam
Rage
*Raging Bull*
1970s films
Al Pacino
Eyes like Woody Woodpecker
Cartoons of the 1940s
Ultraviolence
*A Clockwork Orange*
Heaven 17
Pop hits of the 1980s
Pet Shop Boys
London
Plagues
Ebola
Y2K
Hype
Lies

. . . and so on.

**Assignment:** Discuss Your Job with Somebody
Who Probably Doesn't Care about It

**"Flog the Dead Donkey"**

by Kaitlin Anna Boyd Joyce

**Jim Jarlewski** is my boyfriend's father. He's a fiftysome-
thing former financial consultant turned agricultural entrepreneur, a ballroom dance legend and a movie acting extra.
Phew! Jim's a busy guy. I found him in a trailer in North
Vancouver on the set of a Heartland Channel cable-access
movie in which he portrays a convenience store clerk
gunned down by Jane Seymour, who is, in that scene, por-
traying her evil twin.

**Kaitlin:**
Hi, Jim. Is this a speaking role?

**Jim:**
Fucking hell, no. I asked if I could moan or something, but
it breaks union rules. Kaitlin, why are you here?

**Kaitlin:**
School project. I have to discuss my job with an outsider.

**Jim:**
All that gaming shit? No way. It's such a snooze.

**Kaitlin:**
Too late. I'm here, and I don't have time to find a replacement interviewee.

**Jim:**
Crap. Okay, then, what do you and Ethan and all you gaming chowderheads do out in that mothership thingy in Burnaby?

**Kaitlin:**
Could you at least ask it like you care? Pretend it's a line in a film.

[NOTE: Jim's weak spot is his desire for a speaking role in a TV or film production—any role at all. *Anything.*]

**Jim:**
Okay how about this . . .

[Jim spends the next five minutes delivering the same line.]

**Kaitlin:**
Enough already. Here's the deal—I have to discuss my job with you, so I'll begin by telling you that I'm working on this videogame called SpriteQuest.

**Jim:**
As in Sprite, the beverage?

**Kaitlin:**
No. A sprite is technically a fantasy creature one notch lower on the food chain than elf but two notches above pixie.

**Jim:**
Right.

**Kaitlin:**
It's set in the year AD 100,000—among the ruins of what we call Earth. Superior sprite beings from a distant galaxy have crash-landed here and now have to survive in a confusing apocalyptic world where right is wrong and wrong is right.

**Jim:**
[Jim is not paying attention.]

**Kaitlin:**
Jim, I specifically said something dumb to see if you're listening, and you aren't.

**Jim:**
Sorry. I was attempting to prep the emotions for my corpse scene. It won't happen again.

**Kaitlin:**
Thank you. Anyway, Earth also now has two moons—the one we know, and one that was stolen from Mars.

**Jim:**
I'm listening.

**Kaitlin:**
The hero of the game is Prince Amulon. He's neither a sprite nor an elf. He's the prince of a small band of earthlings who have survived across those hundred thousand years. Prince Amulon works with sprites and other characters, and they go through complex perils that will allow him to crack the two moons together. From the resulting cosmic rubble, Prince Amulon will destroy the bad guys, and the energy released will allow the sprites to fix their spacecraft and return home.

**Jim:**
Wait a second—didn't this used to be a skateboard game starring a turtle?

**Kaitlin:**
You are correct. But first it was a *generic* skateboard game. Then we wrecked it by adding a charismatic turtle named Jeff. And then we basically had to convert the whole game into a fully immersive fantasy gaming environment called SpriteQuest.

**Jim:**
Isn't that kind of a dumb thing to do to a game?

**Kaitlin:**
Absolutely, but it's what I'm told to do by marketing.

**Jim:**
Have you no shame? Have you no sense of decency?

**Kaitlin:**
Stop being silly.

**Jim:**
Who are the bad guys?

**Kaitlin:**
They're called the Zorrs.

**Jim:**
[Sighs.] What magic powers do the game's characters have?

**Kaitlin:**
Using his psi powers, Prince Amulon can win a game of Scrabble using only three vowels. He can also bring fresh air into an unventilated bathroom, *and* he can renovate castles and huts on small budgets using knick-knacks from thrift stores and some well-chosen latex paint colours.

**Jim:**
You made all of that up on the spot.

**Kaitlin:**
Okay, so I did. It's—it's just so depressing what we have to do. But I don't want to marinate in shame. Our characters have other properties, too.

**Jim:**
Like . . . ?

**Kaitlin:**
There's a servant class of characters called Twix. All they do
is have sex and week-long orgasms.

**Jim:**
Really?

**Kaitlin:**
Yeah, but because the game is for kids, we can't use the
word "orgasm." Instead, we have to say the Twix are
"twinkulated." We also can't use terms that might freak kids
out.

**Jim:**
Like what?

**Kaitlin:**
Radiation. Terror. Blood. Hell. On the other hand, our
characters can fly.

**Jim:**
[Sounding bored.] Really?

**Kaitlin:**
But they can fly only in trios, squished uncomfortably
together while reading boring magazines and eating cheap
food that's been badly prepared.

**Jim:**
Hmmmmm . . .

**Kaitlin:**
But if they fly more than ten times, they can then fly solo
while selecting from a wide array of DVD entertainment
and drinking a crisp California Chardonnay.

**Jim:**
Hmmmm . . .

**Kaitlin:**
Jim! You're not listening to anything I'm saying!

**Jim:**
Kaitlin, I'd love to, but I have to be honest—when you say
the word "gaming," my brain goes to the same place it goes
when people say "country and western music."

**Kaitlin:**
You're an actor. Can't you pretend to be interested?

**Jim:**
Oh, all right, then. *Tell me, Kaitlin—what do your sprites eat?*

**Kaitlin:**
Sea monkeys. But if they eat too many, they become drunk
and vulnerable.

**Jim:**
[Jim is utterly uninterested.]

**Kaitlin:**
Well, let's discuss sex again. SpriteQuest is a barebacking sexual environment. Condoms are forbidden, though we can't say that, as such. Instead, the characters kind of melt together into a blob of light. It's all pretty pre-AIDS 1978. *But* if too many characters make out, then the game clicks into a "prude mode," where all the female sprites have to wear unflattering footwear, the male sprites have to have six-dollar Toppy's haircuts and the "un-baby'ed" young female sprites have to go to endless baby showers, where they're humiliated into reproducing.

**Jim:**
I don't believe that last one.

**Kaitlin:**
Finally, you're listening!

**Jim:**
Hey, I'm not totally evil.

**Kaitlin:**
Good. For what it's worth, there are spells galore, and a large palette of characters you can custom design, and everyone spends the game battling and betraying everybody else.

**Jim:**
You're starting to lose me again. Is there anything *Star Wars*-y about it?

**Kaitlin:**
You're too old for *Star Wars*.

**Jim:**
You didn't answer my question.

**Kaitlin:**
Okay, then, it's generic Hollywood Screenplay 101—Prince Amulon wasn't always a prince. He was born poor in the Mukki-Mukki village, near the Harkka Mushroom, and one day a war-hardened Yalli Sprite told him his destiny . . .

**Jim:**
Kaitlin, sorry—I just can't listen to any more of this. Do you have enough for your homework assignment?

**Kaitlin:**
I think so.

**Jim:**
Do you want to eat from craft catering, here on the set? It's "Flavours of Provence" week. Olive oil, foraged alpine mushrooms and pork loin. But the gummi bears are stale, for some reason.

**Kaitlin:**
Sure. Thanks, Jim.

**Jim:**
Look over there—it's Goldie Hawn.

• • •

We decided to pull an all-nighter to inject bonus gore into Ronald's Lair. It was Bree who had the idea: "What if Ronald was kidnapped and we saw him on Al Jazeera three minutes before his execution?"

"What is Ronald doing in the Middle East, anyway?"

"Secretly spying for Royal Dutch Petroleum."

"I don't know if he'd work for another corporation."

"Do clowns have religion?"

"Maybe clowns are like most people, and they merely adopt their parents' beliefs as their own, all the while flattering themselves that they're the ones who made the decision."

"Maybe he's there as an embedded corporate mascot. When they drive a tank through an elementary school, Ronald passes out Happy Meal coupons to the uncrushed."

"Which country's tank?"

"Good question. Do you think Ronald looks Middle Eastern beneath that white pancake goo?"

"No way."

"Maybe he's like that California rich kid who converted and went to Afghanistan. Rich kids are the most screwed up. When they swap cultures they go viral on their old culture."

"Has anyone here ever contemplated bailing out of Western culture?"

Silence.

"Didn't think so."

"Back to Ronald's plea for mercy. When those al Qaeda guys behead people, it's not like they do it in one swoop, like the Japanese in World War Two. They use a steak knife, and it takes forever."

It was that kind of night.

• • •

Next morning:

Steve brought in the new *Condé Nast Traveler* magazine and in it there's this piece on China by Douglas Coupland. He makes it sound like the country is one big cocktail lounge. "Visit the rural countryside, where old and new brush together, creating an almost sexual friction. There's chemistry happening here, folks. The air is filled with hope and passion flower scent . . ."

Steve said, "I seem to remember the air being filled with scorched rubber boots and charred auto seats, but he's certainly right about chemicals being everywhere."

I was appalled. "Lies, lies, lies."

Mark said, "Ethan, I told you, he's a professional liar. Get used to it. You're just pissed off because you can't buy into his amazing new revolutionary technology."

"I'm *not* pissed off."

We heard a moan coming from the hug machine—a bug catcher from a basketball game team. (NOTE: Workers come to visit jPod all the time now. Kaitlin has to launder the terry cloth cozies every two days. She's getting lazy and doesn't want to do it at home, so she rinses them in hot water in the coffee room sink, microwaves them for a minute and then hangs them by the ventilator intake to dry.)

Steve said, "You might as well know it—marketing is now becoming spooked about SpriteQuest."

"No kidding."

"The eye candy's not good enough, and now they're worried that a fantasy game strays too far from their corporate tradition of sports franchises and licensing deals."

"We told them that ages ago."

"Nobody listens to you people. That's why you're not executives. My point is that they're planning on pulling the plug."

"They can't."

"Yes, they can."

John Doe moaned, "We have to stop them."

"This is rich, isn't it?" Kaitlin said. "Trying to save that stupid game after all we've been through. But they can't—they *can't* kill our Ronald . . ."

Steve said, "If you kids have done your homework, he's unkillable. Unfortunately, he'll be unkillable inside a game that's DOA."

We spent the rest of the day in denial as we competed to find the goriest photos we could online, extra points for subtlety. Winners included:

- No seat belts in Mexico City
- PETA cow slaughter video

- Romanian wedding mishap
- Punch press accident
- Drifter takes a catnap beneath Pepsi delivery truck
- Chickenpox vaccine complications
- Toenail removal surgery
- Thai alligator wrangler gets arm ripped off by alligator
- Whale explodes in Taiwan

I honestly don't know how gore websites could exist without contributions from Mexico and Southeast Asia.

Then I went through a wave of paranoia, imagining everyone in jPod rich, except me. They'll all be using their Coupland money to live on easy street while I'm mopping the aisles of Wal-Mart.

*The aisles of Wal-Mart . . .*

It sounds like an enchanted faraway place, doesn't it?

• • •

The phone rang. It was this guy named Bruce Pao. He's the executive whose gossamer-thin spidery handwriting is famous within the company, and bizarre enough to merit a secret web page fully devoted to interpreting its hidden meanings.

"Ethan, I picked you at random from members of the SpriteQuest team—a quality control call."

"Sure."

"Why don't you meet me for lunch?"

"Lunch?"

"That's what I said. Today. In the cafeteria. At one-thirty, after the rush dies down."

"Sure."

*Click.*

Steve was drinking Zima with John Doe in John's cubicle, the two of them porn trawling using Steve's executive override code. I said, "Hey, that was Bruce Pao. He wants to have lunch with me today."

This wowed Steve. "That's three cherries in a row, baby. That guy can make or break the project. What does he want?"

"Quality control he said. Random interview."

"I doubt that. Just make sure the game comes out of it sounding good. By the way, he made $3.6 million last year in stock."

• • •

Why do companies like Toblerone or Pepperidge Farm bother having websites? As if people are going to say to themselves, "Gee, I wish I knew more about Milano cookies. I know! I'll go to their site!"

Just a thought.

• • •

Oh God, I succumbed . . .

**Milano® Cookies**

Milano®, our most popular Distinctive cookie, is a satisfying combination of rich, dark chocolate sandwiched between two exquisite cookies.

• • •

Bruce and I met by the coffee command centre at the cafeteria's entrance. He was in his suit, looking out of place, like your parents at a wedding party, dancing to gangsta. I said, "You came all the way from downtown to see *me*?"

"I'm a caring executive. What are you having to eat?"

The special of the day was veal Prince Orloff with baked pears Felicia for dessert. "I'm going to go straight to dessert."

"Smart."

We got our food and sat down. "So, tell me about Sprite-Quest. Tell me something passionate. Something inspired."

I realized I had to make a plea here for Ronald's life. I began to speak, and as I did, I felt like I was taking a shit in the woods—you know, it's fine, but it also feels totally wrong at the same time. "Bruce, SpriteQuest is just the best project ever. It rocks. It's kickass."

"Really?"

"Oh yeah. We're so stoked, and, I don't know . . . It's got this great aura about it—like we're making some sort of big leap forward game-wise."

Bruce said, "You know, Ethan, incremental improvements never win. We have to be vision busters."

*Vision busters?* "You said it, man."

"Tell me, Ethan, what are your favourite parts of the game?"

This was going to be a toughie, as I had none. *Think, Ethan, think.* "I like the way a player really gets inside Prince Amulon's head. *Why* does he want to find the sword? Sure, he needs it to enter the fire level, but the backstory of his father being killed battling with the Dark Warlord makes it personal. And the sprites' storage vault? Man, that place just *smokes*. And the way we retroed converted skateboards into Happy Carpets was totally inspired."

Bruce seemed mildly interested, so I said, "Hey, there's a rumour going around that the game's in trouble."

Now he seemed mildly surprised. "Oh?"

"Yeah. You can't kill it. It's such a great game, and the company needs it to establish itself as a creator of a quality fantasy franchise."

I didn't know what more to say, nor did Bruce. I ate a bite of dessert while he began to look bored. *Shit. I wasn't being enthusiastic enough.*

Bruce said, "Your brother, Greg, sells real estate."

"Yeah. You know him?"

"Slightly."

"Did you go to school together?"

"No."

More bites of dessert. What a disastrous meeting.

Then Bruce said, "Actually, your brother's selling this place up at Whistler that I have an eye on. A nice little chalet."

"Oh?"

"Yes. He is."

The meeting was suddenly making sense. "Which part of Whistler?"

"The Maui North development."

"Pricey."

"You can't put a price on a dream."

What is it with these marketing executives and their love of crap phrases? "Any specific house or property?"

"Lot 49."

"Have you bid?"

"Yes. But someone else bid before me."

"Bummer."

"Yes. It is."

"Why Lot 49?"

Bruce looked around the room and lowered his voice. "Because I don't believe in the future. I think we're all doomed. A survivalist organization I belong to singled out the Whistler/Pemberton Valley region as the most hospitable given a multiple global warming, dirty bomb, crop failure and SARS Classic scenario. Especially properties like Lot 49, which has a year-round stream capable of generating twenty thousand kilowatts of electricity using only a minimal rotary conversion system."

"I see."

During the pause that followed, I felt adult—*me* being in on a secret and being powerful enough to pull strings. "Why don't I call Greg tonight?"

"Yes. Give him a shout. But don't take too much time away from your work. We want SpriteQuest to be a smash."

• • •

I walked back to jPod to phone my brother. Kaitlin was fluffing some recently washed hug machine cozies, Cowboy was chugging acid pink cough syrup, Evil Mark was watching hockey fight MPEGs on some Russian website and Bree was glued to starswithoutmakeup.com, a site that she estimates has sucked a half-billion people-years of productivity from the global economy.

Steve was sitting at my desk, speaking on the phone in his "old Steve" voice to somebody in the marketing division. "All right-a-roony. That's a yes from this camper . . . best team in the country. Workaholics. I tell them to slow down, but their drive is unstoppable. You got it." Steve hung up, looked around and said, "Come on, you lazy little fucks. You have to do *something* here in this wretched pod. I can't cover your asses forever."

Cowboy said, "Steve, fuck off."

The rhythm of John Doe's typing was growing more manic over on his side of the baffles.

"John, are you okay in there?" Steve asked.

It turns out somebody had sent John the first million digits of pi, and the beauty of it had reduced him to a jittery mess. I said, "John, pi is cool and all, but how come you're falling apart over it?"

"Ethan, pi is essentially a string of random numbers. Here's a fun fact: the chances of finding your phone number inside the first hundred million digits of pi—minus the area code—is 99.997 percent. To find your number *with* area code becomes a bit less than one percent—even to find fake movie numbers like (212) 555–1234."

"I know you have the autism thing going for you, but what's the big deal?"

"The *deal,* Ethan, is that news like this will spur people on to buy lottery tickets."

"How?"

"If people locate their phone number inside pi's first million digits, it'll make them feel lucky, and before you know it, they'll go out and throw money away on lottery tickets."

"John, regardless of your mathematics, somebody always does wind up winning the lottery, so what's the point of stressing?" Kaitlin said. "And while we're on the subject, what exactly is your beef with lottery tickets?"

"My *beef* is that my father won the Irish Sweepstakes when I was two and left my mother, who overreacted and became a power lesbian. It's a family legend. As a result I was home-schooled and didn't even know that capitalized letters existed until I was ten."

"What do lesbians have against capitalized letters?"

"Capitalization implies a hierarchy, that some letters are more special than others."

"Oh."

Meanwhile, Mark—possibly the most pragmatic of anyone in jPod, located a pi website with the first hundred thousand digits of pi. "Everyone listen up. I've just emailed all of you the first hundred thousand digits of pi. Into this list I've inserted one incorrect digit. The first person to locate this rogue digit will win"—Mark looked into his desk drawer and picked something up—"this bag of Korean shrimp chips. At the count of three, search. One, two, three—*search*!"

```
3.14159265358979323846264338327950288419716939937510
58209749445923078164062862089986280348253421170679821
48086513282306647093844609550582231725359408128481117
45028410270193852110555964462294895493038196442881097
56659334461284756482337867831652712019091456485669234
60348610454326648213393607260249141273724587006606315
58817488152092096282925409171536436789259036001133053
05488204665213841469519415116094330572703657595919530
9
```

21861173819326117931051185480744623799627495673518857
52724891227938183011949129833673362440656643086021394
94639522473719070217986094370277053921717629317675238
46748184676694051320005681271452635608277857713427577
89609173637178721468440901224953430146549585371050792
27968925892354201995611212902196086403441815981362977
47713099605187072113499999983729780499510597317328160
96318595024459455346908302642522308253344685035261931
18817101000313783875288658753320838142061717766914730
35982534904287554687311595628638823537875937519577818
57780532171226806613001927876611195909216420198938095
25720106548586327886593615338182796823030195203530185
29689957736225994138912497217752834791315155748572424
54150695950829533116861727855889075098381754637464939
31925506040092770167113900984882401285836160356370766
01047101819429555961989467678374494482553797747268471
04047534646208046684259069491293313677028989152104752
16205696602405803815019351125338243003558764024749647
32639141992726042699227967823547816360093417216412199
24586315030286182974555706749838505494588586926995690
92721079750930295532116534498720275596023648066549911
98818347977535663698074265425278625518184175746728909
77772793800081647060016145249192173217214772350141441
97356854816136115735255213347574184946843852332390739
41433345477624168625189835694855620992192221842725502
54256887671790494601653466804988627232791786085784383
82796797668145410095388378636095068006422512520511739
29848960841284886269456042419652850222106611863067442
78622039194945047123713786960956364371917287467764657
57396241389086583264599581339047802759009946576407895
12694683983525957098258226205224894077267194782684826
01476990902640136394437455305068203496252451749399651
43142980919065925093722169646151570985838741059788595
97729754989301617539284681382686838689427741559918559
25245953959431049972524680845987273644695848653836736
22262609912460805124388439045124413654976278079771569
14359977001296160894416948685558484063534220722258284
88648158456028506016842739452267467678895252138522549
95466672782398645659611635488623057745649803559363456
81743241125150760694794510965960940252288797108931456
69136867228748940560101503308617928680920874760917824

9385890009714909675985261365549781893129784821682998948
7226588048575640142704775551323796414515237462343645
42858444795265867821051141354735739523113427166102135
96953623144295248493718711014576540359027993440374200
73105785390621983874478084784896833214457138687519435
06430218453191048481005370614680674919278191197939952
06141966342875444064374512371819217999839101591956181
46751426912397489409071864942319615679452080951465502
25231603881930142093762137855956638937787083039069792
07734672218256259966150142150306803844773454920260541
46659252014974428507325186660021324340881907104863317
34649651453905796268561005508106658796998163574736384
05257145910289706414011097120628043903975951567715770
04203378699360072305587631763594218731251471205329281
91826186125867321579198414848829164470609575270695722
09175671167229109816909152801735067127485832228718352
09353965725121083579151369882091444210067510334671103
14126711136990865851639831501970165151168517143765761
83515565088490998985998238734552833163550764791853589
32261854896321329330898570642046752590709154814165498
59461637180270981994309924488957571282890592323326097
29971208443357326548938239119325974636673058360414281
38830320382490375898524374417029132765618093773444030
70746921120191302033038019762110110044929321516084244
48596376698389522868478312355265821314495768572624334
41893039686426243410773226978028073189154411010446823
25271620105265227211166039666557309254711055785376346
68206531098965269186205647693125705863566201855810072
93606598764861179104533488503461136576867532494416680
39626579787718556084552965412665408530614344431858676
97514566140680070023787765913440171274947042056223053
89945613140711270004078547332699390814546646458807972
70826683063432858785698305235808933065757406795457163
77525420211495576158140025012622859413021647155097925
92309907965473761255176567513575178296664547791745011
29961489030463994713296210734043751895735961458901938
97131117904297828564750320319869151402870808599048010
94121472213179476477726224142548545403321571853061422
88137585043063321751829798662237172159160771669254748
73898665494945011465406284336639379003976926567214638
53067360965712091807638327166416274888800786925602902

2847210403172118608204190004229661711963779213375751
49595015660496318629472654736425230817703675159067350
23507283540567040386743513622224771589150495309844489
33309634087807693259939780541934144737744184263129860
80998886874132604721569516239658645730216315981931951
67353812974167729478672422924654366800980676928238280
68996400482435403701416314965897940924323789690706977
94223625082216889573837986230015937764716512289357860
15881617557829735233446042815126272037343146531977774
16031990665541876397929334419521541341899485444734567
38316249934191318148092777710386387734317720754565453
22077709212019051660962804909263601975988281613323166
63652861932668633606273567630354477628035045077723554
71058595487027908143562401451718062464362679456127531
81340783303362542327839449753824372058353114771199260
63813346776879695970309833913077109870408591337464144
28227726346594704745878477872019277152807317679077071
57213444730605700733492436931138350493163128404251219
25651798069411352801314701304781643788518529092854520
11658393419656213491434159562586586557055269049652098
58033850722426482939728584783163057777560688876446248
24685792603953527734803048029005876075825104747091643
96136267604492562742042083208566119062545433721315359
58450687724602901618766795240616342522577195429162991
93064553779914037340432875262888963995879475729174642
63574552540790914513571113694109119393251910760208252
02618798531887705842972591677813149699009019211697173
72784768472686084900337702424291651300500516832336435
03895170298939223345172201381280696501178440874519601
21228599371623130171144484640903890644954440061986907
54851602632750529834918740786680881833851022833450850
48608250393021332197155184306354550076682829493041377
65527939751754613953984683393638304746119966538581538
42056853386218672523340283087112328278921250771262946
32295639898989358211674562701021835646220134967151881
90973038119800497340723961036854066431939509790190699
63955245300545058068550195673022921913933918568034490
39820595510022635353619204199474553859381023439554495
97783779023742161727111723643435439478221818528624085
14006660443325888569867054315470696574745855033232334
21073015459405165537906866273337995851156257843229882

73723198987571415957811196358330059408730681216028764
96286744604774649159950549737425626901049037781986835
93814657412680492564879855614537234786733039046883834
36346553794986419270563872931748723320837601123029911
36793862708943879936201629515413371424892830722012690
14754668476535761647737946752004907571555278196536213
23926406160136358155907422020203187277605277219005561
48425551879253034351398442532234157623361064250639049
75008656271095359194658975141310348227693062474353632
56916078154781811528436679570611086153315044521274739
24544945423682886061340841486377670096120715124914043
02725386076482363414334623518975766452164137679690314
95019108575984423919862916421939949072362346468441173
94032659184044378051333894525742399508296591228508555
82157250310712570126683024029295252201187267675622041
54205161841634847565169998116141010029960783869092916
03028840026910414079288621507842451670908700069928212
06604183718065355672525325675328612910424877618258297
65157959847035622262934860034158722980534989650226291
74878820273420922224533985626476691490556284250391275
77102840279980663658254889264880254566101729670266407
65590429099456815065265305371829412703369313785178609
04070866711496558343434769338578171138645587367812301
45876871266034891390956200993936103102916161528813843
79099042317473363948045759314931405297634757481193567
09110137751721008031559024853090669203767192203322909
43346768514221447737939375170443366199104033751117354
71918550464490263655128162288244625759163330391072253
83742182140883508657391771509682887478265699599574490
66175834413752239709683408005355984917541738188399944
69748676265516582765848358845314277568790029095170283
52971634456212964043523117600665101241200659755851276
17858382920419748442360800719304576189323492292796501
98751872127267507981255470958904556357921221033346697
49923563025494780249011419521238281530911407907386025
15227429958180724716259166854513331239480494707911915
32673430282441860414263639548000448002670496248201792
89647669758318327131425170296923488962766844032326092
75249603579964692565049368183609003238092934595889706
95365349406034021665443755890045632882250545255640564
48246515187547119621844396582533754388569094113031509

5261793780029741207665147939425902989695946995565761 2
1865619673337862362561252163208628692221032748892186 54
3648022967807057656151446320469279068212073883778142 3
3562823608963208068222468012248261177185896381409183 9
0367367222088832151375560037279839400415297002878307 6
6709444745601345564172543709069793961225714298946715 4
3578468788614445812314593571984922528471605049221242 4
7014121478057345510500801908699603302763478708108175 4
5011930714122339086639383395294257869050764310063835 1
9834389341596131854347546495569781038293097164651438 4
0700707360411237359984345225161050702705623526601276 4
8483084076118301305279320542746286540360367453286510 5
7065874882256981579367897669742205750596834408697350 2
0141020672358502007245225632651341055924019027421624 8
4391403599895353945909440704691209140938700126456001 6
2374288021092764579310657922955249887275846101264836 9
9989225695968815920560010165525637567856672279661988 5
7827948488558343975187445455129656344348039664205579 8
2936804352202770984294232533022576341807039476994159 7
9159453006975214829336655566156787364005366656416547 3
2170439035213295435291694145990416087532018683793702 3
4888689479151071637852902345292440773659495630510074 2
1087142613497459561513849871375704710178795731042296 9
0666702144986374645952808243694457897723300487647652 4
1339075920434019634039114732023380715095222010682563 4
2747164602433544005152126693249341967397704159568375 3
5551667302739007497297363549645332888698440611964961 6
2773449518273695588220757355176651589855190986665393 5
4948106887320685990754079234240230092590070173196036 2
2547564789406475483466477604114632339056513433068449 5
3979070903023460461470961696886885014083470405460742 9
5869913829668246818571031887906528703665083243197440 4
7718556789348230894310682870272280973624809399627060 7
4726455399253994428081137369433887294063079261595995 4
6262462970706259484556903471197299640908941805953439 3
2512362355081349490043642785271383159125689892951964 2
7287573946914272534366941532361004537304881985517065 9
4121735246258954873016760029886592578662856124966552 3
5338294287854253404830833070165372285635591525347844 5
9818313411290019992059813522051173365856407826484942 7
6441137639386692480311836445369858917544264739988228 4

621844900877769776312795722672655562596282542765318300
134070922334365779160128093179401718598599933849235495
640057099558561134980252499066984233017350358044081168
552653117099570899427328709258487894436460050410892266
917835258707859512983441729535195378855345737426085902
908176515578039059464087350612322611200937310804854852
635722825768203416050484662775045003126200800799804925
485346941469775164932709504934639382432227188515974054
702148289711177792376122578873477188196825462981268685
817050740272550263329044976277894423621674119186269439
650671515577958675648239939176042601763387045499017614
364120469218237076488783419689686118155815873606293860
381017121585527266830082383404656475880405138080163363
887421637140643549556186896411228214075330265510042410
489678352858829024367090488711819090949453314421828766
181031007354770549815968077200947469613436092861484941
785017180779306810854690009445899527942439813921350558
642219648349151263901280383200109773868066287792397180
146134324457264009737425700735921003154150893679300816
998053652027600727749674584002836240534603726341655425
902760183484030681138185510597970566400750942608788573
579603732451414678670368809880609716425849759513806930
944940151542221943291302173912538355915031003330325111
749156969174502714943315155885403922164097229101129035
521815762823283182342548326111912800928252561902052630
163911477247331485739107775874425387611746578671169414
776421441111263583553871361011023267987756410246824032
264834641766369806637857681349204530224081972785647198
396308781543221166912246415911776732253264335686146186
545222681268872684459684424161078540167681420808850280
054143613146230821025941737562389942075713627516745731
891894562835257044133543758575342698699472547031656613
991999682628247270641336222178923903176085428943733935
618891651250424404008952719837873864805847268954624388
234375178852014395600571048119498842390606136957342315
590796703461491434478863604103182350736502778590897578
272731305048893989009923913503373250855982655867089242
612429473670193907727130706869170926462548423240748550
366080136046689511840093668609546325002145852930950000
907151058236267293264537382104938724996699339424685516
4832611341461

10680267446637334375340764294026682973865220935701626
38464852851490362932019919968828517183953669134522244
47080459239660281715655156566611135982311225062890585
49145097157553900243931535190902107119457300243880176
61503527086260253788179751947806101371500448991721002
22013350131060163915415895780371177927752259787428919
17915522417189585361680594741234193398420218745649256
44346239253195313510331147639491199507285843065836193
53693296992898379149419394060857248639688369032655643
64216644257607914710869984315733749648835292769328220
76294728238153740996154559879825989109371712621828302
58481123890119682214294576675807186538065064870261338
92822994972574530332838963818439447707794022843598834
10035838542389735424395647555684095224844554139239410
00162076936368467764130178196593799715574685419463348
93748439129742391433659360410035234377706588867781139
49861647874714079326385873862473288964564359877466763
84794665040741118256583788784548581489629612739984134
42726086061872455452360643153710112746809778704464094
75828034876975894832824123929296058294861919667091895
80898332012103184303401284951162035342801441276172858
30243559830032042024512072872535581195840149180969253
39507577840006746552603144616705082768277222353419110
26341631571474061238504258459884199076112872580591139
35689601431668283176323567325417073420817332230462987
99280490851409479036887868789493054695570307261900950
20764334933591060245450864536289354568629585313153371
83868265617862273637169757741830239860065914816164049
44965011732131389574706208847480236537103115089842799
27544268532779743113951435741722197597993596852522857
45263796289612691572357986620573408375766873884266405
99099350500081337543245463596750484423528487470144354
54195762584735642161981340734685411176688311865448937
76979566517279662326714810338643913751865946730024434
50054499539974237232871249483470604406347160632583064
98297955101095418362350303094530973358344628394763047
75645015008507578949548931393944899216125525597701436
85894358587752637962559708167764380012543650237141278
34679261019955852247172201777237004178084194239487254
06801556035998390548985723546745642390585850216719031
39526294455439131663134530893906204678438778505423939

05247313620129476918749751910114723152893267725339181
46607300008902776896311481090220972452075916729700785 0
58071718638105496797310016787085069420709223290807038
32634534520380278609905569001341371823683709919495164
89600755049341267876436746384902063964019766685592335
65463913836318574569814719621084108096188460545603903
84553437291414465134749407848844237721751543342603066
98831768331001133108690421939031080143784334151370924
35301367763108491351615642269847507430329716746964066
65315270353254671126675224605511995818319637637076179
91919203579582007595605302346267757943936307463056901
08011494271410093913691381072581378135789400559950018
35425118417213605572752210352680373572652792241737360
57511278872181908449006178013889710770822931002797665
93583875890939568814856026322439372656247277603789081
44588378550197028437793624078250527048758164703245812
90878395232453237896029841669225489649715606981192186
58492677040395648127810217991321741630581055459880130
04845629976511212415363745150056350701278159267142413
42103301566165356024733807843028655257222753049998837
01534879300806260180962381516136690334111138653851091
93673938352293458883225508870645075394739520439680790
67086806445096986548801682874343786126453815834280753
06184548590379821799459968115441974253634439960290251
00158882721647450068207041937615845471231834600726293
39550548239557137256840232268213012476794522644820910
23564775272308208106351889915269288910845557112660396
50343978962782500161101532351605196559042118449499077
89992007329476905868577878720982901352956613978884860
50978608595701773129815531495168146717695976099421003
61835591387778176984587581044662839988060061622984861
69353373865787735983361613384133853684211978938900185
29569196780455448285848370117096721253533875862158231
01331038776682721157269495181795897546939926421979155
23385766231676275475703546994148929041301863861194391
96283887054367774322427680913236544948536676800000106
52624854730558615989991401707698385483188750142938908
99506854530765116803337322265175662207526951791442252
80816517166776672793035485154204023817460892328391703
27542575086765511785939500279338959205766827896776445
31840404185540104351348389531201326378369283580827193

78312654961745997056745071833206503455664403449045362
75600112501843356073612227659492783937064784264567633
88188075656121689605041611390390639601620221536849410
92605387688714837989559999112099164646441191856827700
45742434340216722764455893301277815868695250694993646
10175685060167145354315814801054588605645501332037586
45485840324029871709348091055621167154684847780394475
69798042631809917564228098739987669732376957370158080
68229045992123661689025962730430679316531149401764737
69387351409336183321614280214976339918983548487562529
87524238730775595559554651963944018218409984124898262
36737714672260616336432964063357281070788758164043814
85018841143188598827694490119321296827158884133869434
68285900666408063140777577257056307294004929403024204
98416565479736705485580445865720227637840466823379852
82710578431975354179501134727362577408021347682604502
28515797957976474670228409995616015691089038458245026
79265942055503958792298185264800706837650418365620945
55434613513415257006597488191634135955671964965403218
72716026485930490397874895890661272507948282769389535
21753621850796297785146188432719223223810158744450528
66523802253284389137527384589238442253547265309817157
84478342158223270206902872323300538621634798850946954
72004795231120150432932662827276321779088400878861480
22147537657810581970222630971749507212724847947816957
29614236585957820908307332335603484653187302930266596
45013718375428897557971449924654038681799213893469244
74198509733462679332107268687076806263991936196504409
95421676278409146698569257150743157407938053239252394
77557441591845821562518192155233709607483329234921034
51462643744980559610330799414534778457469999212859999
93996122816152193148887693880228108300198601654941165
42616968586788372609587745676182507275992950893180521
87292461086763995891614585505839727420980909781729323
93010676638682404011130402470073508578287246271349463
68531815469690466968693925472519413992914652423857762
55004748529547681479546700705034799958886769501612497
22820403039954632788306959762493615101024365553522306
90612949388599015734661023712235478911292547696176005
04797492806072126803922691102777226102544149221576504
50812067717357120271802429681062037765788371669091094

180744878140490755178203856539099104775941413215432844
062503018027571696508209642734841469572639788425600845
31214065935809041271135920041975985136254796160632288736
18136737324450607924411763997597461938358457491598809766
74470930065463424234606342374746660804317012600520559284
93695941434081468529815053947178900451835755154125222359
05906872648786357525419112888773717663748602766063496035
36794702692322971868327717393236192007774522126247518698
33495151019864269887847171939664976907082521742336566272
59284406204302141137199227852699846988477023238238400556
55517889087661360130477098438611687052310553149162517283
73272867600724817298763756981633541507460883866364069347
04372066886512756882661497307886570156850169186474885416
7915459650723428773069985371390430026653078398776385032
38182155355973235306860430106757608389086270498418885951
380910304235957824951439885901131858358406674723702971
49785084145853085781339156270760356390763947311455495832
26694570249413983163433237897595568085683629725386791327
5055542524491943589128405045226953812179131914513500993
846311774017971512283785460116035955402864405902496466930
70776905548102885020808580087811577381719174177601733073
855475800605601433774329901272867725304318251975791679296
99650414607066457125888346979796429316229655201687973000
356463045793088403274807718115553309098870255052076804630
346086581653948769519600440848206596737947316808641564565
0530049881616490578831154345485052660069823093157776500378
07046612647060214575057932709620478256152471459189652236
08396645624105195510522357239739512881816405978591427914
81654263289200428160913693777372229998332708208296995573
77273756676155271139225880552018988762011416800546873655
80633471603734291703907986396522961312801782679717289822
936070288069087768660593252746378405397691848082041021944
71971386925608416245112398062011318454124478205011079876
07171556831540788654390412108730324020106853419472304766
66721749869868547076781205124736792479193150856444775379
853799732234456122785843296846647513336573692387201464723
6794278700425032555899268843495928761240075587569464137056
25140011797133166207153715436006876477318675587148783989
0810742953094106059694431584775397009439883

49144323536685392099468796450665339857388878661476294
43414010498889931600512076781035886116602029611936396
82134960750111649832785635316145168457695687109002999
76984126326650234771672865737857908574664607722834154
03114415294188047825438761770790430001566986776795760
90996693607559496515273634981189641304331166277471233
88174060373174397054067031096767657486953587896700319
25866259410510533584384656023391796749267844763708474
97833365557900738419147319886271352595462518160434225
37299628632674968240580602964211463864368642247248872
83434170441573482481833301640566959668866769563491416
32842641497453334999948000266998758881593507357815195
88990053951208535103572613736403436753471410483601754
64883004078464167452167371904831096767113443494819262
68111073994825060739495073503169019731852119552635632
58433909982249862406703107683184466072912487475403161
79699411397387765899868554170318847788675929026070043
21266617919223520938227878880988633599116081923535557
04646349113208591897961327913197564909760001399623444
55350143464268604644958624769094347048293294140411146
54092398834443515913320107739441118407410768498106634
72410482393582740194493566516108846312567852977697346
843030614624180358529331597345830308455410337010916767
76374276210213701354854450926307190114731848574923318
16720721372793556795284439254815609137281284063330393
73562420016045664557414588166052166608738748047243391
21295587776390696903707882852775389405246075849623157
43691711311761347838827194168606625721036851321566478 0
01476752310393578606896111259960281839309548709059073
86135191459181951029732787557104972901148717189718004
69616977700179139196137914171627070189584692143436967
62927459109940060084983568425201915593703701011049747
33949387788598941743303178534870760322198297057975119
14405109942358830345463534923498268836240433272674155
40301619505680654180939409982020609994140216890900708
21330723089662119775530665918814119157783627292746156
18571037217247100952142369648308641025928874579993223
74955191221951903424452307535133806856807354464995127
20317448719540397610730806026990625807602029273145525
20780799141842906388443734996814582733720726639176702
01183004648190002413083508846584152148991276106513741

5394356572113903285749187690944137020905170314877346
1652879848235338297260136110984514841823808120540961
2527458088109948697221612852489742555551607637167554
8961730168096138038119143611439921063800508321409876
4599309324851025168294467260666138151745712559754953
8023998314698220361338082849935670557552471290274539
7621404931820146580080215665360677655087838043041343
0591804606800834591136640834887408005741272586704792
5831912741573908091438313845642415094084913391809684
2511639919368532255573389669537490266209232613188558
1580832455571948453875628786128859004106006073746501
0262782402734696252821717494158233174923968353013617
6536737606421667781377399510065895288774276626368418
0680190804609849809469763667335662282915132352788806
5776827815958866918023894033307644191240341202231636
5778603572769415417788264352381319050280870185750470
6312933353757285386605888904583111450773942935201994
2197117164223500564404297989208159430716701985746927
8486538334361457946341759225738985880016980147574205
2995801242958105456510831046297282937584161162532562
1657249807849209989799062003593650993472158296517413
7984910471116607915874369865412223483418877229294463
5178653856731962559852026072947674072616767145573649
1210567771689348491766077170527718760119990814411305
6455779105256843048114402619384023224709392498029335
0731845890353397133088446174107959162511714864874468
1124760542867343670904667846867027409188101424971114
6578177242793470702166882956108777944050484375284433
5108828264771978540006509704033021862556147332117771
7441335028160884035178145254196432030957601869464908
6815452856213469883554445602495566684366029221951248
0910605377201980218310103270417838665447181260397190
8846237085751808003532704718565949947612424811099928
6791589690495639476246084240659309486215076903149870
0673533848349550836366017848771060809804269247132410
0946401437360326564518456679245666955100150229833079
4960799498824970617236744936122622296179081431141466
9412341593593095854079139087208322733549572080757165
7187659944985693795623875551617575438091780528029464
0044721539628074636021132942559160025707356281263873
1060058910652457080244749375431841494014821199962764

31068006631183823761639663180931444671298615527598201
45141027560068929750246304017351489194576360789352855
50531733141645705049964438909363084387448478396168405
18452732884032345202470568516465716477139323775517294
79512613239822960239454857975458651745878771331813875
29598094121742273003522965080891777050682592488223221
54938048371454781647213976820963320508305647920482085
92047549985732038887639160199524091893894557676874973
08569559580106595265030362661597506622250840674288982
65907510637563569968211510949669744580547288693631020
36782325018232370845979011154847208761821247781326633
04120762165873129708112307581598212486398072124078688
78114501655825136178903070860870198975889807456643955
15741536319319198107057533663373803827215279884935039
74800158905194208797113080512339332219034662499171691
50948541401871060354603794643379005890957721180804465
74396280618671786101715674096766208029576657705129120
99079443046328929473061595104309022214393718495606340
56189342513057268291465783293340524635028929175470872
56484260034962961165413823007731332729830500160256724
01418515204189070115428857992081219844931569990591820
11819733500126187728036812481995877070207532406361259
31343859554254778196114293516356122349666152261473539
96740515849986035529533292457523888101362023476246690
55816438967863097627365504724348643071218494373485300
60638764456627218666170123812771562137974614986132874
41177145524447089971445228856629424402301847912054784
98574521634696448973892062401943518310088283480249249
08540307786387516591130287395878709810077271827187452
90139728366148421428717055317965430765045343246005363
61472618180969976933486264077435199928686323835088756
68359509726557481543194019557685043724800102041374983
18722596773871549583997184449072791419658459300839426
37020875635398216962055324803212267498911402678528599
67340524203109179789990571882194939132075343170798002
37365909853755202389116434671855829068537118979526262
34492483392496342449714656846591248918556629589329909
03523923333364743520370770101084388003290759834217018
55422838616172104176030116459187805393674474720599850
23582891833692922337323999480437108419659473162654825
74809948250999183300697656936715968936449334886474421

35008407006608835972350395323401795825570360169369909
88671132109798897070517280755855191269930673099250704
07024556850778679069476612629808225163313639952117098
45280926303759224267425755998928927837047444521893632
03489415521044597261883800300677617931381399162058062
70165102445886924764924689192461212531027573139084047
00071435613623169923716948481325542009145304103713545
32966206392105479824392125172540132314902740585892063
21758949434548906846399313757091034633271415316223280
55229729795380188016285907357295541627886764982741861
64218789885741071649069191851162815285486794173638906
65388576422915834250067361245384916067413734017357277
99563410433268835695078149313780073623541800706191802
67328551191942676091221035987469241172837493126163395
00123959924050845437569850795704622266461900010350049
01830341535458428337643781119885563187777925372011667
18539541835984438305203762819440761594106820716970302
28515225057312609304689842343315273213136121658280807
52126315477306044237747535059522871744026663891488171
73086436111389069420279088143119448799417154042103412
19084709408025402393294294549387864023051292711909751
35360009219711054120966831115163287054230284700731206
58032626417116165957613272351566662536672718998534199
89523688483099930275741991646384142707798870887422927
70538912271724863220288984251252872178260305009945108
24783572905691988555467886079462805371227042466543192
14528176074148240382783582971930101788834567416781139
89547504483393146896307633966572267270433932167454218
24557062524797219978668542798977992339579057581890622
52547358220523642485078340711014498047872669199018643
88229323053823185597328697809222535295910173414073348
84761005564018242392192695062083183814546983923664613
63989101210217709597670490830508185470419466437131229
96923588953849301363565761861060622287055994233716310
21278457446463989738188566746260879482018647487672727
22206267646533809980196688368099415907577685263986514
62533363124505364026105696055131838131742611844201890
88853196356986962795036738243130113317533053298020 16
68881748134298868158557781034323175306478498321062971
84251843855344276201282345707169885305183261796411785
79608888150329602290705614476220915094739035946646916

23539680920139457817589108893199211226007392814916948
16152738427362642980982340632002440244958944561291670
49508235812487391799648641133480324757775219708932772
26234948601504665268143987705161531702669692970492831
62855042128981467061953319702695072143782304768752802
87354126166391708245925170010714180854800636923259462
01900227808740985977192180515853214739265325155903541
02092846665925299914353791825314545290598415 8176370589
27906909896911164381187809435371521332261443625314490
12745477269573939348154691631162492887357471882407150
39950094467319543161938554852076657388251396391635767
23151005556037263394867208207808653734942440115799667
50736071115935133195919712094896471755302453136477094
20946356969822266737752099451684506436238242118535348
87989395673187806606107885440005508276570305587448541
80577889171920788142335113866292966717964346876007704
79995378833878703487180218424373421122739402557176908
19603092018240188427057046092622564178375265263358324
24066125331152942345796556950250681001831090041124537
90153329661569705223792103257069370510908307894799990
04999395322153622748476603613677697978567386584670936
67958858378879562594646489137665219958828693380183601
19323685785585581955560421562508836502033220245137621
58204618106705195330653060606501054887167245377942831
33887163139559690583208341689847606560711834713621812
32462272588419902861420872849568796393254642853430753
01105285713829643709990356948885285190402956047346131
13826387889755178856042499874831638280404684861893818
95905420398898726506976202019955484126500053944282039
30127481638158530396439925470201672759328574366661644
11096256633730540921951967514832873480895747777527834
42210910731113518280460363471981856555729571447476825
52857863349342858423118749440003229690697758315903858
03935352135886007960034209754739229673331064939560181
22378128545843176055617338611267347807458506760630482
29409653041118306671081893031108871728167519579675347
18853722930961614320400638132246584111115775835858113
50185690478153689381377184728147519983505047812977185
99084707621974605887423256995828892535041937958260616
21184236876851141831606831586799460165205774052942305
36017803133572632670547903384012573059123396018801378

25421927094767337191987287385248057421248921183470876
62966720727232565056512933312605950577772754247124164
83128329820723617505746738701282095755443059683955556
86861188397135522084452852640081252027665557677495969
62661260456524568408613923826576858338469849977872670
65551918544686984694784957346226062942196245570853712
72776523098955450193037732166649182578154677292005212
66714346320963789185232321501897612603437368406719419
30377468809992968775824410478781232662531818459604538
53543839114496775312864260925211537673258866722604042
52349108702695809964759580579466397341906401003636190
40420331135793365424263035614570090112448008900208014
78056603710154122328891465722393145076071670643556827
43774396578906797268743847307634645167756210309860409
27170909512808630902973850445271828927496892121066700
81648583395537735919136950153162018908887484210798706
89911480466927065094076204650277252865072890532854856
14331608126930056937854178610969692025388650345771831
76686885923681488475276498468821949739729707737187188
40041432312763650481453112285099002074240925585925292
61030210673681543470152523487863516439762358604191941
29697690405264832347009911154242601273438022089331096
68636789869497799400126016422760926082349304118064382
91383473546797253992623387915829984864592717340592256
20749105308531537182911681637219395188700957788181586
85046450769934394098743351443162633031724774748689791
82092394808331439708406730840795893581089665647758599
05563769525232653614424780230826811831037735887089240
61303133647737101162821461466167940409051861526036009
25219472188909181073358719641421444786548995285823439
47050079803088538860831035719306002771194558021911942
89992272235345870756624692617766317885514435021828702
66856106650035310502163182060176092179846849368631612
93727951873078972637353717150256378733579771808184878
45886650433582437700414771041493492743845758710715973
15594394264125702709651251081155482479394035976811881
17282472158250109496096625393395380922195591918188552
67806214992317276316321833989969380756168559117529984 5
01320671293924041445938623988093812404521914848316462
10147389182510109096773869066404158973610476436500068
07710565671848628149637111883219244566394581449148616

550049567698269030891118568798692947051352481609 17432
430153836847072928989828460222373014526556798986 27767
968091469798378268764311598832109043715611299766 52153
963546442086919756737000573876497843768628768179 24974
694384274652563163230055513041742273416464551278 12784
577772457520386543754282825671412885834544435132 56205
446424101103795546419058116862305964476958705407 21419
852121067343324107567675758184569906930460475227 70167
005684543969234041711089888993416350585157887353 43081
552081177207188037910404698306957868547393765643 36319
797868036718730796939242363214484503547763156702 55390
065423117920153464977929066241508328858395290542 63768
766896880503331722780018588506973623240389470047 18976
193473443084374437599250341788079722358591342458 13144
049847701732361694719765715353197754997162785663 11904
691260918259124989036765417697990362375528652637 57337
635269693443544004730671988689019681474287677908 66979
688522501636949856730217523132529265375896415171 47955
953878427849986645630287883196209983049451987439 63690
706827626574858104391122326187940599415540632701 31989
895703761105323606298674803779153767511583043208 49872
092028092975264981256916342500052290887264692528 46661
046653921714820801305022980526378364269597337070 53922
789153510568883938113249757071331029504430346715 98944
878684711643832805069250776627450012200352620370 94660
234146489983902525888301486781621967751945831677 18762
757200505439794412459900771152051546199305098386 98254
284640725554092740313257163264079293418334214709 04125
425335232480219322770753555467958716383587501815 93387
174236061551171013123525633485820365146141870049 20570
437201826173319471570086757853933607862273955818 57975
872587441025420771054753612940474601000940954449 59662
881486915903899071865980563617137692227290764197 75517
772010427649694961105622059250242021770426962215 49587
264539892276976603105249808557594716310758701332 08861
463266412591148633881220284440694169488261529577 62532
501987035987067438046982194205638125583343642194 92322
759372212890564209430823525440841108645453694049 69271
494003319782861318186188811118408257865928757426 38445
005994422956858646048103301538891149948693543603 02218
109434667640000223625505736312946262960961987605 64259

9639461386923308371962659547392346241345977957485 2464
7837980795693198650815977675350553918991151335252 2987
3611277918274854200868953965835942196333150286956 1192
0122988898870060799927954111882690230789131076036 1763
4779489432032102773359416908650071932804017163840 6449
8787175375678118532132840821657110754952829497493 6214
6082155832056872321855740651610962748743750980922 3021
1609982633033915469494644491004515280925089745074 8967
6032409076898365294065792019831526541065813682379 1984
0906457124689484702093577611931399802468134052003 9478
1949866202624008902150166163813538381515037735022 9660
7462795291038406868556907015751662419298724448271 9429
3310048548244545807188976330032325258215812803274 6796
2002814762431828622171054352898348208273451680186 1317
1959332471107466222850871066611770346535283957762 5997
7446721857158161264111432717943478859908928084866 9491
4139097716736900277758502686646540565950394867841 1107
9011610400857274456293842549416759460548711723594 6429
1058509099502149587931121961359083158826206823321 5615
3086833730838173279328196983875087083483880463884 7844
1884003184712697454370937329836240287519792080232 1878
7448828728437273780178270080587824107493575148899 7891
1739746129320351081432703251409030487462262942344 3275
7126008664250833318768865075642927160552528954492 1537
6517514921963671810494353178583834538652556566406 5725
1363575064353236508936790431702597878177190314867 9638
4082881020946149007971513771709906195496964007086 7667
1023300486726314755105372317571143223174114116806 2286
4206388906210192355223546711662137499693269321737 0431
0598722503945657492461697826097025335947502091383 6673
7728944386964000281103440260847128990007468077648 4408
8711341352503367877316797709372778682166117865344 2317
3226463784769787514433209534000165069213054647689 0985
0502030150448808342618452087305309731894929164253 2293
3612431514306578264070283898409841602950309241897 1209
7160164926561341343342229882790992178604267981245 7285
3458013382609958771781131021673402565627440072968 3406
6198480676615805021691833723680399027931606420436 8120
7990031626444914619021945822969099212278855394878 3538
3056468648816555622943156731282743908264506116289 4280
3501661336697824051770155219626522725455850738640 5852

99830379180350432876703809252167907571204061237596327
68567484507915114731344000183257034492090971243580944
79004624943134550289006806487042935340374360326258205
35790118395649089354345101342969617545249573960621490
28872893279252069653538639644322538832752249960598697
47598823299162635459733244451637553343774929289905811
75786355555626937426910947117002165411718219750519831
78713710605106379555858890556885288798908475091576463
90746936198815078146852621332524738376511929901561091
89777922008705793396463827490680698769168197492365624
22608715417610043060890437797667851966189140414492527
04808819714988015420577870065215940092897776013307568
47966992955433656139847738060394368895887646054983871
47896848280538470173087111776115966350503997934386933
91197898871091565417091330826076474063057114110988393
88095481437828474528838368079418884342666222070438722
88741394780101772139228191199236540551639589347426395
38248296090369002883593277458550608013179884071624465
63997948275783650195514221551339281978226984278638391
67971509126241054872570092407004548848569295044811073
80879965474815689139353809434745569721289198271770207
66613602489581468119133614121258783895577357194986317
21084439890142394849665925173138817160266326193106536
65350414730708044149391693632623737677770958503132559
90095762731957308648042467701212327020533742667053142
44820816813030639737873664248367253983748769098060218
27857862165127385635132901489035098832706172589325753
63993979055729175160097615459044771692265806315111028
03843601737474215247608515209901615858231257159073342
17365762671423904782795872815050956330928026684589376
49649770232973641319060982740633531089792464242134583
74090116939196425045912881340349881063540088759682005
44083643865166178805576089568967275315380819420773325
97917278437625661184319891025007491829086475149794003
16070384554946538594602745244746681231468794344161099
33389089992638411847425257044572517459325738989565185 7
16575961481266020310797628254165590506042479114016957
90033835657486925280074302562341949828646791447632277
40055294609039401775363356554719310001754300475047191
44899841040015867946179241610016454716551337074073950
26044276953855383439755054887109978520540117516974758

13449260794336895437832211724506873442319898788441285
42064742809735625807066983106979935260693392135685881
39121480735472846322778490808700246777630360555123238
66562951788537196730346347012229395816067925091532174
89030840886516061119011498443412350124646928028805996
13428351188471544977127847336176628506216977871774382
43625657117794500644777183702219991066950216567576440
44997940765037999954845002710665987813603802314126836
90578319046079276529727769404361302305178708054651154
24693952651271010529270703066730244471259739399505146
28404767431363739978259184541176413327906460636584152
92701903027601733947486696034869497654175242930604072
70050590395031485229213925755948450788679779252539317
65156416197168443524369794447355964260633391055126826
06159572621703669850647328126672452198906054988028078
28814297963366967441248059821921463395657457221022986
77599746738126069367069134081559412016115960190237753
52555630060624798326124988128819293734347686268921923
97778339107331065882568137771723283153290825250927330
47850724977139448333892552081175608452966590553940965
56854170600117985729381399825831929367910039184409928
65756059935989100029698644609747147184701015312837626
31146774209145574041815908800064943237855839308530828
30547607679952435739163122188605754967383224319565065
54608528812019023636447127037486344217272578795034284
86312944916318475347531435041392096108796057730987201
35248407505763719925365047090858251393686346386336804
28917671076021111598288755399401200760139470336617937
15396306139863655492213741597905119083588290097656647
30073387931467891318146510931676157582135142486044229
24453041131606527009743300884990346754055186406773426
03583409608605533747362760935658853109760994238347382
22208729246449768456057956251676557408841032173134562
77358560523582363895320385340248422733716391239732159
95440828421666360232965456947035771848734420342 27706
65383738750616921276801576618109542009770836360436111
05924091178895403380214265239489296864398089261146354
14571535194342850721353453018315875628275733898268898
52355779929572764522939156747756667605108788764845349
36360682780505646228135988858792599409464460417052044
70046315137975431737187756039815962647501410906658866

162180038266989961965580587208639721176995219466789857011798332440601811575658074284182910615193917630059194314434605154047710570054339000182453117733718955857603607182860506356479979004139761808955363669603162193113250223851791672055180659263518036251214575926238369348222665895576994660491938112486609099798128571823494006615552196112207203092277646200999315244273589488710576623894693889446495093960330454340842102462401048723328750081749179875543879387381439894238011762700837196053094383940063756116458560943129517597713935396074322792489221267045808183331376416581826956210587289244774003594700926866265965142205063007859200248829186083974373235384908396432614700053242354064704208949921025040472678105908364400746638002087012666420945718170294675227854007450855237772089058168391844659282941701828823301497155423523591177481862859296760504820386434310877956289292540563894662194826871104282816389397571175778691543016505860296521745958198887868040811032843273986719862130620555985526603640504628215230615459447448990883908199973874745296981077620148713400012253552224669540931521311533791579802697955571050850747387475075806876537644578252443263804614304288923593485296105826938210349800040524840708440356116781717051281337880570564345061611933042444079826037795119854869455915205196009304127100727784930155503889536033826192934379708187432094991415959339636811062755729527800425486306005452383915106899891357882001941178653568214911852820785213012551851849371150342215954224451190020739353962740020811046553020793286725474054365271759589350071633607632161472581540764205302004534018357233829266191530835409512022632916505442612361919705161383935732669376015691442994494374485680977569630312958871916112929468188493633864739274760122696415884890096571708616059814720446742866420876533479985822209061980217321161423041947775499073873856794118982466091309169177227420723336763503267834058630193019324299639720444517928812285447821195353089891012534297552472763573022628138209180743974867145359077863353016082155991131414420509144729353502223081719366350934686585865631485557586244781862010871188976065296989926932817870557643514338206014107732926106343152533718224338527

635202177354407152818981376987551575745469397271504 88
46979361950047772097056179391382898984532742622728864
71088832701737232588182446584362495805925603381052156
06206155713299156084892064340303395262263451454283678
69828807425142256745180618414956468611163540497189768
21542277224794740335715274368194098920501136534001238
46714296551867344153741615042563256713430247655125219
21803578016924032669954174608759240920700466934039651
01781348578356944407604702325407555577647284507518268
90418293966113310160131119077398632462778219023650660
37404160672496249013743321724645409741299557052914243
82080760983648234659738866913499197840131080155813439
79194852830436739012482082444814128095443773898320059
86490915950532285791457688496257866588599917986752055
45580990045564611787552493701245532171701942828846174
02736649978475508294228020232901221630102309772151569
44642790980219082668986883426307160920791408519769523
55534886577434252775311972474308730436195113961190800
30255878387644206085044730631299277888942729189727169
89057592524467966018970748296094919064876469370275077
38664323919190422542902353189233772931667360869962280
32557185308919284403805071030064776847863243191000223
92978525537237556621364474009676053943983823576460699
24652600890906241059042154539279044115295803453345002
56244101006359530039598864466169595626351878060688513
72346270799732723313469397145628554261546765063246567
66202792452085813477176085216913409465203076733918411
47504140168924121319826881568664561485380287539331160
23229255561894104299533564009578649534093511526645402
44187759493169305604486864208627572011723195264050230
99774567647838488973464317215980626787671838005247696
88408498918508614900343240347674268624595239589035858
21350064509981782446360873177543788596776729195261112
13859194725451400301180503437875277664402762618941017
57687268042817662386068047788524288743025914524707395
05465251353394595987896197789110418902929438185672050
70964606263541732944649576612651953495701860015412623
96228641389779673332907056737696215649818450684226369
03678495559700260798679962610190393312637685569687670
29295371162528005543100786408728939225714512481135778
62766490242516199027747109033593330930494838059785662

88447874414698414990671237647895822632949046798120899
84857163571087831191848630254501620929805829208334813
63840542172005612198935366937133673339246441612522319
69434712064173754912163570085736943973059797097197266
66642267431117762176403068681310351899112271339724036
88700099686292254646500638528862039380050477827691283
56033725482557939129852515068299691077542576474883253
41412132800626717094009098223529657957997803018282428
49022147074811112401860761341515038756983091865278065
88966823625239378452726345304204188025084423631903833
18384550522367992357752929106925043261446950109861088
89991465855188187358252816430252093928525807796973762
08456374821144339881627100317031513344023095263519295
88680690821355853680161000213740851154484912685841268
69589917414913382057849280069825519574020181810564129
72508360703568510553317878408290000415525118657794539
63317538532092149720526607831260281961164858098684587
52512999740409279768317663991465538610893758795221497
17317281315179329044311218158710235187407572221001237
68721944747209349312324107065080618562372526732540733
32487575448296757345001932190219911996079798937338367
32425761039389853492787774739805080800155447640610535
22202325409443567718794565430406735896491017610775948
36454082348613025471847648518957583667439979150851285
80206078205544629917232020282229148869593997299742974
71155371858924238493855858595407438104882624648788053
30427146301194158989632879267832732245610385219701113
04665871005000832851773117764897352309266612345888731
02883515626446023671996644554727608310118788389151149
34093934475007302585581475619088139875235781233134227
98665035227253671712307568610450045489703600795698276
26392344107146584895780241408158405229536937499710665
59489445924628661996355635065262340533943914211127181
06910522900246574236041300936918892558657846684612156
79554256605416005071276641766056874274200329577160643
44860620123982169827172319782681662824993871499544913
73020518436690767235774000539326626227603236597517189
25901801104290384274185507894887438832703063283279963
00720069801244365116394086922207453202446241211558 0
43545420642151215850568961573564143130688834431852808
53975927734433655384188340303517822946253702015782157

Douglas Coupland **JPod** 431

37326552318576355409895403323638231921989217117744946
94036782961859208034038675758341115188241774391450773
66384071880489358256868542011645031357633355509440319
23672034865101056104987272647213198654343545040913185
95131451812764373104389725070049819870521762724940652
14619959232142314439776546708351714749367986186552791
71582408065106379950018429593879915835017158075988378
49622573985121298103263793762183224565942366853767991
13140108043139732335449090824910499143325843298821033
98469814171575601082970658306521134707680368069532297
19905999044512090872757762253510409023928887794246304
83280319132710495478599180196967835321464441189260631
52661816744319355081708187547705080265402529410921826
48582138575266881555841131985600221351588872103656960
87515063187533002942118682221893775546027227291290504
29225978771066787384000061677215463844129237119352182
84998243509208918016855727981564218581911974909857305
70332667646460728757430565372602768982373259745084479
64954564803077159815395582777913937360171742299602735
31027687194494449179397851446315973144353518504914139
41557329382048542123508173912549749819308714396615132
94204591938010623142177419918406018034794988769105155
79055548069538785400664533759818628464199052204528033
06263695626490910827627115903856995051246529996062855
44383833032763859980079292284665950355121124528408751
62290602620118577753137479493620554964010730013488531
50735487353905602908933526400713274732621960311773433
94367338575912450814933573691166454128178817145402305
47506671365182582848980099512139193995633241336556770
98003081910272040997148687418134667006094051021462690
28044915964654533010775469541308871416531254481306119
24078211886900560277818242350226961893443525476335735
36485619363254417756613981703930632872166905722259745
20919291726219984440964615826945638023950283712168644
65617852355651641277128269186886155727162014749340522
76946595712198314943381622114006936307430444173284786
10177774383797703723179525543410722344551255558999864
61838767649039724611679590181000350989286412041951635
51108763204267612979826529425882951141275841262732790
79880755975185157684126474220947972184330935297266521
00156625145529947451276315509176367302594621329301904

```
02837954246323258550301096706922720227074863419005438
30265068121414213505715417505750863990767394633514620
90828889349383764393992569006040673114220933121959362
02982972351163259386772241477911629572780752395056251
58160313335938231150051862689053065836812998810866326
32719806112715488587980934879129137074982305759290918
62939195014721197586067270092547718025750337730799397
13453953264619526999659638565491759045833358579910201
27132045839032008538788816336376851820837278851311752
27769609787962142372162545214591281831798216044111311
67140691482717098101545778193920231156387195080502467
97257924976057726259133285597263712112019057207714091
48645074094926718035815157571514050397610963846755569
29897038354731410022380258346876735012977541327953206
09711545064842121859364909979177668747744818828706323
15515865032898164228288232746866106592732197907162384
64215348985247621678905026099804526648392954235728734
39776804957740914495383915755654854590589764951985138
01007958010783759945775299196700547602252552034453988
71253878017196071816407812484784725791240782454436168
23452395706895142722697504318736332630111030534233358
21609333191218806608268341428910415173247216053355849
99322454873077882290525232423486153152097693846104258
28497149634753418375620030149157032796853018686315724
88401526639835689563634657435321783493199825542117308
46774529708583950761645822963032442432823773745051702
85606980678895217681981567107816334052667595394249262
80756968326107495323390536223090807081455919837355377
74874202903901814293731152933464446815121294509759653
43062842153194457271186149000176505581770953024688752
63250119705209476159416768727784472000192789137251841
62285778379228443908430118112149636642465903363419454
06571835447719124466212593926566203068885200555991212
35363718226922531781458792593750441448933981608657900
87616502463519704582889548179375668104647461410514249
88702521399368705093723054477341126413548928068410591
07716677821238332810262185587751312721179344448201440
42574508306394473836379390628300897330624138061458941
42276947479316657176231824721683506780764875734204915
57628217583972975134478990696589532548940355615613167
40327647246921250575911625152965456854463349811431767
```

0257295661844775487469378464233737238981920662048511B

025729566184477548746937846423373723898192066204851 18
9437886822480727935202250179654534375727416391079 1972
952950812942922205347717304184477915673991738418 31171
036252439571615271466900581470000263301045264354 78659
032907332054683388720787354447626479252976901709 12007
874183736735087713376977683496344252419949951388 31507
487753743384945825976556099655595431804092017849 71846
854973706962120885243770138537576814166327224126 34423
982152941645378000492507262765150789085071265997 03670
872669276430837722968598516912230503746274431085 29343
052730788652839773352460174635277032059381791253 96915
621063637625882937571373840754406468964783100704 58061
344673127159119460843593582598778283526653115106 50416
232953290477721740835593497237585521380483050900 09646
676088301540612824308740645594431853413755220166 30581
211103345312074508682433943215904359443031243122 74713
858420303901060709403152355561727679941600203939 75099
897629335325855575624808996691829864222677502360 19325
797472674257821111973470940235745722227121252685 23842
958742735015636600931880454933389897415714905441 82559
738080871565281430102670460284316819230392535297 79576
586241439270154974087927313105163611913757700892 95648
233236482982630246079758757677453771601024908046 24301
856524161756655600160859121534556267602192689982 85537
787258314514408265458348440947846317877737479465 35801
699607794055687011923286080411309046293508718271 25934
668712766694873899824598527786499569165464029458 93506
496433580982476596516514209098675520380830920323 04873
427034682887516040715466538346196112230137594515 79252
696743642531927390036038608236450762698827497618 72357
547676288995075211480485252795084503395857083813 04769
378813211236742813194879502280663201700224603319 89671
970649163741175854851878484012054844672588851401 56272
501982171906696081262778548596481836962141072171 42149
863619187747545096503089570994709343378569816744 65828
267911940611956037845397855839240761276344105766 75102
430755981455278616781594965706255975507430652108 53015
979080733437360794328667578905334836695554868039 13433
720156498834220893399971641479746938696905480089 19306
713805717150585730714881564992071408675825960287 60564
597824237702424698053280566327870419267684671162 66879

46348695046450742021937394525926266861355294062478136
12062026364981999994984051438682852589563422643287076
63299304091723100725471764188685351372332667877921738
34754148002280339299735793615241275582956927683723123
47989894462743304545667900620324205163962825884430854
38307201495672106460533238537203143242112607424485845
09458049408182092763914000854042202355626021856434899
41454399504109805918179488826280520664410863190016885
68155169229486203010738897181007709290590480749092427
14101893354281842999598816966099383696164438152887721
40852680887574882932587358099056707558170179491619061
14001908553744882726200936685604475596557476485674008
17738170330738030547697360978654385938218722058390234
44435088674998665060406458743460053318274362961778625
18081893144363251205107094690813586440519229512932450
07883339878842933934243512634336520438581291283434529
73086529097833006712617981303167943855357262969987403
59570458452230856390098913179475948752126397078375944
86113945196028675121056163897600888009274611586080020
78033415914517970730368351969777660763737853330120241
20112046988609209339085365773222392412449051532780950
95586645947763448226998607481329730263097502881210351
77231244650953496536930900186377640940943498373132513
21862080214809922685502948454661814715557444709669530
17769043427203189277060471778452793916047228153437980
35396798614243709566832214914654380145938292773

Bree won the chips within a minute: "I did my grade-seven science fair project on pi. I knew them all up to about the two thousandth digit, and then I thought it'd be sexier to play it dumb. It's one of my life's biggest regrets that I never got to remember up to the ten thousandth digit. It was like I made pi my special friend and only he and I could hang out together. How could I ever forget that first love affair?"

***Shocked silence.***

Bree's fling-with-pi victory quickly dimmed when Evil Mark sent us all another strand of numbers. He said, "Yes, pi is special—but so are randomly generated numbers. Inside this list of 58,894 random numbers I've substituted a capitalized letter O for a zero. Without using your FIND command, the first person to locate the 'O' will win the chance for me to karaoke to any song of their choice. Ready? One, two, three, go."

```
83942944535915708827565988180941171602977603437305136
21390047883372351427540720286989526875002292431461936
28239543068022427756058855794286015641989324467102372
25800297273097452429449908354301203870218835442507269
71817267033807989955253172496140238364116161423181682
86982808407565975161585144202085355149342513247112612
62079419135677167536171122565377241995606589838856267
89484108233086396286519881244321698503451868918275599
45693838724723947627414601973463201880989088103467559
43172243275949869026574482711121777978590275781242362
84928956533274793627437438735316526413098229234408689
28887217037671153990108722496354202652724375929936788
92290871394521390144540502256604694347888604907974363
29512081493764832809724352980551105265480439093656304
78508195730154902412472099169385710606542264784205773
75727097574973421978171214630016390433685178774343388
53171732362990470250513103069541983416465927279348761
13073458150617381024767818187141443182834655540638060
41157908237062429275730482362939596344864638839942661
96491322624462011076422558940899387410866060547160120
67376447378242683959804866194844238299973782158735436
75450289593519307895499163233776173799169416449746294
68006072450537953965035821115047930533914535480656429
81038719608184148324108789344586583567268477620753590
52209126688479186107784567803229087297402655371784819
68698633707223635025553892516394097271202752698510189
```

66460931390455977355476392535776123630429612695232001
56914304831972943283176430942963118692924752881873025
21612059759622473333230226249723608636220824233272622
93961075871756743334679879663200891657347075771305636
92273861497705439378643580851325181025896791202514663
80625861253952857619816268750366155799210498426341830
43789750872542718322672965519850728514160390984202336
36598688572570143595073905538839710812176805186905049
65457121972336316099714985695110126155153392330511559
50605798886339411314828765447043992122877196733503964
16263652559665551567386173914160001756333599945392510
69342908024452560587198519233029633872989555969983968
62474581434975861872696797559447651461581526788424119
57925328450941048522932614555719036666615199562955746
59764615250983044917868541232596722659563831593225125
48556479117384547327488732895473230863640722300319315
17681936294445146776869037298748352876562763481713933
74820291873061474289852724910397043076496298812190634
19392803144225172519616708931346582620122274299495031
52498838837454117404763586907326669902199900369554941
15947981777093826325295710472557733194925825308415253
44010073145122062261825099742872675259387610966959730
16711571379873872267683074917032261043033189817399637
38092861095522494285829767836888164107557389551499799
2989887915531538385374501987920662970371802952017187
69650481938155482059267087582563615609993329285625742
42755542867689137607801728107565036157508615952221211
40830004629234111942926153490640801824182231528337696
30939442745226661120216459324442920633226531656579660
41859684686391625915911569544794947285159497512384779
65697681796114844586131004654419950174329804930253935
70991396832574340947166899457427769251406829876118698
63334418272675477556782660667569840472938569008318224
03217765811833871453484666002372567649671924959395445
62774508144862803422084317894136382117641490574110182
87761661493088924906429484453952879005668088908222402
36783038657313494467010351884170509563366287038527489
95019951494573395170946171869993844196273187012768478
15729393306356925651505818527793809043045439906246848
21402743865728184477422121731585824952766968940603787
37100793834096228571723567854670834747091142567551140

7736141334427744448387122384378288003469515166557831 9
7470372846972479337317652432897778745790304246292984 9
3853702523298894626128055835824799659495055647275552 9
0023986624078467740648628708668556885454901336451933 7
9457888871851738388052328658307885590782970932864947 4
9303077791304471606701492333532592212951772411283887 8
6774520549078408290904885240023938451622893198168501 4
7060208515112850984769313948895817227043452952047739 8
8147437114799813564077063773795326017097725333065361 7
3520127708164970028254320945597221790994863924491269 8
9273174733210360993632993694166404118209818198884934 3
2350928487854862079735632507225062496241705801335373 2
4497706779441368256330589311574146199521453608402911 4
6760413534631336309388266374104593621571256702465745 4
5307781178925954967162446374502668701708074359445467 2
3465282719076820144744423508586023936530121297556367 9
9516477453111485252378011615959673788525553370693732 8
4181459091295930679233971735371265943011381074354092 5
0355856967263602659208584763208282364655013904911208 9
3766609865949220712303341890056957688572893888365470 6
3750386895924297393152571800667197629804348459851132 6
6396112257762206819553564907814362101431255657511996 5
5428781835276906504390628071429406281568741234943630 2
6513191358326692973105249133696548745514480962179540 2
7234786511362406029134965737448236723187490413076559 8
5832019023449722879551544147293421581079894285196909 4
3507994313560337023816230823142920992916891942988143 8
6660647585749196314972072974744749541786987958774059 7
7400678928289153495982899268655452525430581327940787 0
8003009317238739515713959810466618069594613833646407 1
8846408621388191341896253576267470726394602530625840 5
2077266553834330241537339663304746432396323197188340 2
0254361711001495845764932064851447462319578797689968 2
9671143053892860029827632303667762418988493257435433 3
5490524329672076284135245501936858794582581548854489 0
3506546762379553152789247759653592201988155725203574 8
8457327889518361923784140060992052408020575479945461 1
3224470651542116012408789043939811083123932701932532 6
5703456407760852612801229969253836590762620547584366 2
9481532061023183468177554668393435472696544704019179 1
6335996666987482338389730178479773373115330878872229 9

0631810819404415114060243890775439287552176543374041
4576177526954836571875188005730018432855562441130239
4513527417218285331376694352306606176655597763207754
366104546772479051038239976318859544905289471164833105
1415482452079575058858997692963654635632322164689598
225873286161468255875676235659231590310853967805247295
39055629513621081925173488852199766074723355883965501
40332574492471728244931800189369758814330749525847843
41487999637694347348294564416520287463316653555408372
6217077032480373426618469549795504253297230910228891

13350672732527022547093888598913435969693324789263238
6178496923665339207709674768386976116794674560913759
3848816589639219580268420077181662941483609059250254
06932145799111801324851151877477824993176746193247030
5642064984070405446998602966433731442367229476315323
5337658867169755354287471948242258915942947355328051
45972017635356075818111785422470647569535549851730584
62394081578187453719873667787873049136199020959929787
41430188324885095031064555945437204570320423258094981
087486881183290756240138441611487171945113896446459096

816190978128025890505540784001602925451259959495952056
81355429130704739341491913865076354825747798991269967
849427098291111645491318096196884122227317641266501756
263998816224885977890655579996546851883230886589142
32837919620134043655679923055523818551066861680968437
04911264045385662993641913637729889621318094331272464
3475883303397428572731121212160391677845334155970157
0479491467172191032055695104545857742115439148299065
58751025884862528031022920629226456827813710417495215
990877112475552377671085662177792429132559657753984535

06222861366774895493811816128933225124426415224356451
95837450907800777596653833302456327066932462535805612
6567959430158288373743502741645252695800564764162809
1173527774487976428679742401922375582134864337779108
34076288223392638046632692119711256318119203527920795
07389741445122254330749917012888536567353760973284292
858415193094006368231904756648365974103099150727156293
7695327798765889986840190213186799103473653282985489
771988507607075174610321198710333101398963541483562533
6763404080964754225219377669199825246294418942012299
31841875341031977872969374777050236284829967950007450

79686246310862323289541215334361442492539436510700699
28756360761172664122142618629036232793929379512145410
09632654857077435474692531846733672117180523400066157
13819173194793669737171532759031236571186683656558618
77128420273419793492319405055275374670260881637800673
59294224827749236667585004132600009616639763814090775
14743556429289442128813505332817026125184342685801754
69475125139193938987728171877406098036743179506182623
48334290053629074226744727699375452846543508341215437
35090690215152318479279256298473587153154584030461509
91290601784163427738719382233858036883836735997825328
36022785701423804587134738891836292854686792879845596
19119611443193536984728784761377008958566199165547213
45966720937439383227163716675923830185359677882854862
23784284547953661328402803255746807185209106936569008
95182263839085552221523136736493381384304208043741547
75462070415910104013966712744539612920444480409752328
44343437166860296134768889724764639696927113492945166
63387654291921665064133508638915886943866901429903384
42579117703884608266737980467074009976981559092524813
67162839551814692746027807536105247697748235023156069
72240493234856371989459360762124779552140794848952730
41357523075390804408789441602875309013369550219687117
89641188059305357297139520816769783340567897991937098
79909163277561083661215601542790017675188579965009451
81433284434533212391493817109587585385299928170445507
15578617650729291588271660801114019166111768268544607
27158978398741823481785618282391325446133320141456351
40691547920325152896402199925725636918340169373246801
08526701918868734999679724308653499377716739038494955
63406273568241199715197184674375136310252309242923120
80397194662298953688578560125472279321353300914247574
96485617658366563524286116274487335047197463979882218
18552928549605991603273244622161556840580786026363744
85697280933360726324364802830443280486993847427719175
14428381592337537314801279485369497226584263839791711
78949703606282280898537318800530701956590172334395761
40265896318581943406690808260084301843627228526278854
97240397495804925917293882431460296512773695972254968
72381046414571870334739245384602350475818082726416390
56681082008326984819746550183442522110694219187726535

440 JPod Douglas Coupland

5443639379571048471060643063977981496626662370 3179817
8724379034414979316299269621830686847712893922 7192688
2503554469736966105338455569644484705843403657 09896585
3740267734843572441500972244265834262804382796 4316072
6800684493802824337490105628025616773765855325 9009969
8591555780480328019789099637227626288213998283 1845436
9822008341676076184322294851191175569477730716 2121562
6485200258441958450784686825125851189549989420 6366276
9684122704259230470113348599932958294797196182 6681952
2432811942482433351333675772743570771486646980 1398163
3527009484173907752920696806323813315477822816 1859184
7979442015158597719753719850479048518282348624 4948231
7240012272747228045565928269534729977853210758 5341347
1187363100247158186590287754949102531372984638 4469940
8797822499546940976441982889824679818644099632 2550700
6429254135522699416331890693877412635036045137 8560230
5468860450733691219613881022147906405427581996 7776497
6243165701924037295169199968014228144531501382 8348174
1994117974631097762736882793823317142061267786 762529
4777354309980036539315928047937896607128590944 4622627
1642705752962432732089858797236128226941078395 6571750
8422449089168468731872243334947594992735155198 4666018
9981455166287918266021758295650654078976802799 9097607
5428961240499490458732704668965079584490664995 3488501
9832335126815999042930002257948095191033070553 3820756
0535038311621739343033591371414264175786428881 6533124
5274181887211778645243828147234854208254958037 9283755
7633092748310259667234701555481698755981050249 0124110
4946676731846023915967025061731454424755977113 2194914
8009217742751895012492071181569561412256456099 1635819
4789157597434709731042586813644859799209164612 7251027
9029180833744441768039102336282703674391377527 8528849
8484554195305233879696721699365803096842404708 0299827
1647472806801823708543596401312992120705010074 553075
3895995392080005236190112637052467695568269126 8585790
0560612287273516556049871030398107339098431688 1427194
6817526348258515757334663491593962093768180198 5956744
2448218459003823206517453248715534350290636905 2354755
1541225869322538614551709375009584452638846628 2263383
1228222376260041132026250816969019652538234405 9016425
5228944053869904491078330751449342505107508959 7296612

0962796065788357441677869304129481095963060 0334303765
98231142487695152441087150683476985431163444560629448
23813761636669696278266639121764641475490398130 3781974
04111526800105344962646363737277204342699776806931837
32657037817578835213689711369458563962074056613521222
58151873198528273347205008285292835457686336775116633
34836780951922137866812179944048423730561498149007155
33017549496691673045067282281317334768586785517341782
72092431357557938881690124509134797840668531190742163
22884186444885731943166874787478944035548452302368755
53297942045375709365379168592785363891465134999449395
46718526211371347253436620021993731595611028429933339
48445195093570885025876164289428227741856178940848967
78482848170393547273624173534425554255197528605553540
63017055375281324811171002879934053002680563172585938
98895372688705977117467808026463277902717346954607728
67454459052025731716434367718764784162736361619964390
96855983481526711312530649797036575308176178043127027
32497078792840485312415894837174827903524992878508206
77073479762354640879601427673597767784377907430456955
82095766723022362268996386606449593113120532854463520
17605587996758852921790171037412075328010386410337504
95939561367575570351619849921474854684706038794519209
75154484748916867269126305923446392516354641021047363
59172947324508236843579226664725729003798937023756734
20632834457140487237649440370752271498610531855420310
78696862012531096651136830782260592852044937449607475
09235913911165956133968587001626022704557431870807891
47975787969798162658422018797794330374801245123968888
98828583725463599242590510547645720438998821696843548
96417868926403205927765187983967085795387817497346959
25345987921447226308558102855684769516296620214809826
61560071524741183919193643519480332933165167183035599
93178405130596322445418504288471702772319774004486093
53017167114368019717958265822854920333665591001399325
65017053492370606383760855166830697878514942960041993
70451416659849475334878887445126197643640156872569610
84671651513986882764119957352814116687911654773526714
10976256386700940356008288245321900103480283299582133
74881074968588466992391506025377333591790857046450421
70039332800223336729890662883728337846711152208643964

30495990681841733243063809239675356390645097529844726
77532403852802291739807964572586964863766856245787788
84559840280957861775764809661039267597723555379639104
76697188905707327084986031331513451814345714061237385
92969477567282975362754979628879547260483854930931141
97644449286968231347894835730259052639033420985577848
52999887187175274791692508449409146899789837892460899
93844987114935404804079113046556149105371123812201686
88287255132453629315952339019796213966508837008933673
19239526293084002671216576202550814894489417366499033
42414049655673395426964520957433411766850223834293759
22575184815569449854825464349884845455537562537893200
67086276655415314984815648505587290866963571212114080
04276141567872401949219063315088521160749225314703616
44473689486411855229319794617529278864220039362060950
05291617098108511950566181687834263805918973296010440
03037385773270881977914288342546069872328291972286941
66894139146191379111009150024115367147455419964776858
48636529229743907172622207703974912918957878385774912
75382456714317111496431554020791214212902237422363198
58983220718787593463849908371761364896625258992887999
15007366648401603740986325935394318332843602235722715
34802386043555495982934848172791898882048862902135192
14358954828666309182060751466904789443358804035286652
45520674618380692832412770719455335877708420166505798
99832286717948268665295231981510945145313882268576394
98881711911316897674043454646463204413886907227422264
33756523785274774168996052344285152397446061124330279
86471351427641444385474008674450494022389327389671437
00505465057487918218517901511653279332379793954986524
37879929025085522817838597337390165639203864890868255
94477081951593483657798362281736360065423910780180889
73121138653121157116812023662433027999261387556991017
66310261829007957177956829649314880907204829868139373
56986737912211980083557079365982211442429565267315098
02337838199417625065298095722079158921415953662274657
97018314645241408290772187557675174222848943423423146
17336439900512038560828476077210139623027984397407997
92884113241264908281342252263357555627739532172638135
83944265590086947452137291092796706218220423153514160
93958351410015759126895823623829136353376412927659548

87872405488172965798020267074250269085271739467012894
53466416673002007443746361841739532484701276384876058
56789621996341130454441771641284216952394534134329132
55230840275088954257417051698919924792520719270993497
34253714094954316273388735259079659787386802377837429
03199586298913031559990994950810969485645417973028829
95487328046299524079826299143586626384176122466939112
45976450457525752438174634690441613656278117586153484
39166416442204326690713858955256257358161069290462718
03420147989846937737439511764942862458693786318221227
78451282760066830174096465153886120195342665867713760
62816514468211075761423177216118973724288098479094391
47859840348209630212353446950856664548507868811501724
94479940675099766251662826025880284764706529536330320
53793398890445170869384671032522924331794920988854283
13754903047347031168706641518033734320234414807142844
46108578743606532315135109486624448888189609713845299
70739333707888689141675487372352862526406868560373785
93862761559459094938574977207429619298895561738308851
10656374865753576518226377361938200119264337544443535
07950786660031331156426088104755314413337322633990372
29575323136963794978660819807152686106042397988854160
92925953745854745253509375129337190294665143416344865
62662632510715817890116089844817102516900291854806258
61754014051373696815260248323256712616574937243138440
33389411379834807107577663034580427040383741619726191
80065357882534860273232869588920153331715625309496445
59719162621390872127140677330797647900545688081921955
22227873072385382700715865997147737781893661897108737
12981537222337615679832096756599638973052376677456641
19028319852592763939726082633193416230067073198793215
48283615141217808951339138564848106460772964002970714
52588552215355637381086374771187156896088476728560647
88917741817514989039360424749118269095218516080895869
16115385523398867193459365680759557032616630595013966
41125082497703212983455050912340275365433540927775539
46605862111902113818135609784472869901723878320481701
90891664316495082458489742624188097214349564889100897
61095470211173988532351097798945736537995261551693333
36592563050596612887323494177484758388484792910939108
28738583291199741660973169146787731309939801734543894

4698873871839836682558816889316473998056747806860528

687400848115981552936149364705727401381182722391530 13

69422235848166460115914373407275564713763937010658800

2219438756092999978167504567209658578770902886765766 9

94395335809242020074340082261487646477514367174217043

2126998209646300441807048273153491873212458157218113 1

7840424322065317501448814970655822582293542408935863 3

04403777959412651690406646412391627871724326691498925

07342718092960248276103111520264190499920937257121448

1588392547548594780819116218575066699564615149268135 7

3719465070597334556413394075887772981443721766862983 0

37765190088418246894258275174150751086141396354929219

1422149289234768131191815715097552252257729798442268 1

72597269925726674355098160038549649807275866396868331

7480384245572562645012685071148538714063889191397911 8

44976239639473576730439830348431123361321086388078848

1266431723259742863693026113399908497118893530101896 2

8730776168880856019312561116203439842295225052190850 6

71065434213697979800640969335761309979726865239969030

907736147768425851131309547883507281347247024737601 52

5539631930769705321014235583584675734357637175478708 2

1826913297390172512390135346728683181657588524323916 4

36298161621303909894222934013635221631087584645147549

5455076694731161431675666729562880721777198615343057 1

94725498323045295443658100753640562109257428749462908

4188302076027769858111493454078975251285655706227118 8

4751436673231118481360917345531862635923722860044776 7

7224021818580485204971490966729868280134906881/266248

3594978144882646825697430157423557081531743375228925 5

6416391667875742510222624210076116114393388152582763 4

46680175910800730878053157120380572023810064866481209

5772643984450619230984943752578082381491938445642961 2

96408617494767171190409861499276952316552444311821122

07633993038275439719301808140615850537421785419383026

95489235183330743622433099437125680179225766533719375

7710518741184358074791075393282001781642221782585975

8550705320171241572553137207564835433226524105523243 5

78847273745954211572017851328903267824801361278849784

74249838780874179752585792176704744043941085159592144

83540311879875122472029822619174594505256193635365648

65929271966807890497650834467387993855098649432722782

721957830697405061286393492394650501802333325613401 01
44568108728477810373379888346959991693087434244819061
20796439771420326994475365708060618578338204444254475
82891408495422509750195234861115382140648090741667842
31922053232964370685160073971080948626939831612262338
88048303984111588689731929931993171527127801132820306
66758432446714013865129787783682428900987714385171344
76242574499351995778373673162648017943214299949704598
46403895706119105185072570959411666716553354931876267
29120364036721629701338941657390514449912827937989765
56722557311252604827217300325732489449298682299970971
50944558537126409776558328442844862213191666994272671
48570084196935250299975634513086216528286465235912058
38070367141755663626494992950698440303290963653272146
83643159420349807095596243659588168458965857285851292
13832977334696478151825099274726204275749284779555146
92163715472762314639157452778167372269464949587121784
59658954895461972182127268206910665520589170600080579
77283477702116807212764327281295493415803487908973177
69626835335362667353794397525483637993543733594683104
05664855329857744317730859849793677729764509083759618
15776323488887638288540862071883848445523495528634240
96328078998914863614183459399905135495103082550392421
58641226195959903399439664266017240509787336632497382 8
04713278447476502934469828449892292059917694937177658
71524560327977597540871085889892755402924774545135401
21783971381024368718729007315318654116180888439408259
85580525957393391543235765057101858041593654239614427
57208805441977885483537710308991814899861122449238185
91219198251578899131825859933806439335794926257330814
05964987025345884409487185408974277184784432136827710
85573690430481292726744440395647442549538617676985547
45601534972826151749521332606517615222384524497357738
58677974478255493333297627454874439928876855392171897
21071445236547537676256282719527526660235239688163793
58182214802142330343813123866779152580118155986570733
34568829911772783221520658133033999961499087572165580
45556285860243861716040571286687082584661991625231796
88924358203514625793955343192805535307916312478752271
54909842401695511983148600127659562167313303606202335
29747839245719838504755862031848098443754118634119595

24278479233349598700914328716909209030534173068896044
03998922949731651200312337368259353967617637018883990
96746760141343752619918561083459865584926568455137215
32735324249012136649278587114294942361865932197867193
28796103178129986152542768687435698810786527882761056
57371940274234448350869592011937509983161510041359628
59650557698609495703780607927885065224057458337699008
60210782100953566667186837483145411905705709309198765
15317531978493216625394198823236039310775426893084198
49392809617521095884083261715768896357213406789310310
60439169935584313364127083438462949478959300755590965
06916724172621266876284223801610972763340853680766275
68755430268050040017592997920444097814015679939445235
53942911161624925808546720893980383716487445765353347
91329503088483421991660381583508125568437449202180385
94957665882089889910815430234738438574987700613016897
48998966602261039235781961051795821008057534227470569
06621112879652012962311842884955389593679515809555239
22125874048356123560771865542139886100534238942352125
05752295000655657487245944152873396204929540113311778
34087407037222100238119250964480015295617478213035059
27167495844190483864409728894853191964454520998245543
96483478366646356747974890159371716755501073995631250
58708018579951429792948140473301747885699514734181429
90635303195887826448729267517299087092059014721188503
05567901065124927918061134004871103969304711936325198
52676387159365081752241045787046010786056142129867529
40725166673409997722923667364334678841502216481193302
28326899431152897461345877335317845738573857473035863
73443119552855632558196514703410681387546397106853170
29833341849159201566496315724045567354645857581483189
39059789818487775649872352926758873909741669357202060
45818681069204595695983741606738625063819190321805934
97403620929350554140212727095229319609811339554306771
54807976362491354761302344696814713435221476921145907
26826319692390326722585170604431474927050414480922181
27159544498084351971015456875478403922555995955529168
16957372213966494335751905362503866922386160494257588
36276567777314940979901172725186025686085993159381973
81290945980881977884077368293132547294448852757764454
26625582933215671888687947471363161146076589754819393

9213911427242587975191579329351014412005239992674722057679944796853583376088514515751791446895355308545866532904862783635312786522345603362091243553568955992408661443514576448290869023870286969157949786214824916474147483847854296568666207733182784352460071986952477631671477974671173588641940206659810887653247211850999363329451342683634412841972516426056048741553305871052652033386498684758699602847542510317988022249946920829300343627048482563262681650355627237823733219108064944917792631077155648975775825332079934335289926634823916532744531012622872037874428610096054652957155472454302065524185879975573816008486599384943943148549339785295831500433521410925462840985433467393902235675341641188761550107784616532439319177274250884410228346133772974918590945785904687421560673831828807549704579341406522845752491690932213193651811104166338399079387855781870883113175273204835976447925139573563259523288641293861129962502866881339778889795731119486977595829287394108341223546340385071406350901106125854961608506333556188206625469942093159889722055781763438067736300994186349766988096404715213565779201392369134624558466970094714943983074515323805250303568922534951958880021738838943398822039310799641512112643267201075149381770288256340189651765938901216874696419373099759522396608974691270591994882471042375497397151798430247938151608142990783265934319373389128510500881205582619560543898736562856784600487669755433726843884630071205244152331698209608506117774713619475331597271174868842693500609335619002225091508305126910658647770824176456178883431706988439382921211820042731961748375570637998666985873712401525197647554335271538345747675433596703262024496268984560950512743547865083987864221234640014298038170018403996172067016771155787615191011037967796869226823692439917527436430915889463360848556584147987095943426411807330419033815783813913941717102990920616713376901645205886926826342325103455754682138229226190493470277882159266388385906185919589687088954981101384657422550456211423377982004825460455421273214817585859709892014491057464493928441989437453708176950109527542931366891135672110918574284345387171648383185314311477210938826713207361338403480845468601

2851224472270639797935191967213950239450713725861559
2835445243699911538457577644622265011621065342116675
4987360538214187706532595168554651971153700286387409
44423792021075397599967238086873236575679315954798856
74012604608610270423169954917267667789412350070536347
95646610307106669307282021364803851181246571792052721
07300471774859770392774261014061115785657304083815696
96781403764143194655640425551509138923111126014605068
69776780991236341965609318071933283940386184367980736
83203466794472491857327274999289567979188388499229963
40546631822357399638626664764111134365302028197632433
29899062959001358165820578773029651142506204803974234
14264894136031446299747977257696909564205575356921800
33674269248087414115484715568858127429552119266429229
23177240827286752184732795192809616437295834567122818
30947676994409688873485838973619867254647005857858112
55433914362013278370193318492738163491811855524876795
57539671715963485216952048871802990096283381920113953
24486698182322801203531975443547947084492271885147499
48295513381121252481098879301334715832135435229498092
70618260710351829949673987866682596520280138742928016
88682397611434769838844477417338035482444515866844613
75892575118279663701415825098242856370703075594120372
44362649067937898274775924457057612835297378541021879
83873022149545190021654634124757243244810217355289345
09642367539769337285638053174572452034799404552813459
32277673856197371315442330623713651022525013390727185
09796713578444510179801076891244874737299213247181361
88581634697797260482283888991817617777227409138704655
92173664111772806209212079673532967641555831664969678
47701531028101537145769321486372713781677666985243058
53919241533057491617569255005647906641191509395374625
18123134519444444232776389636951438952794439590563986
32431210513408931003173801114229560980839898287459284
79383502963978156436409241642325973620780861734670108
78797152282436386434868726355527655647829317898291727
54931562718254619018279177493734912994662952325053129
59785146443675380217064975726530606539324856343921950
92913947588365011906067036879479656616531431100751742
43654364434891903071655331252237217248471437471145356
45952328707412562494970939404109346149968607433846591

01824977413602192191248001363383831244642910984089197
11252499606395288561449614066028069039817370644653254
55302239645583701149954199010823146464794433038369531
72323469243898678568024916994515224648507210425745852
08374449059694311716403870701499669624700511474813222
95880438310983417459057658952100771178199541484000841
36642909427684081875483706409925736381214575457263164
54204854911127875448367030707635540969014969897254087
84428191667523642253842201165073351463212492961563943
58862610927026556476957344905429618502452842753850557
49254410577927828860386347341738396723687402985493356
64337043421793920857331042885275982709938473659568651
33582620914572460955433464280812908835403239228811483
36639870754080860071116762936342640620576540330163682
66640341735401624929745050563423724813359854733924387
24155604829657571532497396001663925673292917625202746
79133776240538563651953248726710138371904218459395959
00764113478892834715814078764456965665930460857635796
04736532588543664328743973289530510868163460350620865
84988955663915518488516559439432055894895601929314843
54734596336663454927267781436413746934312885434230584
54186783441488158585687580760944918670153984130172251
40429851969870901555417535924773746813433687437351109
67474735292679553597617595068824832927832855665871364
14120140144102429874330427303290417356581025570561945
59588487738593747043627260902074201723727689385685589
51244009581974050527489153899536407225093249055853130
24414112511251123936323287561016322754050987259087022
41023072354583906979665249319965926202356944932592702
88952958255709115573679928229897264201118536692785162
44957127468379397963840536678454996754922174411758605
81922941210840848659361478293812698651139359835388415
62171764093516436325804565950484682834181569836656068
01804076180809459043309197860114394395949429880782075
77687649313799331818183787943308201975733752420812305
13981880670191491584892851868619369171041493342931829
06674504934804104191738258807951312729079782460952917
91708518945686434511846688824109237189888409958089200
56591848216832550804734662790146605609558764622993887
67719242164702793859802292410764847381993706836041970
36668815977612913361581993227096704533041277379958205

17117003325360178298802962585979740758035555699457117
55524756688523320203605734384627521328965723753743626
47615407876991416082808508220650953380553974818435491
16638215372366250618802091379294608012294222544266709
39960773484018494253639910516550544277715524590958410
80583339227479655159573284609758873965301408707424650
79911091034867442975974577546606340032937817361535393
37794965522253204333276346879944831674006979292727364
75865737393574277036582473586646561442053278858272700
49476728906085901978346120868637582056702412514691099
01873049474166381282970640860879607089307094757258944
04279567857025154284683952212756403743734628602634511
84722603628007763106070913752741831764417578930545520
28984565864353942185351167815858530624662902379911109
60752280135867325972461975351651939803933913037806314
22357027510026382152595619051114329874715085488698409
25304676637642829540581322314632481248692446245867115
41680134355814443667558776549033569355526905815937926
29820365786671050103790176475632021450073660602963160
71653715806623415635252969252089284247335988925917208
79487638729098924577604349738410718112182326144677287
20464055911240316140596969330965702084587530930864967
67444354139713268552663787564582578642102772693800228
62554663495066980572264482920615426265118089045940483
08752792176436293383862319253632502857042029970773848
46161320630673982638615363235093696407396149196211971
28526617796571950192512384768838564348398584790990273
79386354974332886017331698389912688403190508890268189
30434626684696765215656279059634979511536337320034832
28873058356476764427946946246399351987287220201292768
92207868600305786145514374790436433218225922138654955
42216348286620788189245387954848467630412475853459732
50620460565885683035322718438444094220998666024179521
83141561142577571136613296173832658531791853598724960
93404173768875913820195981277919552322413164119560147
28404254507008905404140022811959005148828462456876496
09502065107971673407578043381156118164415323757888652
33214947862606117606297895282642217842344252282449679
32205102632888694853268729679009964866869895690735173
43024979033226171840236007419052633119923183518309559
10797642442811558851057919789335977459455898822326145

53465004558157545883354453435167687734629057339766782
05327429233621496453993295041470012853575302475724153
46975392874716063363295355411346333617363578988352259
99343066079434425217636758897275768952342091625680912
98790234988596033543557329496605242059791895122261095
81609248246845876674227189893160740789144207098166716
13733142325578400403856210295956400887856500744572780
22788984266245432331027433068074889905978781783032821
92269932978972319242543455471805492171652636476458118
62164511585886765161503678519139175078990626109215462
91138899803353218138624648465754818929211109057990031
47692716223451591547466906054444868685370925125299628
84468045659523171558103025985147235625577888056325356
16385652602973389217651616770668423981800357003793098
58357855038584062115655908671234793761378999123617810
21526756197568114879877191033851373370515675535719103
59380507800415555398739012164649580406231832064385247
36256348697332148704627547280594387371798232374400849
59786269272869640404231604772152980918343397781340467
98901570360317363823616383183103779382600059103681160
44163890207228422822169709859037996255519206768497757
47910369702725760509321581931214799919630442307768591
65344295558905572537851174775294654218762800726295257
34505072159978183628845198079250047573867494243302410
41625012743128565642647469039099586284821421634189866
97095743517935658061843041429553095101184553226351875
31772900084038197758544301466331066387163507097221185
41741394934841632161485173264393315213803433933278793
61638539693770531913908079190624649721973059833695776
16518848717769531538519628509952980169745162778244386
76213536852246634056901473745288752399216163051820968
01941769384978176822446664449575857776036079196960033
97827400267499521424430721330743665865333224896553449
83250123122135146027270809817888199413045111485303789
76678799221498951363570557934195577374800195370820680
56331899199373449504012832418886952285646783220992604
68440332898428493933182893375715641909605809319635851
29822197231577101512731763996866407445111021605257383
80868930572422651592628060934299802944715602708354917
71970526126160691849806997136490297596104825578278405
43122582365762248025493316582765072760247837314653680

08457435868949923878231808798013233067158124471632178
45574125966967601555160188718856653636203809338513618
63281368479366912473932385202875062619438656322716055
15764951646600807974734579365817320182180672705091898
11991790656511335228380566556035734138965039139645100
92395008852172366139163488894840653823372536379475894
59646061652701352228467849171466973892216895113254577
06621929865334570641146592930875936862649979210293816
81700179303084664225999845149508558837344688585460158
36341002496524426351924497766716385579223256647772549
05681161792101926334063613322170896656137447427743099
51088359422145341400228401781310972847563299963016634
80649680892251802878308539009869275911275256235472905
15400165940571792938121652352840714419075555126873506
63786980380719635826756900215930639816687745962854873
20648960799264064174854177817775958360427897132490651
51308914784445830850940639972738356623434837178507835
39035212424670341772896140455520130822168277064698260
19580530491139072461977316235338445812303198072191203
62981297911643576941915582223432785852223909075203051
49473543081420165286548173676417440782997584741432207
90270274677952865368188474737510100824917852442960535
89589748623167479741689835809921173336613427361728957
60156505524877676590072770922468580693216422164119897
70485385651962564482501356958726142599559364141768773
99924115677250623198814685413801175517360058765673013
54847885934496079314963051548118546371521207988915413
69894894994741745866826670839315093233876662502308246
70806682157322701076319209359221255519422016559769405
72085172595261810208385994529915714522926124193679031
73727553753610113608510540974848739246925335821363720
65072323788073157859478258368189092634263552544644874
17691373453864877056099953122899471023257051362055807
95318818135559641225744407553267922488172211917116685
35204712988436860924773218093924918799105280979192381
78741925153321258462950874816238246827793534416974711
24618720738456775974274958501117583121219473432381866
92619163778543420005914962181103376716457926452877664
01835059436800899412962111845239927145695728050559971
26982544990852884175547613788516039617855961825071319
72804315956904136789027596413013500154361495092307821

6863443226406466464166548846528398938836188183 6678341
3347155418273979486525224365883439609779517887 3105505
6483781331882129412836331723091277020782161059 9315362
8018615627818897395336654911568141739055395985 6120054
0595117800980900819729758620450099559646932642 3609293
4956993294795918615842050963586867584541100458 7256023
0057221196884729063795756170699329794781799426 0563119
3415783882672818128754791527666929622501341552 4868082
8479754346875028651321935295797552825132055055 6098872
5346327666193373380663930006566049803696165320 9900964
9927525197970746826044568744246110884010954182 9652612
5370388414513771955839313220554233846399293443 9601867
7605955559834684178252408346004592081245137225 4557836
4787499800290791826627393699829842663274088156 4957717
6557001274798253097201324548939900181966637271 3636654
5068747166379033741168579395059857155990984600 5154629
1481704165019634351810048937305729048000235790 2367314
9174731521109975934167014720854383959061742772 7051155
8599111858722654971545673999448254884680008697 0976877
8540831721911253274210327052571610768285829712 9464818
5936258675779633478395286989994501960156116943 4781902
4615656012813125817688845411775492412676049583 9088681
5616844604248665216660044453364018416142867863 0986134
6596697455826828370519852533204056351039250572 9113762
6990616347828315595592922535062581244243552585 3456272
0393993930745439720528531235706261165164763148 3840481
9998587299007446918611550724333178628972648864 6688719
2188967969613133242166712612770530544797195718 6186702
7395196841024998961989035933708847352773212023 4884459
3534623101130711724495305186502944551167365597 5250714
3573424910936000599868250829220266262764208275 6188985
8177260446820479806455032376942285527149959752 1052660
6442121478888558189135384124529991372209956429 1118442
3274916697796995623700978094402801465229706236 2725457
2436586236358566248477873868641716398937839197 4325684
8917356239917387765394146084913988322810799117 8293690
6222509788298173629704272395375955813256651795 0197949
2899734691741390096375570507014641261842004400 5776574
9845378040274016482925646058700779016443065182 5429990
3925481415253371965522273604697600634148159069 9740462
8658069727306656668794185375601740419566812373 8405140

42714185468388391924330888510394698231771154952982958
73069936248418858209369975776056974691974559162155770
99258458235684617661236000252699345380100183539697316
27716772719647804541480074385955983523651343156887278
27050381266919193257734621938252648088321526481949657
93970427985653797025995621516478374023920133263168061
96136985630387858255084599130476618876841220855731536
96129719741280367342726389107403747181184566777962297
57578840597194378106836396506289241303127818101518676
26620960091265573934048700458928143408819335182859756
18768213807875573303174102149533268876998984971940961
89734534228358149915531705664536052048232268087566475
58868647057324642193856384428912002512022835306262909
60744842143555195369873553432736234362473800374614678
03894958856757230590834963333138536869437919511158640
26681122647395355837763244632231428148036406889463376
23094069692892275279496873259169902395453458230554813
96263296158182356185394530249282779551899008337234544
47004998462157227170063411785997547652817854286428378
82853163179500382383594493542633347281851554714537138
55651366706417771060248091338076488604667188525899775
77373942178920786938139102506482720124578440620538548
38437252546871499768215095674989344404177994989819174
79134147612086628868420290377281746473726551790985706
63185613690977008426890781160761041644968147364629091
28916211776365182616124951067968057945274418191053001
19215005472559450496125515653390401374631956446166091
79203562845116210938215637996876347769073501027139212
17196220544272782389810570723750965319890245938175674
06268239684251124420317487776326206471334315467976255
74599431491159444883195195118865972937358171896548613
41606062001899586236113381709969265742738713059108685
95567522832558807691376917244377796675563534089704166
63179059292869390310783962828521812026136646028892416
50487593565750152796778754792799731896046067292511413
96343277235652327428313013373259241469826106375249111
94953207566227472622869983090497150135327133931827915
49416284470401778928590397641557213328404329702731529
93379964763098013707745502245146740242590934610781151
00461470351162259154887337206539710403825531857299467
31249599170570792868420095412433585511319402430202937

30919472368149698103499995251169585901276214691381728
26273314914892415874390035027688779240856930184961928
71458903386715681139853116843955627809545819484178403
52538857215344484853917699615651008456032940574314354
70268644213388281440116752941614793916466289331135100
49054348404723449086734975176291403472327115842475514
66329536971131397598389198463451777659576187072683355
08616869895036850679992383476142481577312403953532905
91801302811567757156233949918348780705630726129642849
81685237162947837772411014884967806653236995259061431
04359122257701530545140297693511855461286354758951366
33829106098443343164156850748192063889641893110324231
18397488539202682370882096151311769354558450457439563
23014992170745906646975254596777390443895206793702178
87965120903096040717793317164841582953698778486236271
93422368706995807409326634428904704949531123510771556
09707364659127408881089999974806565979136927827135357
75437235293555155616398781120831162610289059336990419
03085882037785076016299029573575911966861851942752636
05469657883677392048796491798468718029907541635375789
35888698369287964316909712496838378745519002298995177
98837137624011284647364251611761616989493236172511821
15118258301529817507677765817998450177377353734740523
31444554553255423939253484180473240030194445293998836
99212159615467702818311496865196197201027048299559926
63685842467533424277481605543440571448259322661851368
12640190622033667785067031165262284134385566622656070
48318061412365925982084927511487879745785907753029423
05314269045026458499333558253506743187115127370509885
19627167714870649481536566275349252489625414688972677
41881677116282382555290938905211502839742980886794601
98948379823687641496843268112264087836223911798383124
56189262936182745872117076244638849461137360812427378
70774322228112663073338536401300549924842127361100186
90410545263150990867572809244009056540532254134727692
94658217097666077205069618054847892710030025923425463
13246379394829136201439555658522557447964133299171965
47663611881610625191354295957345994207845620254201555
49220552320258942857915149042326900857182363836468502
34831760277773108491918698355470284593814582506332195
57489449238532956654489547295822519497211195832805548

60645539391155487274150259263649337528989668823458444
29572211621394337619860920152821170911140517598826428
12272648698184473564129025915866584009455145162418764
62295151711630136769288731737412801398011050174992 7700
70923681197805619424731209606000844491638671386518572
88756495486428596511129667639206358472124045679017364
60273001532052361908406853353363359003389290635235718
53152401761854841379465235131163627746962394627364610
60130442635600779681546917885148687585788390828198360
59779865028631004154979721456084374700652323161297398
38898304081264393723489739803183695741277211351031099
96694484914442075215490849310438678836668998714908079
36916547283457029085449734088097986062693602312896682
09081312118579341005244529021506252304662272969045617
06339598340465495363382812702725111866915538260952916
74800094880298479218830469453036321280201815226517803
97322343334235024242153608696672811629024736129092674
55048660733296750914169630583853540138288937170811858
79644253109928020412559529521629235858034454730888487
22816555717102079574588146360328605779169848636870175
59195279130079905949547415138342306491199575818416549
41175156065335857815060838171125345890542828762204211
44957346818142554545927868510731739544704349068361784
68980797672092147863331826934092431277508375058682319
09003246160872878948725004416366811897608246327440138
42579773568036747744101761806853527255145650122859169
21222457689623184933730006702393320185491742263918747
38329254626767260721403017233376G41415582254086645098
54978575026923673339432735936335676784679855679119616
88925393046779491659533799217895789120543772818573979
29720067112394002101014956123611443031336551019566751
96414194130831510716406194169079403067719728036074206
68332486271149391542911325383634558124715934753769513
16317751148271658329570571012030977367727755111127867
66532950662897515466143665730513799798493644127238992
14485372302246540429799231327983601531862416577809163
26564554990386185651271213021194934297522235383888315
94112210426396455622858319698412687319171950270678546
29760090174848935537226137108867548246816876005139173
35936676945178620269969218489944591259941179694809465
92858888657314591681153200335800218565381509741898572

861890282315383768094226411211776294873206947909662687636015532356249167845200678308716580589812655765401141373371799766346551523179549465486919987632067521607130615331296434531592992063734048799670769158982486162210654012568781388656229260543926753099349133885635203756337134226418401137419661117798292148831446923686697394304323561422031510218604660828370423075581970811233755695986115937073708878408791798602916737164066010583925141749769903576601408549167289285298075073566616955630768268292328570774625028958726780987332772138653226312958656224958283297278355892417164337953107663333836444337492474824600968114528211035981311687734925844410668975446460795764232725634578106033795558470313626405189456081433323947380856147372001137330575956857584734418884989687070384582378363708551323080478538362669137803904410516534872497166958891895733476696506555571576572477612277219818319714149078926423529883429662709622562431558283301949392234497567191000428734585410339742505921388319057600255674294042936346081659674999585772343934125989157778569800316333087308029412177253265038746352325439133394727892792164060585604199514684409508320274499711635153138196177483764131598353563598785014541418489994525697371413608785787425323064301455905209849561950891487977890022298409500174760419587768182032044317261371016923673030382248764428900849411589843532027267538115283687642392966204619517873352383373754344300958652379312702848228967342744591280012798931648684967274930590386806866192729778427303545947256926786280784460247085614270745245952328669627662301253634081089383480657131722890971731563179337298816271835109893597448396828325646534814446145608165337056869383817674671861774648356520228324967160793764668482602382683952775459326198564803042430239435017946828217645953349576763947764542205878106792100271597450433468475587533258178009562442379191989454853054378331237542332775599558901802799163576791111948104283740131476948612375809803775559936604575989553170927556314952449580583497789784597525521972235680621913611394967148182403370188860615356068334481189872586495538139141819913524520021036645385424191769199370583291555687804891337632724148537265495505232168025205169999

68645473427776907138579522972017267198319512793879265
96748820115571094271182610148391403237761597086323616
72593988910125470913957708823957716473933308693833127
30572897021349658347255978422170579715661088024679210
07555514167597162113271167529355571490514895110431809
40746132368605560946084419664468525612289013299854023
22828491310183873415572444657614975958101406432538058
08949725319007870902601103891204526486123466210218444
02893217586257773423696931318578694317327612491065319
81290379858956947773450457202416100605288709680193413
05592793338873188547785749872167690519424360494279482
22929830711444342079955117357884417183748559012427061
83770020304963849751378579531818481081701338340952339
13267255764114922356670129624593306318906035938726178
76377113589767629947929714246798746499949544425224267
55710638739526385331545653402511852695310788648024366
34465193976061372531425988576415492828610915173237875
67117409022522071984146118214979849474691329084348083
12411041612353304670799961492875175059629274224198489
35858200577835749623538932063565103677264900490551434
87916915055279518202342769768567177147346604433642556
70338317726966779635331563789638702017626361176355117
63302050743536706201245057900071837353172062665595400
03715209281042236319125747218687563158897498614674099
12004698337479721591111661370471907434262798982868477
29528309819685257778504928386805571571111254453052711
78558298976623745910374681281375392856176492986428296
82864905267611157697574114658492816932388918964356770
95380669613784366656814490750949846641925012169028272
45375031079738028733233383868195302561319450706187737
07313204659105717192533862663357602835775520312504944
19049563784519798103980771709431588906707856235292169
65118751555303976335498024674426548388872733747737164
98146349273125497648513303788249059046469093120235299
37195011616325779716464314165044122858587259922563494
52322404279631765558699987124935134208336952167743386
25319885951931845332547666665495665757570177683312679
10187861850774450487854913461386924245468266981788844
34518195224674615831278837238654588743836885018467156
12175456874789696593616594907872521456407778088157907
50406947001529081833396507911648394570243860873729797

113451818750353894705166893490304052780203787384 48361
377455182686372263318449187374413353325182664399 00178
348438347467419925647363617343896311637562999787 99280
387737333075362424135388336271994461421256706597 95090
662084071823790354061909940754983491415477337037 34852
569853175497192144922211533987308804003752782245 45636
154615141966886503242169251289182757409722203264 40330
380783642297033223912618852365939579169890770291 14251
385737863243327258498723725736307977873198839641 38575
498764753745960350279857536833017993505420423571 62884
511108672932089562790932475099823709533878420870 71468
253774689948258810428776742649479598554141401622 10798
587514269527654895646467082950497637036498279877 41403
879103874254197889582626878941084644975814423661 87125
398231821308496188676365919405675139148285472743 69989
888396427499989817111971543536246480481709155242 33794
963731432571466892618264564696427131172477035885 50777
255710343112115089842579719804494416062709561326 30708
888614219726087121258139615756025398428064068563 86118
695722242239369048538031820626291846982721321346 46773
349699520201451029963565144524988309780064087715 32395
682362237793452537674435485896193368527237997403 38772
687145815670079328022915130936750408336276170382 17538
481586517852775374512745719888950655809965284837 38383
797782012430414834133921696865585996130252839348 22064
369258740955060465946509559681336969079603882339 74075
597415898652636325067197765216680334522419520959 68973
337581769921613866899426248260810733934654633837 78861
954078495573049474183611529100816697947621304900 23030
808260249487799892054259644541204021883070008346 40784
556521928017974473267573731304744847148097328585 60278
437374005836794355087144259967502885866574681788 84709
190963602285642345985401147569652302909109354233 73753
711287233883273205479629896702219413731368430832 20117
686589741513055931973322687714974316190729098987 73969
459115419181645263028654642538573483817975104662 89839
992783374954295998415617973171828950754264411673 83132
125985627040547198549184912285397412498479871173 59047
466074415711649835598415074283996316363255711218 04584
848582912659294283467786446348263975597171559683 56887
408483135049864436298626984947564366320369802564 14883

32541538720666610544926673815830639235003737664417330
12033888044948322804540411288960913262184669129757628
41288347499787400611457166257543802748456677185578925
8640233416441272269537265826887398051289558478779340
80933697505561285697991332617177390647630339645671616
03534963545123647196522123375334189318788909496297935
33976421897840182464272423244415411370108044121496336
29361635705286349742344237755261727806292914645125633
62609274899042305848112364302118023159977959377847269
44628722651472961341777413873102718076173388340952906
02134508307163902671897961295115245924191655657038484
90056894139940321621943821446996551925279278143834287
42774639795616251288314392431535279390126821577184675
81449324438455114497094788670288688078162318507327972
06855365757793269165164699280393675924613055923975184
83154929334981095425597863177664098735498698150514982
00307318371139533909815472693656895369463058247475144
80252585800734933510950590567777303513125292909629312
62241515703358377345883890599262146814349860216759446
86524743180313225976765581036561858778130762201918409
46733231445643078986332625818862820109474144358231011
39315092522214476416940271511665410854303931444533724
72733507709566452971863924423441651628114848606854285
13828316336739207887658456470651341775664443051753803
02260866942735682425866171754550560610232363738355881
62845375114503092629383619358396855097756203049966724
27809090503663126465141500361082762249678644015556122
90143335292964306654721292148181448522165551962418364
22822659884732041970421529760570806401623788266892928
31244657730114592978304510753974158466612668445669433
65309689974202575477632330975796173484136815051586019
13175012358911166860662818163107163805367943667231101
59290143996064275330168459707141101974866490542430219
61619595830987418508890441784674737469544877219737382
62850067101606041167569629049137468593698018732989337
96575919344011255001250815087202728731083291736556123
05943409706247611034591933513612442294038333286028058
06169228103380506678392716753984651160630844882751468
71244185893524830516308854094007514084590126984798736
31565766437714430935309131572259822615642596935260094
634541548906316983940414922293555092778733451460728871

99174271227577318373376817379697236267431779846997034
58127146150276536383807664792398866109632282959584837
82426755363713200968283466192805214339472038742374687
34444351721731321680590724224961072914116923136644027
25207673151566470993062799073329481267596729592738187
17866240275747465043837767301554561816498858295784974
25061772339287591857693838192078923930128877090916907
82819446326584294654872148752499421228058155589091738
70890337226665312232593270978282372360646372443771133
97615472294744421845327684147255837983568447448002214
14026026054541131197662308032157526085857173575046256
46919658167031462370695255969729128593310337109016857
78466855860683812714604125667805097211420939462088138
01593471247896314369626956676853203229887888648202409
54707767561058891312920562757996444841184173136241344
24001504303338923608312324650497100164876029717938637
26976515805948226045778127507741620645601547175458518
27226923688248040921127365157678335862261387018424797
39647958905665871315584115486699650567130231226917814
52990326332566791506910668798508429791160349157704823
60665542775469437124203731179854953816175124771702249
92713095821170261653719822356149244939386244970527639
56132172713933233621951776204763664396473407116681441
59854338752363818887597167485649704428695516844952165
97045891543931376176850514313440863735252586424714276
01235866568954651132344892856185189076811465533722099
53335667690567863809337551212960023759804500884624192
24706134576045788089405648187120503162569526052063755
88426995499433976770212096128346027260241553212426788
88092969272879168708368978449570695306325650978959780
71678557869624194112832555362646706195089687941074578
60501738231187354552877789198318051552796386663672247
95565348236712974250115606857278595212834984749834081
04486338978971474272118858182978911849570678892949832
28494201107362741129471796748221117431114614913706112
49126547643813057261796104275783354485866417947212612
09868813890305722893884183721327340384835472347006682
90057564350178956478236805431143400883571002852981637
36672068968817369557872359909389566378351641460622165
75523989267015955471344122946689253978015968440514648
41026693782943426836824299287058645361540189483533214

3377340556816113262359702439561627013431433492353026 8
6029594779953540347279329808786218901724391867233681 6
0956537443017703444989084828802127680788937655716323 6
2611687488577297709565839038182538775812536365922789 9
9647930216603228677556164783975472800759269979191914 4
4949960039205101684657095130422738142550329123935146 5
6836481478556706223932783158520509709167213187877887 6
7762697177967629955695987335089743945763748026552457 2
3594537964496769462164556229737287329323911146418689 6
3769992957819332399840408133623954944406713169524538 2
8513417274032787679291711631695550074836933553960319 1
8627241177368088289894345966571561749989327173624747 8
1248039563548044165103895267611941822736641830669047 2
0135241668158017417125320025973731665988782379118597 5
5855174188061330556849448944868263152226150615365937 4
3805574035738934974419933488944183892336419622727340 5
1905432181631898235249416865526258657450078041592656 2
7217969029974470863623486479210861582988297919536269 1
8372087966771177478221628035618893843317608437987016 6
37128590607

Bree won again and made Mark sing along to the cell-phone ring tone version of Alanis Morissette's "Hand in My Pocket."

• • •

Greg didn't answer his phone. Just after I hung up, Dad called. "Your mother's left me for some crazed dyke."

"*What?*"

"You heard me. I've been ditched for Fred Flintstone's fetus."

"Dad, are you drinking rum and Gatorade on the living-room couch with the lights off?"

He was.

"Dad, she hasn't even known the woman for fifteen minutes. She probably went out to buy groceries and you're misinterpreting it."

"She left a note."

"She did?"

*"Dear Jim, I need the passion and intimacy that only a woman can bring to my life's journey. Please don't judge me harshly. And don't forget that tonight the seedlings need their root booster growth formula."*

"I'll be right over."

When I got there, Dad was in the living room, lights out, in the process of switching from orange to green Gatorade, but there were no labels on the plastic bottles. "Dad, where are the labels on the Gatorade bottles?"

"I may be pissed to the gills, but there's no way I'm going to pay full retail when I can get bulk powder at Costco."

"Jesus, Dad—are you cheap in your dreams at night, too?"

I looked at Mom's note, blotched with damp spots from melted ice cubes. A dismal and baroque scene. I'd just sat down on the sofa beside Dad when Ellen, the stalker of yore, scampered across the lawn, wearing a bright pink Gore-Tex pantsuit and shaking spruce needles off her purse.

"Just tell that pesky bitch to take a hike," Dad said.

I went to the front door and called, "Ellen, we saw you."

Her head popped out from behind an azalea.

"Ellen, today's not a good day for stalking. Dad's really depressed about something, and whatever you're up to, today's just not the day."

"Oh. Okay. I'll come back tomorrow."

"Thanks, Ellen."

I came back inside. "Did Mom say where she's staying, Dad?"

"No."

"Any phone number?"

"No."

"Did she pack a bag?"

"Nope."

I was mentally scrolling through all of Mom's infatuations, living and dead, all of whom Dad was clueless about. "If she didn't pack a bag, how long can she be planning to be away? Relax."

Dad was inconsolable. "She's been so pure and trusting all these years—and me bopping every little crumpet I share a gig with." He gulped a few shooters, then passed out, leaving me with the job of tracking down Mom. I phoned John Doe. "Hi, John."

"Hi, Ethan. What's up?"

"John, I need to track down my mom, and I think she's visiting your mother's place. Something about fertilizers."

Silence.

"John?"

More silence.

"John?"

"Oh dear."

"Why are you saying *Oh dear*?"

"I've seen this happen many a time, Ethan. You might as well accept the fact that you're soon to be my stepbrother."

"What?"

"Ethan, once my mother strikes, she becomes an irresistible force. Your mother is powerless. Oh dear, oh dear."

I faked naïveté. "You're nuts. She's simply getting information on boron phosphate hydroponic fertilizers."

John sighed.

"Where does your mother live? I've got to go see my mother, or my father's going to pop a vessel," I finally admitted.

John gave me an address up the coast, at the end of a one-hour ferry ride. "Ethan, I'm coming with you. You'll see why when we get there."

The ferry was almost empty. We thought we'd try to get some work done at sea, but instead we bought Sunshine Burgers and slept in the car on the car deck. We were honked awake by the ferry's bullhorn.

The drive up the coast was glorious: ferns, massive cedars, a sparkling sea flecked with eagles and seagulls. I noticed that John, however, was clenching his fists. "Uh, John, what should I be expecting here?"

"I don't want to colour your perceptions, Ethan."

"Jesus, John. What are we driving into—*Planet of the Apes*?"

"Just don't try to give a clever answer on any topic at all. Any."

"Come on."

"I didn't change my name and identity for nothing, Ethan."

We forked off the highway onto a secondary road, and from there onto a tertiary road, and from there onto a quaternary road, finally ending up on a weedy, overgrown lane, which went on for a half-mile through an alder forest and ended in a small cul-de-sac covered with mulched bark chips. At its end stood a chain-smoking dwarf clad in purple nylon, her ears aglint with silver rings. She saw John coming. "Oh, it's *you*."

"Hello, Yarrow."

"Who's that?"

"That's Ethan."

"You're gay? Finally some good news from you."

"Not gay. Just here to see Mother."

"Right."

We passed the enchanting Yarrow and headed towards the house, a hundred-year-old dump sheathed in long grey planks, the structure beginning to sag into itself, and decorated with a collection of colourful nylon vaginal motif banners. What had once been the lawn was a tangled meadow. Trees didn't look so much naturalized as they did homeless.

I asked, "Is that Yarrow with a capital or lower case Y?"

"Actually, it's capitalized. Long story."

Inside the house John called out for freedom, but there was a nobody-home feeling. The place smelled of eroding fabrics and vegetarian cooking. The coloured crystals and knick-knacks everywhere highlighted my sense that here, people could stop taking their prescription medications without fear of being judged.

We looked out back and spotted a circle of maybe eight women sitting in sun-bleached Adirondack chairs. Mom was at the far end and saw me. "Ethan! Hello."

She came over to hug me. "You're so sweet to drop in unannounced like this."

"Mom, what's going on here?"

"I know what you're thinking, Ethan. I haven't become a

lesbian. I just think it's really important at this point to explore my she-power. freedom is a good teacher."

freedom came over. "Can I help you?"

"Uh, hi, freedom. I just came to visit Mom."

"We're busy."

Mom said, "freedom helped me collect from that fellow who sold me bum seedlings. She didn't even use a gun."

"She helped you on a collection? I could have helped out, you know."

freedom cut in, "She didn't need you or a metal death penis—just a bit of confidence." She put her arm around Mom's waist and kissed her quite luxuriously on the neck. "Do you have business here? We need to go back to our circle."

Mom said, "It's Uterus Week. You can't imagine what I've been learning."

"I'm sure I can't. Can you at least phone Dad?"

Mom looked unsure. "No phones here. freedom says I need to be away from my stifling home environment."

"How could home be stifling? It's never stifled you."

"Ethan, you're always so critical. I know—here's an example—doors."

"Doors?"

"Doors are *very* stifling."

"How are doors stifling?"

"Inside the house here, the bathrooms have no doors, and it's a liberating feeling to be in them, it really is. Doors are nothing more than flat wooden burkas invented to keep women from feeling proud and fallopian." She looked behind her. "I have to get back to the circle. I know you'll figure out something to tell your father. Bye, dear."

Yarrow snickered as John and I walked back to the car. As we drove away, John said, "You can't say I didn't warn you. Now can you understand how I got to be the way I am?"

I grunted.

"I know," said John. "Let's go out and buy a statistically average meal from a large multinational restaurant chain. That usually fixes about seventy-five percent of life's problems."

In a weird way, eating a Whopper did feel vaguely retaliatory, but as we left the restaurant, I realized I was forgetting something. "My new coat. Crap—I left it back at your mother's house. Kaitlin'll kill me if I lose it. It was a present."

John stayed in the car, engaged in a stare-off with Yarrow, while I ran in. I looked around but couldn't see it. I called out, "Mom?"

One of the women pointed upstairs, and so up I went, taking great pains not to accidentally look into a bathroom. But when I glanced into a bedroom, there she was, naked on her stomach, while freedom, clad only in a pair of boxers, gave her a back rub.

"Oh jeez . . . sorry." I backed downstairs, with Mom yelling, *"I am not a lesbian, Ethan!"*

I found my coat on a table near the front door.

As we drove back to the ferry, John Doe insisted on listening to the Top 40 on the car radio while I tried to digest the afternoon's implications.

"Isn't Yarrow a freak?" John asked.

"I can't say I disagree."

"She's my sister."

Kaitlin thought the day's field trip was a hoot.

"It's a phase, Ethan. She'll get over it."

I wasn't so sure.

We were back in jPod, staring into Evil Mark's cubicle. "It's so clean. So ordered. I bet he makes his bed every morning."

```
//called each frame and updates camera position based on position of its target and the cur-
rent camera cut void GmMsCameraFollow::vUpdate(TReal rTimeDiff)
{
//              vUpdate2(rTimeDiff);
//              return;

GmMsPosKeyFrame *poCurrentDesiredKeyFrame;

poCurrentDesiredKeyFrame = m_oCurrentCut.poGetCurrentPosKey();

m_oActiveKeyFrame.vSmoothToKeyFrame(poCurrentDesiredKeyFrame,rTimeDiff);

//get a pointer to the target GmAcActor *poTarget = m_poGmAcActor->poGetTarget(); ASSERT
( poTarget != NULL );

//get a pointer to the camera actor
GmAcCamera *poCamera = (GmAcCamera *)m_poGmAcActor;
ASSERT(poCamera);

if (
poPhantom &&
(RealAbs(poCamera->rGetLookVerticalDesired())< 0.2f) &&
(RealAbs(poCamera->rGetLookHorizontalDesired())< 0.2f))

g_bGoToBox = True;
\else
g_bGoToBox = False;

m_nUpdatePositionOfCameraDelay++;

AtMaPos3 oPosTarget,oPosPlayer;
AtMaVector3 oLookPos;
TBoolean bUpdateTarget = True;
//set camera offset from target and look at target
GmMsPosKeyFrame *poPosKey = &m_oActiveKeyFrame;;

//get the desired look and at offsets
poPosKey->poLocationAt()->vGetVector(m_oAtOffset);
poPosKey->poLocationLook()->vGetVector(m_oLookOffset);

//update the camera's FOV
poCamera->vSetFOV(poPosKey->rGetFOV());

//get the current vectors from the actor
vGetVectorsFromActor();

//set our initial destination position to be that of the target
poTarget->vGetVectors(&oPosPlayer, &m_oFwd1, &m_oUp1, &m_oRight1, NULL);

// BVOL prediction and Rising
{AtMaVector3 oTemp;
oTemp = oPosPlayer;
oTemp.vSub(m_oState.m_oLastTargetPosition);

if(RealIsApproxZero(oTemp.m_rZ))
// If the player's Z position hasn't changed,
// then slide the box up
{oTemp.m_rZ = rTimeDiff*400.0f;}
else
// If the player's Z position is changing, leave
```

**Assignment:** Discuss Your Notions of Good and
Evil with Somebody You Consider to Be One or the Other

### "Through Darkness and into Light"

by Kaitlin Anna Boyd Joyce

**Mark Jackson, thirty-ish,** works with me, designing
videogames. He has typical geek attributes, the strangest
being a need to have everything in his immediate environment be edible. He has a marzipan stapler and Post-it notes
made from sour lemon chewing gum. More importantly,
Mark's in-office nickname is "Evil Mark," and frankly, where
there's smoke, there's fire. Let us explore this:

**Kaitlin:**
Why are you called Evil Mark?

**Mark:**
It's ridiculous. You said that my personality was boring, and
so then Bree [a co-worker] decided to arbitrarily call me
Evil Mark. And then last year your boyfriend, Ethan, caught
me looking at something on my computer monitor, but I
was able to hit QUIT before he saw what it was.

**Kaitlin:**

What was it?

**Mark:**

I can't even remember.

**Kaitlin:**

Oh, *please*. Something shameful?

**Mark:**

Why does it have to be shameful?

**Kaitlin:**

Sometimes you can be so sucky, Mark.

**Mark:**

Gee. Don't tell the media.

**Kaitlin:**

Tell you what—I'm going to throw guesses at you until you crumble and tell me what it was you were hiding. Here I go: cunt-o-rama, cumsicles, golden age shit-eaters sucking Satan's teat . . .

**Mark:**

Stop!

**Kaitlin:**

Getting a bit too close to the truth?

**Mark:**
Why does it have to be something shameful?

**Kaitlin:**
What planet are you from?

**Mark:**
I am *not* evil.

**Kaitlin:**
Perhaps, but then why won't you tell me what you were looking at?

**Mark:**
For God's sake, all right. I was looking at new treatments for . . .

**Kaitlin:**
Yes?

**Mark:**
I can't tell you.

**Kaitlin:**
Don't wimp out now. Kleptomania? Pedophilia? Bedwetting?

**Mark:**
!!!

**Kaitlin:**

It's bedwetting, isn't it?

**Mark:**

That's ridicul—

**Kaitlin:**

!!!

**Mark:**

I did it back when I was a kid. It's nothing to be ashamed of.

**Kaitlin:**

It's not that you wet the bed, Mark, it's that you can't discuss it, and the fact that you'd rather have everybody here in jPod call you Evil Mark for almost a year, instead of simply telling us to screw off and deal with our own problems.

**Mark:**

It carries such a stigma in our culture.

**Kaitlin:**

Maybe you could turn it around and work it to your advantage. I bet there are all sorts of people out there who'd pay for you to come visit their house for a . . . *nap*.

**Mark:**

Thank you, Kaitlin.

**Kaitlin:**

Do you think there's a connection between your childhood experiences and your disturbingly undecorated cubicle?

**Mark:**

Probably. I've never thought of it that way before.

**Kaitlin:**

What about a connection between bedwetting and your having an edible mattress?

**Mark:**

I doubt it.

**Kaitlin:**

Michael Landon, that guy from *Little House on the Prairie,* did a TV movie once about bedwetting.

**Mark:**

Little House on the what?

**Kaitlin:**

It was a 1970s TV show.

**Mark:**

I don't watch shows from before 1990. Otherwise, you could spend the rest of your life watching TV. The TV archives are too big now.

**Kaitlin:**

He was this guy with really good hair. Anyway, in this movie, his mother hung his bedsheets out the window when he was in high school, and he'd race home after class to take them down before anybody could see them. He became a championship athlete as a result of it.

**Mark:**

Can we change the subject?

**Kaitlin:**

We're supposed to discuss good and evil. How does this relate to the game we're all working on?

**Mark:**

In what sense?

**Kaitlin:**

Well, we're supposed to be building this sucky fantasy game with elves and rinkly-tinkly lucky mushrooms and stuff, but what we're really doing is secretly embedding a monster inside the game who will come in and pervert the game into a total gorefest.

**Mark:**

It's a great idea, isn't it?

**Kaitlin:**

I agree, but let's narrow the good/evil debate down to this one question: Why is gore more fun than its opposite?

**Mark:**

The opposite of gore?

**Kaitlin:**

SpriteQuest is the opposite of gore.

**Mark:**

That's true.

**Kaitlin:**

I repeat: Why is gore more fun than the opposite of gore?

**Mark:**

I think that beneath your question is the assumption that gore is bad. I'm not sure I agree.

**Kaitlin:**

Possibly.

**Mark:**

Look at nature. Nature is one great big woodchipper. Sooner or later, everything shoots out the other end in a spray of blood, bones and hair.

**Kaitlin:**

Agreed.

**Mark:**

Gore is Nature's way of saying, "There are too many human beings on the planet, and I'm trying to rectify this any way I can. SARS didn't work, but trust me, I'm cooking up something better. In the interim, please kill lots of yourselves."

**Kaitlin:**
So gore is good?

**Mark:**
Absolutely.

• • •

The next afternoon, Kaitlin showed me a gory new room she'd added onto Ronald's Lair.

"What's it called?"

"Dentistry."

Bree's eyes were red.

"Bree, what happened?"

"I emailed a long, scary letter to the Frenchman."

"So?"

"I've burned that bridge forever. I never should have sent it."

"Nonsense. Guys never read any email from a woman that's over two hundred words long. You're totally safe." Mark and John Doe nodded their agreement.

Bree said, "I think computers ought to have a key called I'M DRUNK, and when you push it, it prevents you from sending email for twelve hours."

Kaitlin said, "I've got another one: a key called FUCK OFF. You press it every time your computer does something annoying—in turn this would somehow force your computer to experience pain. And if you pushed SHIFT/FUCK OFF, you'd end up with FUCK OFF AND DIE, the computer equivalent of a razor being raked across your nipples."

On the corkboard by the coffee machine was a poster announcing the new Tetris season. Tetris, retro as it is, remains a big-deal game here at the company. The plan was to rig the condo lights of a tall, empty downtown tower to simulate the Tetris grid. Greg found just the right place—what a stud. He confirmed an empty tower: 156 condos owned by offshore residents, and all of its units empty. Cowboy and John Doe planned to hack a Tetris algorithm into the building's lighting system so that we could play on the building's front facade while stationed across the street in a park. Talk about stoked.

I got kind of sentimental looking at the layouts of the empty condos. It reminded me of my summer jobs in university, going into Greg's condo towers, rearranging the patio furniture and randomly turning lights on and off to make the buildings look occupied. Buyers don't trust empty buildings. It's bad feng shui. Or maybe it's just bad feng. Or shui.

# Tetris Challenge Tonight, 7:00

# Folders
# vs.
# Crumplers

• • •

John Doe asked, "What's a folder or a crumpler?"

"Both are technical terms used by the pulp and paper industry," said Kaitlin.

"Meaning?"

"Toilet tissue manufacturers divide end users into two categories: people who crumple their paper and people who fold it. Each is fifty percent of the market."

Mark said, "What about you, Bree—crumpler? Folder?"

Bree said, "This is like the white vs. black 'Spy vs. Spy' thing."

"You're changing the subject."

"I'm a folder . . . *obviously.*"

"No! I would have had you down as a crumpler."

"Surprise."

"Do geeks skew in any particular direction?" I asked.

Kaitlin said, "I suspect they're more likely to be folders."

A quick and highly viral email campaign throughout the building revealed that game builders are eighty percent folders, but the few crumplers took pride in their stance. Dylan from server maintenance said, "When I crumple my paper, in my head it feels like a particle-based onscreen effect, like an explosion. That's not just a wad of paper in my left hand—it's a non-dimensional pyrotechnical *event.*"

I read that one out loud. Bree looked at me and said, "Did he really have to specify which *hand*? I mean, nobody's left-handed when it comes to toilet paper. That's just plain wrong."

That's how everybody in the office found out that Bree

had set her sights on a brand new conquest. Dylan, beware.

My phone rang. It was Greg, calling from Mom and Dad's place. "Ethan—Dad just told me that Mom's gone off the wiener."

"She's *what*?"

"She no longer digs man-muff."

I blurted out, "Mom is *not* a lesbian." I could hear my podmates' antennas rising as if commanded. "I went up the coast and visited her. She just needs time to do some kind of . . . life enhancement seminar."

"Man, it's so weird thinking of parents as being sexual, let alone dykey."

"Mom is *not* a lesbian."

"You're doing way too much protesting here."

"Okay. It appears that way."

"I knew it."

"How's Dad?"

"I don't know if it's the cheating or the lesbo part that's got him more freaked."

Greg, like my father, had no idea about Mom's flings, living or dead. But God only knows what Greg knows that I don't. Does Mom divvy out her psychoses to her children like Christmas gifts?

I remembered Lot 49. "I'm coming over right now."

• • •

When I arrived, Dad and Greg were loading up Greg's Hummer with duffle bags. It was a gorgeous afternoon.

"Hey—where are you guys going?"

"Up to Whistler. And you're coming with us. We need a change of scenery."

A perfect chance to ask Greg about fixing that real estate deal. "Where are we going to stay?"

"A client's place."

"Great."

Drunk or not, Dad was fulfilling his masculine parental duty by checking Greg's tire pressure. "Greg, your back two tires are a bit low."

"Dad, I'm not sixteen any more. Just leave them alone."

"Jesus, Greg, I'm just trying to save you some money. Boy, when I think about the two of you, gallivanting about town on your underpressured tires, needlessly accruing excess wear and tear—like you were made of money."

"Dad, I moved a hundred million bucks worth of residential space last year—"

"So I guess you're too fancy for your lousy old father, who's just trying to help you out in his own little way."

"Everyone get in," Greg ordered.

We were soon on Highway 99, headed up Howe Sound into the Coast Mountains. The alpine environment was already making me feel healthier than I really am—which I believe is the secret allure of skiing as a sport.

Dad was in the front seat, swigging from a hip flask. He was slurring his words, and finally lost the will even to berate his spendaholic children. I, however, was thrilled that he was actually using the flask, my Christmas present to him a few years back. Hip flasks are the juice machines of the alcohol world—everyone has one and it never gets used.

"So who is she? What's she like?" Greg asked.

I was about to say she looked like that old TV character, Alf, but caught myself in time. I don't really know what sort of description of freedom would disturb Greg the least. "She's, uhhh—"

"She's what?"

"Kind of average."

"In what way?"

"In an average kind of way."

Greg said, "You're the most pathetic liar, Ethan. Is she hot or not?"

Dad blew up. "Don't talk that way."

"Talk what way?"

"About your mother's—" In a blink, Dad knew that saying the word would confirm it once and for all. "Whatever. I don't feel like talking about it right now."

Suddenly we were doing a hundred miles an hour to pass a Pepsi delivery truck. "Greg—what the *fuck* are you doing?"

"Ethan, be quiet."

"Greg, slow down."

We squeaked past the truck, narrowly avoiding a head-on collision with a white stretch limousine filled with Japanese college students on a pot holiday. My nerves were in ribbons.

"There, now—that wasn't so bad, was it? I also got an extra five thousand points for an insane stunt bonus."

"You could have fucking killed us."

"Ethan, I'm a roadrageoholic, but I'm really trying to overcome it with therapy. When I lapse, could you at least try to be supportive and find some joy in my rageoholism?"

A lemon yellow Supra with all sorts of silly spoiler attachments sped past us. Greg went nuts: "I'll kill you, you little fuckhead!"

*Now's not a good time to ask about Lot 49.*

When we arrived at Whistler, my toes were still so clenched inside my shoes that I had to bang them on the back seat floor to loosen them. My spirits rose when we turned into a street bordering the Maui North subdivision. Our particular ski cabin was mall-sized and resembled the Swiss pavilion at the 2020 World's Fair. "Hey, Greg—who's the client?"

"I've actually never met him or her. It's a registered off-shore buyer who only goes by a number."

The keys were plasticized electronic cards, like in a hotel. We walked in the front door and turned on a light and— *boom*—we were suddenly in what seemed to be Oprah's chic Nordic retreat: everything was perfect—furniture, art and lighting. It reeked of untold volumes of spare cash. Greg said, "Okay, laddies, pick your bedroom. There are eight to choose from."

I walked up the grand staircase and selected a large bed-room with an ensuite bathroom and a magnificent view of the forest out back. But I sensed something weird going on. I couldn't put my finger on just what until I began sneezing. I looked more closely and realized that every surface in my room—and all of the other rooms—was covered in a gentle felt of dust. Sunset beams coming from the west hit windows caked in dirt, spiderwebs, birch leaves and guano streaks. Down in the kitchen, Greg was on his phone. I went to the stove, turned the electric burners on maximum and watched as the dust on them burned away.

Greg clicked shut his cell. "Ethan, what are you doing?"

"Greg, when was the last time anybody was ever actually in this house?"

"Here? Let me see—" From the kitchen counter he picked up a yellowed, desiccated newspaper. "August 10, 1993."

"Nobody's been here since 1993?"

"Why would they? On the other hand, if Taiwan or China or Singapore implodes, there'll be a family of thirty living here in a flash."

Suddenly the house felt like a coffin. "I have to go get some fresh air."

"You do that."

• • •

Sometimes what at first seems like a coincidence isn't really one at all. I say this because I decided to walk over to the Maui North project and check out the lots. I heard Lot 49 before I saw it: a roaring stream. I was walking there to have a magic moment between nature and myself, when who popped out from behind a boulder? *freedom*.

She looked at me. "Well, well, if it isn't the Penis come to rescue Mumsy-wumsy from being brainwashed."

"freedom, what are *you* doing here?"

"I might ask you the same question. Me? I'm here because I'm buying this lot."

"*What?*"

"Kam Fong put me on to this place. I can already taste the wattage this little trickle is going to give me. You?"

I was too confused to say anything cogent. "Where's Mom?"

"Over there."

freedom pointed to a patch of moss embedded with pine needles and chipmunks. A cinematic sunbeam lit my mother in end-of-day magic light.

"Ethan! Come feed a chipmunk!"

And then, from behind me, I heard Greg calling to freedom. "freedom! Glad you could make it." Greg looked at Mom and said, "Mom, what are you doing here?" Gathering his wits, he said, "freedom—have you met my mother?"

• • •

Before I forget, Bree came up with this new trick—how to create your name if you become a stripper. Basically, just figure out the least expensive form of sugar or sweetness you ate today . . .

*"Molasses"*

*"Sweet 'N Low"*

*"Vanilla Wafer"*

*"Tang"*

*"Brown Sugar"*

*"The Doublemint Twins"*

*"Cling Peaches"*

*"Cinnamon"*

My own stripper name is "M&M."

• • •

We decided to let Dad sleep it off while the four of us went to a coffee place that catered almost exclusively to astonishingly attractive young people from Australia and New Zealand, all of whom were baked on local weed. In the middle of the café, freedom gave Mom a lusty back rub while Mom explained to Greg, "I know what you're thinking, but I am not a lesbian. I just need to reclaim my ovarian inner landlord."

This was too much for my brother. His form of denial is to begin speaking like a real estate ad. "Lot 49's such a honey of a property—a prestigious ski-in ski-out location with Whistler Village close by—it's ideal for a luxury chalet. Think vaulted ceilings! Think river-rock fireplace and wrap-around decks! Think Ultraline professional appliances and beautiful detailed log work—a chalet to be proud of!"

"Greg, you know how bored we get when you talk like a brochure," Mom said. "And besides, don't sell something that's already sold."

freedom was cackling. "I'm certainly the chalet type, aren't

I? Ha! I'm going to make a box out of concrete and pack in as many plants as I can. High style is for pantywaists." Her hands were disturbingly close to Mom's chest.

"Greg," said Mom, "as a favour to me, be sure you never ever sell that lot to anyone but freedom. I know how cannibalistic real estate sales are in Whistler. Even if someone offers you twice the asking price. You promise? On my grave? And that if you sell it to someone else, it means you don't love me?"

Greg promised.

An awkward silence ensued.

I was miserable. I saw no way to get Greg to ditch the sale to freedom.

More unnerving was the sight of Mom possibly being turned on by freedom's body rub. What a mess.

freedom barked, "Okay, we need to go now. We have just enough time to make it to *The Passion Cycle of the Mons*. I'm working the breast puppets this season."

Neither Greg nor I had the will to pursue that gambit.

"Give your father my love, boys." With that, Mom was gone.

Greg turned on me. "Why the fuck didn't you tell me Mom was freedom's—"

"freedom's *what*? Her shag bag? Her meat treat?"

"Nothing."

"Let's not tell Dad about what just happened."

"Deal."

Rank
2
Skill
1579
Skill bonus
134
Total kills
585
Total deaths
245
Suicides
0
Souls crushed
4
Rounds survived
190 / 411
Life expectancy
46.73%
Kill streak
14
Death streak
5
Kills per death
2.37
Kills per minute
1.08
Kills per round
1.43
Deaths per round
0.60
Skill increase per round
1.08
Teammates killed
0
Death by teammates
0
Last man standing
4
Play time
8h59m
Longest session
1h5m
Terrorists joined
35
Killed VIPs
0
Planted bombs
33
Bombed targets
(91.38%) 31
Killed hostages
2
Killed terrorists
156
Saved VIPs
0
Defused bombs
(33.33%) 1
Grabbed hostages
9

I'm so fucking sick of Google.

. . .

In the end, the chalet's dust overwhelmed my sinuses, and I caught a bus back to the city. I was alone in jPod, looking up gory websites at which to park my brain for a few hours. Around eleven o'clock, everybody arrived back at work in high spirits.

"He's so funny, isn't he?"

"I know—it's like he has no OFF button."

"He can take anything and just *run* with it."

They saw me and clammed right up. "Uh . . . hi, Ethan."

"Don't tell me—it's Coupland, right?"

Bree went over to her desk and began Swiffering her shrine. "It's as if he knows everything about us—he listens to us and *cares* about us."

"Let me guess again—you've been at a shareholder meeting."

"Did you have a nice trip to Whistler?" Kaitlin asked.

"I would have told you about it already if you'd been around."

"Don't get pissy on me, buster, because I can tell with one glance that you've been having a gorefest. Even if I'd been here, I might as well have been a stacking chair."

She had a point.

My phone rang, and everybody dissolved into their own spaces. It was Bruce Pao: "Hey, Ethan, buddy—how did things go?"

"Hi, Bruce."

"So, how did things go?"

"I'm working on it, Bruce."

"He's not going to sell it to me, is he?"

"Nothing's final yet, Bruce."

"You have twenty-four hours or your game dies."

*Crap.*

• • •

I phoned Greg to plead my case. "Greg, come on—pleeeeez. This guy, Bruce—he'll top anything Mom's girlfriend pays."

"Ethan, no. Mom asked me specifically not to sell it to anybody else, so I can't."

"You'll get double your regular commission."

"No can do, bro."

*Shit.*

**Assignment:** Discuss Love with an
Unlikely Person

**"Dial 888-LOVE"**

by Kaitlin Anna Boyd Joyce

**Kam Fong, thirty-four,** is a friend and international businessman operating in most countries of the Pacific Rim.

**Kaitlin:**
Hi, Kam, thanks for agreeing to be interviewed.

**Kam:**
No problem.

**Kaitlin:**
The topic for this assignment is love. Have you ever been in
love?

**Kam:**
No.

**Kaitlin:**
In like, then?

**Kam:**

I like people, but I have yet to love one.

**Kaitlin:**

Do you wonder if you're missing out on something?

**Kam:**

No.

**Kaitlin:**

How old are you?

**Kam:**

[Pauses.] Thirty-four.

**Kaitlin:**

Thirty-*four*? That's bad luck in Chinese, isn't it? Three is okay, but four is a terrible number.

**Kam:**

It is. Forty-four is considered the worst year of your life; thirty-four is second-worst.

**Kaitlin:**

When was your birthday?

**Kam:**

The day of the hug machine's launch.

**Kaitlin:**

You never told us!

**Kam:**

It's okay. That's why I put a quarter-pound of uncut medicinal-grade cocaine into Cowboy's cola—as a celebration of life.

**Kaitlin:**

That was so great, by the way. Everyone had a blast, and nobody had a clue why. I'm still finding glitter in my keyboard.

**Kam:**

I try to bring joy to people.

**Kaitlin:**

You really do.

**Kam:**

[Makes motions indicating he's about to do an impersonation.] *If caring about your friends is a crime, then come and arrest me right now.*

**Kaitlin:**

That's a perfect John Doe! [Another friend.]

**Kam:**

Thanks. Did you meet John's mother?

**Kaitlin:**
Yes.

**Kam:**
Believe it or not, of all the people I've ever met, I think I could actually fall in love with her.

**Kaitlin:**
Really? Now this interview is truly getting somewhere. You mean to say you could make it with freedom? [freedom (lower case f) is an ultra-lesbian.]

**Kam:**
She's a powerful, confident woman in a way that Chinese women aren't.

**Kaitlin:**
If things work out, freedom could end up as my mother-in-law.

**Kam:**
What?

**Kaitlin:**
You don't know?

**Kam:**
About what?

**Kaitlin:**
Ethan's mother ran off to live with freedom in a rural lesbian communal love shack with no A/C, electricity or running water.

**Kam:**
[No response.]

**Kaitlin:**
Kam?

**Kam:**
Really?

**Kaitlin:**
It's true. Ethan's dad is a mess because of it. He sits in the house, drinking rum and Gatorade with the lights turned off.

**Kam:**
He *did* miss dance class. [Kam and my boyfriend's father are professional-level ballroom dancers.]

**Kaitlin:**
In desperation, Ethan even allowed this stalker named Ellen, who's been hounding Jim forever, into the house. She got so bored that she left and quit the stalking.

**Kam:**
I see.

**Kaitlin:**

Let's go back to love. If you don't think you're capable of love, you must be doing something with all that love energy inside you.

**Kam:**

[Pauses.] I like to play matchmaker. If two people are right for each other, I hook them up. If things aren't working out, I can come in and help . . . ensure that things end peacefully.

**Kaitlin:**

So you're like the Internet then—except you're a real person.

**Kam:**

You flatter me. But yes.

**Kaitlin:**

What about your family? Where are they?

**Kam:**

*Pffft*. I don't really have one.

**Kaitlin:**

You're an orphan?

**Kam:**

In a way.

**Kaitlin:**

That's so adorable! You should let word get out—girls would swarm you. It's even better than walking around shirtless holding a puppy.

**Kam:**

I prefer the dignity of silence. I've actually made you numskulls in jPod my family.

**Kaitlin:**

Oh God, I'm getting teary.

**Kam:**

Here . . . [Reaches into pocket in search of Kleenex, finds none, then brings out wallet and removes a scarlet wad of fresh fifty-dollar bills.] Use these.

**Kaitlin:**

Thanks, Kam. [I blow my nose.] Hey, are these real?

**Kam:**

No. Pretty good forgeries, huh?

**Kaitlin:**

They're great. I'm impressed. My parents got hosed with a suitcase of fake fifties on this shipment they sent down to the States via Spokane. I took one look at the bills and then looked at my parents and said, "How could you be taken in by such pathetic forgeries? You deserved to be shtupped! They look like they were done by a toddler running a tonerless Lexmark Pro they found in a garage sale."

**Kam:**
What did your parents say?

**Kaitlin:**
My mom said, "Well, they had a bumper sticker that said PROUD TO BE AMERICAN, and someone had just blown up an embassy somewhere, and we felt sorry for them."

**Kam:**
Parents.

**Kaitlin:**
Tell me about it. So for Christmas that year I gave them a Samsung Model CPC 993C-1 banknote counter with built-in forgery detection system. It can do over a thousand notes per minute.

**Kam:**
Is that the one that has banknote-width sensors that detect undersize notes to prevent accidentally mixed notes from being counted incorrectly?

**Kaitlin:**
No, that's the Model OMAL 75D.

**Kam:**
Of course. What was I thinking?

**Kaitlin:**

So, if we're discussing love, we really do have to discuss your parents. Can you tell me anything?

**Kam:**

I was the second male child from Wife Number Four.

**Kaitlin:**

Is that good or bad?

**Kam:**

I suppose bad, because all alone I had to claw my way up and out of Beijing's unlubricated pre-capitalist sphincter, cockfight by cockfight—but, then, it was also good because I found my own way in life. I think that's important.

**Kaitlin:**

What about the first male child from Wife Number One?

**Kam:**

His life is so boring.

**Kaitlin:**

What does he do?

**Kam:**

He runs a chain of maybe five hundred massage parlours across the southern provinces. I went to one once. He cuts the baby oil with canola, and they charge you extra for a shower, and even then the water's the temperature of spit.

**Kaitlin:**
And he gets repeat customers?

**Kam:**
You'd think he'd simply offer better service to withstand a free market, but instead he kills his competitors. Where's the challenge in that? But I take some satisfaction in selling him his canola oil from here in Vancouver.

**Kaitlin:**
You're always helping people.

**Kam:**
I try. I really try.

**Kaitlin:**
Did you ever spend time with your father?

**Kam:**
No. Number One Son took care of him.

**Kaitlin:**
His own father?

**Kam:**
I know—where do you draw the line? But in all fairness, it was an accident. They were at the launch of his five hundredth parlour, and Dad showed up and got whacked out on Japanese apricot sake and some leftover date rape drug from a Chanel fragrance launch the night before in Hong Kong.

**Kaitlin:**
And . . . ?

**Kam:**
Suddenly someone wheeled out a helium canister and a stack of party balloons, and Dad thought it would be really funny to do a squeaky voice. He inhaled the helium, and all the capillaries in his lungs exploded, and he died on the spot.

**Kaitlin:**
!!!!!!!!!!

**Kam:**
What?

**Kaitlin:**
!!!!!!!!!!

**Kam:**
What?

**Kaitlin:**
You don't know?

**Kam:**
Know what?

**Kaitlin:**
That's how somebody from jPod died once.

**Kam:**
No shit. Fuck off. You're spooking me.

**Kaitlin:**
It's true.

**Kam:**
!!!!!!!!!

[NOTE: Kam excused himself here and went to his room for a few minutes. He came back in a much better mood.]

**Kaitlin:**
Sometimes drugs help us deal with our problems.

**Kam:**
I agree. Can we end the interview now? Too many painful memories.

**Kaitlin:**
No problem. Thanks, Kam, and thanks for helping everybody in so many ways.

**Kam:**
It's my job in life.

• • •

I was wondering what electrons are actually doing when they sit in your hard drive in an old laptop at the back of your closet. I mean, how does an electron sit still—is it like a cartoon M&M leaning back in a folding beach chair? Is it like an angry little steel ball bearing hovering there, just waiting to go nuts on protons? What's the mechanism that starts and stops the electron? Who's its dungeon master? And if an electron has only a negative electrical charge, how can it possibly even exist? It'd be like a bar magnet with only a north or only a south pole. A monopole. It's impossible.

I voiced these concerns in the pod one day, and Bree didn't even look up, just said, "Quarks, aisle three."

"I think I hear the sound of someone who didn't make the high school math stream," added Evil Mark.

"Gee, Mark, pass me the bong. I just had this really profound idea about subatomic particles."

"Bree, why does water feel wet?"

"Mark, why are kittens fluffy and cute?"

"I like fluffy wuffy kittens."

"Don't worry your pretty little brain, pudding, no one's going to say anything ever again to make you feel small."

"Okay, guys, you can stop now."

I felt so stupid—and I still don't know the answer! What's worse, I couldn't find the answer on Google, which always drives me nuts. Then I made my situation worse. "Do you guys think they'll ever invent some form of wireless electrical power transference?"

Bree said, "Well, actually, it exists right now, Ethan. It's called x-rays."

Then John Doe googled and found these great photos of people standing on top of their apartment buildings in

Chernobyl on the night of the big meltdown. They were a mile away, yet they were still absorbing the equivalent of ten chest x-rays a second.

"Goners," John Doe said.

• • •

Bruce Pao killed SpriteQuest today, Friday, at 4:30 p.m.

Ugh.

After everybody heard the news, it took only forty-five seconds for them to adjust. Evil Mark is already designing a new goal post for a football game, and Bree vanished to hit on guys at the local pub.

Kaitlin said, "It's as if the game never existed."

I had to agree. I felt . . . *blank*. Just blank.

intentionally blank

M

o

t

H e

R

F

uck

E

• • •

Steve refused to believe the game was dead, but there was something more going on than just denial. Around midnight he came to my place and told me to accompany him to my parents' house.

"Steve, Mom's not there. She's at her commune."

"I don't want to see your mother. I want to see your father."

"Why?"

"You'll see."

Dad was moaning drunk when we got there. Steve asked me to help drag Dad into Steve's Touareg.

I said, "Not until you tell me where we're taking him."

"A recording studio. We need to get Ronald's voice tracks laid down. Your booze-soaked heartsick dad is the dream voice for Ronald we've been searching for. I'm paying my own money for the sound session."

"What if he pukes in the back seat?" I said.

"He won't. Members of the Greatest Generation never puke. They just internalize their nausea, then squeeze it out in the form of freeway infrastructure and tightly indexed pension plans."

"Dad is a boomer, not a member of the Greatest Generation."

Dad's body was about as stiff as a garden hose, which made it hard to carry him. Just before we plunked him in the back seat, Steve gently nudged Dad's liver, and Dad parped out a hoarse, mucousy *goddammit*.

"Need I say any more? If he isn't Ronald, then who is?"

Steve was right. A drunken, utterly fucked up Dad was Ronald to a T.

Once Dad was inside with his door closed, Steve and I stood there in the moonlit darkness. The only sound was the faint roar of the Trans-Canada Highway to the south.

"Ethan, over the past year you've made crap, you've made shittier crap and you've made three-layered crap sandwiches—but don't forget for a moment that with the creation of Ronald and his Lair, *you* and the jPod crew have been making the finest form of art—a blood-soaked communion that allows weak souls and lost lambs across the globe to give vent to their inner rage as surely as Jackson Pollock threw household enamel onto raw canvas, or Jack Kerouac scrawled his druggie maunderings onto Woolworth's foolscap."

"I'd never thought of it that way, Steve."

"You, Ethan, dammit, are an *artist.*"

"I am!"

"Okay, let's drive off with boozie here."

The drive downtown was uneventful. Steve needed a fix big time, but the recording studio adjoined his favourite dealer's alley—convenient. After lugging Dad into a small room covered with grey carpeting, Steve popped outside for his vein treat, and returned with a bit of zing in his step. "Let the voices begin."

I sat in the recording room with two techies while Steve circled Dad, who was slumped over on a teal-coloured Naugahyde sofa. He bent down and screamed in Dad's face: "Ronald, who the fuck are *you*?"

"Wha—?" Dad's body hopped like a cricket

"I said, WHO . . . THE . . . FUCK . . . ARE . . . *YOU*?"

I cut in over the intercom. "Dad, just say you're Ronald, okay?"

"I'm Ronald."

Steve said, "No, you're not, because the Ronald I know is *angry*. The Ronald I know is pissed off. *You,* you disgusting maggot, are a flaccid, docile fetal pig splayed out and waiting for the first incision." He whacked Dad on the back of his head.

"Steve, Jesus Christ, go easy on him."

Steve kept talking to Dad. "Ronald gets the first speaking role of his life, and what does he say? Nothing."

The words "speaking role" seemed to rouse something deep in Dad. He grabbed Steve by the neck and pulled Steve's head down to his own.

"This particular Ronald does *not* blow his chance for a speaking role. I will ace this goddam role, or I will snap your legs into slivers like the stems of cheap wine glasses."

Steve looked at me. "Did you get that on tape?"

"Got it."

From there, Ronald's/Dad's words flowed smoothly.

I am Ronald, of Mordor, the Mage, the Destroyer.

Taste the scorched fruit inside my pies.

Chew the bitter towelette of truth.

Die, you seedy little elves who refuse to accept any new menu items added after 1975.

I scorch your loins with
coffee that sears like a
molten steel patty
flipper.

I smash your bones on
rocks of ice churned by
spews of cola.

I till your soil, steal your
potatoes, circumcise
their skins, cook
them in tallow
and tell you
they're vegan.

I shall castrate your bulls, rendering them more juicy and docile, and I shall salt them with hormones, making them girly-cows.

*You* shall wander the wastelands in search of fishwiches fallen from the sky, frozen and plump with weevils and sauce of fiercest tartar.

My face is stripped of pancake makeup, staring at the sun, burning, awaiting balloons and a helium canister that will never arrive.

Your ears shall hear only the sound of a french-fry computer that beeps eternally.

*You* shall remain forever parched with a bottomless Styrofoam drinking cup.

*You,* my imprisoned sprite servants, I shall deprive of both minimum wage and nutrients. My cooker writhes with yellow frybabies your lips shall never taste.

I shall pierce your being with shakes made of ground bones, nay, chalk.

*You* shall beg for death, but instead shall receive only laughter and choking hazards disguised as plastic toys.

In my costume of yellow bib and coarse enormous red feet, I will smite you with burgers laced with thorns.

Inside your bird nuggets you will find razor blades, rats and tumours.

# The only real clown is a dead clown.

唯一的真正的小丑是一个死的小丑

# I ONLY MAKE YOU FAT SO THAT YOU'LL SIZZLE WHEN YOU BURN

我只做您油脂以便您将烧得发嘶声当您烧

. . .

"Hey, Ethan, there's some really great stuff here—"

It was three a.m. Cowboy and I were listening to Dad's work.

"Thanks. Dad is such a star. Steve really coaxed it out of him."

"I had no idea Steve had all this pent-up bile. It's wild."

Cowboy was dressed in weird beltless rugby pants. "What's with the pants, Cowboy? You look like a 1982 liquor store clerk with herpes."

"Since I've laid off the sex, I've had to come up with all sorts of ideas to help me out. Allison downstairs told me about these special undergarments worn by Mormons. They're specifically designed to unflatter the body, so that if you end up with someone, they'll snuff out any urges."

"Right. How's the no-sex thing going?"

"I hate it."

"Are you at least allowed to, er, fly solo?"

"Nope."

"So what happens?"

"Meaning?"

"Meaning—can you sleep or think or anything else?"

"Nope. The thing about abstinence is that *all* you think about is sex, whereas when you actually have sex, you don't think about it nearly as much. Which do you think is the more religious option?"

"Sex."

"Thank you, Ethan. That was the permission I needed!"

Cowboy leapt up and was gone. I made a mental note to turn off my cellphone for the next twenty-four hours.

Mark came in. "Where'd Cowboy go?"

"At the very least he's gone out to stock up on Kleenex."

Mark and I worked until dawn, generating new moves for Ronald. Now that he had sound effects, it was impossible not to work on the project. Ronald had become real to us.

**Assignment:** Describe Your Life Quickly

**"Ma Vie"**

by Kaitlin Anna Boyd Joyce

Another day passes. Everyone picks away at minor tasks. The cafeteria makes nutritiously stylish meals. The crows arrive by the tens of thousands to roost in the alder forest across from the Willingdon off-ramp. Endless cars drone by. I once saw the Oscar Mayer Weinermobile, but never again. I say hello to people in the hallways, and they say hello to me. We all go home and watch *Law & Order*. New pairs of Pumas and Nikes arrive, and idle chat begins. The sun rises and sets and the moon changes phases. Someone comes home from Tokyo or E3 with a new electronic toy and everyone says, "Ooooh." People move from one office to another office on another floor in another building. The TVs in the lobby blare whatever league games are happening. One day is much like the next and the one after that. Somewhere along the line you buy a new sofa at a store maybe two notches above Ikea, but then its cushions get dull and have a wear pattern from your butt. Nothing's new. You wonder how much the guy you're talking to is making. He wonders if you have stock options. The guy at the cafeteria table beside me wonders if he should initiate a conversation with me, whereas I wonder if he would have been out of my league pre-Ethan.

Life is dull, but it could be worse and it could be better. We accept that a corporation determines our life's routines. It's the trade-off so that we don't have to be chronically unemployed creative types, and we know it. When we were younger, we'd at least make a show of not being fooled and leave copies of Adbusters on our desktops. After a few years it just doesn't matter. You trawl for jokes or amusingly diversionary .wav files. You download music. A new project comes along, then endures a slow-motion smothering at the hands of meetings. All ideas feel stillborn. The air smells like five hundred sheets of paper.

And then it's another day.

• • •

The phone rang at 6:12 a.m., and I knew it wasn't going to be an ordinary phone call.

"Mom?"

"Ethan, honey, I need your help."

*Oh God.* "What's up?"

"I'd rather not discuss it on the phone."

"Where are you?"

"I've left the commune and I'm back at the house."

"Where's Dad?"

"Greg took him to a 'Swing-Step and Pivot' seminar in Seattle to try to cheer him up."

"Mom, it's 6:12 in the morning."

"Ethan, I need your help right away."

"Doing what?"

"Something only you can help me with. I don't want to discuss it on the phone."

"I don't want to get up."

"Don't be such a lazybones."

"I've got to eat breakfast."

"Breakfast is for losers."

"No, it's not, Mom. I know for a fact that every family on earth eats breakfast."

"Who told you that?"

"You never served breakfast because you didn't want to get up."

"That's not fair, Ethan. I've got low thyroid."

This is still a sore spot in our family history. Greg and I got all the way to high school without ever eating or being served breakfast. However, having stayed over at friends' houses, we finally realized that our family was aberrant in its rejection of a.m. dining. When we confronted Mom with the fact that everybody else eats breakfast, she was like a bird trapped in the house, trying to escape. Then one afternoon she came home with a bag of chocolate-flavoured Carnation Instant Breakfasts, plonked them on the kitchen table and said, "There, I never want to discuss this again." Greg and I figure we could have had master's degrees at MIT or Harvard if only we'd gone to school properly fed. But the past is the past.

"The last time I helped you like this, it was a pretty shitty experience."

"Ethan, don't swear. I wouldn't have called if it wasn't urgent."

"How urgent?"

Mom started to sniffle.

*Oh God.* "Okay, I'll come over."

"Thank you. Dress warmly and wear sturdy boots."

Boots? *Dear God.*

• • •

When I pulled into the driveway, Mom was loading shovels and turf-hedging tools into the K-car. Before I could say anything, she said, "Ethan, we have to go dig up Tim."

*"What?"*

"You heard me. He's got a safety deposit box key in his jacket."

"What's in the box?"

"Don't be nosy."

"Why don't you just call Kam and explain it to him? I doubt he'd care."

"I did phone him." Mom was loading a tarp. "His acupuncturist said he's down in Oregon, foreclosing on some small town that got wiped out by cheaper manufacturing costs in China. At least he won't catch us digging up his prized New Zealand tree fern."

"Do you have any idea what Tim is going to look like by now, Mom?"

"Don't be a sissy. Hasn't the Internet toughened you up at all? Kaitlin says you practically live in all those gore sites. And in any event, I packed a few bottles of Febreze to help mask the odour. So just get in the car."

"Okay, okay, already."

"I knew you'd help me. You've always been the responsible son."

We got in the wagon. "Mom, how come Greg gets to swear as much as he wants, but I can't?"

"Ethan, that sort of thing was decided long before you were born. Use your nervous energy for better purposes, like trying to figure out ways to make the world a better place. Wait a second—did I pack both plastic tarps?"

I looked in the back. "Yup."

"Good."

Off we drove to Kam's fabulously bizarre Canterbury neighbourhood, past an endless succession of homes even larger, more garish and more bizarre than Kam's. "I find it highly suspect that, of all the houses in the city, Kam ends up buying Tim's burial plot," I said.

"It's not a coincidence at all. I showed it to him when he was house hunting. I told him it had good kung fu."

"Feng shui."

"That, too. Wait a second—Ethan, *stop! Stop the car!*" Mom was screaming.

I jammed on the brakes. "What! *What!*"

"I saw a sign for a garage sale just up the hill. We can sneak in as early birds."

So we did, and Mom haggled like a Microsoft accountant over a stack of 1980s-era *National Geographic* magazines.

"Mom, why are you buying *National Geographic*s? We got rid of ours ten years ago."

"I know, and I've been sick about it ever since."

I helped her load them in the back. When she slammed the

door, she said, "I got them to throw in a set of used Cuisinart blades for free."

As we resumed driving up the mountain, she said, "Your father *would* have to go AWOL the one day we really need him."

Finally, a natural point for me to ask a question or two.

"So, Mom, how is, um, freedom doing?"

"Ethan, I am not a lesbian."

"I'm not saying that, Mom, I was just asking how she is."

"She's fine. She's in Seattle today, delivering a speech."

"On what?"

There was a note of challenge in her voice. "It's called 'Revoicing Yesterday's Vagina: Towards a New Theory of Birth, Post-Industrial Economics and Clitoral Praxis.'"

I remained mute.

"I am not a lesbian."

"I'm not saying you are."

"freedom is an enlightened woman and has given me range to expand both my autoandrogyny and my hormonal slope."

More silence on my part.

"It's very scientific, you know."

I played silent.

Mom said, "If you must know, the food at that house was awful. A bird feeder has better food than there, and every bite came with a lecture. After a while I began dreaming of having potato chips and Tang for lunch in silence."

"Kam's house is over there."

We parked the car. "What if people question us?" I asked.

"Ethan, I'm a well-nourished rich-looking white woman. I could burn polka dots onto Kam's front door with a crème brûlée torch and nobody would question me."

"Good point."

And so we began to dig.

• • •

Four hours later:

"Ethan, this digging is boring, and it's going nowhere."

"I'll never make cruel jokes at the expense of gravediggers again."

We were only maybe a foot down in the blend of premium-grade topsoil, rock bits and construction debris that was Kam's front garden area. All that digging, and Kam's New Zealand tree fern hadn't even begun to list.

"Mom, we need help."

"But who?"

"I'll call Kaitlin."

Mom gave me a look. "Are you sure?"

"She's got the bone structure of a Ukrainian peasant. Her family's in the business, too. She'll understand."

"Leave out the main details." Mom dropped her shovel. "Curse it. TV makes gravedigging look so easy."

The phone rang. "Hi, Kaitlin."

"Hi, Ethan. Where are you?"

"I'm over at Kam's with Mom. I'm helping her out with something."

"With what?"

"It's probably best not to discuss this on the phone. Can you come over?"

"Actually, I've got this, uh, thing I have to go to at noon."

"What thing?"

"It's a, well—"

"It's a Coupland meeting, right?"

"Well, yeah. Ethan, we've been through this a thousand times. Stop taking your resentment out on me."

"Sorry. Who else is going to be there?"

"All the podsters."

"Okay. See you later." I hung up.

Mom asked what was happening, and I told her about the meeting. "The meeting! I forgot about it. *Phooey.*" She brushed herself off frantically, as though the dirt stains were leeches. "Ethan, you carry on. I'll be back around two-ish."

"What!"

"Oh, calm down."

"Can I come?"

"No. You have to dig."

At least if I was digging in a videogame, I might find a piece of a puzzle or treasure. A fermented dead biker? Some prize.

• • •

I carried on digging, and by two o'clock the hole was finally up to my waist, but there was no way I was going to be able to finish the job. I got out my PDA and was trying to locate a place where I could rent a Bobcat or some other kind of tractor when I heard jPod voices coming towards me from up the driveway.

"Ethan?"

"Guys?"

"Ethan," Mom said, "your friends are going to help you dig for a while."

This alarmed me, for obvious reasons. *"What?"*

"Not the entire hole. Don't worry. I stopped by the house and got some more digging tools for everybody."

"Uh, great."

Kaitlin said, "It's so sweet of you to swap Kam's tree fern for a Himalayan windmill palm. You're such a good friend."

"And digging the hole your*self*," Cowboy added. "Now *that's* friendship, and *that's* commitment to being Green."

Tim's corpse weighed heavily on my mind. "You know, I thought I might get a tractor and dig it that way. I don't think I'll need any help."

"Nonsense, Ethan," said Mom. "We're all adults, and we all care about Kam. Digging will be fun, and you young people all need some fresh air and exercise. Poor John Doe here looks like a telethon child."

"Thank you, Mrs. Jarlewski."

"Well, it's true, John."

I asked Mom if I could speak to her in private. We went to her car.

"Mom, what are you doing getting everyone to help us? Are you insane?"

"Don't be such a worrywart. Once we begin to smell Tim, I'll have everybody leave."

"I'm going to rent a Bobcat."

"Over my dead body you will. What if it accidentally cuts through Tim's body? Have some respect for the dead."

And so the gang jumped in and digging began, but it was slow going. There were only two real shovels. Bree had a spade, Kaitlin had an edging tool and John Doe was using this pole-shaped thingy Dad had bought off the Shopping Channel during a three a.m. rum jag. Bree looked at the pole and said, "I think it also French braids your hair if you hold it upside down."

An hour later we decided to trash the fern. The six of us (with Mom as overseer) managed to lug it out of its pit and roll it across the adjoining rockery. I wondered what Kam was going to make of this. It wasn't going to be pretty.

Everyone was being friendly and co-operative, and despite our sad little tools, the hole came along nicely. Cowboy, for once, wasn't off in a corner, contemplating death (or broker-ing a quickie skankwich); John Doe was full of vim and revealed to us a heretofore unknown talent for mimicking dial tones; Bree was describing her doomed second date from the previous evening ("You think you know somebody, and then all of a sudden they start talking about crop circles . . ."). Mark, bless him, was happy simply to be doing a dis-proportionate share of the work.

Mom made a snack run to Whole Foods, and I couldn't remember the last time I'd had so much fun, but then sud-denly the amount of fun we were having made me suspi-cious—and only then did I figure out why they were being so jolly. My blood turned to Freon. I put down my wheat grass smoothie and glared at them: "You're all quitting the company—aren't you? *That's* why you're all being so nice to me."

Silence.

"It's *true*. Come on, now—tell me."

Everybody lowered their tools and looked at Kaitlin.

"Ethan, uhhh—"

"I *knew* it."

Kaitlin said, "Ethan, this has nothing to do with how any of us feel about you. Working for Doug is going to be the best gig ever. We'd be nuts not to move."

"Doug, Doug, *Doug*. Could you at least tell me what that fatuous prick's idea is?"

"Ethan, I've told you a thousand times already, we signed nondisclosure agreement forms. You know they're sacred. And let me state in public that I don't want Kam thinking I was the one who spilled the beans."

Curse Kaitlin.

"When are you leaving?"

"Effective today."

"I'm sure your friends will figure out a way to bring you along once they get settled in. Won't you?" Mom said.

The others nodded just a bit too agreeably. I felt like the last dog remaining at the SPCA.

"Don't be such a gloomy Gus, dear, and besides—" Mom was fishing around her brain for something, anything nice to say. "Learn to take pleasure in life's little accomplishments. Just look at how much progress you've made digging this hole!"

Kaitlin was heading to a tap to rinse off her hands. "Ethan, we'll discuss this tonight. Bree and I have to go get facials."

The guys bailed, too. "It's new shoe day. Some limited-edition Adidas coming in from Argentina. We have no free will here, Ethan—we have to leave. Sorry, buddy."

It was back to Mom and me.

"Dear, don't sulk. It gives you a second chin."

"Mom, for the love of God, why can't you just break the stupid NDA form and tell me what this—"

My words were cut short by a syrupy waft of decomposed flesh scent.

"Mom, I think we've just found Tim."

"I'll go get the Febreze."

• • •

Fifteen minutes and two bottles of Febreze later, we'd scraped enough dirt away to reveal a few square inches of the rolled-up carpet from Dad's den.

"Ethan, all you have to do is yank on the carpet and we're done. It couldn't be simpler."

"Mom, it's not going to come away in one little tug. The whole torso needs to be lifted."

"What's your point, Ethan?"

"Mom! *I'm* the one who has to do this, not you."

"That's right, Ethan, but *I* was in love with him."

I poked the carpet with the blunt end of my shovel. Mom asked why I was doing that. "I don't know—I suppose to see if he's crunchy or chewy."

"I suspect probably more on the chewy side, dear. Bones take a long time to decompose. Those steak bones I put in the azalea garden for calcium back in the 1980s are still hard as quartz."

I looked more closely at Tim's back. "He's not bloated, is he? It looks like the weight of all that dirt kept him quite slim."

"You know, Ethan, maybe if we thought of Tim as a science project we might move along a bit faster here. I think we're being too fussy."

Mom's purse farted. "Excuse me, dear—cellphone." She began rummaging, then checked the number of the incoming call. "It's the Vietnamese fertilizer dealer. I really have to answer this."

I prodded a bit more at Tim's cocoon. From out of the blue above us came an extended manga-like shriek from hell.

"上帝！您異教徒的豬做了˹

什麼的母親對我心愛的結構樹蕨？"

("Mother of God! What have you heathen pigs done to my beloved tree fern?")

Of course it was Kam—Kam and a short fire plug of a blonde-wigged woman in white go-go boots, Jackie O sunglasses and a tasselled white leather jacket who resembled a hooker I saw in Las Vegas a few years back. She was buying twenty-four boxes of Sudafed in the Albertsons on Sahara Boulevard.

"freedom?" I exclaimed.

"freedom?" Mom squeaked.

"Hello, Carol. Hello, Penis."

Kam's language became more intelligible as his first burst of rage died down. "What the fuck have you people done to my baby?"

Mom was taken aback by freedom's new look; she viewed Kam's temper as might a nursery school teacher a toddler's wail. "Now, Kam, don't be angry. There's a good explanation for this."

"There'd better be, and you'd better tell me right now."

Mom remained distracted. "freedom, I thought you were delivering a speech in Seattle today."

"I was going to—until Kam phoned."

"Carol! *What about my goddam tree fern!*"

"Kam, cool down, I'll buy you a new one."

"What the hell are you doing digging up my front yard?"

Mom and I swapped glances. I wasn't going to be the one to break the news.

"Kam," said Mom, "last year I had a fling with this biker chap I did business with. And then he refused to pay me, and push came to shove, and he was accidentally electrocuted, and so I buried him here. Except I just realized he has a safety deposit box key in his pocket, and I need it rather badly."

There was a pause.

"Why didn't you say so?" Kam said. "I could have had some of my, uh, travel associates come here and dig it up for free in ten minutes."

Kam and freedom walked around to the other side of the hole. Mom said, "freedom, I barely recognize you."

freedom actually blushed and then giggled. It was a dreadful thing to see. "Kam told me that if I wanted to be a true radical, there was no point in fogging my bourgeois inertia under a mist of stillborn and archaic dialogues from the twentieth century."

"Did he?"

Kam smiled as if to say, *Look, fools! You think you're so smart and politically correct and all of that, but the Chinese mastered the art of jargon-twisting-to-get-what-you-want back before your sweet Jesus was a holy zygote.*

freedom went on. "Oh yes. A truly radical act on my part would be to infiltrate and hyperbolize the concepts I consider to be my opposite. Hence this new look."

What is it about lesbians and jargon?

freedom continued. "Next week we're off to Palm Desert for a brow lift, a nose softening, an eye lift, fat removal from the cheeks, a breast augmentation, tummy tuck, removal of fat from the thighs and calves . . ."

Kam completed the sentence: " . . . and fourteen Da Vinci porcelain veneers."

"Isn't that rebellious, Carol?" freedom had become a thirteen-year-old girl in search of approval. "Oh, and my new name is Kimberly."

Mom mouthed the word "Kimberly," but no noise escaped her throat.

Kam asked, "Ethan, have you reached that guy's body yet?"

I tamped the patch of carpet with my shovel. "Yup. I should have Mom's key within the hour."

Kam said, "Do me a favour. Just put a little bit of dirt on top of him once you're done. I have a few things I might as well put down there while there's a hole happening."

"What kind of things?"

"Don't you worry about that. I'll get one of my, uh, associates to fill in the hole after that."

"Thanks, Kam."

"Excellent."

Kam bowed to Kimberly/freedom, and then took her arm. "Very well, then. Kimberly, shall we go kick up our heels?"

Kimberly tittered. Small birds in the sky witnessed this and fell to the ground, dead.

Kam and his new girlfriend walked in the front door. Mom still stood in the hole, mute.

"Mom?"

No response.

*"Mom?"*

"Ethan—"

"Yes?"

"Ethan, I . . . I think I might be a lesbian."

"Mom—listen to me—Mom? *Mom?*" I grabbed her by the shoulders and shook. "Look me in the eye. Okay?"

She did.

"Here's the deal. You are not a lesbian. You do not have a crush on Kimberly. You will go home right now. You will cook Dad a hot, nutritious meal, and you will watch an episode of *Band of Brothers* on DVD with him, and you will enjoy that episode. And life will be just like it was a few months ago, and you will feel free and happy because of that. Okay?"

"Okay."

Mom teetered towards her car, bits of dove-grey soil trickling down the hole's edge in her wake. After she'd driven off, I remembered that she was my ride.

And so I toughened myself up and pretended Tim was a particularly well-designed gory website. I must agree that everything experts say about the Internet and violence and games is true—it *does* make you a little bit callous—the first gore makes the second gore easier. But the stench!

I retrieved Mom's key and tossed a bit of dirt back Tim's

way. And then I simply sat at the hole's bottom, wondering about life, wondering about death and wondering about curious raccoons passing through the neighbourhood on their nightly rounds, snacking on Tim's remains.

And then I sat thinking about nothing.

Finally I heard a car pull up, a door slam, and someone approaching.

His face appeared above the hole, his dead eyes and his cruel mouth. Coupland. "Well, if it isn't the happy wanderer. Trying to dig your way back to China?"

"Fuck off and die."

"Temper." He was dressed like a 1960s TV father—glen plaid jacket and matching wool pants. He was holding, of all things, a pipe.

I said, "Kam's inside."

"That's nice. So, tell me, Ethan, why are you digging a hole, and why have you trashed Kam's tree fern?"

"That's not your business."

"Isn't it?"

I picked up a shovel, realizing that there was a part of me that wanted to whack this guy on the skull. "Just go inside."

"Maybe *you're* the one I want to speak to."

"Huh?"

"Come on. Ask yourself if there's some practical reason why I might be here to see you."

"You've lost me."

"Why don't we go for a ride?"

I did need a ride. "Okay."

I got into his Jaguar XJ12 ("Take your shoes off first, and don't touch any of the knobs or dials! Jesus Christ, you've got ants crawling off you"), and we drove down the mountain. I was tired and just wanted some peace and quiet.

"Where are we going?"

"North Van."

"Why?"

"There's something there you need to see."

**Term**
**Type**
**Meaning**

Bsh
Cmd
Sound made when CD ejects from burner

Execle
Fct
Discontinued Popsicle flavour

.osc
Cmd
C++ (indicates that file contents have received an Academy Award)

Diff
Cmd
Rhymes with piff

PPP
Prot
Larger than normal urination

Qdaemon
Cmd
Nomeadq spelled backwards

Scanf
Fct
Misspelling of skank

Eval
Cmd
Opposite of goad

Glob
Misc
Biannual Windexing of monitor screen

.i
Ext
Low self-esteem version of "I"

ARP
Prot
Your seal needs a herring

• • •

We ended up at a building near the Second Narrows Bridge that, until recent currency fluctuations, had been a film studio used primarily for TV movies. The signage near the roof had been removed, leaving an off-white rectangle behind it. The offices up front had the stripped-to-the-bone feel of commercial space undergoing a total overhaul.

"Welcome to the offices of Dglobe."

"Dglobe? Can you spell that?"

"Capital D, lower case g, l, o, b, e."

"What does the D stand for?"

"Doug, you dumb shit. Dglobe is where your friends are coming to work."

"Some friends they are."

"*Tsh, tsh*. Nobody gets rich on software in the twenty-first century. The only money remaining is in hardware, and only hardware made offshore at that, preferably in some unregulated, uninvestigated Asian backwater where you can get a day's labour and a hand job for the cost of a bag of Skittles."

"So, then, what happens here in Vancouver?"

"Here is where the Dglobe gets its *soul*."

"All I see is a big empty heap of a building. Show me something real."

"With pleasure. Come this way."

We stepped over a pile of removed drywall and a tangle of beige phone cables. The carpeting was stained and lying in piles—bright orange steak restaurant carpeting from the 1970s. The rooms smelled like a cold, dank used bookstore.

"This way, if you will." Coupland opened up a set of double doors leading into what was once a fair-size sound stage. In the centre of the room was one small light, enough to illuminate veritable kelp beds of abandoned electrical cords on the concrete floor. Leaning against the wall across the space were dozens of pieces of scenery, stacked like toast slices.

Coupland turned to me. "There, in the centre of the room—that's the Dglobe."

We walked towards it: a beach-ball-sized globe lit from within. "Big deal."

"Fair enough. But watch this."

Coupland pulled a key fob from his pocket and clicked it at the globe. Suddenly the continents vanished, and in a blink the globe reconfigured as one big land mass. "Look closely at—"

"That's Pangaea . . . continental drift."

"Yes, it is."

Pangaea began separating into continental chunks, all of which began moving away from each other. Over the course of sixty seconds, I witnessed the creation of the world as the land masses dragged across long-vanished oceans. Some of them collided, some of them barely moved. South America and Africa crept away from each other. After two minutes the Dglobe showed Earth as we currently know it. And then— and then—the continents *kept* moving. And moving. California touched Alaska; India smushed itself into oblivion into the concertina'd ridges of the Himalayas; South America rested in the middle of the Pacific.

Coupland said, "That's Earth three billion years from now. Hey—let's look at it again in fast motion!" He clicked the fob, and we watched the continents form across a thirty-second span.

I said, "Again."

We watched it again.

Doug said, "Gee, Ethan—I wonder what Earth would look like if Antarctica melted completely? Why, let's find out! And let's do it in sixty seconds."

Before me Earth's land masses lost their familiarity. Florida vanished, as did much of Asia and all the planet's coastlines.

"Do it again!"

"With pleasure."

The continents submerged once more.

"Show me more stuff!"

"*Hmmmm* . . . I wonder what the most recent Ice Age looked like from start to finish."

"Show me the Ice Age!" I shouted.

"With pleasure."

Bingo! Fifty thousand years squished into sixty seconds.

Coupland said, "Gee, Ethan—how about an instantaneous real-time picture of all the weather on Earth at this moment?"

"You can do that?"

"Watch me." With a click, the Dglobe turned into Earth as seen from thirty-two geosynchronous weather satellites. It was stunning.

"Let's go back thirty days and see a whole month's worth of weather leading up to the present moment." With a click, the Dglobe showed thirty days of weather, with the planet rotating to show night and day, the cities of Earth twinkling when cloud cover permitted.

He said, "Let's see what happens if we throw a class 5 hurricane towards Florida . . . yeehaw! Disaster! Better still, what does Mars look like?"

Earth became Mars.

"What does the moon look like?"

I saw the moon.

"The sun? Flame on!"

Next came a succession of morphings: a glitterball; a mirror image of Earth; a graphics light show; political maps of the planet in various languages; a colour-coded slow-speed mapping of human populations on the planet since 5000 BC.

I looked at the Dglobe up close. "How does it work?"

"By using a spherical liquid crystal screen programmed with proprietary 3-D cartographic algorithms. They're going to be made in China . . . obviously. And your friends are writing and designing the globe's various uses."

"How does this particular model here work?"

"It's a mock-up with internal projectors. It cost me a bomb."

I asked, "How come you're hiring jPodders? Why not get eggheads from Yale or Stanford or India?"

"Because it's not that hard to program, so I might as well have fun people doing it instead of robotic geeks."

"And you really *can* make these globes?"

"Yes, I can. And every school on earth is going to want one. And anyone with a kid is going to want one. What am I saying—everyone in the *world* is going to want one."

"I want in."

"I knew you would."

"I also know you're evil, Coupland, so what's the catch?"

"There's no catch, but there *is* a price."

"I knew it."

"I want your new laptop, the one you bought after you returned from China. No erasing allowed—if you mail-ordered a DVD of *Sandra, the Living Chunnel,* I want to know about it. And I also want all of your files from work. *All* of them. Business and personal."

"Hang on a second—you already have my old laptop. Why do you want my new drives so badly?"

"Because my contract says I have to write a book, and it's easier just to steal your life than to make something up. So I need to find out what happened in your life after China."

*My life a story?* "Really?"

"You have ten seconds to make up your mind. One, two, three—wait! I think I hear marketing phoning with a new idea on how to dilute your latest game ideas with crap—four, five, six—wait, none of your friends are working there any more. You're alone in jPod—seven, eight, nine—"

"It's a deal."

"Good. You're living in Doug's world now."

"Not yet. I want your word on paper."

"Fine. No problem." In the parking lot Coupland hand-wrote an appropriate document, then handed it to me. "By the way," he added, "you're going to be filling in that hole tonight, aren't you?"

"Kam's people are doing it tomorrow morning."

"Do you think Kam would mind if I threw in a couple of things of my own?"

"Not at all. Just chuck them in and cover them with a tarp or a bedsheet so nobody can see what they are."

"Marvellous."

## Three Months Later:

And so here I am. Dglobe is a blast. Life is good—so good, actually, that I have to ask myself, why do I worry so much? In fact, everybody in my universe seems happy, including our glamorous new receptionist, Kimberly. Kam is happy, Mom and Dad are happy, Kaitlin and I and all the ex-podsters are happy. Woohoo! Happy, happy, happy!

As for Steve, my old employer decided it needed to enter the gore sector of gaming, and wouldn't you know, Steve had our Ronald package all ready to go. He's golden and is going to turn around yet another company. He also got us all paid as consultants on the project, and we earn money doing sweet fuck all. *Wheeee!*

Yesirree, life sure is good.

Yesirree, nothing could possibly go wrong with everything being so good.

But of course, in books, good is boring.

Good is a snoozer.

Good makes people close the covers and never reopen them.

But you know—you'd think that just *once* when life finally started going my way, that cosmic writer out there would allow me and all of my co-characters to simply enjoy things for just a little while. I mean, what kind of a prick would end a book just when everything's going so well?

# Play again?
## Y/N

## A note on the author

Douglas Coupland is a novelist who also works in visual arts and theater. His novels include *Generation X, Microserfs, All Families Are Psychotic*, and *Hey Nostradamus!* He lives and works in Vancouver, Canada.

Douglas Coupland's novel *The Gum Thief*
is published in autumn 2007.

**www.bloomsbury.com/douglascoupland**